POE

POE

A novel

J. Lincoln Fenn

Published by

47N❂RTH

Text copyright © 2013 Nicole Beattie

Published by 47North
P.O. Box 400818 Las Vegas, NV 89140
ISBN-13: 9781477848166
ISBN-10: 1477848169

Library of Congress Control Number: 2013940591

For my parents, the living and the dead.

Dearest friend, do you not see
All that we perceive
Only reflects and shadows forth
What our eyes cannot see.
Dearest friend, do you not hear
In the clamor of everyday life
Only the unstrung echoing fall of
Jubilant harmonies.

Vladimir Soloviev, Russian Gnostic and philosopher, 1892

We people are the children of the sun, the bright
source of life; we are born of the sun and will
vanquish the murky fear of death.

Maxim Gorky, *Children of the Sun*, 1905

PROLOGUE

link. it sounds like someone just put a penny in a jar. Unfamiliar voices in the distance, fuzzy and hard to pinpoint. My ears are ringing. Damn, why is it so cold? There's something else too, a putrid stench, like shit and rotten pizza mixed together. *Focus.*

I was breathing water—it was cool and felt good in my lungs. I was drowning, dying, and strangely I didn't seem to mind. And there was a woman in the water—ice-blue skin, blond hair floating like tendrils of seaweed. She wanted to tell me something, and I could see a solitary word bubbling from her frigid lips—my name, Dimitri. Then something else, something *important*, but I can't pull the memory to the surface, and it is so cold, so very, very cold.

Gradually the ringing in my ears stops. My hearing starts to clear. There's a whoosh of something like a fan, and a refrigerator hum. I try to open my eyes, but they refuse.

Clink, clank, clunk. Someone is humming. *Humming?*

Then a low voice. "So my wife is, like, you need to take a shower before you come home from work, you smell like cadavers, and *I* said, you don't seem to mind cashing the checks."

A lighter voice, feminine. "Um-hum." Obviously not listening.

"She can't say anything then, 'cause she's got a new Gucci purse she doesn't want to tell me about. Like I don't read the credit card statements—*hey*, do you mind turning that thing off while we're working?"

A sigh, then a click. "It keeps me focused."

"Can't believe your iPod still works after it fell in that guy's stomach. You'd think the acid would have shorted the battery."

"Waterproof case. I did have to get new earbuds though."

Deep-voice guy snorts with laughter. Then a sudden intake of breath. "Damn, have you ever seen a stab wound this deep before? The knife splintered her rib."

Thumpity thump thump. My heart starts to beat. It's cautious, like it's not sure whether there's much point, but methodically plods along anyways. Each throb pushes more of the fizzy darkness aside with a familiar staccato rhythm that's reassuring. Suddenly, every nerve in my body kicks in, tingling with a fiery determination—it's a rush. I realize I'm naked. I'm lying on something cold, metallic, and decidedly uncomfortable. I try a breath, and the air burns my lungs, but they seem functional.

"What kind of knife would do that?"

"A very sharp one."

"Ha-ha, very funny."

Pause.

"Check out the spleen. It looks like something was *eating* it."

"Maybe she had cats. Cats are heartless."

"Cats are not heartless," replies the feminine voice.

"When's the last time you heard about a dog eating its dead owner? Never."

Snap, crack, clink.

My eyelids finally flutter—a fuzzy light glows behind something white and cottony. I gather my jangling neurons, point them at my right arm—*Move, arm, move*—and manage to jerk at the sheet that's covering me. A new chemical stink wafts by—formaldehyde—and above me a bright, round fluorescent light nearly blinds me. I slowly turn my head; it feels like my brain is sloshing inside my skull, and it takes a moment for the dizziness to clear enough for me to see.

A man and a woman in surgical scrubs stand in front of a gray naked body. Bright red blood spatters their sleeves and gloves. The man holds a large pair of shears, also covered in blood, and the woman has a white dangling earbud that trails from beneath her surgical cap to a bulge in her right front pocket. They both stare, perplexed, into the abdomen of what appears to be the corpse of a fiftyish woman; her frizzy gray hair is badly permed, and she stares at me with the glossy eyes of a dead fish. A flap of thick, yellowed, and fatty flesh hangs from her waist, and I can see blue veins crisscrossing the tissue, while some kind of white, viscous liquid oozes onto the linoleum floor. A bloody heap that looks like raw hamburger rests on a hanging metal scale. Ten pounds.

I'm in a morgue. My stomach heaves, but there's nothing to throw up. My body is completely drained. Empty.

"Hey, did you do that?"

"What?" Something squishes.

"Drowning dude's sheet is off."

"Well why don't you go fix that? My hands are a little tied, if you know what I mean."

The woman mutters, "I'm not some kind of first-year resident . . ."

A scream builds in the back of my throat and dies there.

Footsteps softly pad across the linoleum floor. I can feel the rough sheet being pulled back up and over my feet, my legs, my chest. I need to move—I need to move *now*. Somehow I turn my head, look at the woman in scrubs directly in her eyes. Blink. I open my mouth, and a small rush of water pours out.

"Holy shit!" She jumps back, knocking the scale. It swings like a pendulum, and the hand on the dial swerves wildly as the bloody heap slides to the floor with a wet plop.

My eyes roll toward the back of my head, and I reach one hand out, grasping nothing. Suddenly I remember what the woman with the ice-blue skin said in her strange, watery voice.

"*Dimitri. He's coming. He's coming for* you."

Then the darkness wells up, envelops me, and I'm gone again.

HALLOWEEN

Twenty-four hours earlier

CHAPTER ONE: NEW GOSHEN

There's not a lot of opportunity to get creative with obituaries. Take Mrs. Porrier, aged eighty-five, an elementary school teacher who committed suicide by locking herself in the garage of her four-bedroom colonial house with the car running.

She had terminal pancreatic cancer, but that's not the point. The point is that the most interesting part of her life—the moments leading up to her death—I can't write about. I can't write that she got the car keys out of the brown leather bowling ball bag cherished by her husband—Mr. Porrier, otherwise known as "Doc" to his league—and opened the familiar latch of the screen door. That she pressed the yellowed plastic button of the electric garage door opener, got into the car, and pulled the heavy door of the ancient but still functional Cadillac behind her—the scent of cigarette smoke still in the carpeting, although her husband had quit smoking ten years before. I can't write that she rolled up the windows by *hand*—nothing automatic in that car—and started the engine. And the moment before her eyes got heavy, when she still could have gotten out of the car but didn't, the moment she decided *enough*, I can't include in her obituary.

Instead, I have to write the mundane, perfected-life details. She taught school for forty years. She is remembered by her grandchild Harris in Colorado, her daughter Stella, also a teacher, in California, and her beloved husband, who served two years in the Korean War. She enjoyed knitting, horticulture, and baking. She died of pancreatic cancer. I reduce her to a palatable bit of print, ready to be absorbed, digested, and quickly forgotten.

Christ, I wish I didn't take this shit so seriously.

———

I try to avoid the newspaper office in the flatiron building on New Goshen's Main Street as much as possible—probably because I'm supposed to work there. So over the past year I've suffered periodic intestinal episodes from bad sushi. My car has a habit of being borrowed by my (nonexistent) roommate, or the tires are flat, or the battery needs a jump. I'm susceptible to migraines, increasingly bad episodes of asthma, and my back needs regular appointments with a chiropractor, who keeps changing my appointment times. As long as the deadlines are met, Mac, the editor (who really lets themselves be called Mac anyway?), doesn't threaten me too much with firing, which is bullshit anyway because there aren't many people in this town who could string together one sentence, let alone two.

After my parents died and I flunked out of college, it was either this or the crab boats in Alaska, those being the best employment opportunities presented by my frazzled college counselor. She was obviously trying to rush me out the door—completely understandable given she had a long line of actual students waiting. And to be honest I was ready to grab onto anything. But whenever I push open the brass office doors and gaze upon the dusty metal file cabinets resting on the equally dusty olive carpet, with Myrna in the corner pretending to type when she's really checking the clock for her smoke break, I imagine myself in one of those orange deckhand suits on the Bering Sea, my eyebrows singed with frost and realize I've made the biggest mistake of my young life.

But sometimes, like this morning, I have to face reality. For the third time this year I've been given my two weeks' notice.

"Morning, Myrna," I say, wondering if her optometrist has ever heard of those newfangled thin plastic glasses, as opposed to the glacier-thick glass ones she wears. Tinted a delightful gradient pink.

Myrna pulls a sheet of paper from her printer with a *snap*. "You're gracing us with your presence today? Fired again so soon?"

"Is that a new sweater?" I say. "It really brings out the color of your eyes."

Her sweater is red.

Myrna gives me a look. "Smart ass," she mutters.

I head toward my ostensible desk, which doubles as a paper stand when I'm not in. I stack the reams on the floor and then look for my chair. Nowhere to be found. Myrna must know something, but she's studiously applying Wite-Out to a sheet of paper, dabbing at it with a corner of tissue and pointedly ignoring me.

Which leaves Bob.

Bob has a gut that hangs over his leather belt, and his standard attire is tight oxford shirt and penny loafers. He prides himself on dated practical jokes. I've found all my paper clips hooked together, an actual pink whoopee cushion on my chair, and, on my very first day, I got an electric shock from the buzzer he had hidden in his palm. When Myrna's on her smoke break, sometimes I'll find a miniature plastic television on my desk with two large breasts poking out from the screen and the words "Boob Tube" at the base, which I think is Bob's way of testing my heterosexuality, since my hair is on the shaggy side and there are questions. The local barber has one standard style, military buzz, so I pay my "bachelor" neighbor Doug twenty bucks every now and then to cut it. Doug's an actual hair-stylist and a refugee from a long-term relationship in San Francisco that ended badly. He says that if it weren't for the dark circles under my eyes, I would have potential, what with my high Russian cheek-bones and thick brows. Which gender he's talking about my having potential with is unclear. All I know is that I'm the tall, thin, un-naturally pale and dark-haired sensitive-looking type, instead of the rock-bodied, square-jawed testosterone type—a tragic genetic disadvantage that usually results in stilted conversations with girls, who smile politely while obviously clocking the muscular guys chugging beer through funnels.

My mind clicks through various places in the building where my chair could be—emergency stairwell, bathroom stall, the alley that smells of dead cat where the newspaper trucks pull up. Basically, a pain-in-the-ass way to start my day. I decide *screw it* and loudly pull my desk over to the Victorian metal radiator that hasn't worked in, say, a century, balling up my jacket to serve as a cushion. Problem solved.

I pull out my laptop, a device that always causes a certain furrow in Myrna's brow, she who swears by her antiquated IBM, because the Internet is causing the rapid degeneration of society's youth, and wireless frequencies cause cancer. Unlike smoking, of course—her pack-a-day habit is perfectly healthy; Reagan said so.

Bob waltzes in. The cat-that-ate-the-canary metaphor applies rather well here.

"Nice chair," says Bob, barely able to repress a chuckle.

"Yeah," I say, "it's so SAC."

I enjoy making up nonsense acronyms that I know Bob will attempt to use with his ten-year-old niece in an attempt to be "down with the kids."

"You know," I add casually, "sustainable and cool."

"Right," says Bob, and I can tell he's now feeling off his game, having been reminded poignantly that he is pushing his late fifties. I almost feel sorry for him, but then again I'm the one who writes the obituary notices, and I'm sitting on a radiator.

Bob, on the other hand, practically *is* the newspaper, especially since Mac likes to keep the writing staff lean (our value is slightly above janitor and way below the sales and accounting departments). Bob writes the local news, features, and sports; he even writes the occasional "investigative" piece that profiles our highest-paying advertiser in glowing terms, neatly avoiding actual journalism while painting a portrait so rosy it would make Norman Rockwell vomit. A pale accountant fills in to cover the rare event of business news, usually a bankruptcy or store closing, which we call internally YABBTD (Yet Another Business Bites the Dust). Film reviews are written by Sandeep Banerjee, who charges five dollars an article and e-mails his copy from somewhere in the heart of Mumbai. Mac would probably love for Sandeep to write the obits, too—his new favorite acronym is ROI (Return on Investment)—but he knows that in a small, some would say close-minded (I would say borderline racist) town, nobody would want their beloved relative's life-and-death story written by anyone other than a full-blooded American. Which is why my byline is D. Peters instead of Dimitri Petrov. Go figure.

And in New Goshen, where 75 percent of the local population is over sixty-five, there are so many obituaries they fill up two full pages of the newspaper—sometimes three, if we really stretch the prime advertising space. Death here is the proverbial cash cow. It wasn't always that way—when industrialization hit New Goshen in the early twentieth century, it must have been a rocking place to be. Thousands of immigrants and children of rural farmers poured into the city to work in the mills. Fourteen was a great age to start, and if you lost a finger or two in the process, you'd have considered yourself lucky that you still had part of a hand. Of course, now all that manufacturing is done in China, which has an even greater and cheaper supply of fourteen-year-olds, so the mills here are boarded-up shells with broken windows. Anyone under thirty wisely got out while the getting was good, and the aging population has caused a boom in hospice care, funeral, and other "death industries," including my own meager position writing obits.

Lucky me.

"Well," says Bob, trying to salvage his dominant spot as chief jokester, "I'll give you a hint." He leans in close, and his breath smells of fried-egg sandwich. "Next time you want to take a *dump*"—he whispers the word "dump" so he won't offend the delicate sensibilities of Myrna—"you might want to use the stall by the window."

He cheerfully gives my shoulder a punch, like he's the coach and I'm the high school rookie, and then thuds over to his desk, where he has a grinding first-generation laser printer that makes more noise than an artillery range.

I look out the window and wonder if, assuming I survived a jump from the second story, I'd be entitled to disability payments.

———

This much we know about Muriel Sheridan. She died in her sleep at Crosslands Nursing Center at 1:05 A.M. on a rainy Monday morning. At least we hope that she died in her sleep and didn't wake up alone, unable to call the nurse because of her advancing Alzheimer's, gasping for a last, rattling breath as pneumonia filled her lungs with fluid.

When I say we, I mean Lisa and me.

Lisa is the receptionist at Crosslands, one of four nursing homes that make up the Quadrant of Death. All four are located within the same city block, just a stone's throw from the hospital, mortuary, and cemetery. Lisa is my main point of contact and supplier of scoops when it comes to the dead or nearly dead. She hears all the good gossip about the inmates (excuse me, residents)—things that of course can't, but should, go in the obits.

"Relatives?" I ask.

"Bitchy niece who's got her eye on Muriel's Victorian," says Lisa.

Lisa's voice is smoky, and I know she's about my age, but I haven't yet gotten the nerve to ask her to coffee and meet her in person. I like to tell myself that I'm working up to it.

I tap my pencil on my desk. "So what's the story?"

"Well," says Lisa, and I can hear her pause as she checks to see if there's anyone within earshot, "apparently Muriel was loaded. She was a burlesque dancer in Vegas."

I drop my pencil on the floor with a clatter, causing Myrna to glare in my direction.

"No shit," I whisper.

"But she really made her money playing poker. Word is she was a card counter, and when the Mafia found out, they got her a one-way ticket to New York and told her if they saw her again, no one would ever find the body."

I whistle through my teeth. Go Muriel.

"So she just settled down and got married, never had kids, and played Suzie Homemaker until after her husband Harold died. Then she went back to Vegas one last time."

"No one would recognize her," I say.

"Exactly," says Lisa. "Who'd suspect a nice little old lady with permed gray hair? I wouldn't. Bitchy niece said she made over two hundred grand her first week, but the thick-necked guys started following her with walkie-talkies, so she decided it was time to clear out. A year later the Alzheimer's started."

I jot notes as we talk. Not that any of this will make the paper. But still.

"Anyone else close?" I ask. As in close to dying. I like to keep track so that if there's a flurry of deaths in a short period of time, I can have some prep work done and easily make my deadline. I'm that sick.

"Umm . . ." says Lisa. "Mrs. Jameson has been dying forever . . . She seems close, but then I think I said that last month."

"Two months ago," I say. I already have a file on Mrs. Jameson with some preliminary research, so I could wrap her up fairly quickly. "Nothing new?"

"No," says Lisa with a sigh. "I found out she did some charity work at the hospital, nothing else."

I make a note to do some digging. There's always "the thing" that separates a person out, makes them unique, different. It's not always stories about Vegas gambling, although you might be surprised at the number of adulterous relationships, incarcerations, and illegitimate children of the Greatest Generation currently stationed at Crosslands. Sometimes the thing is as simple as a mastery of French cuisine, a collection of rare butterflies pinned on a piece of velvet in the living room, or a stay in the White House during the Nixon years. Finding the thing gives me a strange kind of thrill. It's finding the story behind the façade, even if I have to spin it so that the raging alcoholic was "the life of the party" and the drug addict dies "suddenly of heart failure." I know the truth. Someone knows the truth before they're buried. I think everyone deserves that.

"Dimitri, you there?" says Lisa.

I have once again completely spaced out. This happens often in my line of work.

"Hey Lisa, I wanted to ask you—"

Suddenly the line is dead, and I see a large, familiar, thuggish index finger pressing the receiver's button. Fuck. Nate.

"Talking to your girlfriend on company time?"

I look up to find Nate, Mac's son and the senior editor, aka Senior Asshole, or Senior Douche Bag, or Senior Beneficiary of Nepotism, standing in front of me. There is a characteristic dumb smirk on his squarely-jawed face, and a gleam of unexpressed sadism in his eye. If there was a nuclear war and people resorted to a *Lord of the Flies* barbarism complete with cannibalism and rampant destruction of whatever civilization remained, it would not surprise me in the least to find Nate at the head of the ruling clan with a scavenged thigh bone in hand and automatic rifles strapped to his back, screeching through the ravaged streets in some kind of assemblage of truck, a la *Mad Max*. As it is, Nate's proclivities toward violence are limited to editing my writing with bloody, indecipherable marks made with a red Sharpie.

"She's a source," I say.

Nate hugs himself and makes obnoxious kissing noises. "Just kidding, slugger," he says, giving my other shoulder a punch, so now I'll have a bruise to match the one Bob gave me.

I try to hunch over my laptop, like I'm right on the verge of something truly incredibly important or at least more absorbing than starting a discussion. Nate, as usual, misses (or ignores) the cues. He settles on the corner of my desk, his balls frighteningly close to my stapler.

His eyes furrow in some kind of bad caveman impression. "I don't get it, Shakespeare. Why do you spend so much time on this crap?"

"Crap? What crap?" I say.

Nate pulls out a handful of crumpled and sweaty-looking obits from his back pocket. Nate likes to edit while he's on the treadmill at the gym. He's often said he does his best thinking while pumping iron. Seriously.

I hate to admit it, but I'm a little jealous of his ability to work the phrase "pumping iron" into everyday conversation. I wish I could randomly drop lines like, "Yeah, I was in the middle of a triathlon," but I have a long-standing aversion to any activity that involves pain and an increased heart rate.

"This crap," says Nate, pushing a pile of my writing at me. "Do you know how long it takes me to edit this shit?" Nate pulls a sheet out and squints at it. "He died of an unidentified prosodemic illness. Who talks like this? Every other sentence I have to use a dictionary."

I take one of the pages and try to flatten it back out.

"It's like a fucking never-ending game of Scrabble. And I hate Scrabble." Nate picks up my pencil and starts scratching the back of his ear with it.

"Maybe you should rethink your vocation," I mutter.

"There!" says Nate, pointing my pencil back at me. "That's exactly what I'm talking about. What the hell is a vocation?"

"It's a kind of candle," I say without hesitation. I have no mercy.

"Oh yeah," says Nate. "Those little ones . . . Anyway, we can't print all this shit. No one cares. It's just dead old people."

I swallow everything I'd like to say. Hard. "So what would you like me to change?"

"Just take out some words. The big ones."

I look at the pile in front of me. "So you want me to just *take out some words.*"

Nate's face brightens measurably. "Now you get it." He does an excited drum roll on my desk. "Just get it down to the designer before deadline. We cool?"

I have no intention of editing a word. "We cool," I say.

———

My parents' obituary was sparse—they got one paragraph combined, as if their dying together had somehow melded their lives into a single conglomeration, punctuated by my father's country of origin (Russia) and a vague allusion to my mother's interest in baking. An ad for Dalton Discount Motors pushed hard into their column: 0% DOWN, NO PAYMENTS FOR SIX MONTHS, DRIVE AWAY HAPPY. I don't know who gave the details to the writer at their local paper—I was a little blown out at the time—and the whole experience had the feel of a bad hallucinogenic trip. Not that I have a lot of experience with that kind of thing, but before I failed college last year I did a little experimenting.

In fact, the night my parents died I'd been to a disastrous Halloween party at a frat house. There was this hot girl from my English Lit class with long, wavy hair who'd decided the best costume was none at all. She gave me a hallucinogenic pill called a disco biscuit, along with a shot of warm vodka to chase it down with. I was completely disguised as a Wookie, and she'd obviously mistaken me for one of the frat brothers—a mistake I was more than happy to play along with—so I downed it all in one gulp. What happened next is a blur. There were blobby colors that seemed to wish me ill, threatening blues and

purples, and if I stared at anything long enough, the edges started
to bleed, as if the pulsating boundaries of reality had become loose,
unstrung. My tongue got thick and everything I said came out
garbled. I thought I said "I think I'm going to puke," and instead I
actually said "Russia has a nuke"—truly unfortunate, because the girl
laughed instead of running to get me a bowl to be sick in, and when I
removed my mask to clumsily kiss her neck, I lost my lunch instead. I
still don't know how I got home.

And then when I got the call at four in the morning from Aunt
Lucy—not literally my aunt; more like my mother's best friend—and
she said my parents had died in a car accident, time took on this quality that's hard to explain. It was as if time became thick, like water—
not that it slowed down, but everything got all liquid, including my
knees before I dropped to the floor. I could hear Lucy's concerned
voice through the end of the receiver, all tinny sounding and distant:
"Dimitri, are you okay? Dimitri? Dimitri?" And I guess I'd have been
worried too, because it wasn't like I lived in a dorm surrounded by
actual people; by then I called an isolated trailer on the outskirts of
town home. I wanted to have a first draft of my novel done by the
time I graduated, which was not going to happen in a dorm where
every Friday night reggae, punk, and metal competed to see which
overblown bass line could shatter the windows first. That, and the
fact that every time I hit the head there were pails of vomit. (The pails
provided by janitors who were tired of unplugging the sinks from
undigested chunks of Chickwiches.)

After the call I didn't really eat or sleep for a couple of weeks.
Lucy and some relatives I'd never heard of—ancient cousins with pa-
pery, white skin—made all the arrangements, and a funeral, I found
out, is like a wedding in reverse, with less time to plan. Once the
bodies were identified—eternal thanks to Lucy for taking that on; the
car wreck, I understand, beheaded my mother—there were flowers to
be ordered, coffins to be chosen, the mortuary and catering company
to be coordinated with. I remember soggy meatballs, bread that tasted

like paper, all with the strange ticking of the bodies' inevitable decay pressing over the proceedings. There is a rush to see it done, over. I wore a black rayon suit—itchy and thin—at my parents' gravesite. I held a bit of dirt, which in retrospect must have been some kind of gardening mulch, because the ground was rock-solid frozen. Words were said, coffins were lowered, and I tossed the dirt into the neat rectangular plots, wiping my hands on my pants after.

The next day, with a bad, pressing feeling in my intestines from the aforementioned meatballs, I had a meeting with the executor, a reedy, thin man with very thin hair. In his cramped, dim office, he explained that there was a will, but also X amount of debt, which meant that the estate would still be in the hole after everything was liquidated—that word again, "liquidated." He said I should go and pick out a few things that I wanted to keep. It was hard to understand—the words themselves seemed to move so slowly that I could almost see them hang in the air, and I found myself inordinately distracted by a patch of tape holding together a tear in the leather seat. There were papers to sign—scratch of pen on paper—and my hand was gripped in a meaningful way.

I spent the next few days sorting through the house and putting things in five oversized cardboard boxes.

My mother, I discovered, was surprisingly sentimental. The attic rafters were crammed with every Mother's Day card I had ever made with crayon, Christmas ornaments, my red tricycle, battered from several ill-planned trips into the gulch behind our house, along with the odd antique, like a moth-eaten bowler hat and a croquet set that looked well used, although we'd never played. Eventually I started to rush through the debris like I was on one of those crazy shopping game shows, pulling out photos by the handful and tossing them in the boxes without looking, making split decisions. Baby teeth? No. Kindergarten macaroni necklace Mother's Day present? What the hell, sure.

My father, on the other hand, kept surprisingly little.

Contents of my father's closet: ten identical short-sleeved polo shirts in muted colors and six pairs of wool slacks (black and gray). Contents of drawer (he had one, and only one, in the mahogany dresser): six pairs of boxers and six white T-shirts, folded with military precision. In a shoebox under the dresser I found a tarnished silver ring and a broken pocket watch. The ring was engraved with some kind of Celtic knot, and there was a dull red stone in its center. He'd always worn the ring on his right hand, a mirror of the plain gold wedding ring he wore on his left. It was oddly missing from the baggy the funeral director gave me after the wake, jewelry taken from their cold bodies and presented like some kind of corporeal parting gift. I thought he'd nipped it and even sent a few heated texts that were never replied to. So, on rediscovering the ring, I decided to do the smart thing and slip it into the zipped pocket of my messenger bag, which I keep on me at almost all times. I put the shoebox in one of my large cardboard boxes, leaving the rest for the executor to donate. Of course when I went to look for the ring later, it wasn't there, and I never did find it again—something that haunts me in a recurring dream where I look down and see it on my finger, only to watch it slowly disappear.

The boxes are currently sitting in my apartment closet, taped shut. I haven't opened them in a year, and in fact I don't even use that closet. I find that the floor works perfectly well for coat storage and umbrellas.

Two weeks. Everything you love, own, and cherish, can be gone, *liquidated*, and lost forever in two weeks. Give or take a day.

———

By the time four o'clock hits I'm wondering if it'd be worth it to pull the fire alarm and get an extra hour of my life back, when suddenly Bob, uncharacteristically ashen-faced and sweaty, roughly pulls on his jacket and bolts out the door.

Myrna inadvertently catches my eye.

"What's up with him?"

She icily swivels her chair out of my sight line.

My phone buzzes. I hope whoever died is someone I have a file on, because there's no way I'm staying past five.

But it's just Mac. "Kid, you still here?"

Mac likes to call me "kid," which makes me wonder if I could sue him for age discrimination. For a moment I consider gently placing the phone back on the receiver and ducking out the back through the fire exit, but then I remember my rent is due.

"Sure I'm here," I say in a busy, curt voice, tapping loudly on my laptop. "Got a lot on my plate. What's up?"

"Bob's gotta go to the hospital for a colonoscopy, for Christ's sake. Afraid he's got polyps in his ass."

This brings up the single most disturbing visual image of my life. I rub my forehead. "That really sucks."

"You bet it sucks, 'cause it's Halloween and I already paid Maddy sixty bucks to do her psychic voodoo thing at the Aspinwall place. Huge *fuckin'* feature in the Saturday paper, and Bob's freaking out, 'cause he's got blood in his shit."

Second most disturbing visual image of my life.

"So, guess what? Today is your lucky *fuckin'* day. I'm gonna put your two-week notice on ice and let you write the feature. How do you like that shit? I mean, no offense to Bob and his polyps, but I gotta have something to print or all the fuckin' advertisers will pull out, and it's not like we can fill up those pages with obits unless there's, like, some kind of fuckin' bus accident or something. We should be so lucky, right?"

"So this feature—"

"Yeah, you need to get your ass down to the Aspinwall mansion by seven, otherwise Maddy will pitch a fit. She's my fuckin' wife's hairdresser, and damn, she's got a mouth on her. I'm sending Nate,

too, 'cause he's driving me up the *fuckin'* wall. He wants to start a
gym-and-donut franchise. Can you believe that shit?"

I have nothing to say about that.

"I swear to God my wife fucked around behind my back, 'cause
that idiot doesn't even look like me. But what the hell can I do,
right?"

I try to get the conversation back on track. "So what's the angle?"

"Angle? It's a fuckin' Halloween story in a fuckin' haunted house.
You sure you went to college, 'cause you're starting to sound a lot like
Nate."

"Right," I say, trying to think if I've ever heard of Aspinwall mansion. I haven't. "So—"

"Just don't fuck it up, because I swear to fuckin' God this is your
last shot."

Click.

Great. Me, Nate, and a psychic hairdresser spending the first an-
niversary of my parents' death in some kind of decrepit mansion that's
probably a death trap and will certainly set off my mold allergies.

My life could not *possibly* get worse.

CHAPTER TWO: SPOOKY

I'm twenty minutes late, because the address of the "haunted" mansion isn't on Google Maps, and I drive right by it two or three times. The entrance is completely overgrown with thorny, hostile-looking bushes. In my messenger bag I've got a notepad, pencil, and thermos full of coffee made with eBoost caffeinated water, my special concoction that would be illegal if anyone paid attention and will probably cause my heart to beat erratically. But after the séance or whatever, I still have to get the copy in by midnight, so it's a price I'm willing to pay.

I look to see if there are any other cars parked on the street—nope—which means that even though I'm late, I'm also the first to arrive. That's assuming Nate will be able to find his way here, which I doubt, given his seventh-grade reading level and presumably poor map skills. I should be so lucky. But then I'd be clueless myself how to find Aspinwall if I hadn't called Lisa—font of wisdom that she is—because there wasn't anything on the Internet except for a few digital pictures taken by drunk teenagers who apparently have made it their party destination.

Lisa told me that Delia Aspinwall was admitted to Crosslands two years ago. She was the daughter of Captain Aspinwall, who built the mansion after he made his fortune with evil South American coffee plantations that doubly exploited the indigenous tribes: first by forcing them to cut down the rain forest, their main source of sustenance, and then by making them pick coffee beans on the cleared land so their families wouldn't starve to death. Now seventy-eight, Delia is only semilucid, but she is remarkably bossy and sharp tongued, so none of the nurses want anything to do with her. Her habit of saving feces to throw at staff hasn't helped her popularity much either.

Delia lived at Aspinwall until she was eight, when there was a tragic fire of undetermined origin that claimed the lives of six rich socialites, including her mother. Some said her father started the fire (harsher tongues whispered it was Delia herself), and from age eight to nine Delia didn't speak a word, which made her "queer" (not the kind that immediately comes to mind). Finally at age ten she broke her silence, demanding to go back to Aspinwall, because she said her mother wasn't really dead; she had seen her at the movie theater watching *Animal Crackers* with the gardener. At this point her father sent her off to an English boarding school until she was eighteen and ready to be married to a respectable oil tycoon ten years her senior.

Captain Aspinwall apparently didn't have enough cash to fix the mansion, a dictatorship in Guatemala having put a dent in the family business. Delia, rich and unforgiving, was unwilling to lend the money. So there the house sat, home to mice and climbing ivy, until her father finally passed away in the seventies from a well-deserved bout of liver cancer. (What was left of his wealth had been blown on expensive Scotch whisky.) Delia unloaded the mansion for the first lowball offer she got, from a couple of hippies fresh from Amherst College who wanted to start a New England commune.

But—and here comes tragic death number seven—at Aspinwall the hippy dude was apparently killed by an animal, possibly a bear but more likely a rabid dog, and that was the end of that. There was talk of razing the building to the ground, but although it was officially condemned, there wasn't enough tax revenue for the demolition, so Aspinwall stood. Of course, with a tragic fire and grisly deaths, ghost stories ran rampant, and many of the aforementioned drunk teenagers claim to have heard footsteps, been attacked by an invisible entity, and seen lights flicker, even though electricity hasn't run to the place since Carter was president. The horror, however, apparently isn't enough to put an end to the midnight bashes.

Suddenly I hear a car slowly making its way down the street. It's a battered Ford Escort that was probably white at one point in the distant past and has a right front tire that's going flat. Maddy.

But no, the person who gets out of the car is definitely *not* a sixty-year-old psychic. She's young—my age, maybe younger—with long auburn hair, ultra-short bangs, green Lennon glasses, and ripped jeans. She wears a bright red wool hat, navy-blue scarf, and actual mittens.

"Hey! You must be Dimitri," she says, and I immediately recognize her smoky voice. Shit, she's better looking than I imagined.

"Lisa?"

She smiles and walks forward, holding out a mittened hand. I take it. "Nice to finally meet you in person," she says.

"What are you doing here?" I ask and then immediately wish I hadn't, because damn, what do I care?

"I'm crashing your spooky party," she says. "Plus I forgot to warn you about the floorboards. A lot of places in there where you could fall through."

"How do you know?" Stupid, stupid questions.

"Oh, I used to come here," she says, charmingly shifting from one foot to the other. "You know, high school keggers."

"I didn't know that."

She shrugs, looks almost pensive for a moment, and wraps a tendril of her hair behind her ear. "Not that I was partying. I was in a band at the time."

"You sing?"

"Nah," she says, "I drum."

Awkward pause.

The phrase "out of my league" doesn't even begin to describe how I feel at this particular moment in time. And before I can come up with something witty and insightful to say (I'm mentally trying to scan the last issue of the *New Yorker* I read, oh, six months ago), another car pulls up, this time a massive black SUV with military-grade round headlights. Behind it trails a beige Pinto that sputters and stalls in the middle of the road.

"Shakespeare!" shouts Nate, jumping out of the black SUV. Lisa looks at me curiously.

Nate pulls out a giant camouflage backpack, looking like he's ready to hike the Seven Summits, shoot some commies, or drop out of a helicopter into enemy territory. My messenger bag now looks like a man purse.

"You Shakespeare's girlfriend?" he says as he approaches, seeing Lisa.

"Friend," says Lisa, neatly putting her hands in her back pockets.

"Right," Nate says, keeping his gaze directly at breast level. "What'd you say your name was again?"

"I didn't," she replies coolly. No mittened handshake for you, Nate. Ha.

Nate turns on his biggest, whitest, thousand-dollar-a-year-at-the-dentist smile. (Nate has a notorious sweet tooth, and we're often treated to the sound of Mac screaming into his phone about "*what a fuckin' racket*" the poor local dentist is running, and "*there's no fuckin' way*" he'll ever get paid.)

This is the smile he flashes at Lisa. "Anyone ever tell you that you could be a model?"

"Creepy guys in bars tell me that all the time."

"You're going to the wrong bars then," says Nate smoothly. His timing, I hate to admit, is perfect. "I could show you where the cool people go."

"Oh," says Lisa innocently, "and *you* would know that?"

Damn, I might just be in love.

This must not be the usual response to the Nate playbook, because I can almost hear the gears in his mind starting to grind, as if thinking were an exceptional activity in the life of Nate Cheney.

A raspy voice calls from the now-defunct Pinto. "Do you boys mind giving me a push over to the side of the road?"

We all look over, and a massive woman heaves herself out of the Pinto, carefully maneuvering the biggest platinum-blond beehive I've ever seen through the tiny car door frame, holding the top of it protectively. She wears bright pink polyester pants with matching candy-pink sandals, and a giant diamond-like brooch in the shape of a turtle is pinned above her white pleather jacket pocket. The impressive layers of caked-on makeup would be perfectly suited for, say, a drag queen audition.

"Holy shit," whispers Nate.

For once, Nate has perfectly summed up the situation.

The woman shakes a pack of cigarettes from a glittering studded purse and expertly slips one out, tapping the end of it on the plastic wrapper. I notice she smokes the same brand as Myrna, and that voice—why is it oddly familiar? It's the way she flicks the lighter that makes the connection, because I've seen Myrna do that a thousand times before in the emergency stairwell of the *Eagle*. Maddy must be Myrna's sister. Goddamn, there are *two* of them.

"Sometime today?" she mutters, obviously annoyed. "It's in neutral." As she puts the cigarette to her pink-lined lips, I notice there are small white daisies painted on her hot pink fingernails. Lisa is trying hard to maintain an appropriately serious expression.

Reluctantly, Nate and I go to push the car over. I wheeze more than I would like to admit.

"Myrna was right," she says as she watches us.

No further explanation is provided.

"Hon, who the hell are you?" she says, apparently noticing Lisa for the first time.

Lisa swallows. "Lisa Bennet."

"You don't look like a Bennet." Maddy squints her eyes, staring. "Hmmm. I thought so."

Again, no explanation.

"Well," says Maddy, taking a long and serious drag on her cigarette. "Let's get this shit over with."

———

The driveway is at least ten or fifteen miles long. Of course, my daily
exercise consists primarily of walking across the street to the local
donut shop, so I may not be the best judge of distance. But it is inter-
minable, and for a time I wonder if we've entered a parallel universe
or singular ring of hell, like I died and don't realize it—cursed to
spend eternity trying to find the Aspinwall mansion in the company
of Nate, crazy Maddy, and Lisa. Not that I'm complaining about Lisa,
but she strangely hasn't said more than a few words, and it's awkward
between us, because we know each other by phone only. In person it's
different. I wonder if she's disappointed. Which makes me trip over
an overgrown root. Very manly.

Finally the mansion comes into view and my first impression isn't
house of horrors—more like crack-den money pit. It looks as decrepit
as one might expect for a five-thousand-square-foot Tudor that hasn't
been maintained for the past seventy years. There are gaping holes in
the roof (Was there a war I'm unaware of? With bombs?), most—if
not all—of the lead-paned windows are broken, and thick ivy ob-
scures the massive oak entry door. Beer bottles and cans are scattered
across the overgrown field of a lawn, and the remains of a small
bonfire are evident, with plastic buckets arranged into seating around
charred logs.

Lisa bravely leads the way, stepping gingerly over something that
may or may not be a used condom, and I'm hoping Nate has a gun
in his pack, because we just might need it. The front lock is broken,
and the door easily opens with a push from Lisa's shoulder, giving a
horror-movie-quality creak of protest. Lisa waves her hand as if she's a
tour guide.

"Welcome to Aspinwall," she says.

The foyer is truly enormous and designed in filthy rich Victorian style. It's two stories high (in case you had the occasional need to house a circus tent), features a seven-foot marble fireplace (perfect for roasting medium-sized children), and the ceiling beams are ornately carved with lions, cherubs, and more than a few immodestly bare-breasted women. Every flat surface is plastered and painted to look like an Italianate fresco, continuing the theme of gamboling cherubs and Grecian women. Dangling precariously overhead is an over-wrought crystal chandelier that would be amazingly painful if it fell, *Tom and Jerry* style, on one's head.

But then it looks like the mansion had a psychotic break, a schizophrenic episode of sorts, because the walls are papered in paisley and trippy tones of brown, orange, and yellow. The lighting fixtures are red, blobby plastic affairs, and there is one framed Led Zeppelin poster. Spray-painted next to the poster is the quiescent observation "Led Zeppelin sucks." Next to that someone wittily responded "Suck my dick." Then, in the true spirit of adolescent repartee, is scribbled, "I would if you had one, asshole."

"It's completely hideous," I say. "I've never seen anything as wonderfully demented."

"I knew you'd like it," says Lisa.

Is this us clicking?

"Everyone stop!" shouts Maddy. Strangely, we all do. Apparently psychic hairdresser is in charge. "We need to get in a circle and hold hands."

Lisa expertly inserts herself between Maddy and me. I really don't want to hold Nate's hand—that's way above my pay grade.

"Now," says Maddy, glaring at us.

Nate grins evilly, reaches for my hand, and gives it a bone-crushing squeeze.

Maddy closes her eyes, and I idly wonder if she'll be able to open them again with all that mascara. "Oh sweet Jesus, we ask for your heavenly protection in this den of sin and immorality. Give us thy guidance, oh Jesus. Keep our immortal souls safe in thy heavenly bosom." Nate sniggers at that. "This we ask in the name of the Father and the Holy Spirit. Amen."

"Amen!" shouts Nate, like it's a military call and response.

I say nothing. Maddy looks at Lisa, who is equally quiet.

"I'm an atheist," says Lisa.

"I admire that," says Nate. "But I could never give up hamburgers."

Lisa opens her mouth and closes it just as quickly. She gives me a look, and I shrug to confirm that, yes, this idiot is my editor.

Maddy just pulls out her cigarettes and sighs. "It's going to be a long, long night."

———

We decide that since there is no plan of action per se and the floorboards are dicey, we'll settle into the former dining room, which has a couple of rotted, questionable chairs and plenty of spider webs. The psychedelic wallpaper theme continues, this time with purple blobby colors that trigger a flashback to my hallucinogenic trip. Just looking at them makes me queasy. Maddy sits on a child-sized stool, rolls of butt fat hanging over the edge, and keeps her eyes closed while she mutters a rapid prayer that blurs the words into one barely intelligible sound.

"OhsweetJesusletthespiritscomeandprotectusinthynameamen."

Meanwhile, Nate proceeds to pull a large battery-operated lamp and inflatable chair out of his massive pack. Impressive. The inflatable chair has a built-in air pump, and in about three seconds he's seated comfortably. I try to pick up one of the dilapidated chairs for Lisa, but the whole thing falls apart as soon as I touch it.

"Nice one, Shakespeare," says Nate. "That was probably an antique."

"As if you would know."

"I'm perfectly comfortable on the floor," says Lisa, sitting down and arranging her legs cross-legged. I join her, but there's hardly anything perfect or comfortable about it. My ass is instantly chilled.

Nate leans back. The chair squishes. "Dad said if nothing happens to just make some shit up."

"Oh, that's just great," I mutter. "He could have told me that to start, and we could have saved ourselves the trip."

"Are you kidding?" says Nate, pulling out a bag of chips from his bag. Of course he also has a cold six-pack in there. "This is going to be a blast. I could stay here all night."

Even Lisa's casting a few envious looks at the inflatable chair.

"You want to switch?" he asks her.

"I'm fine," she says firmly, but we all know she doesn't mean it.

"Suit yourself," says Nate. "Chip?"

If Lisa goes for the chip, then the beer isn't far behind. Next thing you know, they'll be cuddled up on the inflatable chair, feeding each other Lay's from the bag, talking about bars where the cool people go.

"You want some coffee?" I ask.

Lisa shakes her head. "I wish, but I can't take the caffeine. It'll keep me up for days."

"It's decaf." Now I'll go to hell for sure. But desperate times call for desperate measures.

"All right, *Shakespeare*, just a little," says Lisa wryly. "Maybe it'll warm me up."

Nate glares at me. Two points for Dimitri.

I pour a steaming cup of my extra-caffeinated coffee into the thermos top and hand it to her, hoping she doesn't suffer from a heart murmur and that she has excellent health benefits. She takes a sip.

"This doesn't *taste* like decaf," she says, peering suspiciously into the thermos top. "Tastes Colombian. Like premium dark roast."

I give my most innocent shrug. "Maybe because it's organic." But I can see Nate suspects something's up.

"So, Lisa," he says. "You must be the friend that works with the elderly." Is this the same guy who said, "Who gives a shit? They're just dead old people"?

"Yeah," replies Lisa cautiously. "I've been working at Crosslands for a few years now."

Where's he going with this?

"I really admire that," says Nate. "You know, my grandmother was there before she passed away last year." He seems to choke up on this last bit.

"Really. What was your grandmother's name?"

"Beatrice, Beatrice Cheney," says Nate. "It was cancer. Cancer left a hole in the heart of our family." He presses a meaty paw across his eyes, as if there might be tears.

Lisa's brows furrow. With concern? Is she actually falling for this crap?

"Beatrice? I don't remember a Beatrice—"

"Probably before you started there."

"I thought your grandmother lived in Florida," I say pointedly, twisting the cap back on my thermos. "Near Orlando."

"She did . . . before . . . she died."

Such an evil, unfair play—now I must look like an insensitive jerk. I'm in a bad, *bad* mental place until Lisa catches my eye and gives me a questioning eyebrow.

Hallelujah. There is a God.

Nate sniffs. "Do you have a tissue?"

"Right, tissue," says Lisa dryly. "You have an arsenal in your back-pack but not a single paper product."

"I just didn't think I'd get so emotional. But this place reminds me of her. It's so old-timey." He sighs heavily and snuffles.

"*Okay*," says Lisa, getting to her feet and brushing the residual dust off her jeans. "I wanted to stretch my legs anyways. I can look around, see if anyone's left some TP or something." She grabs her bag and gracefully slides it over her shoulder.

"Want some company?" I ask hopefully. Last thing I need is quality time with Nate.

"I'm good," she says with a half smile. "Plus I could use a little break from the whole competing-over-the-girl caveman vibe."

Damn. Damn. Damn. She's onto us.

Of course, as soon as she's out of the room, Nate snaps open a beer. He is suddenly dry-eyed.

"She totally digs me. Don't worry, Shakespeare, I'll be gentle with her." He pops a chip into his mouth, crunching loudly. "You know, I bet she's got great tits somewhere under that jacket."

I wince. But to be honest, I'm thinking the same thing myself— I'm a guy; our brains go there. Plus, I haven't *been* with anyone recently. For one thing, the dating pool in New Goshen is dismally limited, unless I want to consider a retiree as a prospective love interest. And I've told myself that a relationship would distract me from finishing the Great American Novel I started in college, which is now nearing the one-thousand-page mark, with no end in sight.

It began simply enough—write your thesis on a historical person of interest. I chose Grigori Rasputin, partly because I'd recently watched a magician hypnotize a frat brother into squawking like a chicken (an obviously useful skill), and partly because I thought that it would finally give my father and me something to talk about— them both being from Russia and all. After buying a few thick, dusty books from eBay on Rasputin, I quickly discovered that actual research is mind-numbingly dull, so I opted to make my book fictional, which allowed me to incorporate unsubstantiated rumors from the blogosphere. Much easier. Maybe the opening chapter with Rasputin's resurrection while his corpse was burning, having just been poisoned, stabbed, beaten, and drowned, *was* a bit much, but after the syphilitic prostitute disemboweled him, I began to think I was on my way to making my first million (gore never having hurt Stephen King's career). Then I thought—what the hell?—let's make him a zombie (a vampire would be so . . . cliché), which would logically explain his pale skin, creepy stare, and inability to be properly killed. "Rasputin: Secret Tsar of Immortal Zombies". Shit, this could be a *franchise*. My professor quickly dismissed the book as trash, which only added to the appeal, but now at page 985 I realize that it's become what we in literary circles call a hot mess. Every night I spend two or three hours feverishly typing, hoping that some Kafkaesque logic will eventually manifest. All I need is another ten pages. Or maybe another ten. I'm like the guy who has lost his life savings at the roulette wheel and is going to the pawn shop to unload his wedding ring—one more roll will make it right.

I look over, and Maddy pauses her chant long enough to take a drag on her cigarette. If she were really psychic, she'd quit smoking, because even I can figure out what her obituary headline will be: PSYCHIC HAIRDRESSER DIES OF LUNG CANCER.

Nate shoves another handful of chips in his already-full mouth. "You getting this all down, Shakespeare?"

"Getting what down? Nothing's happening." A cockroach scuttles along the baseboard, as if it's waiting for us to be distracted long enough so it can make a run for the potato chip crumbs—thrilling stuff. I hear creaking footsteps overhead, which for a few tantalizing seconds gives me hope that there might actually be a ghost and, more importantly, a story to write about, until I realize it's probably just Lisa on her quest for bathroom tissue. I hope she's up to date on the rotting floorboards situation. Given the piles of termite dust in the corners, I'm surprised the place hasn't collapsed entirely.

"Night's still early," says Nate. He opens his pack and pulls out a high-end video camera. "It's got night vision, so I can catch all the action. Figured I'd need to make sure you get the story right."

"You're worried *I'm* not going to get the story right? This from someone who just lied his ass off about his grandmother dying."

"Shakespeare's jealous," he says, wiping a greasy hand on his jeans. "When's the last time you got laid anyways?"

"I really don't think I need to tell *you*—"

"So not recently. This year? Ever?"

I cup my hand to my ear. "Hear that, Nate? That's the sound of my lawyer calling your dad and filing a hostile work environment lawsuit."

"If this is a workplace, then get to work," says Nate. "You're supposed to be a reporter; what are you going to report *with*?"

"Fine," I mutter. I open my messenger bag to dig for my notepad, but my hand comes across something else instead, small, round, and hard. I open my bag wider and see a rip in the lining. There is something silver glinting within. My heart skips a beat. I widen the tear, and yes, there it is—my father's ring. Fuck, I *didn't* lose it. The ring's been in my bag all this time. It somehow feels right to slip it on my finger. It's heavy and strange but solid too—reassuring.

"You going to put a necklace on next?" asks Nate.

But before I can respond there's more creaking, closer this time, which announces Lisa's return. She holds a slightly yellowed roll of toilet paper, and Nate quickly resumes his traumatized expression.

"Best I could find," she says, tossing the roll to Nate.

"Thanks," whispers Nate. He tears off some tissue and pretends to blow his nose, loudly. "I just get a little emotional talking about Granny."

"I *so* believe you," she says, taking off her jacket and making a cushion of it before sitting back down. "Did I miss anything good?" she adds casually. But for some reason she seems a little shaken, and I notice that her mittens are now stuffed in her jacket pockets. Her hands are also covered with dust, and a raw, mean-looking scratch crosses the back of her wrist.

"Wanna check out my video camera? It's got *night vision*," Nate says proudly.

"Hey, you okay?" I ask quietly.

"Sure, I'm fine," she says. "Why?"

"Well that scratch looks like it could use a Band-Aid or something."

"It's nothing," she says tersely. "I was opening a cabinet and a rusty nail got me."

"It doesn't *look* like nothing."

"Is that thing on?" shouts Maddy from her corner.

"It's rolling," says Nate, pointing it at Lisa. I see he's working the zoom around her chest.

"Well, why didn't you say so?" says Maddy. She slowly heaves herself to her feet and then raises her flabby arms up like she's about to catch something—a chunk of plaster from the ceiling perhaps—and her voice takes on a strange staccato cadence, like she's a bad actor in an equally bad community theater production.

"*Spirits*. We come as *friends*. We come in *peace*. If you can hear my *voice*, then give us a *sign*. Show us your *presence*. Show us what happened *here*." Her eyes roll to the back of her head, and we're treated to a view of her upturned nostrils.

But of course nothing happens, except for a few dust motes drifting tepidly in the wake of a slight draft.

"That could get infected," I whisper to Lisa. "Or you could get tetanus. I can drive you to the doctor."

"What part of 'I'm fine' don't you understand?" she hisses back.

"The spirits require *silence!*" says Maddy loudly, glaring at us. But just as she finishes the word "silence," she's struck with a deep smoker's cough and has to hit her chest a couple of times, like something is firmly lodged there—a lung tumor perhaps. All that chest thumping causes her beehive to lean slightly to the left, so it's hard to keep a straight face as she raises her hands again and intones, "*Spirits*. What do you have to *say?*"

The ghosts here must be a shy bunch.

"I just don't see why you want to stay here," I whisper, "and risk lockjaw when I can easily take you to the doctor. We could grab something to eat afterward."

Oh God oh God, I think I just asked Lisa out. But just as she opens her mouth to respond, my dear friend Nate chimes in.

"That *is* a nasty scratch you got there. I have Band-Aids. And Neosporin."

Lisa gives him a look. "You have Band-Aids, Neosporin, a six-pack, chips, and an inflatable chair with an air pump but no *toilet paper.*"

Nate smirks and pulls his bag onto his lap. "You can thank me later."

Lisa's mouth just hangs open in disbelief, but I want to get back to the dinner part. Was she going to say yes?

"Let's see," says Nate. He pulls out a road flare, bungee cord, a set of jumper cables, a pair of handcuffs (handcuffs?), small silver packages of wrapped emergency food, a cigarette lighter, a well-worn paperback—*The Complete Survival Handbook: Protect Yourself Against Revolution, Earthquakes, Hurricanes, Riots, Famines, and Other Disasters*—and finally a small first-aid kit.

"You're not one of those creepy package bomber survivalists, are you?" Lisa finally manages to say.

"Nah. They wouldn't take me after my buddy blew off a couple fingers. Give me your hand."

Lisa pulls it back defensively.

"I'm *just* going to put a Band-Aid on it. Shakespeare's right about getting an infection. All these rats around here, you could probably get that flesh-eating bacteria or something."

"You could just *give* me the Band-Aid and Neosporin."

"Yeah, you could just give it to her," I say, my voice definitely pitching to a fourth-grade decibel.

"But that wouldn't be any fun, and my buddy Shakespeare likes fun. He was just bragging that he'd have you in the sack by the end of the night. That's why he gave you some of his jacked-up java: so he could keep you up all night, have his way with you. We bet twenty bucks on it. I personally thought you weren't that kind of girl, but Shakespeare, he's *so* immature."

I'm so shocked that I open my mouth, but the words won't come.

Lisa turns to me and narrows her eyes. "I *thought* that didn't taste like decaf."

"Lisa," I sputter, "I didn't—"

"Almost like slipping a girl a roofie," says Nate.

And then the unimaginable happens, the unthinkable. Staring me down coolly, Lisa reaches out her hand and actually places it in Nate's meaty palm, as if she's daring me to complain. Nate grins at me, dabs a bit of Neosporin on her scratch, and then rubs it lightly—no, pornographically—with his thumb.

Holy mother of God I need a miracle. "C'mon, spirits, *do* something," I mutter.

And that's when Maddy's convulsions start.

CHAPTER THREE: LADYBIRD

It's like watching someone being electrocuted, but there is no blue arc of light, no sizzle of an electrical wire. For a moment we all stare in shock as Maddy lies on the floor, her body convulsing furiously. But then Lisa suddenly jumps to her feet and I do too; together we race to Maddy's side. With the professional touch of someone who's worked, even as a receptionist, in a nursing facility, Lisa kneels and expertly cradles Maddy's head, while I do my best to hold down her shaking body—not an easy task, since underneath the rolls of fat, Maddy is apparently built like a tank.

Nate, though, just keeps the camera rolling. "Man, this is some great shit."

"Should we call an ambulance?" I ask quickly.

"It looks like some kind of epileptic seizure," says Lisa. "Let's get her on her side so if she throws up she doesn't choke on her vomit."

The idea that there might be vomit involved soon is disconcerting to say the least. I try to roll Maddy over, and I get an elbow in the chin for my pains. "You thinking about helping, Nate?"

"Kinda busy," says Nate. "See if you can hold her head steady so I can get a close-up."

"*God*, what an asshole," mutters Lisa, and I feel a thrill of joy. Thank you spirits and convulsing Maddy, thank you.

"A minute ago you didn't seem to think he was an asshole," I say smugly.

"A minute ago I couldn't decide which one of you was the *bigger* asshole."

Ouch. "C'mon, that's not even remotely fair—if this was an asshole contest, he'd win hands down."

"Thanks, Shakespeare," says Nate with a cheerful wave.

Lisa grips Maddy's head firmly and gives me an equally firm look. "I'll be the judge of that. And if you're going to mess with me, then I'm going to mess with you. Got it?"

I swallow hard. "Duly noted."

Just as suddenly as Maddy's seizures began, they abruptly stop. The room falls into a deathly quiet. There's a gentle creak as the wind brushes around the corners of the house. The glass that remains in the windowpanes shudders, then is still. For the first time I really think about how far out in the countryside we are—no living human within a ten-mile radius. And the sun is starting to set. *Fuck.*

"You think she's dead?" whispers Nate. "'Cause if she is, we can put her obit on the front page. Dad would love that."

I can feel Lisa invisibly seethe.

"We can kill him later," I whisper.

"Promise?"

"I'll hold him down and you can beat him in the head with his night-vision camera."

We both look over at Nate and the annoying, owl-like lens that is recording us.

"Deal," says Lisa with a hint of a smile. "But I guess I should . . . check."

It hadn't occurred to me that Nate might actually be right, but now I notice that Maddy *is* uncomfortably still, and it's impossible to tell under the stiff pleather jacket whether she's breathing.

"*Okay,*" Lisa whispers. She takes a slight breath before she reaches a tentative hand out to Maddy's neck to check for a pulse.

But as soon as her finger makes contact, Maddy jolts upright with an astonishing speed, like a marionette pulled roughly on a string.

She stares straight head, unblinking, unseeing. Her right shoulder twitches, as if she's still processing the current from an electric shock, and her beehive slowly sags even farther to the left.

"Maddy?" asks Lisa hesitantly. "Are you okay?"

Nothing. Silence.

Lisa catches my eye—this is not a good sign.

"Maddy?" asks Lisa again, carefully.

Maddy inhales suddenly, fiercely, like there's not enough air in the room to fill her lungs. She *is* breathing.

"Gotcha," says Nate cheerfully. "Dad wasn't kidding when he said she was good. Our web traffic's gonna go through the roof."

This is all just part of the act? Lisa glares at Nate, looking highly pissed, but something like relief starts to wash over me, a giddy "We made it" kind of vibe.

But apparently the show's not over. Maddy opens her mouth— forming a small, almost perfectly round O—and begins to sing in a lilting, childlike voice:

On a mountain stands a lady,
Who she is I do not know,

Appropriately creepy—I'm impressed. One of her arms darts out madly, clutches Lisa's shirt, and she jerks Lisa to her with a strength that seems unusual for someone courting emphysema.

"This is so cool I'm going to piss myself!" whispers Nate.

Lisa tries in vain to pry Maddy's fingers off her shirt, but Maddy's deep in character—too deep in my opinion.

"For fuck's sake, Nate, we got enough footage, don't you think?"

All I know is she wears golden slippers,
And her skin's as pale as snow,

"We can string it out," says Nate. "Make it into a series."

"*Maddy!*" I grab Maddy's shoulders and give them a shake. "Let her go. Let Lisa go." Instantly she does, and her hands hang in the air for a moment, suspended, as if she's frozen. But then she closes her eyes and begins to giggle.

Lisa straightens her shirt and falls back on her heels, visibly annoyed. Damn she looks cute when she's annoyed.

But then Maddy's on her feet in less than a second, and I swear to God I never saw her move. A new wave of panic—real panic—sets in, and my heart begins to thud loudly against my chest. Suddenly I'm thinking of that story by Edgar Allen Poe, "The Tell-Tale Heart", where the guy kills an old man and buries him underneath the floorboards, only to be haunted by the sound of the victim's beating heart. For a few horrific seconds I can't tell whether what I'm experiencing is real or some kind of literary déjà vu, but then I realize that it's not *my* heart making that noise; it's *actually* something pounding loudly against the sagging floor beneath us. And not only is there a thunderous pounding, but a slight push accompanies it, as if something is straining to get out, like a great white shark bumping against the bottom of a sadly inadequate dingy.

A frigid breeze rushes through the room, lifting Lisa's hair—I see her breath form a small cloud of mist. It feels like the temperature just dropped below freezing, and a wave of nausea hits me.

Take her by the lily-white hand,
Save her from the water,

"Whoa, did you see that?" says Nate, face pressed to the viewfinder.

"See what?" asks Lisa, but her voice sounds far away, like I'm hearing her underwater. My ears buzz, and a sharp pain pushes against my temples.

"This white light just flashed on the camcorder. So fuckin' cool," says Nate.

Maddy stands in the middle of the room, swinging her arms in an absent, almost childlike kind of way. Does anyone else see how black her eyes have gone? She pulls at a tendril of hair that has come loose from her beehive and twirls it around her finger.

Leave her and you might just find,
There's no end to the slaughter.

The pain in my head is turning into a roar, the floor seems to tilt, and vomit rises at the back of my throat. I think someone says "We should go"—Lisa maybe—but it's hard to tell where sound is coming from, and as I fall to the floor, I don't really care. I feel disassociated from my body, like it's someone else watching Maddy rip the brooch from her jacket and toss it across the floor, where it skitters like a living thing. It's someone else watching Maddy skip in an unearthly kind of hopscotch, like gravity doesn't apply, like she's an astronaut on a moonwalk. And the evening reaches a new level of surreal when her voice takes on a singsong cadence that fades into and out of my consciousness.

Ladybird, ladybird
Fly away home.

Lisa's voice is urgent, almost deafening. "*Nate!* Call 911!"
I cover my ears with my hands. There's something I want to say, but it's a struggle to remember the words or to think about forming them.

Your house is on fire
Your children are gone.
She stops then, looks at me, or maybe through me would be a more accurate description. What the *fuck* happened to her eyes?
"*He's coming for* you," she hisses.

And then I find the words. "Leave her alone!" I shout.

Maddy gives one last, tremendously impossible leap.

I say last, because next I hear a splintering crash, and Maddy disappears through the floor entirely.

———

Relief. Silence. I tentatively blink. Dust rises from the gaping hole in the floor, but the pain is gone, as is the roar in my ears. I'm able to push myself up to a sitting position, and the floor only tilts slightly. Something soft is holding my arm.

I look to see that something is Lisa's hand. She's so close that I can feel her gentle breath, and her warm brown eyes are beautiful, amazing—there are small gold flecks that catch the fading light.

"Dimitri, are you okay?" she whispers.

And in that moment, I am.

"Can you please say something? Because you're really freaking me out right now," she says, her eyebrows furrowed.

"Something?"

Lisa sighs and then sits back, tucking her hair back behind her ears. "Well, I can see you're only partially brain damaged now."

"No more than usual."

The shadows in the room are lengthening, but the hole in the floor is a completely dark abyss. There's no sound from below.

"Do you have a flashlight?"

"Flashlight. No clue what I was thinking, but no, I didn't bring one."

We both turn to Nate, who, to even *my* amazement, is still rolling tape. The large, battery-operated lamp still sits by his feet.

"Do you mind if I borrow that?" asks Lisa.

"Knock yourself out, babe."

He pushes the light over with his foot, obviously not wanting to lose his shot. Lisa inhales deeply, like she's considering whether she wants to preemptively knock him over the head with it, and flips it on. Immediately it's like a supernova exploded—I think I can actually feel my retinas burning.

"Pretty monstrous, right?" snickers Nate. "Four thousand one hundred lumens. Should be illegal."

"Christ, Nate," I say irritably. "Couldn't you have given us a heads up?"

He chuckles. "You should have *seen* the look on your faces—like two deer in the headlights."

Lisa turns to me. "How have you *not* killed him before this?"

I shrug my shoulders. "I have an aversion to penitentiaries. Weak coffee. No donuts."

"Right," she says. "I could always smuggle some in."

We turn to Nate, who is slurping a beer.

"I'll give it some serious consideration," I say.

Lisa starts toward the gaping hole, but I put a hand on her arm to stop her. "It's not safe."

"We need to know if she's . . ."

Dead. An uneasy shudder runs down my spine.

"I'm light," she continues. "And I know where the bad floorboards are."

"Lisa, you're not—"

"I'll be *fine*." And there's something final about the way she says it that makes me realize it's pointless to argue.

"Be careful."

"I'm not an idiot," she says with a half smile. Bravely she approaches the gaping hole where Maddy disappeared, testing the floor as she goes. When she finally gets to the edge, she holds the blinding light over it and calls, "Maddy, can you hear me?"

Nothing.

Shit. I mentally start to pack my suitcase, because there's no way Myrna will do anything other than make my life a living hell after I've gone and killed her sister.

Then there's the sound of something stirring. "Ahhhh," moans Maddy.

"Are you okay?" calls Lisa.

"For Christ's sake, I just fell through the goddamn floor. Of course I'm not okay."

Apparently unpossessed, Maddy is back.

"Can you move?"

A loud hacking cough is the immediate response. "Christ, I need a cigarette. But no, hon, I'm pretty sure my ankle's broke. Maybe your hunky friends could carry me out. Or your *one* hunky friend— that skinny Ruskki doesn't look like he could lift my poodle."

"Don't look at me; I got back issues," says Nate.

"You're always talking about lifting weights," I protest.

"Exactly. Weights. Not stinky fat women. Did you get a whiff? Smells like she stuck her head in a bathtub of Aqua Net."

"All right, don't move," Lisa calls down to Maddy. "We'll figure out what to do."

"I don't think I'm gonna be doing much moving with a broken ankle, hon."

Carefully, Lisa makes her way back to us—every creaking step makes me catch my breath, but she has the athletic confidence of a gymnast. She plops the lamp on the floor, puts her hands on her hips, and thinks for a minute, all business. Very sexy. "Who's got a phone?"

I pull mine from my back pocket. It's dead, even though I charged it in the car on the way over. "Not working."

Nate keeps his eye on his camera but searches his front pocket and pulls out an iPhone. "Mine's dead too," he says.

"So it's getting dark fast, we have no phone, and one battery-operated light," says Lisa. "One of us could take the light, walk to their car, and go get help. But that would leave the rest of us here in the dark."

"My camera's got night vision," says Nate.

That's only what, the third time he's mentioned that?

"That could actually be useful. Nate, you can use the camera to go to your car and then call for help. There's a drugstore that's open all night a couple of miles off the highway; they'll have a pay phone. Me and Dimitri will go down to the basement and stay with Maddy. You got anything else in that pack we could use?"

The idea of trekking down to the basement is not very appealing. "What if there are more bad floorboards?" I say. "Wouldn't it be wiser to stay up here?"

"Chicken," says Nate. "Shakespeare's afraid of the ghosties."

I turn to Lisa and try, but fail, to keep a defensive tone from my voice. "I'm just thinking practically."

"Well," says Lisa, "she might go into shock. We need to keep her warm, maybe give her what's left of your coffee. That should keep her conscious."

I nod, but my head starts to buzz just at the idea. I suppress the urge to grab the light and run from the house, screaming girlishly.

"Let's see what else we got here," says Nate as he digs through his pack. "Extra batteries, road flares, glow sticks, hand-crank emergency radio, Mylar blanket, leg splint."

"The Mylar blanket and leg splint would be good. Just leave everything with us."

"Plus I got some bandages." As he pulls them out, a condom drops to the floor. He grins and slips it into his back pocket. "A *real* man's prepared for anything."

Lisa looks over her shoulder and asks innocently, "Oh, is there a real man here? Did I miss him?"

"Ouch." Nate clutches his hands theatrically over his heart. "That really hurt." He pulls out his car keys from his back jeans pocket, twirls them around his finger, and then swings his pack in my general direction, hitting me so hard that it knocks me a few steps backward.

"You two kids don't do anything I wouldn't do. Not that Shakespeare here would really try anything; I was totally kidding about the bet. He's a little rusty, if you know what I mean."

"Not everyone's a manwhore, Nate," I say.

Nate gives me a wave with a middle finger as he exits.

"Don't get lost!" I call after him, hoping he does.

For a moment Lisa and I both stand in front of a broken window, watching him head down the overgrown driveway. The sound of crunching gravel echoes in the still night air, and the red light of Nate's camera floats away into the quiet darkness, then disappears. A cold wind blows through a nearby tree, which taps, taps, taps against the slate roof.

"Well, *this* has been an interesting night so far," says Lisa with a brightness she can't possibly mean.

"I'm sorry," I say. "This wasn't exactly what I had in mind. For meeting you."

"You had something in mind? You were sure taking your time."

"I was working up to it," I say defensively. "And I was thinking of something more along the lines of dinner and a movie. Like a regular-people date."

Lisa laughs. It's a good laugh. "Dimitri, that would have been so, well, *boring*."

"Second option was bungee jumping off the New Goshen Bridge. Blindfolded."

"Been there, done that," says Lisa, entering the gloom of the foyer.

"You're kidding, right?" I say.

She doesn't answer. And despite my erratically beating heart, which is caused by either fear, Lisa, or the life-threatening dose of caffeine in my coffee, I follow after.

———

In the kitchen it's easy to see where the fire spread from the basement to the walls and ceiling—the path is charred black. The back part of the roof caved in a long time ago and is now a rotting pile of debris, leaving part of the room open to the dark sky above. A lone, perfectly preserved teacup glistens in the twilight.

Some coarse and weathered plywood has been crudely nailed to the floor, creating a path to a wooden door decorated with a spray-painted skull and crossbones. Underneath are the words "This way to hell."

Why do I have the bad feeling that's where we're going?

"It's the only door to the basement," Lisa says. "I've never been down there, so no clue what the stairs are like. We should be careful."

"Careful. *Right.*" Personally my concept of careful would be waiting outside for professional paramedics.

"You okay? You're looking a little pale."

"Me? I'm fine. Never better." And to prove it I bravely cross the dubious planks and reach for the knob. It burns my hand.

"Shit, oh shit!"

"What, what's wrong?" says Lisa.

The pain is searing. "Oh God, I think I've got a third-degree burn."

"What? Let me see."

Gingerly I turn my palm over, expecting to see red bubbling flesh. But in the beam of the supernova light there's nothing wrong. My skin is perfectly normal. Damn, I thought the freaky stuff was over.

Lisa whacks me on the arm with the lamp—hard.

"What? What'd I do?"

"Payback. I *told* you not to mess with me." She reaches for the knob.

"Wait Lisa, don't . . ."

But before I can stop her, she's already gripped it, and the door opens with a mild creak of protest. "This *really* isn't the time for asinine behavior," she says, barely containing the irritation in her voice.

"I'm innocent, I say. Innocent." In fact my hand still stings.

Lisa snorts and starts down the stairs. I swallow and reach for the railing, which has a disturbing amount of give for something made of wood.

Now if you're going to die, fire's not the way you want to go. It's no stretch to think that if you burn to death, the spirit part of you is going to be so pissed that you'll hang around to take out some of that anger on anyone you can. Completely understandable. I pause at the top step and reach out to the wall; part of it crumbles in my fingers, releasing a dark cloud of smoky dust. Anyone who died down here went the hard way.

"The stairs are fine," calls out Lisa, and I see she's already at the bottom.

"Great. That's really great news."

She stands in her halo of supernova light, like some kind of hipster girl angel, looking at me expectantly. I give what I hope looks like a *hey, I'm totally cool with this* smile and reluctantly head down the creaking steps to join her.

And that's when the sickly sweet smell of rotting flesh hits, something I'm familiar with because my slumlord is too cheap to hire an exterminator, and every few months a rat dies in the wall by the dishwasher. My stomach heaves and I cover my mouth.

"What's wrong?" asks Lisa.

"That stench—it's unbearable."

"I don't smell anything," says Lisa. "Am I going to have to hit you again?"

"No, no," I say. "I'm . . . sensitive to mold." Guess it's just me again—maybe *I'm* having a psychotic break. It would explain a lot.

Finally I reach the bottom of the stairs, trying hard to focus on the curve of Lisa's Roman nose, which looks so kissable. The basement turns out to be one long, dark, and empty space that must lie under the entire width and breadth of the mansion. The ceiling is low, so I have to stoop slightly.

"Ewww," says Lisa.

She holds the light over two distressed and sagging mattresses. There are candles melted in the base of several cheap wine bottles, and a lone pair of women's underwear.

"Classy," I say.

"I *so* don't even want to know."

"You sure dinner and a movie wouldn't be better?" I tease.

"Yes," says Lisa. "But I have to admit I'm finally creeped out. Hand?"

She holds out hers and I grasp it firmly. It actually makes me feel a little more upright myself. "Maddy?" I call.

"Over here!" Maddy shouts from what sounds like the far end of the basement. "Sometime today would be nice."

"How come you never came down here before?" I ask Lisa as we head in Maddy's general direction. Hard to tell exactly where she is—there's something about the basement that sucks the bright light into its murky depths like some kind of black hole, and I can't see more than a few feet in front of me.

Lisa raises her eyebrows. "Are you seriously asking me that?"

I swallow. "Let me rephrase. Have you ever heard of any reason why the basement would be especially dangerous?"

"Well," she says, "besides the dead hippy guy, people who fried, and the obvious threats to one's chastity"—she nods at the mattress—"there were rumors."

"Rumors. Perfect. Nothing like unsubstantiated rumors for a newspaper," I say.

Lisa studies me closely. "You know, you don't look like what I'd imagined."

"Is that a good thing?"

"You're a little Jimmy Gneccoish," she says. "Ours is a seriously underrated band, don't you think?"

I haven't the slightest clue what she's talking about, but I hope there might be a compliment in there somewhere. I'll have to Google this Jimmy later, but right now I just change the subject. "So, the rumors . . ."

Lisa shrugs. "You know, scary demons, portal to hell. The usual stuff guys use to creep girls out and get laid. Is it just me or is it particularly freezing down here?"

It is remarkably colder—my nose and lips are becoming numb. Must be because we're below ground. *Below ground.* Like the bodies of my parents. For the first time I think about how cold it must be to lie in a coffin six feet under, the frigid iciness of it. Suddenly I can't breathe; I feel as if I'm being buried alive or am drowning—the air's taken on the quality of water, pressing in on my lungs.

"Dimitri, you don't look so good again," says Lisa. Concern clouds her eyes.

"Fine," I manage to gasp. "Allergies." Calm down, Dimitri. Not the time or place to freak out. Gradually I hear the thump of my heart rebooting.

"See?" I finally manage to say in a passably normal tone of voice. "I'm fine." To prove it I drop her hand and take a bold step forward beyond the sphere of light.

Bad idea.

My feet feel something softly wooden beneath them that bends, sags, and gives way—*Where did the cement floor go?*—and then I'm falling, falling, falling down into a deep, black abyss. My head knocks against something impossibly hard, then crash—I'm in arctic-cold water that's fetid and choking. It pushes into my nostrils, fills my mouth. Water that's *colder than a witch's tit*, Mac would say. My body registers the shock, my ears ring, and I instinctively reach out, feeling cold and slimy stones, but I can't stop my descent, until finally my feet hit something muddy but solid that yields and sucks at my boots. I kick. I need air—all the breath was knocked out when I hit the water—but there is nothing to see, no way to know which is up or down. I can hear my panicking heart thudding against my ribs, but there is something strangely comforting too about the darkness now that it's come and I don't have to think about it ever again. I release a weight I never knew I was carrying—I can actually feel it drift from my mouth—a small black spot that's heavy as sin, and even as my lungs burn, I feel lighter, happier. For a moment I have a lingering thought about Lisa—*Damn, just when things were starting to get interesting*—and then I think about my novel—*Thank God that's over with*—then I think about the five boxes in my closet—*It's all trash now anyway.* Something reflects against the slime, and I look to where up might be, and there's a dim light in the brackish water. It seems to be at the end of a long, thin tunnel, so maybe I'm dead already. But if I were dead, there probably wouldn't be bubbles, which I can now see rising from my nostrils. So that *is* up, but it might as well be the moon—too late, game over. Still, I weakly try to push my way there. I don't want Lisa to feel guilty. I know that feeling all too well.

But something grips my leg and pulls me back down, a burning cold hand like a vise, with nails that dig into my numb flesh. I look down. Two eyes, glittering like ice, stare back at me.

My last thought:

OBITUARY WRITER DIES IN HAUNTED HOUSE.
NO ONE MOURNS.

CHAPTER FOUR: AWAKE

Squeak, squeak, squeak. The room is moving. No, wait—it's *me* that's moving. My right hand begins to shake—I feel the neurons trembling, filaments that are jumpy, nervous, like a radio with bad reception. I want to reach behind my head and see if it's still there, but my arms won't cooperate. In fact, I can't feel them at all, which is strange—what was I dreaming again? I was on a slab in a morgue and there was a flayed corpse and a nurse in bloody scrubs, the stink of formaldehyde. Was that a nightmare? Some kind of hallucinogenic flashback? And then the deeper dream, the woman in the water. My leg burns where she gripped me—*impossible*.

"Is he conscious?"

Am I? My eyes flit open. Guess so. The ceiling is covered by cheap beige panels, which pass by in a blur. My head jiggles to the right. Two men in light blue scrubs; one has a cheesy seventies mustache and hobo-style stubble (did the Village People recently lose a band member?), and the other is Nordic and blond, like he just stepped out of a J. Crew catalog. They clutch the side of the gurney, faces beaded with nervous sweat, and there's a frantic edge to the way they look at me. I want to reassure them, but my mouth won't cooperate, so instead I just lie there. It's comforting somehow, not being able to do anything, handing it all over.

"Mr. Petrov, can you hear me?" asks Village People doctor.

Why are they talking to my dad? Oh, that's right, I'm Mr. Petrov these days.

A woman now comes into view, all angles and loose skin, as if she stopped eating years ago. She's very corporate in a prim black suit with small glasses perched on her pinched nose.

"Mr. Petrov, if you can hear me, I want to let you know that Grace Memorial is going to do *everything* necessary to make sure you enjoy a speedy recovery." Her voice is smooth and practiced.

"I've got you a private room on the top floor. I'm putting my personal assistant Jessica at your complete disposal, so if you need anything—and I do mean *anything*—she'll see to it personally. If there's anyone you want to have visit, we'll be more than happy to fly them out and put them up in the finest nearby hotel."

There's a fine hotel nearby? Where, Boston?

"Do you *mind*," J. Crew doctor says curtly. He has one of those testosterone-square jaws and is probably sleeping with a few nurses, damn him. "He's still a patient and not a litigant yet."

"My card," she says, studiously ignoring him. She slips it in my pocket (apparently I have a pocket now) and pats it firmly, as if she wants to make sure it doesn't escape.

Then, *whoosh*, she disappears as I'm pushed into an elevator. There's a mirror on the ceiling, so I get a good look at myself.

I look like shit.

There's no, and I mean *no*, color in my normally pale skin. I am freakishly white, blindingly arctic-tundra white—in fact an albino who'd spent his entire life in a cave would look positively tan next to me. Ditto my lips, which have a cadaver-quality blue tint, and—hold on—even the irises of my eyes have gone from a deep, earthy brown to something approaching a wintry dull gray. I'm sure I could easily terrify everyone in the confines of the elevator by holding my breath and not blinking, because damn if I don't resemble a newly resuscitated zombie. I try a grin. Impressively creepy. In fact, the overall effect would make Stephen King fall over and have a heart attack from fright.

I glance over at Village People doctor, and his eyes nervously flick to mine. Is that a tremor in his hand? Muzak plays in the background, a symphonic version of "Dancing Queen." Irritating. I stare at Village People doctor and bare my teeth, try a frightening hiss. Instantly his back is against the stainless steel elevator wall, and he holds up his hands defensively.

J. Crew doctor tries, and fails, to contain a laugh. "Good one."

"Thanks," I croak.

Hey, my voice works.

Now the elevator doors open, and I'm pushed onto a floor that I never knew existed in hospitals. The music changes to something classical, Bach maybe, and the walls have gone from industrial beige cement bricks to expensive shiny oak paneling. Swank. An extraordinarily, and I do mean *extraordinarily*, hot nurse with light blond hair, Barbie doll figure, the works, joins my gurney procession, and I decide that my speedy recovery will be as slow as I can possibly make it. In fact, I may never get better.

"This way," she says perkily to J. Crew doctor, and suddenly I'm in a private room that has a wide expanse of tall windows overlooking the deep chasm of the Goshen River. Very pretty from this distance—you could almost forget that a quick dip in that industrial sewage trough would immediately burn all the flesh off your body. There are also a variety of machines, which I'm immediately plugged into, and while hot nurse tapes electrodes to my chest (her hands are warm, and there's a waft of floral perfume), something sharp pricks my arm— damn!—J. Crew doctor hooks me into an IV, and then, *holy fuck*, Village People doctor is inserting a tube into my penis, which is so not right on any number of levels.

"It's just a catheter," says J. Crew doctor, reading my pained expression. "We're going to be flushing your system with an intense amount of thiamine and glucose."

I try to say "Couldn't you give a guy some warning?" but the only thing that comes out is "Warning?"

"Sorry." J. Crew doctor scribbles something onto a chart. Nurse Barbie is now hooking up the catheter to a clear bag that hangs from the end of the hospital bed. Embarrassingly bright yellow piss starts to gush.

I *have* died and gone to hell.

"Now Mr. Petrov—"

"Dimitri."

"Dimitri," replies J. Crew doctor with a tense smile. "I'm Dr. Conway. Do you have any allergies to medications, or are you currently taking any medication?"

I shake my head no.

"Now, and this is important to answer honestly—I'm not here to judge—but are you doing any drugs?"

I shake my head no again. Village People doctor raises his eyebrows.

"Nothing? Not even pot?"

At this they all look at me seriously, and I can tell that there's more to this question than they're able or willing to tell me. I try to raise my hand and find that my wrists are tied to the sides of the gurney with loops of hard plastic. Son of a bitch.

"Just a precaution," says Dr. Conway. "When you regained consciousness you experienced grand mal seizures, and we need to make sure those are over, since you're now hooked up to the IV."

Seizures I understand, "grand mal" not so much. Sounds like an excessively large size of espresso. Which reminds me, caffeine could be considered a drug, although I like to consider it *my little friend*.

"Coffee." My throat is on fire—why the hell has no one thought to get me some water?

Dr. Conway tilts his head. "Coffee really isn't the best idea right now; we're administering some sedatives."

"No," I croak. Thank God Nurse Barbie is on the scene, because she connects the dots and finally picks up a sippy cup with a bent straw from the hospital nightstand, settling the straw in my mouth. I take a few grateful sips.

My head clears, and I suddenly feel surprisingly lucid. I try a complete sentence. "I drink a lot of coffee."

Success. I'll be out of here in no time.

"Define a lot," says Dr. Conway.

"Seriously intense Colombian coffee. Even the water I make it with is caffeinated."

"I take it you don't care for sleep?"

I shrug. "Overrated." I take a moment before I ask the real question. "Was it just my imagination or did I come to in some kind of morgue?"

Dr. Conway gives Nurse Barbie and Village People doctor a meaningful glance, and they quickly exit the room. Not a good sign.

"Yes," he says quietly. "You were pronounced DOA by the ambulance technicians."

He gives me a minute to take this in. The sky is turning a deeper shade of gray; the sun must be setting somewhere beyond the bank of clouds. I wonder what day it is.

"You'd been underwater for at least two hours before the firefighters were able to pull you out of the well."

"A well." Such a small word for such a terrifying abyss.

"An improperly sealed well in the basement, yes. You fell through the plywood covering into about thirty feet of water. They tried to resuscitate you . . ."

Tried?

"But you didn't have a pulse; you weren't breathing and your body was stiff. So you were brought to the morgue. Prematurely, I guess we can say."

Understatement of the century. "That's what you meant by litigant. The hospital is afraid I'm going to sue."

"Well, yes." Dr. Conway slips his pen in his pocket and grabs a small metal stool on wheels. He sits on it, looking at the polished linoleum floor for a few moments, obviously thinking through what to say next.

"To be honest, we don't know for sure what happened. There are cases of hypothermia where children who've been underwater in extremely cold temperatures have been revived after an hour. But never an adult. And never after such an extended period of time. You didn't regain consciousness for almost twenty-four hours. It's a good thing that the coroner called in sick . . ."

I'm not sure I want to know the reason why, but I can guess. For a moment neither one of us says anything. I listen to the *blip, blip, blip* of the heart monitor.

"Is there anyone you want us to call?"

Is there? Aunt Lucy, who I don't know very well outside of our lovely time together preparing for my parents' funeral, or my neighbor Doug, who could at least tell my landlord to not throw my stuff out just yet. Nate's probably busy getting my obituary prepped for the next day's paper (Mac got his headline, the little fucker). But no, I have no one really in my life, which makes an entirely depressing situation even worse, so that it's hard to appreciate the fact that I did wake up before two inexperienced residents dissected my still living body.

"There was a girl in the ambulance," says Dr. Conway, who is starting to sound distant, but in a pleasant way.

"Lisa," I manage to say as my eyelids begin to droop. I struggle but can't manage to remember her last name. The darkness is softly edging into my consciousness again, and I feel like my body is slowly stretching out, like I'm as long as the hospital room—no, make that as long as the New Goshen River. Me like these drugs.

"Crosslands," I say, wanting to add more, but then I drift to a place where I can't say or do anything else, and I listen as the door quietly clicks shut behind the doctor. I am left partly awake, partly asleep and completely prey to the cold, dark thoughts that creep in through the windowsill, past the door.

———

My parents' obituary gnaws at me. If I'm honest with myself—an act
I try to avoid as much as possible—the painful truth is I wouldn't
have been able to add much more.

My mother had a near-obsessive dedication to the domestic arts,
which in the age of feminism are not arts at all—they're conceptual
chains of bondage imposed by a patriarchal society that serves to
demean women. This translates in my generation to pulling out one's
laundry from the dryer, giving it a good shake, and assigning a kind
of retro-chic factor to wrinkled and worn clothes. But if you had
entered our ranch house on any given day during my childhood, you
would have had to admit that there was an artist at work, or maybe
even a domestic dominatrix. For one thing, every article of cloth,
including washrags, dinner linens, and my underwear, was steamed,
pressed and ironed into submission with a lavender scent. Then there
was the food. If it wasn't rich, decadent, and with a calorific load that
should have caused us all to die of heart failure from congested arter-
ies, then it wasn't fit to be served at our house.

But while every dust-free and lemon-scented corner of the house
was imbued with my mother's passion, my father's passion was—and
remains—a mystery. In fact, the more I try to pin down his "thing,"
the further I feel from knowing him, unless you count knowing
something by its absence—like making a mold of a footprint to deter-
mine the curve of the heel that created it. Here's what I can say for
sure about my father. Every day he left in the morning at eight o'clock
sharp, coming home a little before or after six thirty. Sometimes he'd
go on trips for weeks at a time, returning weary, worn, and pale. He
did not work, my mother explained once, because our income had
been kindly provided by a deceased and wealthy aunt on my father's
side of the family in Russia. But when I asked where he was during the day or why, if we were loaded, he had to travel, my mother
quickly changed the subject and asked if I wanted to taste the cake
batter to make sure there wasn't too much vanilla. Her tone let me

know that there was no point in asking again. Some things were just not to be spoken of—like the burn scars that twisted around the entire length of her right arm and up to the base of her long and lovely neck. I asked only once why she wore long-sleeved shirts on even the hottest days of summer and was offered an impromptu trip to Farrell's Ice Cream Parlor.

My father was ethereally quiet and completely inscrutable. It was hard for me not to jump when I'd unexpectedly find him in the same room with me. One time I thought I was completely alone in the house only to discover him right behind me, reaching past my ear to open the kitchen cabinet. My dad could probably pick your pocket, lift your watch, and knot your shoelaces together in five seconds flat. When I was younger, I often wondered if we were in the witness protection program, because no one would make a better spy than my father—plus he had that soft Russian accent that gave him an international, mysterious edge.

He was such a nonentity that I never gave his life much thought until he was dead, until I was looking through his drawers, feeling part thief, part pervert. I found nothing that could add to my understanding. There were no yearbooks or mementos in the attic, not even a file with a birth certificate or copy of his immigration papers. I'd felt a queasy churning in my stomach. Who the hell *was* this guy, my father? I dove into the metal trunk used to store our family photos. There were hundreds of me, of course, only child that I was. Me as a baby, toddling precariously down the steps holding my mother's hand; me on my red tricycle, gap-toothed with a bad haircut; and there were a series of Polaroids I'd taken of my doomed goldfish (I was the angel of death to fish—none lasted more than a day or two). But none that I could find of my father.

Finally, at the very bottom I discovered one: it was of the two of us, my father and me, taken by my mother. We stood in front of one of her grand Thanksgiving turkeys, an impressive spread on the linen-clad table. We did not look comfortable with each other; there was an awkward distance between us. I was squinting and forcing an impossibly wide grin, and he was looking down at his shoes, brow furrowed, as if he were worried.

None of this, of course, made its way into their obituary, a copy of which I keep in my *Roget's Thesaurus*. I'm the only record of who they were, or weren't. And what stops my heart at four in the morning is the idea that in time I'll lose what little I remember, and then they will truly, and irrevocably, be gone.

————

It's a massive crack of thunder that wakes me up. I open my eyes, and lightning flashes across the night sky. A shattering rain pounds at the windows, blowing sideways. Or maybe it's sleet. If I were outside, it would sting; sleet has a slashing quality I've never been able to appreciate. It makes me wonder why I don't move to Florida, where I could eat grapefruit from a backyard tree—what keeps me here.

I try to move an arm, but it looks like I'm still tied up. Well, that's one thing keeping me here.

Something in the room rustles and I see a shadowy figure sitting in a low chair by the door.

"You are *so* dead."

My favorite smoky voice.

A floor lamp clicks on, and I see Lisa, glorious Lisa, sitting in a very plush, dark purple chair, which almost exactly matches the deep purple bags under her eyes.

"Well, not anymore," I say, flashing a grin. She's clearly not amused.

"Do you have *any* idea what you've put me through?" Her eyes narrow into slits as she speaks. She's trying to look stern but all I can think is, *Damn, that's sexy.*

"Hey, I'm the one who's plugged into a heart monitor." My voice is dry and crackly again. "Water?"

She blows through her nose hard, like she's debating whether or not to take advantage of my incapacitated status and kill me. I don't think I've ever seen anyone so upset on my account before. I'm flattered. She stands slowly and picks up the glass of water that Nurse Barbie has thoughtfully left for me, complete with its bent sippy straw. Way to add to my emasculation.

Lisa stands and holds it out to me, and I shrug, pull at the ties binding my wrists. "Need a little help here."

She gives an exorbitant sigh and then holds it to my lips. I take small sips; there is an oddly sensual dimension to this small and quiet act. When my throat feels like it isn't made of emery board, I nod.

"Thanks," I say.

She places the cup on a writing desk—for critical care patients who apparently need to keep up with their correspondence—and then pleasantly settles onto the foot of my bed. Her shoulders sag. "I'm so damn *tired*."

There's a nice little quiet between us, and I say nothing, because for the first time since I woke up on a slab in the morgue, I feel peaceful. *Blip, blip, blip* goes the heart monitor, regular little peaks and valleys on the screen. It has a mesmerizing quality—it's like watching fish in a tank or a burning log in a fire. It's so here and now, a touchstone that's ambient and reassuring. I wonder if the hospital will let me take it home. Maybe Jessica can pull some strings.

"Thanks," I say again, speaking without thinking.

She turns to me, eyebrows furrowed. "You realize I haven't slept since someone gave me 'decaf,' which actually contained the caffeine equivalent of a controlled substance, and then that someone went and *died* right in front of me."

"My bad," I say. "But I thought you didn't want a regular-people kind of date."

"I'm reconsidering my position."

I want to reach out to her but can't. Still tied up. "You got any scissors or sharp objects?" I ask.

She smiles. "A smart girl always has sharp objects. But I think I like you better this way."

"So do I have to beg?"

"Kinky thought, but no, I'll take pity on you this time."

I watch her reach down for her large brown leather purse, and her hair falls to the side, revealing a delicate, arching neck and pale skin with a paler, but very thick and obvious, scar. I want to ask but don't. She starts to empty the amazingly lethal contents of her purse on the white hospital bed. There's a good-sized bottle of mace, a couple of drum sticks, a Swiss army knife, another knife, larger and sheathed in some kind of leather casing, and to round it all off, a Taser.

I raise one eyebrow, but she ignores me, pulling the large knife from its sheath and then reaching over to my wrist. She holds it steady—her warm hand feels good on my skin—and then slips the knife between my wrist and the plastic binding. She is focused—I can feel her breath on the small hairs of my arm—and then she pulls quickly, snapping the plastic easily, like she's slicing through butter.

I try to raise my arm, and it hovers for a second above the edge of the railing before falling limply back to my side. The small effort exhausts me.

Lisa turns to the other wrist, releasing me.

"Thanks."

"You said that already," she says quietly. I can't quite read her tone of voice, whether that's a good or bad thing. She looks to the heart monitor, like it has an answer. "My heart's been racing. I don't know if it's the stress or caffeine."

"You're beautiful." The word "beautiful" rushes out, seems to float in the air, like mist.

"Ah, the drugs are talking," she replies. But she pushes me over gently, electrodes, wires, and all, and neatly curls up beside me. Then she reaches out and slips her hand under my hospital gown, which causes a pleasant shiver. The gown has cartoon ducks on it, and I momentarily wonder if it's part of hospital psychology to lull one into childlike obedience, but then—ouch!—Lisa pulls an electrode off my chest, a couple of hairs with it. She expertly slips it under her T-shirt, placing it directly across her breastbone so quick the monitor doesn't even skip a beat. Immediately the peaks and valleys of the monitor become more erratic. *Blipblipblipblip*, long pause, *blip*.

"See?" she says.

"Sorry," I say.

She yawns.

Another loud crack of thunder rattles the windowpanes, followed by a flash of light that reflects across the linoleum floor. I don't want to say a word. I can't take the chance that she'll leave, and I feel that this moment is tentative, like a wild bird has just landed on my shoulder. I don't know what any of it means, her being here beside me, and I don't really care. It's enough. It really and truly is enough.

CHAPTER FIVE: BARDO

I once took a religious studies class in college, Tibetan Buddhism of all things, because the professor was known to smoke dope and go easy on the grades. I remember almost nothing, because it was just a filler class, an alternative to the history requirement. But there is one thing that stands out: the *bardo*.

A bardo is a state in between one and another. There is the bardo of birth, of waking consciousness; there is the bardo of dreams and the bardo of death. I sometimes wish I'd paid more attention, but my professor had this droning voice that made it difficult to concentrate in class. I'd start out with the best of intentions, pen in hand, fresh sheet of notepaper in front of me, but once he started throwing around words like *trikaya* and *dharmakaya*, my mind drifted off to other things, like whether it was pizza or turkey tetrazzini day in the cafeteria. But the bardo stood out, this idea of an in-between place. And when my parents died, I felt like my life, up to that point seemingly stable and permanent, was in fact nothing more than a motel room—I couldn't seem to land anywhere solidly. It all felt so transitory, like I could put my hand against a wall and it would pass through.

Lisa changes that.

——

Lisa sits in the purple chair, comfortable. We both know the routine now, and it's strange how this hospital room feels like a home of sorts. We know the nurses by name: Nurse Barbie is actually Pamela (not Pam, not Pammy; you have to say Pamela, or the next time you're due for your sponge bath she will be rough). We've heard all the gossip, (Dr. Conway's marriage is on the rocks—his wife had an affair with her psychiatrist.) And we've learned that Village People doctor is actually Henry. He played lead guitar for a metal band in the eighties—even wore Day-Glo spandex and platform shoes. Sometimes he and Lisa talk music; she rattles off the names of bands that sound like jokes to me, but he nods seriously, like they share a religion.

Time drags in the morning, and early afternoon is deadly boring, but everything lightens when Lisa appears at the door promptly at 3:30 P.M. The outside world somehow clings to her—I can almost smell the light rain that beads her wool hat—and she always carries a paper bag with some treat for me: my favorite donut, the latest issue of the *New Yorker*, or a new addition to the serious vitamin regimen she swears by and which colors my pee different shades of orange.

And although I am getting better, from what no one really seems to know—my diagnosis is being assigned to that amorphous category of "undetermined"—a part of me doesn't want to. A part of me could stay here, like this, forever.

"Oh, I almost forgot," Lisa says.

She digs through the large bag she keeps her laptop in. Yesterday she showed me a video on YouTube; she was playing drums for a band that broke up three months ago, Pandora's Lunchbox. The lead singer got a job at a big insurance agency in Florida, and the guitarist moved to New York to get married.

"I had it framed," she says.

She hands me a black wooden picture frame, but where a picture would be is instead a neatly cut article from the *Devonshire Eagle*.

My obituary.

STAFF WRITER DIES IN HAUNTED HOUSE

Staff writer Dimitri Petrov, known by his byline D. Peters, tragically drowned to death on Halloween after falling into an old well at the Aspinwall mansion. He was 23. He is survived by nobody. Anyone who wants to watch the exciting video of the events leading up to his death can view them online at the *Devonshire Eagle* website, sponsored by Doug's Automotive on Fourth Street. (Half off your next tire rotation.) He will be missed.

"Classy. I take it Nate wrote the piece?"

Lisa smiles. "Anyone else you know who would use your obituary as advertising space?"

I frown. "The 'drowned to death' part really bugs me. I mean, if I drowned and I'm being written about in the obituary pages, then 'to death' is redundant. Don't you think?"

"Check out the back."

I turn the frame over. And there, in the corner, is my toe tag.

"I had to bribe Henry with free concert tickets to Buddy's Holly to get it. The hospital would freak if they knew you had it."

I'm speechless.

"You like it?" she asks, concerned.

"This is the best thing *ever*. I love it."

She visibly relaxes. "I knew you would. Doug says hi by the way. He made you lasagna and put it in your freezer. Also your spider plant is dead. He forgot to water it."

"I have a spider plant?" Oh right, Doug's housewarming present from a year ago, which I believe I killed when I mistook the glass cleaner for the water spray.

"I want to see the video," I say. "The one Nate posted."

Lisa shudders. "No, you don't."

I don't push it.

Somehow parameters have been set between us. We don't talk about "that night," we don't talk about anything personal (my one innocent query about whether she grew up in New Goshen was met with stony silence), and we don't talk about what will happen when I leave the hospital. (Does she only visit me out of pity? Once I'm well, will we still see each other?) We don't talk about if we're just friends or more than that, and we don't talk about feelings in general or feelings for each other specifically. I pretend not to notice the scar on the back of her neck; I don't ask about where she goes home at night or who sends her text messages on her phone that make her frown and swear quietly to herself. I try not to think at all about my cold and lonely apartment or that thing called reality. We exist in a hospital room bubble, paid for in full by the *Devonshire Eagle*'s health insurance company, with fringe benefits provided by Jessica, Grace Memorial ace executive assistant, who really does give us anything we ask for.

Which reminds me.

"What do you want to eat tonight? Should we send Jessica to Worcester for Indian or to Albany for Chinese?"

Lisa thinks about it. "It's always cold when she drives so far."

I reach over for a room service–style menu. I have pleasantly discovered that one of the benefits of staying on the sixteenth floor is that there is a different chef for us VIPs, one who can actually cook.

"Steak?"

"Lobster salad for me," says Lisa.

"Consider it done," I say, buzzing Pamela. "But we only have two more days. We should think of something exotic for Jessica to chase down. Like jellied eel confit."

Lisa flips the page of *Rolling Stone*. "I like Jessica. And I don't see the reason to torture her. It's not her fault you ended up in the morgue."

I don't share the sentiment. Personally I feel like I'm owed millions, or maybe even billions, for emotional distress alone, but my calls to lawyers have revealed that unless you're left permanently damaged, like you get a sex change instead of a Botox injection, the courts don't care much for medical suffering. I'm told I'm lucky to be on the sixteenth floor and to get on with my life.

I sigh. "You've become a lot less fun since I died."

Lisa sticks her tongue out at me. It's a nice tongue.

Two more days. Forty-eight hours. Two thousand eight hundred and eighty-eight minutes.

"Lisa . . ." I start to say, then stop.

She looks up. The lamp casts a shadow over her face.

"Two more days until I get out of here. Into the real world and all that."

She glances down at a spot on the floor, as if there is something suddenly interesting there.

"Do you still want to go on a regular-people date?"

Half smile. "So are you finally asking me out?"

"I guess you could say that." The heart monitor is long gone, and now there is only the sound of a nurse walking down the hallway, the clock on the wall ticking. Lisa slowly puts the magazine down on the table, taking her damn time about saying anything, letting me hang.

Finally she begins, somewhat hesitantly, "I just want to be—"

"If you don't," I interrupt, desperate to avoid hearing the hated word "friends" voiced aloud, "that's cool too. Not cool I mean, just I'd understand."

"Honestly, Dimitri, will you let me finish what I was going to say?" She walks over to my bed, pushes my legs over and settles on the edge. Her sweater is pink and fuzzy. "Are you always this—"

"Neurotic? Yes."

She shakes her head at me as if I'm an impossible case, which I am. A strand of yarn is unraveling from her sleeve, and I tug at it, wrap it around my index finger.

"I'll shut up now."

"*Thank* you. What I was trying to say was I just want to be clear. You keep talking about a regular-people date, and I'm not regular people. My life is . . . complicated."

"Complicated is *fine*; everyone's life is complicated."

"Not to the degree mine is." She sighs and places her hand in mine, turning it over. A deep, inscrutable look passes over her face. "Sometimes when people find out about this *complication*, they head in the other direction. Quickly."

"You want to talk about it?"

"Not yet. I will, I promise, but for now I just want to keep things simple. Like they are now. Does that make sense?"

"Sure, I agree completely." I haven't the faintest idea what she's talking about, but since this is heading outside the dangerous "friends" waters, I'd agree to just about anything. "So Lisa Bennet, would you like to go on an *irregular*-people date with me?"

Now she smiles, a real smile. "What would we do on an irregular-people date?"

"I don't know. I have a feeling it involves garden gnomes, the New Goshen Bridge, and golf clubs, followed by pizza."

"That could be interesting. But people here are very attached to their garden gnomes."

"Very true, and I'd never suggest vandalism for a first date. These would be virgin gnomes, freshly bought from Kmart and ready for sacrifice. How about Friday night?"

"Friday could work."

"What time should I pick you up?"

Again, the shadow of hesitation; she turns her head slightly away, and her hand goes limp in mine.

"Maybe we could meet somewhere?" she asks in a quiet voice.

"Meet somewhere," I say in a rush. "That's actually what I meant to say. Because picking you up would be—"

"Complicated."

"Now you're finishing *my* sentences."

She leans over, smelling like lemon, honey, and something woodsy, like sandalwood. Her lips lightly brush against mine. "Thanks, Dimitri. For understanding."

But seriously I couldn't care less what her complication is, because it feels like home when she kisses me. It feels like I finally have a place, a reason, to stay.

———

A clatter wakes me up; Nurse Pamela pushes an old woman in a wheelchair down the empty hallway. The woman mutters something unintelligible while she pulls nervously at her lank gray hair; she wears a light yellow bathrobe and fuzzy slippers, not the standard hospital issue. I look over to the purple chair, but Lisa is gone to wherever it is she goes at night; she has been painstakingly ambiguous about where she lives. It's always over there, or close by, or around the corner. I hate it when she leaves without waking me first.

The clock says it's midnight, which means no TV, no calls to the kitchen for a snack. And I've discovered that nothing ruins one's circadian rhythm like being in a hospital where there's always something squeaking or beeping, where muffled announcements are constantly made over the intercom—"Paging Dr. Harrison; Dr. Harrison, line one." It's like trying to sleep at the DMV. So although I should try to go back to sleep, I'm as alert as if I just drank a triple-shot latte.

Fuck it.

Then I see Lisa's laptop on the small table by the door, covering her copy of *Rolling Stone* and the hospital's copy of *Reader's Digest*.

I really shouldn't.

Sometimes I'm stunned by the quantity of personal information my own measly laptop carries about me. My photos are all digitized, every blog I read is tracked by my RSS feeds, and every website I visit is documented by my browser history. There is a cookie trail of all my interests lodged in some digital sphere, which will one day consolidate the collected data of six billion souls and vomit out—I don't know—personalized infomercials for deodorant and car wax. I have three hundred and fifty-two virtual friends I've never met and couldn't place in a crowd, kind souls who feign an interest in my snide comments about crappy movies. And this all makes me wonder if the preliminaries of dating could be more efficiently handled if we simply exchanged laptops with one another; we could skip past the mozzarella stick appetizers and awkward moments—"So what was your major in college?" "Any peanut allergies I should be aware of?" It would all be right there, digitized bits and pieces of true biography— no white lies, no need to pretend a liking for cats and *Friends* reruns.

My fingers tap against the rail of the hospital bed. This would definitely be a violation of the "it's complicated" parameter.

What the hell.

It's a relatively simple matter to slide off the bed—cold air whooshes up my hospital gown, peppering my ass with goose bumps—and then grab the laptop and slip back into bed before Nurse Pamela walks back down the hall. If she sees that I'm up it'll be a good dose of sedatives for sure, so I turn over to the window side, pretending to be asleep, and surreptitiously press the power button.

Of course Lisa has a Mac. Already we're at different ends of the universe.

Her desktop background is a hand-scribbled flyer for some punk band I've never heard of, Yuck Fou. So far, so good—I'm glad it's not something cheesy like puppies.

Her documents folder contains mostly music files, so I click on over to her photos. They're blurry cell phone pictures, bands playing in subterranean-style bars and shirtless guys jumping into a mosh pit—that kind of thing. Then there's a series of one lead singer in particular. He wears tight, ripped jeans, his hair is jet black and lank, like he just rolled out of bed and hasn't showered in, say, a month, and he's either shooting heroin or has decided to stop eating altogether, because through his white T-shirt I can see the angular bones of his rib cage. There are three snapshots of him slamming his guitar on the stage, two of him looking off into space, gripping the microphone tightly, and one of him crashed out on a sagging plaid couch. Maybe Nurse Pamela should give me some of those sedatives after all.

A different series of photos, taken outside, show a plain white farmhouse. There's a young girl with pink rubber boots and thick braids; she's working on a dilapidated snowman that sports a Mohawk formed from carrots. Then the girl is throwing a snowball at the holder of the cell phone, and shortly after she must have taken over the phone itself, because next is a snapshot of Lisa. She's wearing my favorite wool hat and mittens, her eyes are sweetly closed, and she's laughing.

A spasm of guilt hits me, but it's not enough to keep me from clicking over to her browser. Lots of band sites bookmarked, but also mental health websites: St. Augustine's Medical Center; Metro West; Odd Fellows Home; a few websites about schizophrenia; and one, disturbingly, called the Sibling Abuse Survivor's Network.

Okay, now I feel like an asshole. I'm about to click out, shut down the whole thing, when I remember that part of my obituary that said there was a video of the events leading up to my death.

Who wouldn't want to see that?

I hop on *Devonshire*'s sadly outdated website, which is primarily loaded with advertising: "Pascali's Fine Liquor—Six-Pack Sundays, Buy One Get the Second Half Off"; "Alizbozek & Sons—New Goshen's Widest Selection of Coffins." I find Nate's video masterpiece slotted under a car commercial and hit PLAY.

Everything has a slightly greenish hue—Nate's camera did indeed have night vision. And oh sweet Jesus, there's Maddy bending over to pick up her dropped lighter. I must have been occupied with pouring Lisa her coffee, because I would never, *never* have forgotten what proves to be a disturbing reveal of Maddy's butt crack poking up above her white leather studded belt, which failed its purpose of holding up her hot pink pants.

I shiver. This is scarier than I thought it would be.

Then blah, blah, blah, Nate and I are trying to score points with Lisa. I push forward past the embarrassing dialog—*Did I really sound so desperate?*—until there, Maddy is on the floor convulsing. It's even worse on replay; at the time, shock must have diminished some of the details now caught on glaring HD video. The veins in her face are swollen and bulging, like she's suffering a rage attack, her thick tongue hangs from the side of her mouth, and her eyes are as flat and empty as the corpse in the morgue.

But there's a moment in particular I'm looking for. I forward the video to the frames right before she jumped to her feet, and there it is.

Impossible.

I push the play bar back, count again. After Maddy's giggling fit and before she's standing upright, there is *barely* one second between the frames. It's even freakier encapsulated on this small video player, because it looks almost cheesy in an ultra-bad B-movie kind of way, which is probably why it's only had about fifty views and a couple of comments, both negative: "This suckz" and "Lamer than *Alien Autopsy.*"

In disbelief, I let the video roll.

> *On a mountain stands a lady,*
> *Who she is I do not know,*

Then a glowing blur flashes across the screen. I remember Nate said something at the time, so I push it back again, but it's so *fast*, it must be . . . what? Maybe a digital hiccup—a good reason to take your night-vision camera back to the pimply-faced RadioShack sales associate who sold you the piece of crap in the first place. But there's something else, something . . . familiar. So I take it frame by jerky frame, but the light doesn't seem to *come* from anywhere. In one frame it's just Maddy standing in the corner, and then the light appears, a small orb that dances across the screen like a firefly on speed.

The orb explodes into a burst of particles, and in the haze I can see something *there*! The face of a woman. I pause the video, bring my face closer to the computer screen.

And gasp.

High cheekbones, long neck, hair that seems to float in the air like it's water; eyes that glitter with a potent, tangible fury—they seem to reach through time and space like she's actually *here*, seeing me now in my ducky hospital gown. My heart freezes, my fingers turn to ice, but there's something else too, a vague intuition, like a dream you can't quite remember. She'd said my name, but then something else—I can hear the words bubble from her lips: "He's coming for *you*."

"*Who's* coming for me?" I whisper.

All the lights in the hospital suddenly flicker, then go dark. For a moment I'm left with just the ghostly illumination of the laptop, the same frozen video image—until all of a sudden up pops one of the blurry cell phone pictures of the punk musician. He's gripping the microphone like he's in the act of strangling it, a palpable rage rippling under his skin.

The lights come back on.

A coincidence—a glitch—a random convergence of completely unrelated events. It must be.

I shut down Lisa's computer with jittery hands and restore it to its spot on the side table. But I have a strong sinking feeling I can't quite will away that this small but happy phase of my life, this lovely little bardo of my hospital stay, is over.

CHAPTER SIX: PICTURES

My last Grace Memorial perk is a black stretch limousine that drives Lisa and me back to my sad apartment in one of the saddest neighborhoods in New Goshen, with its characteristic series of empty brick factory buildings, broken windows, graffiti, and sagging stoops. We pass old cars propped up on cinder blocks in the driveways of scattered tract homes, the occasional trailer park, and broken, empty lots with twisted chain-link fences. A light scattering of snow snakes across the road, and a brown skinny dog pauses on the sidewalk and sniffs around the base of a rusty drain pipe before pissing on it.

I wonder what Lisa thinks as we pull up to the old Victorian, with its peeling blue paint and scraggly dead bushes. In the sixties it was spliced into efficiency apartments, and mine is on the second story, with a good view of the Stop & Shop rooftop and deserted rail yard beyond. I hope someone has thought to pay the heating bill, because the windows are original to the house, and even with the baseboard heaters at full blast, I usually have to wear a wool sweater and scarf.

"My crib," I say.

"I see you live the high life on your obituary writer's salary."

I shrug, uncomfortable. I feel revealed in some way.

"I like it," she says.

It's nice of her to say. The limo driver pops the trunk and gets out; he is actually wearing a black suit and dark sunglasses, like a secret service agent. There's not much in the back; I'm wearing the clothes that were on me when I arrived at the hospital, which feels weird, like bad juju. I thought about throwing them away, but then I wouldn't have had anything to wear except for my favorite ducky hospital gown. The driver takes out a plastic shopping bag filled with what Lisa calls my hospital guilt prescriptions—a ninety-day supply of Valium, Ambien, and Xanax.

I smile at Lisa, awkward again. I take the bag from the limo driver, decide against a tip—*Let the hospital cover that*—and then head up the steps to the familiar entry. Lisa follows.

The hallway is dark, and the stairs, also original to the house, are dusty. It's strange to be back. I notice things that I never saw before, like the way the steps are worn in the middle, and the thin oriental carpet in the entry that is fading away to nothing. The air is stale and heavy.

I have to stop on the second step, take a breath. My body still isn't fully recovered, and my head feels light, even with this small amount of exertion.

"You all right?" says Lisa.

"Sure." Actually I feel like I've just climbed to a high-altitude base camp on Mount Everest. Just think, only fourteen more steps to go.

There are two apartments on the top floor, Doug's and mine. For some strange reason his number is 12 and mine is 18. When we get to the landing, I pull out my worn steel key, an antique in itself, and it takes a few moments to catch the lock correctly.

The apartment is sunnier and smaller than I remember. The sheets that I use for curtains have been pulled aside, there's a stash of mail on the counter, and my dead spider plant rests in memoriam on a small, shaky table by the doorway, gathering cobwebs. My "cozy" one-bedroom consists of three small rooms. Each leads into the other, and there is no hallway to speak of, which is adequate when you live alone, as I do. The ceilings are high, with peeling yellowed plaster, and the cheap plastic light fixtures hold the remains of dead insects. My jackets and umbrella are piled on the floor as usual, and I kick them aside to make a path. To the immediate right is the one small closet, filled with the boxes from my parents' house.

"Are you going to give me the tour?" asks Lisa.

"I'd just like to point out in my defense that I wasn't expecting company when I left."

"What, you scared I'm not going to like you because your bed isn't made?"

Uh, yes, exactly. But I shrug like I don't really care either way. "Here's the living room."

"Convenient. I like the open floor plan."

I physically turn her away from the galley kitchen with its sink full of dishes—I can smell the trash from here, it probably needed to go out a month ago—and gesture to my brown sagging couch, Doug's second cousin's castoff. In front of it is a wobbly bamboo coffee table, with the petrified remains from my last dinner there: crusts of a peanut butter and jelly sandwich. A small thirteen-inch television is propped up on stacks of books. I drop my guilt prescriptions on the coffee table.

"That's actually the casual dining room."

"It looks a lot like your living room."

"And it's also my home office. So I guess you could call it a multipurpose room."

"You could seriously use another chair."

"For what?"

She raises her eyebrow. "For company."

I swallow. Right. Suddenly I'm counting my threadbare towels. There are two, both frayed at the ends.

On the wall are a couple of framed black-and-white photographs —both of the same crosswalk in New Goshen. Lisa approaches them, looks closely.

"Interesting," she says.

"I like that crosswalk." Did I really just say that? Idiot, idiot, idiot.

"Why?"

"I don't know. Random. Like ninety-eight percent of my life right now."

The Xanax is starting to gain some appeal—maybe I should take one, or two, or six. Why was it so easy in the hospital room? Here everything feels strange, like a first date. Why does it matter that she said my photography is interesting? Why does my heart actually skip a beat?

I cough and flick the light on in the next room, which is strangely split in two halves. There's a small bathroom with a shower on one side, a built-in closet on the other. The tile in the bathroom is pale pink, and the sink looks like a scallop. No windows.

"Not awful" is Lisa's verdict.

I snort with laughter.

"Well, it's not all mildewy and gross," she says defensively. "I've seen worse."

Two more steps and then we're in the last room, my bedroom. I can almost, but not quite, stand in the middle, reach out my arms and touch the walls on either side. The mattress is on the floor, covered with an unzipped navy-blue sleeping bag and striped pillows—no pillowcases. Next to it is an overturned milk crate that serves as a nightstand, with a lamp and pile of books. But the window here is tall, and there's a view of the steeple of St. Joseph's Church through the barren branches of a maple tree.

"Your apartment is *sadly* deficient when it comes to band posters," says Lisa, reaching out to touch one of the empty walls.

"It's not much," I say.

"Define much." She turns to the window, catches my eye.

Why is she looking at me like that, like she can see right through me and hear what I'm thinking? It's hard to take. I go on the offensive.

"And what's it like where you live?"

Now she's the one looking down. She takes a deep breath. "I'm jealous."

"Jealous? Of what?"

"You have your own space. It's cool. No roommate; no one to ask you where you're going, when you're going to be back."

"Yeah," I say, "no one to care if I drown in a well."

"Well, there is that," she says. "But you can't say no one. I care."

I take a step closer and wrap my arm around her waist. My hand idly slips up behind the back of her sweater; her skin is soft and warm. "You do?"

"I can't even afford to live on my own," she says quietly, pointedly ignoring my question. But frankly at this moment I couldn't care less where she lives or what her secrets are, or what her name is, for that matter, so although she starts to say something else, she can't, because I pull her to me. My lips meet hers—not softly, not gently, more like a starving man finding bread, a drowning man finding air—and suddenly all I'm aware of is her breath, the curve of her neck, the slope at the base of her spine. My hands have a will of their own; they discover the elastic back of her bra and tug at the clasp.

"Wait," she breathes. "I don't *know* you. And you don't know me."

But my lips are persistent, and I press her against the wall. There is something incandescent about her skin; it tastes like salt, oceanic and breezy. There's too much clothing between us, something I plan on rectifying immediately.

A crash in the kitchen—a splintering, shattering sound. I pause.

"Someone's here," she whispers, putting a hand between us.

I groan, but already the moment is lost. Lisa is running her hands through her hair, straightening her clothing. "My bag, where's my bag?" she says worriedly. "Did you lock the door behind you?"

"Why would I lock the door?"

As if in response, the front door slams.

"Fuck," mutters Lisa.

I grab the lamp from my nightstand, gripping it tightly and suddenly wishing I was one of those guys who keep a baseball bat in the closet, because this fixture was a Kmart special, and the base is a lightweight plastic. Not really an ideal defensive weapon, unless one is being attacked by an arthritic elderly person or young child. Then something clicks, because I remember the lethal contents of Lisa's purse—mace, knives, sharp pointy objects—and I realize that maybe there's a reason she's carrying all that shit.

"Daniel?" she calls.

No response.

"Who's Daniel?" I whisper.

She doesn't answer. Instead she takes a deep breath and strides forcefully past the bathroom into the kitchen/living/multipurpose room, me trailing behind, gripping my forlorn lamp.

The room is empty. Lisa immediately darts to the front door, locking the deadbolt, while I look around—something feels different, but what? Everything looks the same, with nothing out of place. Maybe it was just Doug checking in?

"Your photos," says Lisa, pointing to the empty space on the wall where they had been hanging just moments before.

I notice small shards of glass on the floor and then see the glittering trail that leads to the shattered frames facedown on the kitchen linoleum floor, like they've been thrown across the room.

"Someone doesn't appreciate fine art."

But then I notice something else—on top of my dusty stack of mail is an ominously plain white envelope with just my first name roughly written on the outside. My heart drops—Christ, I did pay the rent this month, didn't I? Maybe not. It's a given that my slumlord—who blusters like an extra in *The Sopranos* when the rent is a little late—is an asshole, but I'm surprised he'd actually trash my stuff. I always thought that was an idle threat.

"For fuck's sake, I *died*," I mutter, grabbing the envelope. "Least he could do is give me an extra week. Lisa, I'm so sorry about all this . . ." I start to say, but then I realize that Lisa's face is as white as the proverbial sheet. She's staring with an odd intensity at the envelope.

"Give me that." She reaches out for the letter, but damn, I can't imagine that sharing my eviction notice will exactly help me in the attraction department, so I hold it slightly over her head, like we're playing keep away.

"Look, I can straighten this out—"

"It's not . . . it's not what you think."

"Well what do you think it is?"

"I think it's . . . complicated."

That word again. "Complicated." It drops like a curtain between us.

"It's from *him*." I don't really know what I'm saying, but the way she grips her purse tighter, the tense flicker across her face, means I'm close to something.

"Fine. Keep it, throw it away—whatever. I've got to go," says Lisa. Her voice is choked, and tears are starting to bead her eyes.

"Go? Where *do* you go, Lisa? Or is that complicated too?"

"I have to check . . ." she murmurs, grabbing her bag, digging through it frantically. Her hands are shaking.

And then a thought strikes me—or not a thought so much as a name. "On Daniel?"

She visibly flinches, like I've cut her.

A sudden corrupt rage rushes through my body—icy and yet strangely victorious. *Daniel's* the complication.

"Is he your boyfriend?"

Her jaw clenches. "Is that what you think?"

"What am I supposed to think?"

Lisa swallows. I cross my arms over my chest so she can't see them shaking.

"We're not doing this," she finally says. "I will call you later, and then we'll talk. But not now."

I don't know who I'm more pissed at—Lisa for refusing to talk, or me for unlocking the door and opening it. "Fine," I say. "It's your funeral."

White-faced, Lisa slides her bag angrily over her shoulder, brushes by me with palpable fury, and clatters down the stairs.

"Tell your boyfriend I say hi," I call after her.

There's a *whoosh* as the entry door opens, I feel a draft of cool air, then *slam*—the door rattles shut.

And what I'm left with is the hollow realization that it's not my slumlord or this Daniel who's an asshole.

It's me.

———

My apartment, which has always been stale and empty, now feels completely lifeless, like a bad motel room with no maid service. The shards of broken glass on the floor glitter in the dimming light, catching the few rays of the setting sun. They're pretty, like the icy sparkle of a fresh layer of snow. *Snow.* For a heart-jolting moment suddenly I'm not standing in my shitty apartment surrounded by broken glass—I'm in my neat childhood bedroom, and my mother stands next to me, an arm on my shoulder. It's winter and there was a storm the night before, so they've canceled school. She opens the window and points to the fairy-tale snow glistening in the morning sun. "Angel tears" she calls it. Her laugh is deep and throaty, and a cold breeze pushes through, which makes me shiver in my flannel baseball pajamas. Then she reaches out and pulls an icicle from the roof, gives it to me to taste; it's slick, like a giant ice cube. In it I can see our warped reflections.

Fuck, not now.

I reel with a visceral, choking wave of grief and drop to my knees, very much alone in my shitty apartment, and press my hands to the floor like a prayer. Distantly I register the glass cutting into my palms, and I sob. I sob in a way that's like vomiting—an overpowering, stomach-twisting, and wrenching pain. Tears stream down my face;

snot runs like a current from my nose. God I miss her, God I miss her, *God I miss you.*

Time passes.

Finally I manage to sit up, back on my heels, and rub my sleeve across my nose. I'm several degrees past spent, but it's an empty, holy kind of exhaustion. I pick up one of the frames that are facedown on the floor, smearing blood on the glass in the process.

I took the picture at the end of summer; the mornings were just starting to be cool in that crisp, near-autumn kind of way. I'd been entertaining the delusion that I could make a few extra bucks from the paper if I shot photos too, so I'd taken to keeping a cheap camera in the car. At the crosswalk on the corner of Main and Ocean, an old woman was crossing the street slowly, holding up traffic. Not news exactly, but something about it interested me. She wore a plastic scarf over her head because it had been lightly raining earlier; her pink coat translated into a light gray on the black-and-white print.

The photo is now torn straight through the middle, neatly halving the woman in two.

But what's interesting, compelling, is that the tear is *underneath* the remaining glass in the frame.

Which is not physically possible.

I pick up the other photo, this one taken a few weeks later at the same crosswalk. A heavyset woman wearing a reflective jacket and blowing a whistle supervises elementary school children crossing the street. I thought it made for a nice contrast, New Goshen's past and New Goshen's future, but when I showed them to Mac and proposed I get paid, he burst into hysterical laughter before promptly throwing me out of his office.

This picture too is ripped neatly in half in exactly the same way.

I sit down on the couch, holding the photo at arm's length. There's something familiar about the heavyset woman . . . What? I close my eyes, picturing her face in my head. And then it hits me—her permed and frizzy hair, her eyes, which I last saw staring lifelessly in the morgue, and her gray, bloody corpse splayed out like a medieval victim of torture. What was it the doctor with the iPod said?

I can't quite remember—something strange and disturbing.

My guilt prescriptions are still on the bamboo coffee table where I left them, so I pop a couple of Ambien, washing them down with a half-empty bottle of water that I find lying on the floor.

And then I remember the envelope. If it's *not* an eviction notice from my slumlord, then what is it?

I pull it out from my jeans pocket and rip off the end. Inside is a small white sheet of notepaper with just two small words written in tight, angry print.

race you

Well that makes no fucking sense.

The Ambien begins to creep through my veins; it's a welcome, sagging fuzziness that tugs at reality. And just as my eyelids start to droop I remember what she said, the doctor in scrubs, as she peered into the abdomen of the corpse: "Check out the spleen. It looks like something *was* eating it."

But then everything, blissfully, fades to black.

CHAPTER SEVEN: RACE YOU

I'm standing in a snowy wood. It's morning, the sun is coming up in the east, and I'm not cold, even though I'm only wearing a pair of plaid flannel pajama bottoms that my mother gave me years ago.

A feeling buzzes through me, powerful and strong. I reach up for a tree limb and break it off easily. Interesting. Then I crush it in my fist, turning it into fine powder that gives off the clean scent of freshly cut pine.

In the distance a sleigh bell jingles, and there's laughter, bright and tinkling, familiar. My *mother*. I race up the small hill—I'm amazingly fast; the trees pass by in a blur—but when I reach the top of the rise, I'm faced with another, steeper hill. Sharp rocks protrude from the even, untouched layer of snow, but no problem, my feet sink deep, reaching frozen ground, and I use the earth to launch myself up the hill faster, with long, powerful strides. But at the top I find a small mountain is now in front of me.

Again the familiar laughter, and another voice now, deeper. My father's. They're close, so close; I want to call out but strangely have lost my voice—what I've gained in physical strength I've lost in my ability to speak.

Then I see the thin punk-rock musician from Lisa's photos standing with preternatural stillness by a thin, barren tree. He stares at me with wild, roaming eyes. His face is ashy pale, and in his bony right hand he grips a long knife that glints in the hazy morning light. His thin white T-shirt is covered with bright blood, and after his eyes register mine, he grins.

"Race you," he says.

He plunges into the dark wood, and as my heart thuds frantically against my chest, a feeling of complete and utter panic rising through me, I run after him. But he's faster, stronger—he's over the hill and halfway up the next just as I get to the top, my chest heaving. If only I could call out a warning; if I wasn't a mute, my parents might have a chance. When I reach a flat clearing, I can't tell which way to turn— the trees are spinning, and my lungs burn with cold. Then I see marks left in the snow, an inhuman distance between each footprint. I want to collapse, sleep, let the drifting snow cover me, but maybe there's time, so I stumble through the clearing and back into the woods, where the trail leads.

I reach the summit of the next hill, spent. And there, in the distance, I see him in silhouette standing on a jutting crag near the peak of the next mountain. He's watching someone below, with a visibly coiled energy, like a lion about to pounce. He turns to me with a jeering grimace, opens his mouth, and lets out an indescribable sound, like the roar of a massive waterfall. The ground begins to shake as he leaps off the edge.

A bloodcurdling scream echoes through the canyon walls. My mother.

Too late, too late, but still I try to force my aching legs to move— they're sluggish, frozen, and I'm overcome with an empty feeling of powerlessness and desperation. Not enough—*I'm not enough*—and then I see the snow on the mountain peak start to shiver. A crack forms, and then a thundering chunk drops off. An avalanche. I don't even bother to move—there's no point—and the torrent of snow hits me with the force of a Mack truck, knocking me into a current of rushing powder. Once again I'm rolled around; once again I can't tell which way is up or down; once again I'm drowning. Dying is becoming a familiar experience.

Finally all is still and dark, like a cocoon, like a womb. My heart still beats, but I'm choking on snow, buried alive.

A sound. Digging. The snow in front of my face gets lighter, brighter, and I can see movement of some kind, accompanied by a deep, guttural growl. A hand reaches down to me, grips me tightly by the wrist, and lifts me with supernatural strength to the surface, where I gasp for breath and shake with wet cold.

It's the woman from the water.

Her skin is so pale it has a bluish hue, and her hair is wet. It clings to her high forehead in damp clumps. She wears a thin cotton shift that's drenched too, as if she just crawled out of the well. She cradles me in her icy arms, staring at me with glittering, ice-blue eyes, then brushes snow from my face, leans down as if to kiss me but stops short.

"Dimitri, he is coming," she whispers. Her accent is foreign but familiar, and I don't just hear her speak—I see blue words drip from her lips, like vapor.

And then she smiles at me, but it's a cold smile, calculating. She reaches into the snow and conjures an icicle, holding it in front of my face. But I don't see my reflection, or hers. Instead I see a warped symbol. It is oddly familiar but also strange.

"*You must be ready.*"

The symbol—it's the symbol on my father's ring. I want to ask her what it means, but just then she places the tip of the icicle on my forehead, and it burns, spreading to a searing, sharp pain that crushes me from within—white hot, blinding.

———

I wake up. Turn on the light. There is a small dusting of snow on the floor, already starting to melt. And at the edge, a woman's delicate footprint, leading from my apartment, out the door.

CHAPTER EIGHT: MYSTERY #5

I have watched enough cheesy detective television shows in my young life to know that when one is presented with an inexplicable mystery, the first order of business (after procuring good donuts and coffee—check) is to create a wall of clues with photos of suspects and article clippings, preferably in an artistic yet seemingly random fashion. This collage is essential to the solution, because it is the ground from which the *aha!* moment comes—a moment which usually occurs fifteen minutes before the hour is up. The lead detective suddenly gasps and goes to grab his coat and keys without explaining the details to his black or female partner.

So, three donuts under the belt and halfway through my second cup of coffee, I grab my obituary journalist notebook and start to make notes.

> *#1—Who is Daniel? Do I need to be jealous?*
> *#2—Dead fat woman in morgue. Identify.*
> *#3—What's up with the symbol on my father's ring?*
> *#4—How is Aspinwall connected with any or all of the above?*
> *#5—POE*

I don't have a name for the ghostly woman in my dream, and I feel vaguely superstitious that committing too much of my thoughts about her to paper will somehow conjure her, make her real. So I decide to use a code word, Poe, for mystery #5, in honor of the author of "The Tell-Tale Heart". Seems appropriate.

Sadly, the best place to start my research is in the dusty basement archive at the *Devonshire Eagle*, where they still use microfiche to catalog articles. This means I probably can't escape a visit with Mac to see what new assignments are on the horizon, which means my hospital vacation is over, which gives me a sad ache somewhere in the lower quadrant of my stomach. But there are things to do, people to see, dead people to write about—they wait for no one, the dead and dying.

———

I pass the bored security guard on the first floor (I can't see the need for security, really, except to keep Mac's legendary creditors from dropping by inconveniently) and give him a wave, which he studiously ignores as I press the B button on the elevator. I'm somewhat in luck, because it's half past twelve, which means most newspaper employees are still on their smoke/lunch break. When the doors open, the elevator is empty.

I've never understood why the lighting is so poor on the basement floor, or why the walls are painted a prison-cell olive green. There is a steel gray desk, behind which sits Ernest, who really should have died about ten years ago. He officially retired from Exeter Academy after forty years teaching pubescent boys Greek and Latin but got bored and lonely at home, so he took a job at the paper, where he is paid to be bored and lonely at work. It's rumored that he's eighty-five, but he jokes that he doesn't feel a day over ninety.

"I thought you kicked the bucket," he says, not looking up from his crossword puzzle.

"Why, you after my job?"

"I'd consider that a demotion," he says dryly.

"You're probably right. Mind if I do a little research?"

Ernest pulls a well-chewed pencil from behind his ear, tapping it on the desk. "Suit yourself," he says absently. "What's a four-letter word for a flat-topped plateau?"

"Mesa."

"Oh, for cripe's sake, I should have known that."

I head toward the back, where the microfiche machines are gathering dust, passing through the narrow corridors created by the steel shelving. Each shelf contains a white cardboard box of archived newspapers and forgotten office files—a genuine tinderbox of paper, which apparently doesn't concern the employees of the *Devonshire Eagle*, because I note more than a few cigarette stubs ground onto the floor. The Stacks, as we call the basement, is a great place to hide from work or engage in an office tryst—I once caught Myrna passionately kissing Barney from accounting, a fact I use every once in a while to get her to vouch for one of my mythical illnesses.

The lone fluorescent light flickers overhead, making a low, ambient buzzing sound. I reach the far end of the room, where an antiquated computer stores the article catalog, and I sit down in a creaky wooden chair, turn on the computer—it takes a good five minutes for it to boot up—type in "Aspinwall," and press RETURN.

A long digital list appears. The archive goes back to the mid-1850s and might have gone back further if not for a fire in 1839 that razed the newspaper office—and most of the surrounding town—to the ground. Fire seems to be a recurring issue for New Goshen.

January, 1930. ICE TRUCK HITS CYCLIST NEAR ASPINWALL
July, 1935. BASTILLE DAY CELEBRATED AT ASPINWALL BALL
August, 1940. BABY CRIMINAL CAUGHT STEALING, RUNS OFF
October, 1940. TRAGIC FIRE CLAIMS FIVE, SOCIALITE MISSING
May, 1970. ASPINWALL FOR SALE
September, 1972. HOW TO TELL IF YOUR CHILD IS A HIPPIE
October, 1972. WILD ANIMAL SUSPECTED IN ASPINWALL DEATH
December, 1980. ASPINWALL DEMOLITION SET

January, 1982. ONE YEAR LATER, AND ASPINWALL STILL STANDS

I decide to skip the first article and focus on the others, jotting down the dates in pencil. "Baby criminal" in particular seems to stand out—how much trouble could an infant get into, anyway? It doesn't take long to find the box with the microfilm reels, and then I settle onto the fabulous fifties plastic chair in front of the reader.

Spinning the articles on the monitor always makes me motion sick, and I wonder why no one has thought to digitize the film and put it online, like a real newspaper. But then I remember that, gee, no one really gives a shit about New Goshen in the early part of the twentieth century. The Bastille Day article yields nothing, unless one is captivated by the ballroom finery and high society of New Goshen circa 1935, although there is a photo snapped in the Great Hall that looks like a film still straight from *Citizen Kane*. Two men with slicked-back hair, one sporting a thin pencil mustache, are decked out in tuxedos, and they stand next to a beautiful woman wearing a satin evening gown and mink coat. The headline reads BASTILLE DAY A GAY AFFAIR.

The second article proves to be more mundane than its title suggests. The baby criminal in question turns out to be a twelve-year-old stable hand who was accused of stealing five silver spoons, a silver creamer, and a good laying hen. Positively tame by today's standards of juvenile depravity.

Finally, I find the most interesting article of the bunch.

TRAGIC FIRE CLAIMS FIVE, SOCIALITE MISSING

One wonders if the town of New Goshen will ever recover following last night's tragic events, marring the traditional Halloween festivities. Downtown businesses put the flag at half-staff, and a funeral procession with all five bodies made its way down Main Street today, with dirges played by the American Legion Military Band.

All Hallow's Eve began in traditional fashion with little tykes playing trick or treat on neighbors' porches. Who would have thought that hours later the town would be mourning five lost souls, the most luminous of Devonshire County's socialites, Mr. Blaine Lomond, Mr. Edgar Sweeney, Mr. Sidney Crane, Miss Eliza Fitzgerald, and her twin sister, Miss Sarah Fitzgerald?

Chester Hurlbut of Hurlbut's Ice Delivery on East Street was on his way home from a late-night church service when he spotted the flames.

"I thought maybe they were having a bonfire," said Hurlbut. "They had some fancy parties there. When Miss Delia turned five, they brought in circus ponies and peacocks!"

Indeed, Aspinwall mansion has seen happier times. Just last September this reporter was invited to the Annual Harvest Gala to help support the Cooke School for the Blind, a sparkling affair that brought high-society folks from as far away as Albany, NY.

In today's burial service, Rev. Dr. William Jersey of Grace Protestant Episcopal Church read the prayer as the five coffins were laid to rest at Folsom Cemetery.

And as if this tragedy alone wasn't enough to bear, police say they're searching for Mrs. Aspinwall, who was last seen being carried from the inferno by the gardener but has subsequently disappeared. Captain Aspinwall attested that when he saw her last, she had suffered horrible burns and seemed close to death. Readers may recall that the Aspinwalls were recently robbed by their young stable hand, who made off with several pieces of silver and some say was seen at the house shortly after the fire began. Any persons with knowledge of the whereabouts of either the groom or the gardener should contact authorities immediately.

Several photos accompany the article. One is an easily recognizable Main Street, filled with throngs of people clad in somber black, watching as the funeral procession passes by the *Devonshire Eagle* flatiron building. There's a hand-drawn pencil sketch of Miss Sarah Brewster, almost cameo-like in its perfection, and then a photo of the Aspinwall mansion with family and staff neatly arranged on the clipped front lawn. The maids wear uniforms and starched white aprons, while the valets or butlers wear stiff black suits and the same sober expression. At the far right is an awkward, freckled twelve-year-old who looks like he's overdue for a growth spurt. He wears dirty overalls and a jaunty sideways cap. The caption identifies him as A. Bennet, the baby criminal. I wonder if he's related to Lisa.

Centered in the photo and seated on white Adirondack chairs are Captain Aspinwall and his wife. Captain Aspinwall sports long side-burns and a fierce, burning expression; an eight-year-old Delia kneels at his feet, her hair looped in perfectly formed curls, a shy smile on her mild face.

And here I find something strange.

The face of Mrs. Aspinwall has been purposely rubbed out, like someone took an eraser to the print. And then to the far left is a man, a blurry figure who at the last moment must have stepped out of the frame so that only his arm and shoulder appear. His shirt is dirty and coarse, and his pale hand holds a trowel.

It can only be one man. The gardener.

———

Bob looks crushed as soon as I enter the third-floor newsroom, like I just stole his favorite Monday morning gag (as if I'd wear Old Fart Slippers to the office). In fact, the whole room stops. Myrna's hands freeze above her keyboard, Nate drops a pencil, and everyone stares, including a few people I don't recognize who are probably from the accounting department—they never leave their floor, *never*. I feel like another head has just sprouted from my shoulders.

"Who died?" I ask.

Silence. And a palpable aura of sulkiness.

"IS THAT MY FAVORITE GODDAMN WRITER IN THE WORLD??!!"

The glass door to Mac's office crashes open, and suddenly he rushes out to greet me, wiping his sweaty palms against his pants—a consideration usually reserved for car dealers when they're looking at a big ad buy. Mac is short, about the height of the average fourth grader, but what he lacks in size, he more than makes up for in volume.

"HOW THE HELL ARE YOU, KID?!"

"Uh, fine," I say. "Better."

"*Great* news, great news, so good to see you. You want anything to drink?" He shakes my hand eagerly, and his grip is almost painful. Nate gives me the evil eye.

"MYRNA GET THE KID SOME COFFEE. WHAT THE FUCK'S THE MATTER WITH YOU?"

Myrna jumps from her chair like she's just received an electric shock (but then with Bob in the office, that's a definite possibility) and scuttles over to the kitchenette with a speed I wouldn't have thought her capable of.

"You take sugar? Cream? We only got the powder stuff. MYRNA, WHY THE FUCK WE ONLY GOT THE POWDER STUFF?"

"Black is fine," I say, utterly confused.

"Got that, Myrna? NO SUGAR!"

"I got it," mutters Myrna. I can only hope she's not adding rat poison.

"Well, come in, come in," says Mac warmly, pulling me into his office. "We gotta catch up, right? Chew the fat, talk shop."

Everyone else stands, frozen in place.

"WHAT THE FUCK YOU ALL WAITING FOR? GET BACK TO WORK."

This seems to be the magic phrase that releases them from the spell, because immediately everyone rushes away; in fact, Bob runs into Nate, which causes Nate to swear quietly.

"Have a seat, kid. Make yourself comfortable," Mac says, settling himself onto his leather executive chair, which squeaks vainly in protest. It's a large chair, too large for his height, and instead of making him look appropriately intimidating (the point, after all, of executive furniture in general), it makes him look like a Keebler Elf. In fact, he has to reach up to grab his pencil off the desk.

I ease onto one of the hard plastic chairs that I generally associate with getting screamed at and fired, since those are the only other times Mac has invited me in. But the vibe now is freakishly congenial. Myrna bustles in with a Styrofoam cup of steaming black coffee. Although I usually don't drink the office stuff, because it tastes like a burnt dishrag, I actually feel guilty for the way Mac's treating her and take a few sips.

"Good?" asks Mac, scribbling his signature on a letter.

Sure, if you enjoy licking the sole of your shoe. But I nod. Mac waves Myrna off, and she closes the door quietly behind her. Then he leans back in his chair, pressing his hands together like he's having an intellectual bowel movement, his brows seriously furrowed.

"I have to tell you, kid, you had us all gravely worried. I've always looked at you like you were a second son, ya know? Family, that's what you are. Family."

He can't be serious. I start to laugh and inhale the coffee into my lungs, which brings on a bout of coughing.

Mac shakes his head seriously. "Look at you, you aren't even fully recovered. What a trooper. Not like Nate, that lazy-ass piece of shit." His eyes actually get moist. "If I had a son like you . . ."

This line of thought needs to end. *Immediately.* I clear my voice. "So you were saying we need to talk shop."

"Exactly," says Mac. "Cut straight to the point, that's what I always say. This whole Aspinwall thing, it's been like money in the bank. The fuckin' bank. Just met with Accounting. They're over the moon." He leans forward, places a stubby hand on his chin and sighs. "I don't know how long we can milk it, now that you're on the mend," he adds somewhat ruefully.

"When you say cash in the bank—"

"I'm talking subscriptions up 34 percent in just the last two weeks. I'm starting to have to turn advertisers away—everyone wants to know, what happens next? I got a reporter from the *Enquirer* who wants to take it national."

He says this like it's a good thing.

"I mean, shit, you woke up in a *fuckin'* morgue. I wouldn't be surprised if you got a call from Jerry Springer. Love that guy. Love him." He slaps his hand down on the desk. "I got it! Exclusive interview. We draw it out over the next three weeks, double the cost of ad space. What do you think?"

I think I need to pay my rent and buy some real furniture. I lean back in my chair, whistle hard. "I don't know, Mac. An exclusive interview. I might want to talk to my agent." *My imaginary agent.*

Mac's fingers start tapping on the desk nervously. "What? I mean, we're family, right?" A small trickle of sweat drips from his forehead.

"Sure, Mac. Of course. But let me run something by you, see what you think."

Now Mac leans back, staring pensively. He obviously thought this would be much, much easier.

"You know, some strange things have started to happen since the incident. I don't know if they're related, but they *could* be."

"Strange things," says Mac, almost choking with eagerness. "What kinds of things?"

"I was in my apartment, and someone, or *something*, threw two pictures across the room. What's weird is that the photos were torn in half."

"That is weird," whispers Mac.

"But the spooky stuff only seems to happen in my apartment," I say, deciding to omit the possibility that an angry boyfriend could be responsible for the damage. "Right now I'm trying to figure out what it could be, or who it could be."

"Like a mystery," says Mac, his eyes widening. "Something that will take six months, a year to figure out." I can see him calculating how much he can charge for advertising over the next six months.

"*Exactly*. But the thing is, I need time, you know? Time to do my research; time to document everything weird that happens. And some funding too. You know, business expenses, that kind of thing."

"HOT DAMN, KID!" shouts Mac. "That's it! You're so *fuckin'* brilliant, I can't stand it." He pushes his phone intercom. "MYRNA! Get Peters here a company card. PRONTO!" I can almost hear her mentally swearing on the other end. "Don't think this isn't going to get you a raise too, kid. Double your salary, at least. I've got to talk to the Board about it, but I don't see a problem." He pulls out a series of keys and opens his locked drawer. The company rumor is that he keeps a gun there to shoot writers who've missed their deadline. But instead he pulls out a fat wad of cash and starts to peel out bills, like an experienced dealer in Vegas.

"Here, take a grand. Consider it a bonus. Myrna will have your card in a week. Just keep it to $2K a month."

Did he just say *month*?

"But you mind staying on obits, too? People have been complaining about the shit Nate's writing. Actually printed that Fred Jenkins died of alcohol-related liver failure. He's a walking litigation magnet."

"Sure," I say, and then casually add, "but do you need me in the office? I get more done at home."

Mac's eyes widen, and at first I think I've overstepped. "Of course! Plus that's where all the weird shit's gonna happen too, right? And there *will* be weird shit, right?"

"I guarantee it," I say. And I will. I'm a fiction writer, not a journalist, damn it.

"Done!" says Mac, eagerly opening the door of his office. "Now you go home, get some rest. You still look like shit, no offense. Take the day, and then show me something by Saturday, all right?"

"Great," I say while slipping the burning cash in my pocket, an act that escapes no one in the office. Psychic daggers hit me from all directions.

Mac starts to chuckle, hits my shoulder with a soft punch. "You'll never guess. Bob didn't have polyps in his ass after all. It was *beets.*" He bends over with laughter. "Bob's wife made him beets and he thought he had blood in his shit."

I look over to Bob and his face is as red as, well . . . a beet does come to mind.

"WHAT ARE YOU ALL STARING AT YOU STUPID FUCKS? GET BACK TO WORK!"

Apparently my cue to exit. It doesn't feel safe to wait for the elevator—a pair of scissors could be plunged into my back—so I head briskly for the stairwell. As soon as I'm down a few steps, I feel a giddy sense of release. There's more money in my pocket than has been in my bank account for the past year, and I'm free from even my sporadic time in the office.

Dying may just be the best thing that ever happened to me.

CHAPTER NINE: DANIEL'S NUMBERS

Outside on the sidewalk I check my watch—it's only two. The sky is a darkening miserable gray, threatening rain, but I feel like celebrating, spreading around some of my newly acquired wealth. Of course, most of the retail establishments on Main Street closed years ago, except for Lombardi's Pawn & Loan, the local Goodwill, and a Christian store, Sacred Heart Collectibles, which specializes in plastic statues of Jesus, Virgin Mary ceramic lawn ornaments, and state lottery tickets. A popular place among the sixty-plus crowd.

Worse still is that I have no one to celebrate with now that Lisa's not speaking to me. But I'm feeling lucky, and Crosslands is only a block away. I pull out my cell.

Lisa's professional voice answers the line. "Crosslands Nursing Center, may I help you?"

"Ditch work and meet me."

There is a pause. She lowers her voice. "I can't. You know some people only get paid *when they show up*."

"Meet me. Pretend you've got a migraine or something."

"Dimitri—"

"Great, I'll be by in ten."

I press END and can feel her cursing me, but I don't care, because I've got *a thousand dollars*. Cash. I'm like Donald Trump with better hair. Which gives me ten minutes to kill, so I head into Sacred Heart to buy fifty lottery tickets—I'm on a roll; why not see how far I can take it? And maybe I'll find something to further annoy Lisa with—a snow globe of Saint Peter perhaps.

A bell chimes as I enter. The place is dimmer than I expected, and it smells cloyingly sweet, like scented candles, incense, and something oily, musty, and exotic I can't place. To the right are a series of paperback books, their covers faded by the sun—*Footprints in the Sand, Sisterhood of Faith, The Christian Book of Questions*—plus a few badly printed folded brochures: *Debunking the Da Vinci Code* and *Talking to Teens about Christ*. To the left is an aisle of bobblehead saints, a variety of wide-eyed plastic cherubs, and a shelf devoted to Mexican-style patron saint candles—the source, apparently, of the sweet smell. There's a spinning display of Christmas tree ornaments and crucifixes, while in the far corner a ceramic Saint Francis of Assisi fountain burbles cheerfully, a fake bird wired clumsily to his shoulder.

In other words, deliciously kitschy.

"Can I help you?" a deep voice calls from behind a beaded curtain that must lead into the back room.

"Lottery tickets." I check out the ceramic gargoyle banks on the glass counter. They are impossibly grotesque, with bulging eyes and leering grimaces, but the question is whether they'd be better than garden gnomes for my irregular-people date with Lisa. I pick one up, judging the weight. With a good swing and the right golf club, I bet it could go a fair distance.

"No one's ever won here." A young guy pushes the curtains aside—not what I expected, with dark skin and long black dreads that reach his shoulder. New Goshen's only Russian resident may be standing in front of its only African-American resident. It's a veritable United Nations moment.

"It's my lucky day."

He snorts. "That's what they all say. How many?"

"Fifty."

He whistles. "High roller."

I somehow get the feeling that he only works here, that's he's not exactly a Sacred Heart customer himself. "What's the most expensive and weirdest thing in the store?"

"Man, that's a tough one. Weirdest is the King David Ken doll."

"That's tempting." Lisa would definitely hate me.

"Most expensive thing is in the back." He takes a step back, eyes me critically. I wonder what it could possibly be. Solid gold crucifix? Diamond rosary beads? I mean, this is New Goshen we're talking about.

"You from around here?"

"I write for the paper," I say, extending a hand. "D. Peters. Actually Dimitri Petrov."

His eyes widen. "The dude who died and woke up in the morgue?"

I nod.

"Holy shit! I knew you looked familiar. Hey, can I get a picture with you? My girlfriend won't believe me."

"Sure . . ."

Before I can finish he's already on the other side of the counter with his iPhone, and he stands next to me, eagerly holding out his arm to take the picture. When did I become a local celebrity?

"I made her watch the video. She says it's fake." He gets closer, whispering as if someone might hear us: "It's not fake, is it?"

"Unfortunately not."

"Ha! Knew it. Well it's been good for business either way. Rosary beads are flying off the shelf."

I smile, nod politely. Glance at my watch. *Ahem.*

"Oh, the tickets," he says, darting back behind the counter. "You want to pick out the numbers or let the computer do it?"

"Computer is fine," I say. "So you didn't answer my question. What *is* the most expensive thing in the store?"

He looks over his shoulder. God, the guy is paranoid. "My boss would kill me if I told you. It's not officially for sale, but she's gotta unload that thing. It's got bad juju."

"Bad juju is my specialty," I say.

For a brief second he appraises me. His eyes fall to my cheap Kmart watch. "I don't know—it's worth at least five hundred bucks."

It's an affront to my newly burgeoning sense of self-importance; he doesn't think I can afford it; he doesn't believe I *am* a high roller. *Moi.* So I pull out my wallet, taking my sweet time, and count out five hundred in twenties. I lay them slowly out on the glass counter, a veritable fan of cash. *Hot damn, that feels good.* "Let me take a look."

He nods, visibly impressed, and slips back behind the beaded curtain. The ceramic gargoyle on the counter stares at me reproachfully, so I cover his face with a pamphlet, *How Well Do You Know Your Bible?* A part of me can't believe that I'm about to blow a month's rent plus electricity on a piece of bad juju crap just to prove to my ego that I *can*. But didn't Mac say I was getting a raise and two grand a month for expenses? Isn't this what celebrities do—spend loads of cash on stuff they don't need or want?

He returns carrying a battered brown leather book; the cover is bound with peeling duct tape. Five hundred for that piece of crap? He quickly reads my expression.

"It's an antique. I don't know much about it, but it's old. And the pages are . . . Well, take a look for yourself."

I open the book, releasing a small cloud of dust. The yellowed pages are thick and roughly cut. There are brightly colored medieval illustrations—an angel slaying a dragon, wizened old men approaching a castle, a field of demons doing battle with knights in armor. The chunky text is obviously Greek—I recognize some of the letters from fraternity row. And on the opposite side of the pages is a different language altogether . . . Russian? I lift one of the pages and look closer at a drawing of a castle—there's a watermark hidden in the stonework of the walls, a symbol . . .

A cold shiver ripples down my spine.

The man gasps, his eyes wide. "Your ring."

I look down at my hand. It's the same Celtic-looking knot.

"My *father's* ring," I correct quietly. I lightly trace the symbol on the ring with my finger. A random coincidence? What are the odds?

"I'll buy it," I say, the words rolling out before I can even think.

"I don't know, my boss—"

"It's *mine*," I say with an intensity that surprises me. But I can't imagine walking away without it. I almost feel like I'd be ready to fight the guy for the book, which is, for me, a very odd feeling. The only time I almost got into a fight was in tenth grade when I accidentally hit weight-lifting, shaving Andy McClure with a Twinkie that I had aimed for the trash can. It took two weeks of lunch money to resolve amicably.

"Still, I should check with the owner," says the clerk hesitantly.

I pull out my wallet and count out another hundred, pushing it toward him.

He gives me a look but quietly pockets the cash while I grab the book and head for the door.

"Wait—what about your tickets?"

"They're yours if you want them," I say, and then I'm back out on the street, buzzing with a weird kind of jubilation. The book feels hot under my arm, like it's alive, like it has a pulsing heartbeat, and I feel a strong desire to go home and pore through it immediately. But I know Lisa is waiting, and she definitely won't wait forever.

———

Great. She's already pissed because I'm a good ten minutes late. But then Lisa looks pretty sexy when she's pissed.

Today she's wearing a vintage forties flower-print dress and the dark blue denim jacket I've seen before. Her hair is pulled back in a neat ponytail, and her black combat boots are the only giveaway of her drummer aspirations.

As soon as I'm near she narrows her eyes. "I just waited so I could tell you that I'm *not talking* to you," she says, her voice tight.

She turns away and starts to walk briskly down the sidewalk. Her combat boots make a clop-clop sound on the pavement. I have to jog to keep up.

"Look, I'm sorry, but I found the most amazing thing . . ."

She ignores me.

"And I've got news—they're giving me a raise; I can work from home. You should have seen Mac's face when I came into the office . . ."

Nada. I'm the invisible man. A trickle of sweat inches its way down my back; I'm not used to walking so fast.

"And then I find out—like I'm famous or something. I went into that weird little Christian store and the guy behind the counter wanted to get a picture with me."

At this she snorts derisively, which I take as encouragement. Technically it's not talking, but it is a *sound*, a form of verbal communication.

"And the guy had this book and he was, like, it's five hundred dollars, like I don't have five hundred dollars, and I was all, like, no problem, and man, you should have seen his face when I laid out that cash on the table . . ."

Lisa stops short at the bus stop, crosses her arms over her chest, and peers down the street. A beige Cadillac lurches by; one wheel is slightly flat, and the exhaust sputters a plume of blue smoke as it turns the corner.

"And then I saw the book, and it's all in Greek *and* Russian, really old actually." I'm now blathering away like the proverbial idiot. "I found some weird shit of my dad's after he died, like this ring, and the symbol on the ring is *in* this book, and I'm thinking maybe this is all happening for a reason. I mean, when would I have five hundred dollars to blow on something as stupid as an antique book—"

"Wait," says Lisa, holding up her hand. "Your dad is dead?"

"Sure, my parents were killed in a car accident. When I was in college. You didn't know that?"

"No," she says tersely. "Like I said, we don't really know each other."

Awkward pause.

"I'm sorry," she adds a little more gently. "About your parents."

"Yeah, well," I say, and here—*Shit, not now, not now*—tears start to well in my eyes, so I quickly turn away from her, look toward the Devonshire Bank. There's an old-fashioned clock that hangs out over the sidewalk, and I watch the second hand tick, gather myself. A lumbering bus approaches, the 49B.

"My car died yesterday," says Lisa quietly. "This is my bus."

It stops in front of us, and there's a *whoosh* as the doors open.

I turn to her.

"I've never had a nickname in my life," I say quickly. "My birthday is September 3, I'm twenty-three, and I dropped out of college senior year when my parents died. I was majoring in English. I have a scar on my right knee from a bicycle accident, I like tomato sauce and ketchup, but strangely don't like tomatoes, and I write shitty obituaries for an even shittier newspaper. In my spare time I pretend to be a novelist."

"You getting on, Miss?" calls the driver.

"I like chocolate cake—never vanilla, *never*—I'm allergic to penicillin and being on time for work, and I don't have a favorite color, because why play favorites? I've been told a few times—okay, *more* than a few times—by the opposite sex that I can be an idiot. Yesterday I admit that I went more than a few steps past idiot to asshole. But I was jealous. Okay, so you *know* me. Now you know me."

"That's all superficial stuff," says Lisa.

"But it's a start, right? Lisa, all I want is a shot to get to know you. Just one. I won't blow it."

The driver leans over his steering wheel. "Either you're getting on or you're not."

Lisa doesn't move—doesn't look at me. Her gaze is fixed somewhere between the second and third step of the bus. A moment passes. Another. But finally she looks up at the driver.

"Not," she says firmly. "He's giving me a ride."

The driver mutters something unintelligible, the doors of the bus close, and I think that maybe, just maybe, doors of another sort altogether open.

———

"Right here—no your *other* right," says Lisa.

We're on the outskirts of town cruising down South Street, and I turn the car onto an unmarked road that's not much of a road. I wish I had a Jeep instead of my Mustang, because with all the teeth-jolting potholes, I can't imagine the muffler will make it out alive. We pass a wide field that's planted with corn in summer but is now just a barren, weedy lot. On the left is a lonely gas station, Friendly Fred's.

The houses are smaller here, single-story ranches and shotgun shacks, not like the looming Victorians downtown. Some are fenced, enclosing a scattering of horses, sheep, and goats, while others have scrubby front yards and wire chicken coops. In one yard a tire swing hangs from the branch of a thick maple tree.

"Right here," says Lisa as we approach an unpaved driveway marked by a tall elm tree. She's tense for reasons I can't imagine, but I know enough not to ask.

The driveway is rutted deeply, gashes in the frozen earth that I try to avoid by driving on the shoulder. A couple of chickens scatter before us, squawking in protest, and then a two-story farmhouse rises in front of us. It's the same house from Lisa's laptop pictures, and its simple white paint stands in stark contrast to the surrounding brown and dormant field. A hulking, abandoned thresher rusts quietly at the far edge of the property near where a forest begins. I put the car in park and turn off the engine.

"This is your house?"

"Not mine. My mom's. Get ready." Lisa opens the car door and steps out into the chill afternoon air.

"Get ready for what?"

No answer.

I get out of the car and feel a gentle arctic breeze brush against my cheeks. It's amazing how quiet it is out here in the country; the sound of my feet crunching across the thin layer of icy snow seems absurdly loud. But suddenly the silence is broken by a massive pit bull, which barks fiercely from the sagging porch. I'm grateful to see that it's chained.

"Buddy doesn't bite," says Lisa. "Much."

"Gee, thanks for the heads up."

Lisa just smiles at me nervously.

A barefoot little girl charges through the front door of the house, braids flying behind her. She clutches a crayon drawing and launches herself into Lisa's arms.

"You're home, you're home, you're home! What'd you get me?"

Lisa gasps in mock surprise, twirling the girl in a circle. "Was I supposed to get you something? I forgot."

"No you didn't, no you didn't!"

"Well," says Lisa, putting the girl down, "there might be a little something in my bag. Where are your shoes?"

The girl ignores the question. "Life Savers, I know it's Life Savers." She stops short when she sees me, an unfamiliar man standing next to an unfamiliar car, and then I recognize her: a little older maybe, but definitely the girl with the pink boots in the photos.

"Who's this?"

"My friend Dimitri."

The girl eyes me warily. "What do you play?"

I look to Lisa; *some help here please?* But she's trying to cover a smirk with her hand.

"Well, ah, what do you like to play, hide-and-go-seek?" I sound like a very bad and transparently phony imitation of Mr. Rogers.

The girl gives an exasperated sigh, like I'm hopeless. "I play bass guitar. See?"

She holds out her hand, and I can see her thumb has a large callous. "But Lisa's teaching me to drum too. I'm pretty good at it."

"I'd like to hear you sometime." At this her face brightens considerably.

"Maybe later," says Lisa. "*After* you're done with your homework. And found your shoes."

"Damn it," the girl mutters.

"Amelia!" Lisa's voice is sharp. "What did I tell you about swearwords?"

Amelia kicks at a clod of frozen dirt with her bare feet. "I can decide if I want to use those words when I'm older and have a record deal, but for artistic purposes only."

"What *kind* of record deal?"

"With a major label," grumbles Amelia.

"*Exactly*," says Lisa. "Now go find your Life Savers and leave Dimitri alone for a few minutes. Think you can do that?"

"*Okay*," says Amelia, mimicking Lisa in a pitch-perfect lilt.

"Interesting parenting style," I whisper in Lisa's ear. I can't miss the fact that the girl bears a striking resemblance to Lisa; they share the same Roman nose and wide brown eyes.

"Interesting *auntie* style," says Lisa.

"This is called getting to know you. I wasn't judging."

"Sure you weren't," says Lisa, heading up the porch steps. As if on cue, Buddy starts to growl at me menacingly, his yellow teeth bared. He looks like he's blind in one rheumy eye, and patches of his mangy fur are missing, revealing pink skin beneath.

"C'mon," says Lisa. "You're not scared, are you?"

"Me?" My voice squeaks. "Scared?"

My heart does start to pound as I take the first step and Buddy continues to snarl, but I think to myself that the hospital wasn't so bad, was it? Maybe they'd put me back on the VIP floor again while the neurosurgeon team attempts to reassemble what's left of my face.

But as soon as I'm on the porch, Buddy turns into a doggy marshmallow, his stump of a tail starts to wag, and he sniffs my crotch in a decidedly interested way. Dogs and kids—now I remember why I avoid them.

"See, he likes you," says Lisa, barely containing a laugh.

As if to further make the point, Buddy heads around behind me and starts sniffing my ass.

"A lovely pet," I say. "I feel violated."

"Buddy!" Lisa whistles, and Buddy settles slowly onto the porch floor with a whine. "Good boy," she adds, and his stumpy tail wags in response.

"You ready for the house tour?" She seems jittery, and I remember how revealed I felt when she was in my apartment, how I saw it through her eyes, all its flaws and imperfections.

"I was born ready," I say.

"I'm going to pretend you didn't just say that." She inhales deeply. "Okay."

Together we step inside the small entry. The walls are paneled with fake dark oak, and the wall-to-wall carpet is a bright Astroturf green, like the house was built on the remains of a miniature golf course. Narrow stairs lead to the second floor, and the banister is clumsily painted white, as if it was primed but no one ever got to the painting part.

She leads me into a tight living room. There's a large seventies-era TV that's built into an armoire, an awful sagging red-plaid couch covered with an orange crocheted afghan, a La-Z-Boy upholstered with cracked black leather, and an oak-veneer coffee table, the kind that comes in a box from Kmart and you assemble with a hex key wrench. Above the TV hangs a tall painting: an owl sitting in a seed-shaped helicopter while a curl of wind blows beneath. I step closer and see that a tree in the background has a human face, and the leaves are actually tiny hands. It's part Hansel and Gretel fairy tale, part surreal Salvador Dali, in a dark green wash that gives it an antique vibe.

"My mom paints," says Lisa. "She has a studio in the barn out back."

"Nice," I say, and Lisa shrugs, as if everyone's mother paints owls in helicopters.

The rest of the walls are covered with photos, the typical family brass-framed portraiture. I see Lisa through different stages of adolescence, including glasses and braces. Her hair was a different color when she was young, more of a mousy dirty blond than the deep auburn it is now. There are photos of a boy growing up as well, his hair the same mousy blond until his late teens, when he starts to sport a jet-black Mohawk. In one picture his eyes are heavily made up, and they stare directly at me, as if the photo is alive somehow. Possessed. I involuntarily shiver.

"Daniel," says Lisa. "My brother."

There are complicated emotional layers in the wistful and sad way she says "brother," but something else as well—a trace of fear, a tangible anxiety. Her finger absently traces the thin line of her scar, which is just visible above her jacket collar.

Suddenly Amelia tears through the screen door; it swings shut behind her with a loud thwap. "I found them, I found them!" She's already pulled at the top of the wrapping and is prying out an orange candy with her thumb.

"Who wants a Life Saver?"

"I do," says Lisa quietly. She reaches out her hand, and Amelia drops one on her outstretched palm.

———

Amelia gives me the rest of the house tour while Lisa heads out to the barn to retrieve her mother. (She loses track of time, Lisa tells me, and can paint all night if no one reminds her to eat.)

"This is the kitchen," says Amelia, dragging me by the hand. It's small but functional, with beige painted cabinets, a scratched yellow linoleum floor, and a matching seventies olive-colored stove and refrigerator.

"I did these," says Amelia proudly, pointing to some watercolors attached to the fridge with magnets.

"They're great," I say.

"Not as good as Nana's," says Amelia, "but she says I have potential if I can develop my point of view."

Before I can comment on *that* I find myself being dragged through a tiny dining room. There's barely any space between the chairs and the wall, but Amelia squeezes through easily, and I catch a glimpse of more abstract owl art, smaller square canvases this time. There's a black owl with demonic bat wings in one, standing in an empty field that's eerily similar to the one behind the house. A figure huddles behind a thresher: a young woman.

"*My* room is upstairs," says Amelia, pulling my arm so hard I'm afraid it will come loose from its socket. The stairs creak as we go up. The green wall-to-wall carpeting continues, but here the walls are covered with different panels of mismatched wallpaper, stripes on one, faded flowers on another. Amelia pulls me into the first small room on the right; it's painted bright pink, and the walls are covered with art and sheet music. A guitar sits on her small white bed, and a few lone dolls are scattered on the floor, looking neglected.

"You can get into the attic from my closet," she says proudly, as if that were the best feature.

Next I'm pulled into a slightly larger room, painted a plain white. It has a queen-sized bed in a Shaker-style bed frame, and the sparse accessories are neatly arranged. There's a Japanese vase containing dried milkweed pods on the simple dresser, a wooden rocking chair on a braided rug, and a carved and painted wooden owl sculpture sitting on a rustic bookshelf, continuing the theme of owls from the canvases. A third, smaller room seems to be primarily used for storage; there are sagging cardboard boxes, an assortment of plastic Christmas trees and garlands, and a sewing machine in the corner that doesn't look like it's been used in the past decade.

"And this is my *dad's* room," says Amelia. The door to this room, unlike the others, is closed.

"Um, I don't know if we want to disturb your dad," I say.

Amelia sighs and rolls her eyes. "He's not *here*," she says, as if my ignorance is astounding.

She opens the door. A small rush of stale air escapes. I peer in past the doorway. The walls are painted black. The ceiling is painted black. The carpeting has been torn up and the wooden floors are painted black. Even the windows are painted black. It's like a dark cancerous cell, and I get a lightheaded, dizzy feeling just looking at it, like I'm back in the watery abyss at the bottom of the Aspinwall well. The closet doors are mirrored, reflecting the light from the hallway and Amelia's small and fragile image. A mattress, stripped of bedding, has been pushed up against one wall. There is a four-pronged candelabra on the floor, and here, oddly, are the only colors in the room: the melted candles are blue, white, yellow, and black.

"Uh, is your dad coming back anytime soon?" I'm hoping the answer is never.

But if Amelia hears me, she ignores the question completely. "You want to see something cool?"

Before I can answer she's pulled me into the room, and then she shuts the door behind us, which is painted black as well. Instantly it's pitch black and claustrophobic. I hold my hand in front of my face and can't see it.

"Maybe we should go see what Lisa's up to," I say, trying to hide the obvious panic in my voice.

"Watch," she says breathlessly. I hear the click of a light switch.

A black light flickers on overhead, casting us both in a purplish glow.

"Look," says Amelia, pointing to the walls.

The walls are literally covered with glowing tables and numbers scrawled with a yellow highlighter, so that they can only be seen with the door shut and the black lamp on. There is something strangely logical in its obvious madness; the same square of numbers is repeated over and over.

6	32	3	34	35	1
7	11	27	28	8	30
24	14	16	15	23	19
13	20	22	21	17	18
25	29	10	9	26	12
36	5	33	4	2	31

"He's getting better," says Amelia in a tiny voice. This is as much of a question as a statement.

"I'm sure he is," I say, giving her hand a squeeze. "I'm sure he is."

CHAPTER TEN: DEVIL IN THE CORNFIELD

Dinner proves to be a simple affair—frozen pizza, frozen peas, with vanilla ice cream for dessert. It's nicely familiar and yet also strange to be eating at a table with people, a family. I've gotten used to eating fast food alone, watching the evening news—my mother would be horrified. The dishwasher hums, the microwave beeps, chairs scrape on the floor, and I feel like an outsider as everyone else maneuvers through their evening ritual— "Amelia, did you put the butter on the table?" "Anyone seen the salt?" "Who drank the last of the milk?" It's all words to a language I'd forgotten.

Lisa's mom, Elizabeth, seemed to stare right through me during our introduction, until Lisa said I was her friend the *writer*.

"I'm trying to find my point of view," I said, winking at Amelia.

Elizabeth sighed, gripped my arm. "I didn't find mine until I was forty. Don't give up."

We eat off paper plates, and Elizabeth and I surreptitiously examine each other while pretending not to. Elizabeth must be fifty but looks forty, with long dark gray hair pulled back in a braid. There are smudges of blue paint under her fingernails, a few spatters of yellow on her cheek, and she wears an oversized man's white shirt over a pair of simple jeans.

"So, Dimitri, what do you write?"

"Obituaries," I say, reaching for the salt. "And I'm working on a novel. But I'm thinking about tossing it."

Her inquisitive gray eyebrows arch at this news. "Why?"

"It's shit," I say.

"Well," she says, as she rises from the table, "you should have someone read it before you throw it away. Stephen King threw *Carrie* in the trash. It was his wife who pulled it out. Of course, she never gets any credit. The woman *never* does."

"Typical," mutters Lisa.

"Everyone who reads my book says it's shit," I say cheerfully.

Amelia bends over to Lisa. "Does he have a record deal with a major label?" she whispers.

"And do you agree with them?" Elizabeth looks genuinely interested.

I shrug. "I can't tell the difference anymore."

"No, sweetheart," says Lisa, answering Amelia's question. "He doesn't."

"Then how come *he* gets to use bad words?"

"I wish you'd stop telling her that," mutters Elizabeth. "Amelia's going to be an *artist* like her *grandmother*, not a musician."

"I'm a writer," I say seriously to Amelia. "Writers can use all the words they want to. It's our job."

"Lucky," says Amelia, kicking at her chair.

"Maybe she'll be a writer," I say, and at this both Lisa and Elizabeth gasp in protest. The identical look of shock on their faces is almost comical.

"For a couple of postmodern feminists, you two are pretty controlling."

"Ha!" says Amelia, giving me a fist bump. She's starting to grow on me. "I showed him Daniel's numbers," she adds congenially.

The room drops into instant and immediate frozen silence. Lisa gives me a nervous glance and reaches for her water; her hand trembles ever so slightly.

Elizabeth sits back in her chair with a tub of ice cream and four paper bowls. She turns to me, her intense green eyes penetrating and serious. "And what did you think of Daniel's numbers?"

I have a feeling this is a pass/fail question by the way that Lisa is suddenly gripping her fork and staring at the table. And I have a feeling I can't pass a lie by Elizabeth.

"He's either crazy or he's a genius. Or both."

"Yes," confirms Elizabeth in a small voice. She scoops the ice cream into the bowls and then passes them around. Lisa relaxes, just a bit. "Madness and art," says Elizabeth quietly, "are the Bennet family legacy. On the male side of the family, that is. The women, we just get the art."

"Do they mean anything?"

"The numbers?" Elizabeth pauses, and we can all tell that Amelia is listening intently for the answer. "You did a good job eating all your peas, sweetheart. If you want to take your ice cream and go watch TV for a bit, you can."

"I want to stay *heeerrre*," Amelia whines.

"Go," says Lisa firmly. "TV."

If Amelia was allowed to swear, I'm sure we'd be recipients of a blue streak, but instead she just grinds her chair against the floor, grabs her bowl, and stalks from the room with dramatic stomps that shake the dishes in the cabinet. Immediately there's the buzz of high-pitched voices and the usual cartoon violence from the living room.

Lisa starts to stand. "She knows she's not supposed to watch cartoons."

"Let her be seven for a minute." Elizabeth waves her back into her seat. "You haven't told him *anything*." The accusation in her voice isn't hard to miss.

"We're still getting to know each other," says Lisa defensively.

"Go get the painting."

"Mom—"

"If he hasn't run away screaming after seeing Daniel's numbers, I don't think he's going to when he knows the whole story."

Lisa doesn't seem quite so convinced. She stares at her mother; an unspoken but obviously old argument hangs between them.

"Fine," she says tersely as she stands and goes to the dining room. I can hear her lifting one of the canvases off the wall.

"More ice cream?" says Elizabeth. She doesn't wait for me to answer and adds another scoop to my bowl anyway.

I'm starting to see why Lisa is jealous of my crappy yet private apartment.

———

"He was twenty-five when the voices started." Elizabeth takes the canvas from Lisa and lays it down in the middle of the table. I recognize it from my house tour with Amelia, the demon in the field with a woman hiding behind the thresher.

"Look closely," says Elizabeth.

Lisa sits, pulls her chair close to mine. It's hard not to notice that she smells like Ivory soap and something else, lemony and fresh. But I look down at the painting.

The demon has the face of an owl. In fact it almost looks like the owl is wearing a black demon suit, which is binding its arms in a straightjacket.

"The owl is the guardian of the underworld; he's the keeper of the spirits. I gave birth to Daniel in this house, and that morning an owl landed on the branch of that birch tree out there. So I started painting them. I liked them. They felt protective somehow. Like they were watching over us. Especially when their dad left."

She sadly traces the painting on the table with her finger, a distant look in her eyes. "But this one is Daniel, after he was diagnosed."

"Schizophrenia," says Lisa.

"So they *say*," says Elizabeth. I feel like Lisa wants to add something, but she doesn't.

"He'd been trying to raise Amelia on his own, working as a mechanic during the day, playing his music at night. Sarah, his girlfriend, wasn't ready to be a mother; she wanted to give Amelia up for adoption.

But Daniel wouldn't hear of it. He hated his dad and felt like giving up Amelia would be abandoning her, something his dad would do, had done. So he moved back here with me, and I took care of Amelia while he was at work or traveling to his gigs across the state."

"You probably didn't tell him about getting into the Thornton School of Music either," states her mother in a flat voice. I notice that Lisa is very, very still. "A very prestigious school in Los Angeles. They even offered her a full scholarship. Daniel was jealous."

"That has *nothing* to do with anything," says Lisa.

"He *was*," insists Elizabeth. "He changed. You can't deny that he changed. He painted the room black."

"He played punk," says Lisa. "That's part of the whole punk *thing*."

"You think I don't know that?"

A very tense silence hangs for a moment.

"Daniel was brilliant," says Elizabeth. "He'd always been the center of everything. He could have done anything he wanted, been anything he wanted. But he made bad decisions. Rash decisions."

"Keeping Amelia wasn't a bad decision," says Lisa with a lowered voice.

"But it limited his options," says Elizabeth. "And when Lisa got into music school, *his* dream, well . . ."

Now they both stare at the painting, as if it will speak to them, provide a definitive answer.

"He didn't talk about the voices at first," Elizabeth continues. "He just seemed tired, a little withdrawn, maybe depressed. I thought it was because of Sarah. But once Lisa started planning her move to LA, he began drawing on walls. Then the walls weren't enough—it was like they couldn't *contain* the voices—so he drew on napkins, his body, the soles of his shoes. The same numbers over and over. He said they protected him, protected us. Then I knew. My father, Archibald Bennet, was a respected artist. Watercolors, some woodblock prints, but he's most famous for his *Amelia* series. He hit a dry spell in his forties though, and then he heard voices too, drew numbers on the walls. They sent him to an asylum. But they didn't have much in the way of treatment back then. He was given a partial lobotomy. He never drew on walls again, but then he didn't remember who any of us were either. A hard trade."

"And Daniel knew about this?" I ask.

"Papa's numbers? I don't know, maybe. I thought I threw all that stuff out, but he could have run across something in the attic."

"Wait," I say. "They're not the *same* numbers?"

Elizabeth nods. "I think they are. But I'm not sure. I didn't memorize them at the time, and I tried to get rid of anything that contained them. I remember there were numbers in tables. 'Magic squares' my father called them."

Elizabeth turns to the canvas again. The overhead light casts a shadow on her face, revealing dark circles under her eyes, a few lines of crow's-feet. Just telling the story seems to age her. "He tried to kill Lisa. One day I had a doctor's appointment for Amelia downtown, and Lisa was home with Daniel. I never thought—*never*—that he would ever do anything to hurt her."

"That wasn't Daniel," adds Lisa firmly.

Elizabeth stares at her uncomprehendingly. "He stabbed her in the neck with a kitchen knife."

The scar. That's where her scar came from.

Elizabeth points to the woman in the painting. "She ran into the field, hid behind the thresher. It was a driver passing by who called police. When they came they found Daniel naked, covered in blood. He'd drawn the numbers all over his body—his chest, his arms, and face. And he was screaming, 'I release thee! I release thee!' Lisa almost bled to death."

"Don't be dramatic," says Lisa. "It wasn't that bad."

I look at Lisa. *Not that bad?* "Did he say why?" I quietly venture.

Elizabeth shakes her head. "There are lyrics to some of the songs that he was working on that make me wonder, but you know anyone in punk has a few songs about demons." There's something too even about her tone; it sounds like she's trying to convince herself.

"It's a disease," says Lisa. "It doesn't matter whether he thinks the voices were demons, aliens, or the CIA talking to him through an implant in his head. He's where he needs to be, getting help."

"If he's . . . getting help, why did you think he was in my apartment?"

Elizabeth looks shocked, and I can tell this is news to her. Lisa gives me a quick kick under the table to make the point.

"Somebody broke some pictures at Dimitri's," she says with measured calm. I notice she doesn't mention the letter. I decide not to either. "I thought maybe Daniel had broken out again."

"Again?" Knife-wielding crazy brother was on the loose?

Lisa reads the expression on my face. "About a year ago Daniel set off the fire alarms by blowing powdered cocoa under the fire detectors, and he got out." She is, remarkably, unable to keep a small hint of pride out of her voice. "His IQ is off the charts."

Now they both turn to me, as if waiting for me to make some excuse, head to my car, maybe run over a few chickens as I speed out the driveway. And it *is* quite the complication. But instead I pick up a crust of cold pizza, take a bite.

"So you going to show me your drums, or is that just a line you use to pick up guys?"

Elizabeth's face breaks out in a warm smile, the warmest of the evening, and she puts her hand over mine. "It's always better to know what you're getting into before you jump into bed."

Lisa throws her spoon onto the table with a clatter. "Really, Mom. I mean *really*."

But Elizabeth just looks into her empty ice cream bowl, trying and failing to hold back a laugh.

———

Lisa is still muttering as we head down the stairs to the basement. "Poking her nose in my business . . . Can't she just leave it *alone*?"

The basement is remarkable in that it looks nothing like the rest of the house whatsoever. If there had been Kelly green carpeting, then Lisa must have pulled it all up, leaving a bare cement floor covered by a few white, looped throw rugs. There's an antique brass bed painted firehouse red, pushed up against the cement wall and decorated with modern pillows and a clean linen comforter. The room's only window lets in a modicum of daylight. On the other side of the room is a white metal desk, and above it a large corkboard covered with Amelia's artwork, a few casually snapped photos, a flyer for one of Daniel's gigs, and some handwritten lyrics on college-lined notepaper.

Impossible to miss, dead center in the room, are the drums. Black and chrome, they're polished to an almost-obsessive gleam.

"They look expensive," I say.

"I'm still trying to pay them off," says Lisa. "One of the reasons I can't afford a place of my own. But the good thing about being way out in the middle of nowhere is that nobody complains about the noise."

"I can understand that," I say. "What made you start drumming?"

"Mom says I was always banging on stuff. She got tired of me pulling the pots out of the kitchen, so she got me my first set."

I hold up a pair of fuzzy bear slippers, arch my eyebrow. "Little big for Amelia, don't you think?"

"I wasn't *expecting* company," she says, snatching them from me. "And just remember I didn't make fun of your bamboo coffee table."

"Why, is there something funny about my bamboo coffee table?" I start to tickle her, and her laugh is infectious, bright, and airy. "It's not polite to laugh."

"Then stop," says Lisa between giggles, and somehow we collapse on her bed. *God*, it feels good to laugh.

"Your bed is so comfortable," I say with a sigh.

Lisa turns over on her side, puts her head charmingly on her hand. "You know I didn't think you'd run off because of Daniel. But my *mother*. She's scared off more than a few prospects."

I wave my hand dismissively. "Wimps all of them."

Lisa tugs at a button on the comforter. "So you're not freaked out?" There is a serious note under her light tone.

"You're talking to the guy who woke up in a morgue, remember? Plus I seem to be attracting some serious weirdness of late. I'm a spooky-shit magnet."

"What do you mean?"

I pause but decide to fill her in. A part of me agrees with Elizabeth that you *should* know what you're getting into before you jump into bed, and now that I know Lisa's whole story, it'd be chickenshit to omit mine. I start at the beginning, which I consider to be the death of my parents. I find the words to briefly describe my mother, my father—it's hard to talk about them, but I manage. Then I bring her up to speed about the ripped photographic prints, how I made the connection that one is a shot of the woman who was on the other table in the morgue. I try to explain the woman in my dream that I'm calling Poe—just saying the word causes a shiver at the base of my spine—and my new assignment for the *Devonshire Eagle* to investigate the story. I tell her about the article on Aspinwall with the accompanying altered photo, the dream about Daniel in the woods, the *real* snow in my bedroom, and the equally real footprints, and I end with the $500 leather book that's sitting on the backseat of my Mustang.

"Christ," says Lisa. She pulls her hair loose from her ponytail, considering. "But you haven't said anything about the envelope."

"Like I'm going to. If I remember correctly, you looked more than a little freaked out when you saw it."

"I *might* have overreacted."

"You recognized the writing. You thought it was Daniel's."

She nods. "But it couldn't be, right? If he's in the hospital?"

"Maybe he sent someone," I say, immediately regretting it because her face falls as she considers this.

"It's possible. What did it say?"

"*Race you.*"

"Like your dream," she says hesitantly.

"Well, I'd just read it before taking some serious sleep medication," I say with a forced note of cheer. "No wonder."

She's obviously not buying it.

"So *are* you freaked out?" I ask.

I can see that Lisa is choosing her words carefully. "You know what I said upstairs about Daniel suffering from a disease? That it wasn't him, it was the schizophrenia?"

I nod.

"Well, he was also starting to get into some really *dark* stuff. Occult stuff. He used to hang out at Aspinwall alone. Said he could write better there."

"And you went with him?"

"Sometimes. I was worried about him. How do you think I knew where all the bad floorboards were? But the termites must have got worse over time; the dining room used to be pretty solid."

An unsettling thought dawns on me. "You were *looking* for something that night. That's why you crashed our spooky party."

"Partly. I thought maybe he'd left something behind. Something that would help me . . . understand."

"I feel so *used*," I say in mock hurt.

"I said *partly*. I wanted to meet you too—"

"Sure, easy to say now that you know I'm such a catch."

Lisa punches me on my arm.

"Ow. First you use me, now you beat me. I think I liked you better when I didn't know you."

She gives me a warning look. "Dimitri—"

"Kidding, okay? Just trying to lighten the mood. So did you find anything?"

She sighs. "Nothing but the usual crumpled beer cans, cigarette stubs. But then I found something really weird in an old saltine tin. Scratched my hand trying to get it out from a hole in the wall."

She leans over the bed and pulls up the tin. It's rusted, dented, but the colors are still remarkably intact and the name clearly visible, Bremner Wafers. I pull off the top. It smells smoky, there's ash at the bottom, and inside is a folded sheet of paper. I carefully open it up. A bad Xerox copy with certain words underlined with red marker:

Dark sigil of the sun,
Numbers end 4, 2, 31,
Lay out the magic square,
Light candles, then beware,
Become a god, become a slave,
Two sides of the same coin,
Become a god, become a slave,
Your soul and his will join.

"Daniel wrote this?"

"No, that's what's weird. I Googled the lyrics, and they're from an eighties metal song, "Succubi Dreams." Daniel *hated* eighties metal—said they were fat corporate bands playing at being dark so they could snort coke and pay off their Beverly Hills mansions."

"But you think it's somehow related. What's happening to me and what happened to your brother."

"I don't know for sure, but *still*. He was looking for something. Maybe he found it."

"Look, Lisa," I say, "a lot of people have listened to this shit. Not everyone—"

"Stabs their sister. I know. But I just think there are some doors you're better off not opening. And just to be safe, I'd feel better if you threw out that book. Leave it alone. Be happy instead."

She traces her hand on my face, and for a moment it seems possible that I could find happiness with Lisa in a small farmhouse on the outskirts of town.

But I place my hand on hers. "The only problem is that whatever *it* is, I don't think it's going to leave *me* alone."

A pause. "That's what Daniel said once. When he was still lucid." Her voice chokes on the last word.

I lightly kiss her cheek. "Play something for me."

"You're trying to change the subject."

"Maybe."

Lisa sighs but sits up, walks to the drums, and settles into a metal folding chair behind them. I prop myself up on the bed.

"Okay," she says quietly, as if she's alone, centering herself. She taps the gleaming brass cymbal with her index finger, makes a circular motion, and it gives a resonant hum. When she's satisfied with the tone, she picks up some drumsticks off the floor, cracks her long, pale neck to one side, then the other, and closes her eyes.

"This feels weird," she says.

"Just pretend I'm not here," I say.

"Yeah, right."

She starts tapping the cymbals with her drumsticks. It sounds like rain hitting the fire escape outside my apartment window, and she sustains that for a few moments, then adds a bigger cymbal with a deeper tone, sliding easily between them, her hands quick and light. While they hum she strikes a few drums lightly, and I realize that this is nothing, just the warm-up—she's feeling how her drums sound today.

"Sometimes they're tight when it's cold," she says quietly.

She flips a drumstick in the air and then starts in earnest, playing a percussive sliding rhythm that's a staccato roll of thunder. Her hands move faster than I can follow; it's like she's looking for something or someone with sound. The sticks fly with relaxed ease, she's incredibly light with her touch, but the vibration is so deep that I can feel it resonate in my ribs. I close my eyes too, letting it fall over me, a liquid rush. And then the sound gets faster, harder, like a storm is letting loose and I'm with her in it; the wind is blowing, the rain shattering in sideways slices, but then she suddenly pulls it all back, shockingly abruptly, into a light tinny rainfall, slipping between the drums and cymbals until they blend together into a riff so fast that is sounds like a word or a phrase. A voice.

And I realize that this tells a story too, using rhythm. Maybe Daniel's numbers are a rhythm the way words are a rhythm, the way my heartbeat on the monitor was a rhythm, the way life and death is a rhythm.

When I open my eyes I see that hers are now half-closed. She is channeling her sound, alone in her private world, and a trickle of sweat drips unnoticed from her brow. If she sees me stand, it doesn't register, and I move quietly behind her. Another small trickle of sweat runs from the base of her neck, past her scar. I lean over and kiss it, salty, like the ocean, like a tear. I hear her quick intake of breath. My hand slips around her waist, the other starts to unzip the top of her dress; her skin here is soft but cool. The drums get fiercer, wilder, like a part of her is trying to push me away, warn me.

"I'm not Daniel," I whisper in her ear. "I'm not going anywhere."

When she drops the drumsticks and turns to me, what takes my breath away is how shockingly instantaneous the loss of sound is, like death itself. But then she pulls at the buttons on my shirt, and nothing registers but her skin, her lips, and we don't even make it to the bed, that first night.

CHAPTER ELEVEN: LIFESAVER

The forlorn chair is a definite find that early morning on the corner of Elm and Main, where someone who obviously had no appreciation for tacky, egg-shaped mid-twentieth-century plastic furniture dumped it for the trash collector to pick up. And it *is* gloriously ugly. The chair is cast in an amber plastic the color of beer, with spindly chrome legs tapering to tiny, lethal-looking points. I manage to stuff it halfway into the trunk of my Mustang and then squeeze it through the narrow Victorian stairway of my apartment building with only a mild bout of swearing and a couple of scraped elbows. But Lisa will love it.

Not that she deserves her own chair after booting me out of her warm bed just around five in the morning into the *freezing* cold, all because she didn't want to have to explain to Amelia or, God forbid, her mother what I was still doing there in the same clothes from the night before. As if they would care. But Lisa promised to drop by after work, which means I have some cleaning to do. The dishes in the sink are growing interesting fuzzy substances—some of which could be classified by the CDC as a health hazard—and I probably should invest in some sheets, maybe a new towel or two. The thought gives me a pleasant buzz.

Which is instantly killed as soon as I open my apartment door. Christ, my place really does stink, somewhere between homeless man in the library and old cheese. I cover my nose with my hand and race to open a window.

But when I turn around I notice that the shards of glass on the floor are different; they're not randomly scattered. Instead they've been carefully arranged to form a symbol.

The symbol on my ring.

My heart starts to pound—was the glass like that when I came in? But I know the answer. It wasn't.

Theory one is that in less than five seconds someone zipped into my apartment, positioned the broken glass, and stepped out again without making a sound or cutting their hands in the process. Theory two of course doesn't seem possible either, but then I've had to recently expand my notion of possible. After all, snow is not a normal meteorological occurrence in crappy apartments, unless there's a gaping hole in the roof.

Time to test theory two. So how does this actually work, communing with the spirit world? Maddy's approach was a little histrionic, to say the least.

I take a deep breath. Let's see how a direct question works. "Poe, did you do this?"

The temperature suddenly drops to just a few degrees below freezing, and a thin vein of frost crackles across the glass of the window.

Fuck. My apartment's haunted. As if my life wasn't complicated enough.

"For crying out loud," I mutter, my breath hanging in the air, "could you do something *useful*, like clean my apartment?" My voice echoes in the empty space, and I don't think I'm crazy, but then again, define crazy.

But apparently my ghost friend is not all that into cleaning, because she doesn't respond. And after I turn up the heat, start to wash the dishes—some are beyond help and get thrown in the trash —I realize that I am probably the worst person in the world to document a haunting, particularly my own, because I know little or nothing about the subject. We never even celebrated Halloween in my family. On October 31 we'd keep the lights low, and if some poor unfortunate kid in a Power Rangers costume happened to ring our doorbell, they'd be treated to a torrent of swearing in Russian by my father, who'd then slam the door in their face and mutter something about stupid Americans not understanding the origin of their commercialized pagan rituals. "What will they celebrate next?" he'd ask my mother, "Hiroshima?"

And there was definitely no mention of how *irritating* a ghost could be. Because irritation is the main thing I feel as I sweep up the shards of glass on the floor and dump them into a can. It's like being stalked by an angry ex-girlfriend, this haunting stuff. Is she here now, watching me search for a clean towel in the hamper? Is she pissed that I'm not scared shitless? She's trashing my stuff, what little there is (I liked my photos without the tear through the middle, thank you very much). And for Christ's sake, if she can toss around my pictures and make it snow in my apartment, why the hell can't she just *tell* me what she wants me to know?

But the darker thought that nags somewhere in the back of my mind is something different altogether, a black little whisper that creeps along quietly as I straighten the mail. Why can Poe reach me but not my parents? Wouldn't they be first in line to haunt me? Would it kill them to say hello?

Maybe I *am* losing my mind.

But in a strange way what happened at Aspinwall, while terrifying, also made me hope that this was a bigger door opening. It doesn't make sense that a spirit I obviously have no connection to has control over my dreams, can even step into my waking life, but my parents—nothing. A part of me feels abandoned all over again. Which is ridiculous, stupid to even think about.

But it does give me an idea. Maybe there's a better way to communicate with Poe, one that doesn't involve the destruction of my personal property and won't bankrupt me with sky-high heating bills.

Poetry magnets.

I don't know where she got them, my mother, but sometime around the time I was in high school she picked up a box of poetry magnets, placed them on the fridge, and we would go back and forth trying to make each other laugh with the weirdest nonsensical phrase. "Raw vivid purple pops puppies." "Lollipops eat city leave memories." Or we'd use them as a kind of visual shorthand—"Would young man use imagination and clean clothes." I know they were among the few things to make it into one of my five cardboard boxes. The ones I haven't opened in a year.

This is going to take a Xanax and maybe a couple of Valium to accomplish.

Evicting a few spiders in the process, I drag each dusty box into the middle of my living room floor and use a dull steak knife to roughly hack at the tape, leaving jagged cardboard wounds on the flaps of the boxes.

"See?" I say to an apparently empty room. "I fucking heard you. I get that the symbol's important. But we are not engaging in some kind of *Poltergeist* cliché. We are going to make this a civilized haunting; we are going to act like two grown adults."

I might need to rephrase that.

"Or one grown adult and one dead adult. Or ghost. Or whatever."

Maybe using a beer to wash down the meds was a bad idea. Or not, because I revise that opinion after drinking another.

I reach an arm into the Styrofoam popcorn guts of box one, pulling out a battered Steiff monkey with an eerie grin, Bunky, who never left my side for most of my childhood. He goes to the floor with a thump. I reach in again, this time pulling out my high school yearbook, which is still wrapped in plastic, thank God, because that year I sported a mullet in an attempt at post-twentieth-century irony. The next find is the VHS copy of our middle school production of *The Wizard of Oz*, in which I played a munchkin; so far the only things I seem to have kept are ammunition for my blackmailers once I'm rich and famous.

Then I hit upon the shoebox that was under the dresser. A few crushed pieces of Styrofoam cling to the top; I wipe them away with my wrist and sit back on my heels.

The box must have been dropped or jostled somewhere among my several moves—first the boxes went into storage at my friend Neal's garage, then into the U-Haul on the way to New Goshen— because the watch inside is even more broken than before. The back has completely sprung open and little bits of machinery are scattered about.

It figures. My eyes are blurry from the beer, Xanax, or both, but I notice something on the inside of the watch: tiny writing—an inscription. A feeling of excitement rises in my chest—here it is, my detective-style *aha* moment—so I eagerly hold the watch closer and discover that the writing is . . . Greek. My head starts to pound. Is *anything* about this going to be easy? Could someone please leave me a *single* fucking clue that makes sense? So, I do the obvious thing, which is to throw poor Bunky across the room with more force than is necessary to kill a stuffed animal. He makes a satisfying thwump on the opposite wall, even makes a small crack in the plaster that will come out of my rent deposit (dang, that Bunky weighs more than I remember), but fuck it.

The afternoon sun stretches across the floor, and I discover that instead of cleaning up my place I've made it a good deal worse, and with my current buzz, I'm not sure what time it is or how many hours have gone by. But Christ I don't want Lisa walking in and thinking that she's got another crazy freak on her (she does, but no need to clue her in on that fact just yet). I check my father's watch (oh, right, broken) and start to shove the Styrofoam back into the box, actually stumbling across the poetry magnets in the process. Thank God *something* went right.

I push, shove, and swear but finally get the boxes back into the closet and sweep most, if not all, of the clinging Styrofoam bits off the floor.

Then, the faintest ticking.

Did someone leave a bomb in my apartment? Because it's that kind of sound, a *don't open that suitcase!* sound; the kind of sound in a movie before there's a loud and violent explosion. I stand for a moment and try to gauge where it's coming from. Not the kitchen, not the closet—too loud for that—but somewhere closer, near the door. I glance over to the bamboo coffee table and see my father's watch. The second hand is moving in a counterclockwise direction. Impossible, of course—half the parts were swept up into the trash. Impossible unless you have your own personal ghost.

If Poe weren't dead already, I might kill her myself.

I press my knuckles into my forehead. *God*, I don't want this. I was feeling so *good* when I was on my way home, practically flying. And it's been so long since I felt anything even *approaching* good. I wonder if Poe isn't just messing around with my dreams, my apartment, and my father's watch, but messing around with my emotions as well. Maybe that's part of the whole haunting experience; she hasn't exactly been a jolly presence to be around. Next time I see her in my dream I know what my question will be: How the hell do I get rid of you?

I grab the poetry magnets and stride toward the kitchen. "These," I say loudly, my voice echoing ridiculously in my apartment, "are called *words*. If there's something you want to say, *use them*. But for Christ's sake, leave my shit alone. Any more fucking around with my personal property and I'm going to pretend I don't see or hear you. I'll move to Florida. I mean it."

There. Ghost girl got served.

———

By the time Lisa arrives I've borrowed a few things from my neighbor Doug to spiff things up and detract from the overall homeless-shelter interior décor. Apparently some people still own cloth napkins and iron them no less. (Not a big fan of the new chair, though, is Doug. One glance and his verdict was, "The point of design is to encourage relationships, not scare them away.")

Anyways.

My first article for the *Eagle* detailing the spooky happenings here on Grant Street (MESSAGE FROM THE GRAVE) is almost done, I've got a pizza on the way from Del Fino's, and I've even discovered a forgotten stash of bottled water that I'd put away in case of snowstorm-induced electrical outages—an amazing find, because I'd hate to serve Lisa water from the tap, which is yellowish from the old copper pipes. And all my effort is worth the moment when Lisa enters, slips off her jacket, and says, "It smells *so* much better."

Then she sees the chair, and her eyes widen. "That is the most hideous thing I've ever seen." She settles happily in the egg and spins it around.

"Jealous?"

"Completely." She stops the chair and then points to the opposite wall, where the photographs had been. "What's up with that?"

In my cleaning frenzy I made the decision—hey, who needs a corkboard when you're living in a low-rent dive and have plenty of pushpins? So I've started my collage, tacking the torn-in-half photos to the wall, as well as the copies of the old *Eagle* articles and my hand-written mystery list.

Lisa puts a finger to her temple with a pained expression. "Are you writing on walls now too?"

Ooohh. Didn't think about that one. "This?" I say, trying to make light of the subject. "This isn't writing on walls. This is writing on *paper*, then tacking the paper *onto* the walls. Completely different. Apples and oranges."

Lisa groans.

"What—you have a corkboard with lyrics? I don't make morbid associations about that."

Before we can get started with another argument—again, is this the Poe effect? We only seem to have arguments here—the pizza dude arrives, blessing us with pepperoni-induced peace and harmony.

"Place mats?" asks Lisa, her mouth full. She seems wary of them, and they do look too expensive; not the kind of thing you want to drip pizza sauce on.

"Doug, my neighbor's," I admit. They don't look quite right on my bamboo coffee table with paper plates and plastic cutlery, but oh well.

She shakes her head sadly. "You spent five hundred dollars on a book you can't even read and you're borrowing your neighbor's table linens? Do you not *know* how to shop online?"

"I got the chair," I protest.

She gives me a serious look. "How much did you pay for the chair?"

"Okay, it was free," I admit. "But you know what they say: one man's trash is another man's treasure. Plus you've got to *see* this book." I jump up to get my messenger bag.

She raises a hand. "No, I *don't*."

"Really," I say, rummaging through my closet. That's something I feel like I can do now—open my closet without wallowing in a pity party for one. Interesting. "It's cool," I add. "Very goth." I find the book and okay, it really doesn't look all that cool, the gray *MacGyver* duct tape ruins the effect, but still. When I turn to show Lisa though, she's got her bag over her shoulder and is opening the door.

"I'm not doing this," she says quietly. Her face is soft, as if she's about to cry.

"Wait," I say. "Doing what?"

"You *know* what. This is *exactly* how it started before."

"For Christ's sake, Lisa, I'm not Daniel; I'm really not. I would never, *never* hurt you. Is that what you're scared of, that I'm going to go crazy and try to kill you?"

"Daniel is not *crazy*. He has a disease—"

"A disease that made him think stabbing you was a good idea." Instantly I'm filled with regret as her face goes a whiter shade of pale. "Look," I add more gently. "All I'm asking is for you to explain. One minute you say he has a disease—that he's schizophrenic, and that's why he attacked you—and then the next minute you're scared I'm going to end up like him just by reading some book. By taping notes on my wall. As far as I know, reading and organizational skills aren't big risk factors for psychotic breaks."

"It's not that simple," she says tentatively. She sits back down in the egg-shaped chair but holds her purse in her hand, like at any moment she might still leave. I settle on the couch and let her think for a minute.

Finally she says, "To Daniel it was all a big game at first, a challenge. He looked at my grandfather's numbers like they were an interesting puzzle, and then, it's like the more time he spent with them, the more they seemed to hold him. Possess him."

"I thought your mom said she'd thrown all that stuff out."

Lisa sighs heavily. "She did. But I wanted some privacy and decided to move into the basement. Daniel helped me rip up the old carpeting, and the numbers were there on the cement floor in white chalk. I washed them away, but Daniel jotted them down in a notebook first." She stares intently at her hands.

"You can't think this is *your* fault."

"Sometimes I'd be sitting across from him," she says softly, "just like I'm sitting across from you, and I knew he was thinking about them. Repeating them in his mind over and over. He was so *sure* of himself at the beginning. He kept saying there was a reason we'd found the numbers, that he could figure out what they meant . . . He was so convincing that he convinced me. But he didn't figure it out, because there was nothing *to* figure out. And a part of me wonders . . . What if I'd done something different? What if I'd said something? . . . Stopped him?" She twists the straps of her bag between her fingers, and for a moment we're both silent.

"Look," I finally say, "there's a big difference here. No family history of mental illness. Okay, maybe my mom was on the OCD side when it came to cleaning, but no schizophrenia."

"But why take the chance?" she asks in a small voice. "Why not just leave it alone?"

A good question.

Two candles also borrowed from Doug burn low on the table, flickering weakly, almost about to go out in a pool of melted wax. A cold wind blows through the eaves of the house, rattling the windowpane. It's a lonely sound.

I pull at some loose thread where the couch is worn away. "My parents died. One minute they were here, calling me to let me know they were coming out for the weekend, and then a few hours later they were gone. Forever. No warning. I had no bad feeling; no black cat crossed the street—it was a completely normal day. I was worried about my novel; I was planning on going to the corner store to pick up some flowers for my mom; CNN was on; there were kids playing on the street. I went to a party. Then, when I got the call, it was like, *what the fuck*? Because the next day nothing changed. The sun shone, the kids played baseball, CNN was covering the same news. My whole life disappeared, and the world went on as usual. That scared me. It scared me more than anything. Because then, what's the point? There is none."

"But that's just it," says Lisa. "It's random. It's all random and there is no point, so you've got to take your happiness where you can find it. You almost died but didn't. So now enjoy what you've got."

"What's happening to me now is *not random*. The symbol on my father's ring is the same symbol in the book."

Lisa shakes her head dismally. "Dimitri, a *dollar sign* is a symbol. Ever see that in more than one place? It doesn't *mean*—"

"But it could—"

"This is all about your father, isn't it?" A statement more than a question.

I swallow. "No. Okay, *maybe*. But let's look at this logically. Hypothesis A: Daniel is completely off-his-rocker nuts. Then there can't possibly be any harm if I read the book, right? Insanity isn't communicable."

Lisa gives me a guarded look. "Well that's Hypothesis A."

"Right. Then we have Hypothesis B, which is that Daniel is *not* crazy. Instead something is going on that has to do with Aspinwall, or the numbers, or my father, or something else we don't understand. But if we go with that assumption, then Daniel spending the rest of his life in an asylum isn't going to help him, because he's not insane."

"Where are you going with this?"

"What I'm saying is that the only way to help him would be to understand what's wrong. There are too many coincidences for all this to be random. I feel like there's a thread that's connecting it all, that there's a direction, a path."

"A thread, a *path*," murmurs Lisa. She looks at me with an expression I can't quite read and then leans over, placing a hand over one of the candles. The delicate skin between her fingers glows an incandescent red. "Let's say Hypothesis *B* is right, and it *is* all connected. What's at the end of that path?"

"I don't know," I admit.

"I do," says Lisa. "And it's not good. For anyone."

"That was the end of Daniel's path. And I'm not Daniel."

"You keep saying that."

For a moment we don't talk—we just sit there silently. An obvious impasse. There's no way for either of us to win.

"I don't know what's going to happen if I really start to pursue this," I finally say. "But I know that I need you, Lisa." I twist one of the couch's threads around my finger. "I need you to tell me if I've gone too far. I need you to throw me a line."

"My track record as a lifesaver is not that great," she says bitterly.

"You'll know," I say. "You're maybe the only one who will."

Lisa doesn't answer. Instead she slowly passes a finger through the edge of the dying flame, making it ripple, playing with it. "You know, Daniel always used to do this when we were kids. I'd wonder why he never got burned. He said it was magic. But there's no such thing as magic."

"Is that a no, then?" I ask softly.

"I didn't say that." She pulls her hand back from the candle, looks me in the eye. "*Okay*, I will throw you one, and only one, line. If I say pull back, pull back. If I say run, you run. Will you promise me that?"

I swallow and nod. The magnitude of this concession is not lost on me.

"Because if you don't . . . I can't be there with you when it ends. Badly."

The flame dies, and smoke curls from the burnt wick.

I stand—hold my hand out to her. "I wouldn't want you to."

————

Around ten, at a reasonably decent hour, I give Lisa a ride home.

"You want to come in?" she whispers, her breath hanging in the cold air. Of course there's not much point in whispering; Buddy has announced our arrival with a fit of barking that could wake the proverbial dead, or worse still, an anxious mother. A light pops on in Elizabeth's second-floor bedroom.

"Yes," I say, "but then I won't want to leave."

"Hmmm," she says, nuzzling my neck while she places a hand on my thigh. "And is that a bad thing?"

"Hey," I say, gently pushing her away. "Don't start the engine unless you're going for a ride."

She eases out of the car and smiles. "I thought writers needed to suffer for their art."

"Well thanks to you I'm going to be taking a cold shower as soon as I get home."

"That's not suffering, that's dating a tease."

She puts her hands in her jacket pockets, and I watch her go up the front steps, slightly hunched against the cold, illuminated by the Mustang's round headlights. She looks smaller somehow, more vulnerable. At the top she gives Buddy a gentle pat but doesn't look back before opening the front door, which briefly casts a warm light on the porch.

It's a long and lonely ride back home alone. The ghostly streets are empty and deserted, except for the liquor stores and bars—today is Friday, the day for cashing welfare and social security checks in these parts. I pass a dirty middle-aged man sitting on the curb in front of Ace Liquor; he drinks from a bottle in a paper bag, swaying slightly. I wonder if he's someone's father. There was about a month in high school where I seriously wondered if my continuously absent father was leading some kind of double life, if maybe he was an alcoholic. I'd seen a television special outlining the signs, unexplained absences being one of them. So I'd ride my bike to the bars, find an inconspicuous spot, and watch the door, imagining myself a detective on a stakeout. I did see other people's fathers, like Mr. Sprague with some woman, not his wife. An occasional teenager would try to get in, but they'd be escorted back out on the sidewalk five minutes later with one less fake ID. But not my father. Never my father.

I could usually tell about a week before he left that he would be going on one of his unexplained trips. My mother would get into a *mood*. The first bad signs were the dust bunnies under the bed. Next came the envelope with cash for me to buy lunch at school. I was the only kid in my class with an industrial stainless steel lunchbox and four-course gourmet meal, but each day leading up to my father's departure, my mother would get up later and later in the morning, leaving me to fend for my own with cereal for breakfast, or if she wasn't looking, chocolate chip cookies. Frozen items would make an appearance at dinner, peas and french fries, and I knew things were really bad when I'd come downstairs to find a tinfoil-wrapped TV dinner at my place at the table.

When he was gone I tried to keep self-contained, not be a burden. I'd take out the trash without my mom having to ask me three times; I'd wash what few dishes there were and put them in the dishwasher, adding my mother's favorite brand of detergent. I folded my clothes and made my bed before school. Tried to make it up to her in my own way.

Which of course made me hate him just a little, my father. He wouldn't call while he was gone and left no way for us to reach him. It was like being periodically and inexplicably abandoned. But what made me hate *her* just a little was the fact that when he finally came back unannounced, appearing one day at the front door with his suitcase in hand, she'd act like he'd never been gone, even if it'd been weeks. Suddenly the vacuum would be buzzing, we'd have roast duck for dinner, and I'd find my underwear starched into near-cardboard perfection. Was he having an affair? Did he have another family stashed away, or was he involved in something illegal, like the Russian Mafia or maybe a Colombian drug cartel? Whatever he was up to drained him completely; he'd stay in bed for at least a week, with my mother carrying his meals on trays to their bedroom. Eventually I realized that whatever he was doing, my mother must have known, or if she didn't know, she didn't care. So to a certain degree I stopped caring, which created a distance between us—my mother and me.

I park the car and head up the creaking stairs to my apartment. Walking in I find the candles have gone out, so I run them under the water for a second to make sure the wicks aren't smoldering, then toss them in the trash. Maybe I'm not different than my dad—here I am abandoning Lisa in a way to chase down some long-dead mystery. Maybe I'll never learn more about my father, his "thing." Maybe she's right, it's all random and there's nothing *to* learn.

The book is on the couch where I left it. I sit down and pick it up. The leather cover is soft in my hands; it has a smooth sheen, and the corners are bent with obvious signs of wear—this wasn't a book that sat unread on a shelf, gathering dust. I open it in the middle, randomly flipping through some of the yellowed pages. It's amazing to think someone carefully traced each line of each letter; it must have taken years for the Greek text alone. But what does it mean? What does the symbol on my ring mean? Why do I care?

"What the hell am I doing?" I say, tossing the book on the floor. "Can you tell me that, Poe? Can you tell me what the fuck this is all means?" My voice echoes through the empty apartment.

There is, of course, no response. There never is when you want one.

CHAPTER TWELVE: AMELIA

There is the glow of a party in the distance and a live band. Not the kind of music I'm familiar with: it's an old-fashioned warble, a woman's voice, rising out to a night sky filled with stars.

> *There'll come a time when you'll regret it,*
> *There'll come a time you'll want to forget it,*
> *'Cause I'm gonna haunt you so,*
> *I'm gonna taunt you so,*
> *And it's gonna drive you to ruin.*

A bright staccato laugh rises out above the murmur of a small crowd. I look down and find that I'm wearing a black tuxedo, with black leather shoes polished to a high shine. A cigarette burns in my hand. I toss it to the gravel driveway and crush it with the edge of my heel. Gold cuff links in my shirt sleeves catch the light of small round headlights coming toward me, and I step aside as a Packard, black with a round hood, roars by. I watch as it pulls up to Aspinwall, where a butler smartly steps forward to open the car door.

I must be dreaming. Or I'm in a really, really bad cliché of an MGM film. I half expect to see Fred Astaire tapping by with Ginger Rogers on his arm.

From behind me a tiny woman in a white silk gown glittering with embroidered crystals approaches. Her platinum hair cascades down her back in highly styled curls, and she grips my arm lightly.

"Are you coming?" she says, her voice like a bird's.

I nod, and she laughs as if I've said something funny and pulls me past the paper lanterns hanging from the neatly pruned elms into a courtyard filled with large white tents. Waiters in white jackets drift by, balancing gleaming silver platters filled with hors d'oeuvres. On a small raised stage I see the source of the music, a small orchestra; all the musicians are wearing fake beards and turbans, while the singer sways in front of a microphone, looking like a recent escapee from a harem, gauzy red silk draped over her head. Her eyes are lined with thick black kohl.

"I just *adore* jazz," says the blond on my arm. "My *mother* says it's sinful. Isn't that a gas?" She pulls out a cigarette from her glittering purse, which reminds me of Maddy's, but with a higher caliber of crystal. I realize she's waiting for a light, and I search my pocket, which remarkably yields a gold lighter.

"Thanks," she says, blowing some of the smoke in my face, a strange form of flirtation. "I'm Alice, by the way."

Suddenly the murmur turns to astonished gasps, then a smattering of applause. I turn to see, of all things, an elephant emerge from the woods with a woman sitting on top wearing blousy trousers and a tight-fitting bodice, like an Indian princess from *A Thousand and One Nights*. Her skin is creamy white, glowing under the paper lanterns.

"She always makes an entrance," says the blond bitterly.

"Who's that?"

The woman turns to me, surprised. "Mrs. Aspinwall. You don't know her?" There's a hopeful edge to her voice.

"No," I say.

"I've never met anyone who didn't know Mrs. Aspinwall. You must not be from around here."

"I'm not." I leave her side to go get a closer look.

I push through the crowd, and time seems to slow—I can see every detail, hear every sound. A woman in her fifties holds a martini too tightly, smelling like she took a bath in musky perfume—"How did she get her hands on an elephant? That's what I want to know." I pass by a tall, gangly man with thin round glasses—"The market will recover; it always does." A little girl zips by, chasing a brown puppy. She's followed by an overweight and much slower maid—"Delia, stop now; time for bed."—until finally I reach the front, where I find Captain Aspinwall, puffed up with pride, standing at the elephant's head—"Spent our honeymoon in Bombay; that's where she got the idea." Mrs. Aspinwall is still perched on the elephant's back, looking away. Her long brown hair is curled into a shiny wave, and I hear her bright laugh again; it sparkles high above the music. She turns to the rest of us.

She has no face.

"Love, can you help me down?"

Shock ripples through my body, but no one else seems to notice. Captain Aspinwall gallantly holds out his arms, and she jumps lightly into them, causing another small round of applause. The shoes on her feet are pointed and curl upward at the ends. She runs a delicate hand through her hair. "Don't encourage me. Next I'll be swallowing a sword."

With what mouth?

But everyone laughs. A waiter holds up a platter with small shot glasses, and I take two.

"Well, I don't know about anyone else," she says. "But I'm completely famished. Have they started to serve?"

"Just the hors d'oeuvres, love," says Captain Aspinwall. "We were waiting on you."

"Well tell them to start serving the duck. I hate it when food is served cold."

"Yes, my heart," he replies, heading immediately for the kitchen, and I wonder if everyone here is her servant in one way or another.

"I don't believe we've met," she says, turning to me and extending a hand.

I swallow, look to where her face should be. "We haven't. I'm Dimitri."

"A Russian name? You must be one of Richard's friends from New York. He doesn't take me there nearly enough. I'm obviously Mrs. Aspinwall, but you can call me Amelia."

A second and apparently visible wave of shock hits me.

"You don't like the name? Neither do I. It's such an old-fashioned name, like Gertrude or Myrna. I thought about officially changing it to Greta, like Greta Garbo, but Richard put his foot down. Come sit with me. We should get to know each other."

And just like that I'm now a part of her cadre, under her spell. As I follow she tosses out greetings, clasps hands, works the crowd— "What a darling dress, Sammy; you must tell me where you got it"; "Oh, hello Doug, so glad you could come"; "Edgar, it's been far too long; you must drop by more often, I insist." She is, I realize, a born politician.

Her long table is at the front of the tent to the right of the band, and she points me to the seat directly next to her. For a moment she hums along to the song, and I try not to stare at her face, or where her face should be. It's like the person who rubbed her image out from the photograph in the newspaper has somehow rubbed her out in my dream as well.

"You're *sure* we don't know each other?"

I shake my head.

"That's funny, because you look *familiar* somehow. But that can't be, because I don't know many Russians. Except for the gardener. But you don't have an accent."

"You have a Russian gardener?"

"He's divine. He can make my rosebushes bloom in winter. He whispers something to them; I've seen him. But he only gives me the red ones. The white ones he saves." She leans forward and says in a conspiratorial tone, "He has jars and jars of the creepiest stuff—Pollie told me she'd never had such a scare as when she tried to clean his room. Said there were actual dried batwings in a jar."

She turns to an invisible waiter behind her, clicks her finger, and he darts forward. "Do tell Pollie to make sure the cream is whipped properly for the mousse."

"Yes, madam," says the waiter, disappearing to wherever waiters go.

"I tell you, it'd almost be easier for me to cook myself. If I don't stay on Pollie she'll send out burnt pork chops. Servants get distracted so easily."

I realize that like any other politician, she's completely self-absorbed.

"Take our stable boy. Twelve years old, the little scoundrel, and he ran away with fourteen silver spoons and a chafing dish. I let Pollie stay, even though he's her brother and she should have known. But it's not easy to find someone who can make a cheese soufflé that won't fall. In this part of the world at least. What do they eat in Russia? Something nasty with beets, if I remember."

"Amelia!" calls out a portly man from the dance floor. "I'm famished! Where's the main course?"

"Coming, Stanley. Give your wife one more spin. It'll be worth the wait, I promise you!" Then to me under her breath, "Not that he needs another dinner. He'll be dead from a heart attack by sixty, like his father."

A large woman comes up behind us, opens her arms.

"Doris," says Amelia, "you look ravishing tonight. Simply ravishing."

While they exclaim over how beautiful they both are, I scan the crowd, wondering what it is I'm supposed to see. Some of the servants look familiar (from the Aspinwall photograph probably), but none of the partygoers, who twirl on the grass with a woozy swirl, and I'm surprised to realize that the two shots of whatever hard liquor I downed earlier are having an effect. This is a dream after all. Still, I loosen my bow tie.

As soon as Doris is out of earshot, Amelia whispers, "God, what a terrible dress. It looks like someone with dull scissors cut up a burlap bag. They lost everything in the crash, sad to say."

A waiter deftly leans between us, puts down a delicate porcelain plate with neatly sliced roasted duck, white asparagus, and julienned potatoes. My mother served something nearly identical every Christmas Eve. The smell washes over me and causes a wave of grief to rise, choke my throat.

"Ugh, a little overdone," complains Amelia. She picks up her fork, and there's something strangely familiar about the way she does this, its studied grace . . . and something else too about the *cadence* of her voice. I try to make the connection, but then her fork spears a slice of duck before disappearing into the haze of her face. I feel like I'm going to be sick.

"Distracted, like I said. Oh, speaking of Russians—I'm going to have a séance here on Halloween. You should come."

There, in between the dancers, I see something for just a split second. My fingers clutch the tablecloth.

"My gardener was the inspiration. He has the oddest book with the most *provocative* pictures—beheaded women, demons dancing around a funeral pyre, very macabre. I've seen him carrying it in his leather bag. He pulls it out when he thinks no one is looking, but of course I'm always looking. I once asked him about it and he pretended to not understand me. *Such* an annoying habit with foreign servants—you have no idea, *no idea* how difficult it was to plan a successful party in India. Still, I managed a peek at this book of his—not that I rummage around the servants quarters, but you can't be too careful. And then Eleanor mentioned that when she went to England, séances were all the rage; anyone who's *anyone* has a salon. They invite *real* psychics who channel spirits—Russians, she said, are very good—and the most *amazing* things happen. Eleanor said she met an actual disciple of *Rasputin*, who was able to make contact with her grandfather Edmond Wright—no connection to the Wright Brothers; they made their money in coal, the Wrights."

A face, caught at the edge of the dance floor, cold and familiar, flashes and then disappears.

"So I asked the gardener if he knew of anyone, and he just stood there, looking for all the world like an imbecile, and I know he understood me perfectly well—he even smiled a bit, like *I* was the idiot, if you can believe such an impertinence—and then he turned on his heel and walked away, just like that. I would have fired him," she says with a sigh, "but I've become somewhat famous for my red winter roses. They're very pretty on the Christmas tree."

Poe. She stands at the edge of the dance floor, haughty and thin, like a severe ballerina. Her clothes are dripping wet, her hair clings to her wet, cold face, and something greenish and slimy drapes around her neck like a silk scarf. None of the partygoers see her; none give her a second glance. She stares at me and her eyes are like glittering diamonds, void of warmth and expression.

I quickly look away, down at my plate. But instead of roast duck, I find the severed head of a puppy sitting in a sauce of bright red blood. A spasm of blinding white light hits, and the world tilts to one side, then the other.

"It was amazingly expensive to get her to come, Khioniya, which doesn't sound like a Russian name, does it? More Italian I would think. She said she already had an engagement for Halloween—a duchess, I believe—but I told her about the funny book and the gardener, and she changed her mind. She's on a ship right now—it takes *forever* to cross the Atlantic. I'm very good on the water. I never get ill."

The dancing crowd parts, and standing next to Poe I see little Delia, her innocent eyes now equally hard—she holds a large kitchen knife in one hand; blood drips to the soft grass beneath. Delia giggles the same ethereally evil giggle I last heard coming from Maddy before she fell through the floor.

Then her eyes turn completely black.

The world tilts again. I feel like I'm going to vomit.

I clutch the white tablecloth, try to steady myself—there's so much I want to know, *need* to know, but Amelia's blurry face is stretching into a whirl of color, and I'm falling again—where, into what, I'm not sure.

"No one will forget," says Amelia. "Everyone will hear about my Halloween party. I'll be famous . . ."

Delia's small, haunting voice sings.

Take her by the lily-white hand,
Save her from the water,

". . . I'll be famous forever." Amelia's voice is distant now, has a floating quality.

Leave her and you might just find,
There's no end to the slaughter.

CHAPTER THIRTEEN: FOOTPRINTS

The old woman's body was found under an old railroad tunnel that was once used to transport coal and timber. The fingers were frozen solid but not the heart, which the truck driver thought might still have been beating when he put his hand to Alice Chesterfield's cold neck to check for a pulse, despite the frozen puddle of blood. Despite the gaping hole in her stomach.

"One of these days your fuckin' luck is going to run out, Shakespeare," Nate mutters irritably into the phone after giving me this delightful news. I wish I hadn't picked up. I'm still groggy from my dream, my head is throbbing like I have a massive hangover, and a lingering visual of the puppy's head served on a silver platter isn't exactly helping. But now there's a frozen dead woman missing most of her internal organs and I'm lucky—how?

"What are you *talking* about?"

Nate either ignores, or doesn't hear, my question. "Just because you're, like, my dad's new favorite reporter, doesn't mean I'm not still the editor. You might think you're hot shit 'cause you get to go cover a fuckin' murder, but if you don't fuckin' get me copy by noon, then I'm gonna tell Dad you've blown your deadline. And no fancy words."

None of this is making any sense.

"Nate—"

"Turn on the TV," he says. "Noon."

Click. I look at the clock—10:10 A.M.; that gives me barely two hours to get it done. And, oh right, I was supposed to get Mac an article by Saturday, which is today. Nate is obviously setting me up for failure, the little fucker.

Of course my TV is crap and the cable bill hasn't been paid, so I have to experiment with a pair of bent bunny ears (thank God New Goshen still is on analog) until I get a fair, if sporadically fuzzy, picture. There are two reporters covering the murder, one all the way from Albany and the second from Rochester, New York. They both have concerned, serious tones but can't hide their excitement, because it's not just a murder, I discover, watching the B-roll of downtown New Goshen and accompanying narration, it's a *slaying*, the difference being the viciousness of the attack—multiple stab wounds—and the rumored ritualistic removal of the spleen.

The slender reporter from Albany is standing at the top of the tunnel, wind whipping her hair in her face, which she professionally ignores. It's so strange to see a place I drive by every day framed and flattened into two dimensions.

I turn the volume up.

"Police are not verifying whether satanic rituals played a part in this tragedy, although we have a report from a first responder that many of the details *are* bizarre. There is also no confirmation whether this death is related to a recent homicide which claimed the life of fifty-six-year-old Celia Jenks. Two murders in one year would be a record, given the town's elderly population and traditionally low crime rate."

A record and an advertising bonanza for the paper. No wonder they want the story in an hour.

"No arrests have been made in that case, and police say they cannot comment on an ongoing investigation. An autopsy report of today's victim is expected to be released by Grace Memorial Hospital later this week. We're waiting to hear if the autopsy report of Celia Jenks will be reexamined as well."

They show a picture of Celia sitting at a kitchen table, smoking a cigarette.

"Holy shit," I whisper. I jump to my feet and race to my wall of clues. There she is again—the woman from the morgue; the woman whose picture I snapped at a crosswalk. I reach out a tentative finger and trace the edge where the photo is torn just below her hand, as if she might just reach back. "Celia," I whisper. "Your name is Celia Jenks."

It's another piece in the puzzle, and a thrill runs through my body. Of course I just solved Mystery #2 on my list, but now I have another. How the hell is she connected to this new dead woman?

Did they say the autopsy report would be released by Grace Memorial?

I gasp like I'm now the lead in a cheesy detective show, grab my jacket and keys without explaining further to my female (albeit dead) partner, and don't even bother to look back as the door slams behind me.

———

"I can't talk to you," hisses Jessica, patently ignoring me as she strides down the hall holding a stack of thick manila folders. The now-familiar hospital fluorescent lights flicker above us, and a nurse passes by in blue scrubs.

"Can I carry those for you?" I ask in my most chivalrous voice. I don't wait for her to respond and pull the folders from her arms. Jessica is pencil thin and probably in her early thirties, but the glasses and mousy brown hair make her seem a decade older.

"Give those *back*—"

"C'mon, all I'm going to do is take a quick look at the files. Five minutes, I promise."

"I can't talk to you," says Jessica, trying to pry the files out of my arms. "We're not supposed to discuss the results with reporters."

"Five minutes. Four."

"No," she whispers. A doctor walks by holding a clipboard, and she gives him a tense smile. "I'll get fired."

"You won't get fired—I'm the morgue guy. You can say you were talking me down from filing a lawsuit. You'd be a hero."

Now she glares at me. "You know what a long drive it is to Albany for fried wontons?" She grabs the files back in a way that's surprisingly manly and heads for the elevator doors, which just opened.

"I'm sorry," I add, trying hard to keep up. "I was emotionally traumatized. *By almost being flayed alive.* And there isn't any decent Chinese food in New Goshen, unless you know someplace and you've been holding out. Hey, did you just get your hair cut? Looks really nice. And those glasses—what can I say but *wow.*"

"Will this man not *shut up*," Jessica mutters under her breath. She stops, looks around. Everyone is suitably busy. "If I let you borrow the files, will you promise to never talk to me again? *Ever?*"

I hold up my right hand. "Cross my heart and hope to die."

She snorts. "I should be so lucky," she says, shoving the bottom three files at my chest in what can only be described as a hostile manner. "Three minutes. Janitor's closet across the hall. Any longer and I'm calling security."

"You're a doll," I say, and her eyebrows rise in surprise. I must be still channeling my debonair dream alter ego—next thing you know I'll be saying she's the bee's knees.

Inside the cramped closet, I prop open the first file, marked "Alice Chesterfield," on a steel cabinet next to a red plastic box labeled "Hazardous." Probably contains leftover radioactive waste or infected needles. Lovely.

The photos from the morgue, in full color, are quite shocking. An old woman's nude body is splayed out on a metal table, and there are circles on the photo highlighting wounds, with arrows pointing to the smaller ones on her hands—"defensive" is written in black Sharpie above them. Her eyes and mouth are still open. Mrs. Alice Chesterfield was ninety-five, a widow, and apparently lived alone in an old motel on Harrison Street called The Hurry Back Inn that mostly rents on a weekly basis, due to the lack of tourists. Room 306.

I check my watch. Two minutes.

I grab my notebook and start jotting down details. Flipping quickly through the images, I note that one is a close-up of her abdomen where her spleen should have been, another shows a bite wound circled on her thigh, and the last is of a series of numbers, scribbled hastily on her arm with a black marker.

7   11   27   28   8   30

Impossible. Jessica raps on the door—one minute.

But there's something else—what is it about her, she looks familiar . . . And then it hits me—I've been looking at that face for months. It's the face of the old woman crossing the street in the other black-and-white photograph—one of the two tossed across the room and torn in half by Poe. How is it possible I have photos of the two victims? I don't get it.

There's no time to think—I can feel Jessica getting nervous on the other side of the door—so I hurriedly open the second file. This one's a little dusty. Celia Jenks—spleen gone, attributed to a pet cat that hadn't eaten in the week it took for someone to notice the smell. Just seeing the first photo makes me gag, and for a moment I'm back in the morgue, overwhelmed by the smell of shit, pizza, and formaldehyde, but I have to keep looking for something, a confirmation. And there it is—the fourth photo. A close-up of her right hand clenching a note with another set of numbers.

6   32   3   34   35   1

My heart slowly petrifies as I recognize the tight, furious handwriting, then the numbers—they're the first row from Daniel's magic square. And I would bet my life that the numbers written on Alice's back match the second row.

The floor beneath my feet seems to tilt, and I drop the files on the floor as my stomach reels. Schizophrenic knife-wielding brother *is* back. There were six rows in his magic square—does this mean four more people will die?

Suddenly Jessica opens the door; a slice of light pours into the dark closet. "Time's up," she says firmly. I can tell from her tone that she's not kidding about calling security. That might not be a bad idea, considering who's on the loose.

"Right," I mutter absently, not even looking her way as I race for the elevator doors.

"You've completely lost your mind, haven't you?" she calls after me.

What little I had left.

———

Time is important—I can feel it slipping by me, *through* me, the precise click of each and every second. The air is electric, like when the sun is shining and there's not a cloud in the sky, but the barometric pressure has dropped. Like a big storm is coming.

I gun my car through the red lights, getting a few honks and causing a couple of near accidents. I call 411, which gives me the wrong number for Crosslands—twice—so when it actually rings through and Lisa picks up, I'm almost rear-ended by the car behind me when I jam on the breaks.

"Is anyone *there*?" she asks in a bored tone. I fondly remember boredom.

"Hey, it's, uh, me. Got a minute?" An Oldsmobile lurches out of a parking space in front of me; I press the heel of my palm against the horn. The elderly driver flips me the bird.

"Sure, Mr. Stevenson, I always have a moment to talk to family. How can I help you?"

A part of me wants to tell her everything I've just found out, but then this probably isn't the kind of news one should blurt over the phone to someone at work. And she's fine as long as she's there; Crosslands keeps all the doors locked to keep the residents with dementia from wandering away.

"Your supervisor behind you?"

"Yes," says Lisa in a bright professional voice. "You're correct about that."

Okay. *Definitely* not the time to break the news. "Do me a favor. Don't take the bus. I'll come pick you up at four."

She must hear a note of my constrained panic. "Is there a particular reason—"

"Yes. No. I mean, I'll explain when I come get you. But wait for me inside, okay?"

There is a pause.

"Just—just *promise* me. Okay?"

She sighs, completely exasperated. God she's sexy when she sighs.

"*Okay*," she finally says. A giddy wave of relief rushes through me. "You better be on time though," she adds in a lower voice.

"Me? On time? I'm always on time."

Lisa starts to snort derisively but has to catch herself. "Oh, that's really funny, Mr. Stevenson."

"In fact, I'm on my way now. I'll be waiting outside."

"You're going to spend the next four hours in your car?" she whispers quickly. "What's *wrong*, Dimitri?"

"Oh nothing," I say as innocently as possible. "More rats in the wall. I can't be there while they fumigate."

"*Right*," says Lisa. "You're a bad liar, you know that."

"Oh, and keep an eye on Delia. No unexplained visitors."

Her voice suddenly goes all formal—her supervisor must be back within earshot. "May I ask why?"

Because after my dream I think there's probably some connection between Delia, my female ghost stalker, and the murders? Yeah, that wouldn't make me sound like her crazy brother at all. "I'm not sure. Let's call it a hunch."

"Do people still actually use that word?"

"What can I say, I'm hooked on *Columbo* reruns."

"That explains a lot," says Lisa dryly. "Is there *anything* else I can help you with, Mr. Stevenson?"

"What are the chances of getting some smokin' sex tonight?"

Click. Can't blame a guy for trying. And I really am on my way to Crosslands (considering my scoop on the autopsy photos, I think Mac will forgive me if I'm late) when an unmarked, very governmental beige sedan speeds by with two serious-looking men in front wearing sunglasses (in winter). They might as well have a bumper sticker that says "Kick Me, I'm FBI." The sedan screeches right on Harrison Street, which means they must be on their way to The Hurry Back Inn.

The light in front of me turns green. I should turn left, toward Crosslands.

But for some inexplicable reason I find myself sitting in the car letting the engine idle, strangely transfixed by the crosswalk light on the corner of Main and Ocean that's blinking a red palm, next to it the digital countdown 6, 5, 4, 3, 2, 1. In the last few seconds, a skinny, blond, teenage girl, looking cold and lonely, trots across the street, pulling the collar of her jacket up against the wind. A car honks its horn behind me.

Lisa will be more than okay for the next few hours; heck, she's in the safest place she could be, a veritable fortress. All I'm going to do is take a quick drive by, maybe add a little flavor to my article. At least this is what I tell myself as the light turns red.

And I turn right.

———

There is, as one might expect, a whole block full of squad cars outside the old motel. It's as if every policeman or policewoman in the county, tired of writing speeding tickets, wanted to take full advantage of this rare opportunity to see an actual crime scene. I immediately recognize the reporter with the whipping hair on the opposite side of the street; she stands next to her white news van, leaning against the hood and sipping a Styrofoam cup of steaming coffee.

I can't shake the feeling that there's something in the apartment I'm supposed to find. Unfortunately it's crammed with people carrying live ammunition.

"Now what?" I whisper.

I pull my Mustang over to the sidewalk and sit for a moment, taking in the scene. The parking lot has been completely cordoned off with police tape, and there are two officers standing in front of the entrance. Several others are just standing around blowing on their hands and chatting idly. An empty plastic bag, caught by the wind, takes sail and drifts down the street.

And then I see her—Poe. Or at least I think it's her; all I catch is a brief glimmer of her pale reflection in the news van's rearview mirror. Maybe ghost girl isn't the housebound sort of spirit. Either that or I *have* lost my mind. Quite the toss-up.

But if it *is* Poe, then she's obviously leading me to the reporter. On the one hand, I hate to let a possible hallucination take the lead, but on the other, I haven't a clue what to do next, so what the hell.

I jump out of my car, put my hands in my pockets, and briskly trot over to the reporter, who is shivering miserably.

"Hot enough for you?" I say cheerfully.

She regards me with an icy stare. "Let me guess, local paper."

I shrug. "I saw you on TV this morning. Weird, huh?"

"Yeah," she says coolly. "You *might* say."

I grin at her, undeterred. If there's one thing I'm an expert at, it's being shot down by the *ladies*. "You know anything you can't say officially?"

She gives me a hard look. "Of all the lazy-assed questions—"

"Hey, we're just the *local* paper. Basically a fifty-cent mat for house-training puppies and pushing coupons. I'm Dimitri, by the way. D. Peters is my byline, which you'd know if you read the obituaries, though no one under sixty-five does."

She steps back, and her eyes squint a bit. "I've seen you before. Morgue guy!"

I hold up my hands. "Guilty as charged."

"I'm Jennifer. Was that for real?" She leans closer. "I didn't see a lawsuit. Did you settle out of court?"

"I can't remember," I say, looking to the sky as if the answer lies there. "Maybe if I knew more about this homicide I might come up with something."

"An interview?"

Damn she's gotten eager and pushy all of a sudden. "*Maybe*," I say. "What you got?"

She looks around, as if Brian Williams might actually be within earshot. "Well, they *are* connected. The murders. Probably some teenagers who've been rolling E and listening to Marilyn Manson. Everyone's pretty much decided Celia was really the first victim, but there's very little physical evidence that's the same. Besides the removal of the spleens."

"And the numbers," I add. "And the bite marks."

"What?" I can see her calculating the potential value of an information trade. She must decide that the risk of a local newspaper printing the story the next morning—*after* she's reported it live on the evening news—is worth it, because she pulls me to the rear of the van. I notice she wears soft, expensive-looking leather gloves that, given her blue lips, are probably useless in actual cold. "Okay, talk."

The rear door of the van is open, and I see a pudgy, bald cameraman—a forty-year-old version of Charlie Brown—eating a sandwich in the back, eyes glued to a football game playing across four video screens. Around his neck is a professional black digital camera with an impressive lens. I catch a flash of movement in the glass, like a shadow. Suddenly the signal on the video is lost and it all goes to snow.

He swears under his breath and roughly knocks the screens a couple of times. "Fuckin' backwater Hicksville . . ." he mutters with a thick Boston accent.

"Have we lost our feed *again*?" asks Jennifer in a tight voice. "Mike, you know CNN is scouting."

Mike grudgingly drops his sandwich onto the control board, wiping the crumbs off his pants. "No need to get all hysterical again; just have to adjust the dish—"

But Jennifer is already a couple notches past hysterical. "Because I swear to *God* if I'm not on at exactly *five* tonight . . ."

Mike pulls the camera off from around his neck and hands it me. His cheeks are ruddy with cold. "Hold this for me, kid." The camera feels oddly heavy, and a chill spreads through my fingers and up my arms. With a surprising agility given his thick stomach, Mike climbs up an attached ladder to the roof of the van.

". . . I swear I will make your life a living *hell*," continues Jennifer.

"Already is," mutters Mike.

I feel something brush against my ankle and look down to see the plastic bag tumbling by—and then something else—*impossible*. Footprints in the snow, but not of shoes or boots. These are delicate barefoot prints that even Columbo would recognize as a perfect match for the strangely ethereal prints left in my bedroom.

Poe again.

The prints lead away from the van down the sidewalk. An obvious trail to follow.

For the first time it occurs to me that this might be a really, *really* bad idea. The kind of bad idea that causes teenagers in a spooky cabin in the woods to decide to split up to investigate a strange sound, or that assumes a land war in the Middle East will be short. What *am* I doing here? Who, or what, is Poe after all? For all I know, she's the reason Daniel went insane.

"I'm not Daniel," I whisper.

Wonderful. Talking to myself now.

But I know I don't have a choice. I *have* to find out whether this is all random or it's connected to my father, even if I lose my mind in the process. And I know what I'm going to do next. It's really not even a question, it's more a perverse exercise to ease the inadequately small amount of guilt I feel about doing something Lisa would rightly call idiotic.

The wind blows coldly as I sling the camera over my shoulder and follow Poe's footprints.

———

Jennifer and Mike are so engrossed adjusting the dish that neither notices as I slip away with my hands deep in my jacket pockets, making off with the weighty camera. The air's so cold that my breath forms a mist in front of me, but strangely I'm not cold at all—I feel distant from reality, like I'm having some kind of lucid dream. I follow the footprints, making my way up the sidewalk past a small group of worried onlookers—none under sixty. I glance at the alley behind the motel and see two local cops standing by the back door. I keep walking.

But when I get to the street corner, the prints stop abruptly, like whoever made them melted into thin air. A frigid gust of wind pushes across the deserted street, and I catch a slight movement to my right—a blue scrap of cloth that's stuck in a frozen pile of debris. I walk over to it, reach down, and pull it free.

A navy-blue baseball cap. White letters on the front: FBI.

Hot damn, *that* can't be random.

"Not bad, Poe," I whisper. "Not bad at all."

I put the hat on my head and then casually stroll back to the alley behind the old motel. The local cops take one look at the hat and the camera and say nothing as I brusquely push past them, opening the door with ease. The lock, I notice, has been crudely broken.

Inside, deep voices echo down the fire escape stairs.

"What's the score?"

"Fuck if I know."

A haze of cigarette smoke drifts past the one small window, so dirty it lets in only a few dim rays of winter sunlight. I climb the stairs to the second floor, then the third, where two more cops lean against the unpainted cement block wall. I nod at them, they nod in return, and then I open the heavy metal door.

The hallway is wallpapered with a spidery, shiny metallic print, like someone took a sledgehammer to a glass windshield. The carpet is a dirty, well-trod brown. A couple of interested elderly neighbors wearing bathrobes stand in their doorways, their silver hair wrapped in identical pink plastic curlers, excitedly shocked.

"She *never* locked her door."

"Never."

As if Mrs. Chesterfield somehow brought this on herself. It's a conversation that's familiar. At my parents' funeral there was much discussion about their decision to buy a convertible, as if the karma of owning a sports car did them in.

I actually breeze into the crime scene. The first room is packed with police officers, busy field technicians wearing latex gloves and men in dark suits with long black coats. And this room has to be the saddest I've ever seen in my life. It has a dusty, gray quality, as if the windows haven't been opened in decades, and it smells of wet dog. All the furniture is obviously cheap motel décor circa 1950. The thin, olive-green sofa sags in the middle, the chrome-accented linoleum table in the kitchen is rusting, and the amber glass lamps are adorned with beige, spidery shades, continuing the theme from the wallpaper in the hall. There were some attempts, primarily with knitted lace, to cover the worn spots on the chairs, and a crystal vase is filled with blue marbles and red plastic roses.

The carpeting is the same dark brown from the hallway. And dead center in the room is a darker stain. Blood.

One of the men in dark suits glances over; his blond hair is military short—obviously FBI. I raise my camera and take a picture of the bloodstained carpet. He's about to come over and say something when his cell phone rings, so I dart into the adjacent bedroom.

A pink polyester bedspread covers the single twin bed. Two unrolled stockings are strewn on the floor, looking like discarded snakeskins, but other than that the room is shabby but impeccably neat. It doesn't look like anyone *lived* here, certainly not for fifteen years, as Alice had done, week to week. She could have easily packed all of her personal belongings into a single suitcase and been gone in thirty minutes. But maybe that was the point.

A cop pokes his head in, so I take another picture, this time of the stockings on the floor. And then something catches my eye—a lone photo in a cheap brass frame leaning against another amber lamp. I can tell that it's old, black and white. I slowly walk over and pick it up.

Aspinwall, of course.

A party, probably in the forties, judging by the hairstyles. Everyone is wearing a costume and sitting around a long rectangular table covered with elegant white linen. In the center is Amelia Aspinwall. (She would never be anywhere but the center.) She wears a tight-fitting sequined gown, and her face is covered with a peacock Mardi Gras mask; its feathers fan out and partly obscure Captain Aspinwall, who's dressed as a pirate, with a real parrot on his left shoulder. Sitting next to Amelia is the needy platinum blond from my dream, dressed like Little Bo Peep, with round circles of rouge on her cheeks and a dainty, painted mouth. In her right hand is a white staff and in her left she cradles a lamb that looks like it would rather be anywhere else. Next are two women wearing black wigs and dressed as geisha, their identical faces blanched white and mirroring the same solemn expression. There's a man dressed as a Roman soldier, and another dressed as the Tin Man.

But it's the woman at the far left who catches my attention, partly because she seems more aloof, more regal than the others, but also because she seems strangely out of place. Her costume consists of a plain black mask and a pair of demon horns, as if she hadn't thought through her outfit or had been handed some props at the last minute. There's a visible edgy space between her and a man dressed as Zorro on her right. He leans toward her; she leans away. She's also the only one who isn't smiling.

I hear a deep voice in the kitchen say, "I thought he was with you."

Quickly, I slip open the back of the glass frame, pop out the photograph, turn it over. A shaky scrawl in pencil.

Halloween, 1940. Right before the fire. Me as Little Bo Beep. Mrs. Aspinwall & Captain A., center, Blaine as Zorro, Edgar, the Tin Man, Sidney pretending to be a Roman. Fitzgeralds as geisha, and K.G., the psychic.

I pull out my notebook, writing down all the names as quickly as possible, but just as I write the initials "K.G." I hear a shout.

"Hey you! Turn around, turn around! On your knees, on your knees!"

Two things happen next.

One, the lights flicker, then go out, which is interesting.

Two, I hear but don't see the click of a gun's safety being released.

CHAPTER FOURTEEN: DANIEL'S ESCAPE

Jail is not a good place to be. There are no snacks in jail and people, police people, feel perfectly free to drink coffee in front of me without offering me a single cup. And it smells like really, *really* good coffee; I have a feeling the good people protecting and serving know their Colombian from their French roast. Plus a jail cell smells like piss and lead paint. There is a single thin and rancid mattress in my cell, which is so disgusting I wouldn't even think about sitting on it unless I was wearing a hazmat suit, which I'm sadly not. So instead I sit on the concrete floor, pressing my head against the cool wall, trying not to imagine all the ways that Daniel might have killed Lisa while I was out playing crappy detective. The FBI weren't too impressed with my theory that Daniel is behind the murders; apparently, he doesn't match their profile for the spleen-eating serial killer, but judging from their hard stares and even harder line of questions—"Would you call yourself a loner?" "Have you ever impersonated an officer before?"—I might.

They did give me my one phone call—on a device called a "pay phone"—and even the *phone* smelled like piss; amazing considering it was made of plastic and stainless steel. But then who to call? It's not like I've bothered to memorize anyone's phone number when they're all stored in my cell phone, which the police unfortunately confiscated—as if I would be able to disassemble it and use the parts to pick the lock of New Goshen's city jail, *MacGyver* style. Lucky for me, Lisa answered the phone for Crosslands, a number that was readily available in the battered yellow pages hanging from the pay phone, and she accepted the collect call.

But I don't feel particularly lucky when I see her expression as the guard walks her down the hallway. Furious doesn't even begin to describe it.

"What's a nice girl like you doing in a joint like this?" I say doing my best Bogart impression, which is really not all that good, I admit.

She inhales *deeply* and glares. Even the guard looks a little leery, as if he's half expecting her to throw a punch—I bet he has more than a few stories. He keeps one eye on her as he opens the cell door, which whines in protest.

Lisa opens her mouth, as if she's about to say something—something which I, in all likelihood, don't want to hear—but then anything would be better than this frigid silence. She visibly struggles to find the words, then gives up and turns on her heel to leave.

Shit, I haven't told her about Daniel. "Lisa, wait . . ."

She ignores me completely, briskly walking back down the hall. I start after her, but the guard grabs my shirt.

"Gotta sign you out first."

"*Lisa!*"

The door slams shut behind her.

"Damn," says the guard. "It might be safer for you to stay here."

"You don't *understand*—" I say desperately.

"She likes you enough," says the guard, giving me a friendly thump on the shoulder. "They don't get mad if they don't like you."

There's an agonizing wait in line—then the printer is out of ink, then they realize they've given me the wrong form and must call upstairs to get the right one. I plead with a cop to send a car to check on Lisa, that her brother is dangerous, schizophrenic—at *least* let me make one phone call—but he just ignores me until I annoy him to the point where he tells me to shut up or I'll be arrested again for disorderly conduct. A teenager accompanied by his harried mother walks sullenly by. I saw him being booked earlier; there was a party, underage drinking.

"If your father was here," she says.

"Well he's not," he replies bitterly.

Something about the teenage angst resonates with me, or maybe it's just the fact that he still has a mother to care. And without Lisa, who really gives a shit these days about Dimitri Petrov, errant obituary writer and college dropout? No one. Why the *hell* didn't I pick up Lisa from work and keep her safe when I had the chance? What was I *thinking*?

Finally after what seems like an eternity, my name is called— scratch of pen on paper—and they hand over a manila envelope with my phone, watch, notebook, keys, and wallet. The ring never left my hand, since no one could pry it off my finger. My cell phone is, of course, dead.

"We're holding the camera as evidence . . ." they start to say, but already I'm through the glass doors, running down icy steps.

The jail is only two blocks from The Hurry Back Inn, where I left my car. The sky is dark as I sprint through the deserted streets, past empty storefronts, the cold air pumping through my lungs. It's like an urban version of my dream in the snowy wood; I can almost feel Daniel watching me. Laughing.

Race you.

Oh God oh God, I hope I'm not too late.

———

Every single blazing light inside the farmhouse is on, casting a warm radiant circle in the lonely field of desolate snow, and I catch a glimpse of Amelia through the curtains, happily drawing. Life—signs of life. I pull my Mustang into the frozen driveway, hydroplaning on a new layer of thin snow and knocking over a fence post before the car comes to a stop.

I take a breath and lean my throbbing head against the front wheel for a moment. I hadn't realized my heart could beat so fast without going into arrest. I sit up, run my hand through my hair so Elizabeth doesn't think she's got a complete lunatic on her front porch, and get out of the car.

What's immediately striking is the ethereal and nearly complete silence; I can hear my boots crunch the icy snow beneath my feet, a lonely sound that seems to echo across the field and into the frigid night sky. Not a single dog barks, even the chickens are eerily silent, and there is no wind to speak of—the trees stand like quiet sentinels. Like the calm before the storm.

Just as I put my foot on the porch step a distant loud crack breaks the silence, like a tree limb has fallen in the woods, something that happens when the ice gets thick and heavy. But we haven't had freezing rain for weeks.

Little Amelia is waiting for me just on the other side of the door. "Dimitri's here! He's here! He's here!" She pops open the door and immediately rushes for my legs, hugging them tightly, and almost causing me to tip over. Buddy grunts from the entry and gets to his feet, his stumpy tail wagging.

"How's your point of view coming?"

She gives a heavy sigh. "Nana says I'm still too literal. What does literal mean?"

Before I can answer, Elizabeth steps into the entry from the back kitchen, wiping her hands on a dish towel. Tonight she looks her age; there are dark, puffy circles under her eyes and her skin is sallow. "I'm actually cooking spaghetti tonight. It could be dangerous."

Amelia regards her seriously. "You remember when you cooked me french fries and they got all black, like coal? And the smoke alarm went off? And remember that time you were boiling an egg, and all the water burned away, and it *exploded*?"

"Thanks for sharing, love," says Elizabeth. "Good artists make bad chefs."

"Were you *really* in *jail?*" Amelia asks me with wide eyes.

"I was. There were handcuffs and everything."

"That's so *cool*," says Amelia. "Did you do something bad?"

"No. Just something incredibly stupid."

"I hope you took good notes," adds Elizabeth seriously. "It's not easy to get that kind of source material for art. You should write it all down while your memory is fresh."

Suddenly a wild, raucous noise erupts from the basement, causing the walls and floors to shake. Something in the kitchen crashes to the floor.

"She's going to get blisters and lose her hearing," says Elizabeth, her eyebrows furrowed. "She's been at it since she got home. We've had some—news."

She catches my eye and then looks pointedly at Daniel's photo on the wall.

Oh. They know.

Amelia covers her ears. "I don't like it when she drums like that. How come Aunt Lisa's *so* mad?"

Elizabeth ignores her question and instead gently takes her hand, leading her to the kitchen. "Go on down," says Elizabeth to me over her shoulder. "Maybe you can convince her to give it a rest."

I enter the living room and press my hand to the dark oak paneling; it vibrates under my palm, like she's trying to knock it all down. I get that. And when I open the basement door, an impossibly fierce wave of sound hits me, makes me take a step back. There's no rhythm; it's as if she's just beating at her drums randomly, creating chaos. I inhale—deeply. Then head down the stairs.

The room is a mess. Her bed isn't made, the blankets twisted like she's been wrestling with nightmares. Pillows, papers, and various items of clothing are strewn about the floor; a single beige Converse sneaker sits on top of a pile of thin, long-sleeved T-shirts. I make a note of the underwear, gray boy shorts with a red striped band (cute), and some work dresses that are jumbled in a heap, still on their hangers. The handwritten song lyrics I'd last seen on the cork-board have been torn into shreds, and on the white rug is a lone open suitcase stuffed with more clothes, piles of music sheets, and a few random photos.

Lisa sits behind the drums, pounding them into submission. Her white T-shirt is wet with sweat, which under any other circumstance would be kind of sexy. I quietly approach, and as she raises one arm to beat the cymbal, I grab her gently but firmly by the wrist, hold it steady. She turns to me. Her skin is pale, so pale, and it takes a good moment for her to register who I am. Too long. I pry the drumstick from her right hand one finger at a time, and she lets me but says nothing.

I don't bother trying to get the drumstick from her other hand; instead I reach under her arms, lifting her up, and I carry her to the bed. She lets me, but her chest flutters in a way that's troubling. She shivers, and I feel her forehead, which is cool and clammy. I find another blanket on the floor and gently cover her with it.

"Daniel's gone," she whispers. "They don't know where he is." Strands of wet hair have fallen out from her ponytail and they fever-ishly cling to her forehead. I smooth them back into place.

"Do you want to talk about it?" I slip under the blanket with her and wrap my arms around her waist. It's like we're back in the hospi-tal, but this time I'm the strong one.

She places one hand on my cheek. "I'm supposed to be *your* life-saver. Not the other way around."

"We can take turns," I say, rubbing the small of her back. It's somewhat shocking to see her like this, vulnerable and small. She groans and leans into me.

"I can't stay here. I just can't. Everything *reminds* me of him."

"You can come stay with me. I just have a ghost. It's almost like having a roomie who doesn't pay rent."

"Her? How do you know it's a her?"

"What, you jealous?"

Lisa laughs, but it's a little high, a little frantic. "So my choice is to either stay here and see if my schizophrenic brother comes back to kill me or go stay with my boyfriend in his haunted apartment."

I stroke her hair. "And who says life is boring?"

"My mom bought a handgun. She said, 'Just in case' . . ." The words trail off, and the empty look returns to her eyes.

I'm stunned. I can't imagine Elizabeth owning, let alone firing, a gun. "*What* does she say?"

Lisa twists a bit of sheet with her finger. "That he might . . . well, the murders."

Apparently Elizabeth and I are completely on the same page.

"Do you think she'd really shoot him?"

"If he tried to hurt me," Lisa says in a small voice. "Yes. She got a little paranoid . . . after. Bought a shotgun that we'd use for target practice. I think she felt guilty. But he's not . . . Daniel is sick, but he's not evil. If I thought for even a minute that he *could* be . . . Oh shit, Dimitri, I don't think I could take it. I couldn't."

It's the way her voice shakes that makes me realize I can't tell her about the numbers on the bodies, the handwriting that looks like Daniel's—at least not now. But it's a thick, weighty secret to carry alone.

"So what happened?" I ask, reaching for safer ground. "I thought you checked, and he was at the institution."

Lisa puts one hand on her forehead, stares at the ceiling. "Apparently he had a seizure about a month ago and they called an ambulance to take him to a clinic. The ambulance dropped him off, but there was a fire nearby, so after they checked him in, they left. Daniel used the opportunity to rifle through the receptionist's desk—he found transfer papers and forged a copy that stated he had been sent to the nearby hospital. He even managed to steal a lab coat and credentials. When a different ambulance came to pick up Daniel Bennet, he pretended he was a doctor and told them Daniel had been sent to the hospital, with complications. Then he handed them the transfer papers and walked back into the clinic. No one remembers seeing him after that."

"And no one at the institution checked on him?"

"That's what I asked. But they said they'd gotten a couple of calls from a physician at Mercy Hospital with a status update on Daniel's 'condition.' That it was going to be a long recovery."

"But it was Daniel making those calls."

"I told you he was smart." Again the small hint of pride in her voice.

"*Christ*," I say, wrapping my fingers in hers. If he's so smart, why is he leaving such a large, obviously bloody trail? The answer immediately comes to me, turns my heart to stone. Because the trail isn't obvious to anyone but me. *Race you.*

As if she can hear my thoughts, tears start to stream down Lisa's cheeks. Her voice is choked. "But he would *never* . . ."

She can't finish the sentence. I pull her closer. "I know," I say, even though I don't, but it's what she wants to hear, what she needs to hear. "I know."

———

Elizabeth is not happy when she finds out that not only will we be missing dinner, but that Lisa is packing to come stay with me, at least for the night. After seeing the look in her eyes when Lisa told her our plan, I am now a believer that, yes, Elizabeth could shoot someone dead.

"You," she says, pointing at Lisa. "Downstairs. We need to talk."

"You," she says, pointing at Amelia. "Go watch TV."

"Man," retorts Amelia. "Nobody tells me *anything.*"

"And *you*," says Elizabeth, pointing a dagger-like finger in my direction. "You just—go keep Amelia company."

"*Mom*," says Lisa, looking a bit more like her old self, a welcome edge of defiance in her voice, "I'm not a kid. I'm an adult—I can make my own decisions."

"Downstairs. *Now.*"

"Oh, for Christ's sake," says Lisa, but she complies, stomping down the basement steps.

"These kids are going to kill me," mutters Elizabeth, following after.

I head to the living room, where Amelia is sitting, glued to MTV. Before I can join her, I hear a creak from the upstairs hallway. Buddy looks up from the floor hopefully, his tail wagging.

"My crotch and ass are off limits," I tell him firmly.

Then another sound from upstairs, like a piece of furniture is being pushed across the floor. Or a body.

Great.

For a moment I think about calling my new police friends, since they're the ones paid by my measly tax dollars to protect and serve, but shit, by the time they arrive we could all be numbered and spleenless. Plus, if it *is* just my overactive imagination, then Elizabeth would have another reason in her arsenal of reasons why Lisa shouldn't leave with me.

So as quietly as I can, I pad over to the kitchen, grabbing a large and hopefully very scary-looking kitchen knife. I also turn off the pot of spaghetti, which, as Amelia accurately predicted, is burning. Passing by the basement door, I overhear bits of a loud argument in progress.

"You're *safer* here . . ."

"I just need to get out, can't you understand that . . ."

". . . and what's Dimitri going to do if Daniel shows up—hit him over the head with his novel?"

Ouch. But my novel probably is the best weapon of choice in my apartment—I could bore someone to death with it. Which reminds me, I still need to write the article for the newspaper, if I haven't been fired already.

Christ, it's going to be a long night.

I step over Buddy and reach out for the banister with my spare hand. A riff from a Justin Timberlake video floats out of the living

room, corrupting the next generation of youth with corporate-pro-
duced nonmusicians (my complete conversion to indie music, thanks
to Lisa, is apparently imminent). My stomach flutters as I go up the
stairs.

Climbing to the top of the stairs of Lisa's house, I experience a
kind of déjà vu in reverse, because not too long ago I was doing something equally stupid in the opposite direction, namely going *down*
the stairs to the Aspinwall basement. But the feeling of dread is eerily
similar. When I reach the second floor I find that all the lights are on,
and all the doors are open. Nothing looks strange in Amelia's room,
and the storage room seems untouched, as does Elizabeth's room.

Which leaves Daniel's.

His door is shut.

I press my ear tentatively against the door—doesn't sound like
someone's spleen is being eaten, but then what the hell would that
sound like anyway? I grip the knife tightly in my hand and cautiously
turn the knob until I hear the click of the lock. The door opens a
crack—no one rushes out and stabs me, a good sign. I give it an extra
few minutes for good measure, then push the door open all the way.

The black light is on, and at first glance everything seems normal, exactly the way it was the last time I'd seen it. But the numbers
are harder to read, probably because the warm light from the hallway is messing with the glowing effect of the highlighter scribbles.
I approach them, squint. I thought they would probably match the
numbers written on Celia's body, and I'm not wrong. The first row is
identical.

$$6 \quad 32 \quad 3 \quad 34 \quad 35 \quad 1$$

A cold draft of air wraps itself around my feet, and I see that one
of Daniel's windows is wide open. I cross the room to close it, registering the creak under my footstep—exactly what I heard downstairs,

only louder. My heart stops and I pause for a moment, listening. There's the drone of the television downstairs, the tap, tap, tap of a tree branch knocking against the house, the sound of my own labored breathing. Cautiously I step toward the window, holding my knife even tighter, and as I reach for the windowpane I notice the tree outside, so close I could reach out and touch it. It's a sturdy tree, the one by Daniel's window. I think even I could climb it.

I poke my head out the window and look down. Several smaller branches are broken. And in the circle of light I can see bootprints in the snow, leading from the tree to the shadowy woods beyond.

Fuck.

I slam the window shut, lock it, my hands shaking, and barely register dropping the knife. But I hear it clatter against the floor, which makes me look down, and I notice something else. The mattress has been moved and is just slightly askew. Beneath it, barely, I can see that part of the floorboards, a neat rectangle, has been lifted and moved aside.

Now the fluttery feeling turns into a jittery scream—*Replace the floorboards, ignore it.* I should walk back downstairs and sit next to Amelia, wait for Elizabeth and Lisa to return to the kitchen and find the spaghetti ruined.

But I don't do that, the sensible thing.

Instead I look into the space under the floorboards, and find a well-worn crumpled black-and-white photograph—a man with scraggly hair and very unattractive beard sits in the middle of a gaggle of plump Victorian women. The way he stares manically at the camera, *through* the camera, almost makes me drop it, but then I *recognize* him—it's my good friend Rasputin, subject of my ailing novel. It's not a photo I've seen before though—he looks fiercer, or maybe a few steps further along in his madness. And on his right hand a glint of silver, some kind of ring with a symbol—*impossible.*

I look down at the ring on my right hand and see the same insignia.

"How?" I whisper.

There's something else hidden away in the floorboard, wrapped in decaying black velvet. I reach in, releasing a small plume of dust, and pick it up, immediately recognizing the weight and feel of a manuscript. Gingerly I unfold the velvet and find a series of loose pages, the edges tinged by fire. They look like they were written by the same author of *my* book—there are pages in Greek and Russian with similar medieval illustrations, although these are darkly violent and graphic. I see a man being flayed alive, three young boys burning on a pyre, a black crow sitting on top of a corpse with a dangling eyeball clutched in its beak. There is a palpable sense of evil hovering lightly under my fingertips, and a part of me thinks that the best thing to do would be to burn it all immediately.

And then I see a man with a knife slitting a woman's throat in a snowy wood, the blood spreading out like a dark, accusatory stain. I hold the page in front of me, hand slightly trembling, hoping I won't find it, but I do. The warm light of the hallway renders the page slightly transparent, and through the stain is a watermark—the same insignia on my ring.

I suppress a sudden wave of nausea.

But why would Daniel leave these here for me to find? It feels like a taunt; he knows something I don't.

Of course the one person I could talk to about it I can't. I can't let Lisa know that Daniel was here, that I think he is somehow involved in—if not directly responsible for—the murders. I need her too much to push her over that edge, an edge I know very well, every narrow, black, razor-sharp inch. I was pressed against it for months after my parents died.

So I take the pages, rewrapping them carefully in the velvet before slipping them with the photo under my jacket so Lisa can't see. It's a theft and a betrayal, I know, on many levels. I quietly replace the boards and move the mattress back to its original position. Now there's only one more thing I need.

I find the gun in the top drawer of Elizabeth's dresser. A Glock. It's the deadliest thing I've ever touched in my life—I hadn't expected it to be so *cold*, like a corpse. At my father's wake I touched his hand—his dead body was shockingly cold and hard, like a stone in winter. But this is colder.

And as I arrange my face into an innocent expression, heading back down the stairs to the relative warmth of the living room, a dark foreboding prickles at the base of my spine, like an omen.

CHAPTER FIFTEEN: THE MAD MONK

By the time we get to the apartment, my nerves are a jangled mess—I think I see Daniel in the shadow of every apartment stoop, every alley. Is that him just behind the dumpster outside Sacred Heart Collectibles? Or looming in the backseat of a passing car? It's like being surrounded by an invisible army—all eyes on me—like snipers are watching my car roll by through their scopes on rooftops. The gun isn't helping much either. I keep thinking it'll go off somehow, that when I turn the wheel I'll inadvertently shoot my foot off.

Lisa, on the other hand, nodded off almost as soon as the heater came on, and already she looks much better; her face is soft and relaxed. In terms of consolation prizes, I'll take it. She doesn't wake up until I open the passenger-side door, letting in a cold blast of frigid air.

I reach out a hand and force a passable smile. "I'd carry you, but that might seem patriarchal."

Lisa gives a small but lovely sigh. "Minus one for feminism. You'd probably just drop me anyway."

I mock gasp. "I would *not*," I protest, pulling out her bag from the backseat. "Okay, well, maybe on the stairs. But you have excellent health insurance." I quickly scan the street—no schizophrenic brother in sight.

Lisa leans her head back, taking in the stars. "Oh *God*, it feels good to get away from the house. It's like it's haunted."

"Uh, Lisa?" I say hesitantly, pausing on the steps.

"Yeah?"

"You remember that whole part where I told you my apartment *is* haunted, right?"

Lisa smiles at me and chivalrously opens the entry door. "But that's your ghost, not mine."

"*Right*," I say, shuffling in after, following her up the stairs. "We'll see how you feel once it starts snowing in my bedroom."

My apartment door is safely locked, and it only takes about five minutes of fumbling with the key to open. I turn on the light and feel a wave of relief—everything is exactly the way I left it. In other words, a chaotic mess. But somehow I've got to slip the photo and pages from Daniel's room somewhere Lisa won't see, and I'm not sure how my superstalker ghost, Poe, will react to having an overnight guest. The blinking light on my answering machine tells me that Mac hasn't forgotten about the article either.

"God I'm *starving*," says Lisa, collapsing into her egg chair. She gives it a good spin.

"Right, food," I say. "Let's see what I've got."

Which is when I see that something in fact *has* changed in my apartment since I left—a few poetry magnets have been pulled from the others, forming the message:

mad monk ring father

"Well that makes completely no sense," I mutter. "Unless the mad monk has a cell phone." My ghost needs a reality refresher.

"You lost over there?" Lisa calls. "I've got a wicked recipe for ramen noodles and tuna, if you want some help."

"Nope, got it all under control," I quickly reply, reshuffling the magnets. Lisa might think a ghost is no big deal, but it's not a theory I want to test at the moment.

I open the fridge, take a quick inventory, and find excellent ingredients for botulism. There's a limp bunch of celery, two slices of moldy American cheese, and a sad tomato that's shriveled down to the size of a prune. I take the opportunity though to slip the photo and pages into the empty vegetable bin. One problem solved.

But that doesn't address the food issue—I know the cabinets are empty because I tossed out all the stale cereal, and I haven't yet gotten to the grocery store. Then I realize the sole clean towel I have is crumpled in the bathroom corner. I'm *so* not prepared for girl company.

I frantically open the freezer door and discover a miracle—a single, perfectly sealed frozen lasagna that I must have bought . . . months ago?

"You didn't eat that?" Lisa is leaning against the doorway, a hint of a smile on her face. She's taken off her jacket, and her sweater is invitingly askew. "Your neighbor Doug brought that over before you got back from the hospital."

"Yeah, well, my freezer wouldn't usually be a good place to look for actual food."

"What'll we do while it cooks?" Lisa yawns, dusky circles budding beneath her eyes.

I have a very clear idea about what *I'd* like to do, but I'd be sinking pretty low to take advantage of the situation. Plus I need some privacy to look at Daniel's pages more closely.

"Why don't you get some rest and I'll wake you up when it's ready?"

"*You're* no fun," says Lisa, lightly pulling at my T-shirt collar. "You sure you don't want to come with?"

I swallow. Hard. "If I don't get this article done—"

Lisa raises her hands. "Life of the artist; I get it." She yawns again, covering her mouth with the back of her hand. "I am pretty wiped out too."

I smile weakly.

She taps me on the chest. "Just don't burn it."

"Thanks for the vote of confidence!" I call as she walks away. She shuts the door of the bathroom behind her, and I hear the faintest gurgle of running water. Lisa curled up in my bed—it's a delicious thought.

Which is disrupted by the swish, swish, swish of the poetry magnets on the fridge.

Now I know the whole communication-via-poetry-magnet thing was my idea, but it's disturbingly creepy to see them actually in motion, being arranged by some invisible ghostly hand. Creepy and annoying. Got enough on my plate without dealing with the undead.

"*Give* me a minute, will you?" I mutter, and the magnets instantly stop. Praise Jesus. I make sure the deadbolt is locked (not really in the mood to entertain Daniel), wrangle the lasagna out of its packaging, relight the pilot (I generally stick with food that can be nuked), and crack open the window just enough to let some of the gassy fumes escape. I notice the bathroom door is open and decide to see if Lisa needs anything, only to find her fast asleep on my disheveled mattress.

For a moment I just look at her. Amazing. She fills the apartment—it feels complete, whole. I lean over and lightly brush her lips with a kiss.

"I love you," I whisper. The words roll out before I can even think about them; thankfully she's unconscious. But I realize they're strangely true.

God, I want to crawl into bed next to her. A wave of exhaustion suddenly hits, and it's so peaceful here in the room, so quiet. But I have articles to write. Pages to decipher. And ghosts to wrangle.

————

I stand in the kitchen trying to look as intimidating and authoritative as possible while also trying, and failing, not to feel like an idiot. After all, I'm talking to an apparently empty room.

"Ground rules. No magnets while Lisa's awake. In fact, no spooky stuff at all."

I watch as the words on the refrigerator are rearranged.

no rules

Funny. Ghost girl is giving me lip? I don't *think* so.

"Look," I say seriously, "I will quit this whole thing and move to Florida. I hate snow. Always have. A schizophrenic, knife-wielding brother isn't really helping the situation. But I get the feeling that *you* want me to be *here* figuring out this whole Aspinwall magical mystery tour. Am I right?"

This time the magnets arrange themselves in what can only be described as a sullen manner.

your world rigid

"Cry me a river," I say. "Is that a yes, you're going to cooperate, or a no, have fun in Florida?"

A magnet drops to the floor.

yes

Good. Second problem solved. Next, with serious misgivings, I hit PLAY on my message machine.

"IT'S TEN AND I STILL DON'T HAVE AN ARTICLE YOU LAME-ASS MOTHERFUCKER—"

I hit STOP. *Okay.* The good thing about Mac is that it's never unclear where one stands with him, even if that standing changes by the hour. I pull out my laptop and do the thing that I'm sure makes every writer sick to their stomach, something scarier than staying overnight at a haunted mansion, waking up in a morgue, or facing a schizophrenic knife-wielding brother.

I open a blank Word doc.

BRUTAL NEW GOSHEN SLAYING CAUSES PANIC IN THE STREETS

That *could* be considered true. I saw two cars on the street driving home—two more than usual. Mac will love the headline at any rate.

Police aren't saying whether a serial killer is on the loose *(This is good—create a rumor; keep the flow, keep the flow).* Friday morning truck driver Vincent Prevey discovered the body of 95-year-old Alice Chesterfield in the street *(Okay, officially under a railroad trestle, but there's nothing threatening about the word "trestle"; it sounds benign, like a Christmas tree decoration)*, the victim of a brutal assault. Preliminary reports show she bled to death, having suffered multiple stab wounds *(Jessica is so going to kill me).* But is this a random act of violence, or, more troubling, the work of a mad serial killer on the loose? *(Crap, Lisa's going to kill me. Strike mad.)*

The FBI is reportedly theorizing that the initial assault took place at Mrs. Chesterfield's apartment at The Hurry Back Inn, and at some point she was taken to a second location, although it's unclear where she died. *(Now the FBI is going to kill me. Or put me in jail. Same thing.)*

Another resident of Goshen, 50-year-old crossing guard Celia Jenks, was also brutally murdered one month ago. Until today, the primary suspect was her boyfriend, local baker Fred Danvers, who, ~~although he makes a mean apple Danish,~~ has a criminal record, including a domestic violence charge from 1998.

But what's the connection? Could it be the ill-fated Aspinwall mansion? Mrs. Chesterfield was one of the few still alive who were there the night of the tragic fire in 1940. In 1970, Celia Jenks and her husband, Will "Wolf" Jenks, purchased Aspinwall, where tragedy struck again when Wolf was killed by a wild animal. (*Kind of ironic when you think about it.*)

It only takes another twenty minutes to finish the article, and I decide that it's so bad I will have to retire the pseudonym D. Peters when I finish my *real* book, but for now that's the best I can do, and I e-mail it to Mac.

Now, back to the spooky stuff. I pull the loose pages I found in Daniel's room from the vegetable bin, along with the photo of Rasputin. If possible, it's even more bizarrely compelling under my bright fluorescent light—a Manson-esque portrait of insanity.

Which makes me think of Poe's magnet message—*mad monk.* "Why does that sound so familiar?" I whisper.

For no reason whatsoever my television flickers on—no signal, just snow and deafeningly loud static.

"What the fuck." *Christ*, I don't want to wake Lisa up. I race to unplug the damn thing but then I see them—of the array of books that I'd stacked to form my no-budget television stand, a few titles stand out. *The Quiet Revolution: Rasputin and the Tsaritsa, Rasputin and Gnosticism in Early Twentieth-Century Russia, Rasputin: Mad Monk or Mystic Prophet?*

I slap a hand against my forehead. Biggest idiot *ever.*

Granted I've been busy of late, what with drowning, nearly being flayed alive, almost shot by the FBI and whatnot, but I can't believe that I've somehow missed the biggest connecting thread of them all. All those hours of mind-numbing research years ago for my ill-fated historical Rasputin novel, my eBay finds that I'd hoped would give it some semblance of authoritative weight, sitting here staring me in the face for *weeks.* The gardener at Aspinwall—Russian. The psychic at that ill-fated Halloween—Russian. The medieval pages are Russian; shit, even my ring, or at least the same symbol, worn by the most infamous Russian of all time—Rasputin. Whom I, for some strange reason, decided to write about, although not so strange when you consider that my father was . . .

Russian.

I jerk the television off the books and quickly pull out *Rasputin: Mad Monk or Mystic Prophet?* Thank God I had the good sense to highlight the good bits to crib from later.

I vaguely remember it was his fellow Russians who dubbed Rasputin "The Mad Monk." Given his rather liberal views in Victorian society—he thought that in order to truly repent, one had to sin and sin often (alcohol and sexual licentiousness being key)—it's no wonder that some members of the Russian royal family were more than a little perturbed about his free access to the daughters in the tsaritsa's nursery. So he racked up a serious list of enemies, including Iliodor, a former friend and rival monk.

I quickly skip through the first few boring chapters (including a long-winded introduction by a professor that's so dull it could cure insomnia) until I get to the pages that made me think Rasputin could successfully be characterized as a zombie.

Because *lots* of people tried to unsuccessfully knock Rasputin off. First up, a seventeen-year-old former prostitute and student of Iliodor, who waited for Rasputin while he was walking along a gravel path, nose innocently buried in a book, and plunged a knife into his abdomen. As his entrails fell out of his stomach, she screamed, "I have killed the Antichrist!" Just a *bit* prematurely, because Rasputin sprinted away, cradling his guts in his arms, and she chased him down the street until he managed to grab something and club her in the face with it.

And *I* get woozy from a paper cut.

The assembling crowd was all for beating said prostitute to death, but instead she was picked up by a constable, put on trial, and sentenced to an insane asylum, where she stayed for a few years, until she was busted out by a different crowd during the February Revolution.

Somehow Rasputin survived—if he wasn't a zombie, then damn, that must have been a good surgeon for 1914—and he went on his merry way, which pissed off the Russian nobles. Considering this was before the February Revolution and the nobles were still in *power*, probably not a bright idea. Finally they decided to band together and assassinate him properly. Led by Prince Felix, they invited him down to a cellar and served him cakes and red wine that had been laced with enough poison to easily kill five men.

But then Felix thought, you know, it takes time to conceal a body—we should really move this along a bit faster. So he pulled out a revolver and shot Rasputin in the back. Which would just about do it, one would think. All bases covered.

Rasputin fell to the floor, and they must have all thought, *Great, mission accomplished.* They headed back to the palace to take a break, murder being harder work than they were probably used to. But forgetful Felix left his coat in the room, so he went back to get it, because *damn*, it's cold in Russia. And he walked into the room expecting to find Rasputin dead in a pool of his own blood—hopefully nowhere near his coat, because as everyone knows, bloodstains are impossible to get out.

But instead he found Rasputin *standing*.

Rasputin then grabbed Felix by the lapels, screaming something like "You bad boy" and tried to *strangle* Felix. The posse heard the ruckus, and they shot Rasputin three more times, and he fell again. They thought, *Okay, mission really accomplished*, but when they approached the body they discovered he was struggling to get up.

Rasputin. The first Freddy Krueger of the twentieth century.

Well, what else is a crew of Russian nobles going to do but try to beat him to death? They clubbed away at him with anything at hand, because this was now well past the realm of vampire horror stuff. They went so far as to castrate Rasputin—ouch—then they rolled up his body in a carpet and threw him in the Neva River for good measure.

When Rasputin's body was eventually discovered, the coroner found water in his lungs, as if the poison, gunshot wounds, beating, and castration hadn't killed him—as if he'd *drowned*.

The tsaritsa was sad, and she gave him a proper burial, to the consternation of all the nobles who worked so hard to kill him. And apparently his popularity wasn't all that high with the common folks either, because after the February Revolution, they dug up his remains so they could burn them. For good measure.

And as the flames licked at Rasputin's bloated, rotting, castrated corpse, the most bizarre unimaginable thing happened.

He sat up.

Okay. I have to admit that this definitely has the whiff of urban legend, a la Mikey's stomach exploding because he drank Coke while eating Pop Rocks. While I'm wondering if there's any possible scientific explanation why a corpse would sit up while it's being incinerated—maybe I should have paid more attention in Biology 101—something else catches my attention.

A small newspaper cartoon shows the tsaritsa on her knees praying to Rasputin, who has horns on his head. He cradles his entrails while staring down a wild-looking woman who holds a knife. But it's the description below that chills me, one name in particular. Khioniya Gueseva. I almost say it aloud, but I get a superstitious shiver that this might be a bad thing.

The psychic at Aspinwall was Russian, and her name—how had Amelia pronounced it in my dream? I quickly reach for my notebook, a flutter of excitement in my throat, and find my hastily jotted notes from the back of the photo in Alice's apartment. "Fitzgeralds as geisha, and K.G. the psychic."

K.G. Khioniya Gueseva? Could she also be the prostitute who tried to kill Rasputin? She did escape from the asylum, which would make her about forty at the time of the Aspinwall fire. Stranger things have happened. But maybe in Russia Khioniya and Gueseva are common names, the equivalents of Mary and Smith.

I'm missing something—I know it. I flip through the pages looking for another reference to Khioniya or K.G., skimming through biographical information that isn't nearly as exciting as resurrected corpses and intricate murder plots. Rasputin was born in Pokrovskoye in 1869, son of a peasant blah, blah, blah—but then another name stands out.

Mine.

Rasputin had a sister and an older brother, Dmitri (the proper Russian spelling), who tragically fell in a nearby river. Rasputin jumped in to save them and also came close to drowning, before all three were pulled from the water by a passerby. While Rasputin survived, his sister didn't make it. Dmitri caught pneumonia and died shortly afterward. And what does Rasputin name his own son? *Dmitri.*

I feel like I'm trying to pull out the vague memory of a dream. I'm surrounded by bits of flotsam and jetsam, but *Christ*, what does it all *mean*?

But there's no time to think about it further, because suddenly from the bedroom Lisa is screaming.

CHAPTER SIXTEEN: BROKEN

Fuck, fuck, fuck. I race to the bedroom, tripping over the light cord and knocking the lamp over in the process, breaking the bulb—I don't even notice stepping on the glass, because all I can think is I'm going to kill him, so help me God if he's hurt her, if he's even *touched* her . . .

But I find Lisa sitting upright in bed, trembling hands covering her ears, eyes shut, and no blood or gaping wound that I can see. I rush to her side and take her in my arms.

"Are you okay? Was he here? Did he hurt you?"

She seems to finally register me and she stops screaming, but her body still shakes with fear. Her mouth opens but can't speak.

Which makes me think he *was* here. And maybe still *is* here.

I run to the closet, see if Daniel's inside, but he's not, which leaves the shower—is the curtain closed? But no, I find it's open, and the window in the bedroom is closed shut and locked from the inside. Guess that's the chief benefit of living in a small, crappy apartment—not many places for knife-wielding schizophrenic brothers to hide.

I take a moment—my heart is still fluttering like a wild bird in my chest, and I start to feel the pain in my feet—but the adrenaline is pumping, and I manage to walk back to the mattress, sit down, and hold Lisa close. She's still shivering.

"You're not dead?" she asks in a choked voice.

"Not the last time I checked." I put her hand to my neck. "Do I still have a pulse?"

She smiles hesitantly. "Then it *was* just a dream . . ."

"Hopefully. What was the dream about?"

"I don't know. I was having a nightmare, then I thought I opened my eyes, and I saw . . ."

"You saw what?"

"A face in the window." She holds out her arm, pointing. "There."

I look at the window. The stark, leafless branches of the maple tree sway slightly in the wind, and a scattering of new snow drifts lazily in the haze of a streetlight.

Lisa whispers, "You don't think . . ."

"Course not," I say, giving her arm a squeeze. "But I'll go look just to make sure."

Slowly I stand, ignoring the pain in my feet, and step toward the window. I press my hand against the cold pane of glass and quickly scan the street below.

And my heart clenches.

There's a cluster of bootprints at the base of the tree, identical to the ones outside Lisa's house. A lone, cracked branch dangles from the trunk, like a broken arm, like something or *someone* was too heavy for it.

"Do you see anything?"

"No," I lie. I turn to her, try for a reassuring smile.

I can see her question me for a moment, the slight furrow in her brow, but then she presses the heel of her palm against her forehead. "Guess it was just part of my nightmare."

I make my way back to the bed, settling in next to her. "Can't imagine why you'd be having a nightmare. We lead such uneventful lives."

"It was so *real*." She hugs her knees, looking distant, like she's underwater.

"You saw Daniel?" I ask casually.

"Yes," says Lisa. "Or I thought I did." She runs a hand through her hair. "I don't know. It was so . . . quick. But in my dream, I saw Daniel. Or it was him, but it wasn't . . ."

I gently stroke her cheek.

"It's hard to explain." She looks at me and steadies herself. "I've never told anyone this before, because it sounds so . . . crazy."

"Crazy as in my crappy apartment is haunted? Or crazy as in I was almost autopsied alive?"

"It's up there," says Lisa.

"I'm intrigued."

Lisa takes a deep breath. "When Daniel . . . attacked me, his eyes were . . . different."

"In what way?"

"Daniel's eyes are green, like mine. But when he attacked me . . . they were black. Freaky weird black—no iris. I thought maybe it was a hallucination, part of the trauma. But lately, with all that's happened . . . I don't know, I can't stop thinking about it."

A cold realization strikes me. "Like Maddy's eyes."

"Maddy's?"

"The psychic at Aspinwall."

"It was so dark, I didn't see . . ." says Lisa. She absently rubs at the scar at the base of her neck, like it's some kind of charm or talisman.

"Lisa," I say quietly, "do you think it's possible someone can really be possessed?"

Before she can answer, the light overhead flickers on. My eyes squint, trying to adjust—either ghost girl isn't following orders, or my Victorian apartment has dangerous wiring. A hard call.

"Oh Christ, your feet!" says Lisa.

I look down, and the blood is much worse than I would have thought possible from stepping on broken glass. Maybe I should invest more in plastic.

"You're *so* going to the emergency room," she says briskly with just a hint of relief, as if she's glad my feet are bleeding, so we can safely change the subject.

"Hell, no. It's not that bad, really. I have Band-Aids, and you know a thing or two about nursing, right?"

"I'm a *receptionist*," she says. "And you probably need stitches."

"Not going to the hospital. Not gonna happen."

She glares at me, but I hold my ground. A standoff.

"Fine," she finally says, "but if it gets infected, you're *going* to the hospital."

I open my mouth to protest.

"Or you can pull the glass out of your feet yourself and I'll just go back to sleep."

Heartless wench. "Fine," I grumble.

"Can you walk?"

"Now that I see how profusely my feet are bleeding, I think not."

"Well, you'll need to get yourself to the edge of the bathtub so I can clean the cuts. Can you crawl?"

"Only if it turns you on."

She unwraps my arm from her shoulders and gives me a look. "You're completely *impossible*, you know that?"

"I've been told." But then I'm out of jokes, and as I lean over to the floor to get down on all fours, I knock my head against the wall.

"Karma," says Lisa smugly as she slips into the bathroom.

———

I manage to crawl the ten feet to the bathroom and haul myself up to the edge of the bathtub, gingerly placing my feet inside. Just looking at the blood makes me lightheaded. Lisa, however, is all business; she's got my Kmart special first-aid kit open and is sorting through its contents, pulling out alcohol wipes, gauze bandages, white medical tape, and long tweezers. She gently lifts my left foot, peers at it closely, and then picks up a brown bottle of hydrogen peroxide.

"This is going to sting a bit," she says, pouring some over the sole of my foot.

Understatement of the century—it's like someone has dipped my foot in acid. The peroxide fizzes and drips into the tub basin, a

nauseatingly cloudy pink. "*This . . . is . . . not . . . a . . . bit,*" I manage
to say through clenched teeth.

"Oh, so you want to go to the emergency room now? Or would
you rather let your feet get infected, contract sepsis, and *then* go to
the emergency room?"

Damn the woman and her valid points. Just as I start to feel
woozy from the blood and searing pain, she starts to gently dab at my
foot with a ball of gauze. "Now I can see," she says, picking up the
tweezers. She pulls out a large piece of thin glass, about the size of a
quarter, and drops it into the small metal trash can. *Clink.*

"So," I say, staring at a tile in the tub, which has come loose from
the caulking, "you had a nightmare that I died? You seemed pretty
upset about that."

Lisa ignores me, and with more force than I would think necessary, pulls out the next piece.

"Are you trying to help me or kill me?"

"Impossible," she mutters in the direction of my toes.

"I'm just saying," I continue, "you must have some feelings for
me, right? To get that upset about me dying."

Holy mother of God! I think she just pulled out a tendon.

She expertly places a square of gauze under the heel of my foot,
tapes the sides neatly. "I like you. *Sometimes.*"

"It's the pad, isn't it? A veritable booty lair."

She lets my foot drop. Ouch.

"Until you say stupid shit like that," she replies, grabbing my
right foot.

I'm seriously reconsidering the hospital visit, because she's treating my flesh like it's a game of Operation.

"So what exactly happened in your dream?"

For a moment she says nothing, peering intently at a smaller
sliver of glass. Then she picks up a sharper pair of tweezers. "Why
can't we talk about normal stuff? Like regular people."

"Since when have you wanted to be like regular people?"

She sighs with a note that hits somewhere between exasperation and exhaustion.

"Okay, fine, I'll start," I say. "How about those Mets?"

"Oh, for fuck's sake, Dimitri, I dreamed he killed me," she says hollowly.

Well now I feel like a moron. "*Christ*, Lisa. I'm sorry."

Somewhat more gently, she plucks out another shard.

"We were in these woods, and it was snowing. He had a knife to my throat and his eyes were black, completely black, just like last time. You were there, but you didn't do anything. Like you were frozen. Like it was all—frozen. It was all so dark . . . so *cold*. But when he slit my throat I could feel how warm my blood was, and all I could think was how strange it was to notice that. Then suddenly I was above myself, watching my body die. Daniel was walking toward you, taking his time. And he had this terrible smile . . . I was screaming at you to run, but you didn't do anything. You didn't move."

Her hand trembles slightly as she pulls out the last sliver. "I couldn't do anything to stop it. I was invisible. Like a ghost."

"Great," I say, trying to tease out another smile. "Just what I need: another ghost in my life."

"Oh *Christ*, Dimitri, it was horrible. Can't you take anything seriously for once?" Her voice is edgy and hoarse.

"Look, if I take any of this seriously, I *will* go crazy. Because it hasn't exactly been the best year, if you know what I mean." My throat constricts at this last word, so I pick at some of the loose caulk and crumble it between my fingers to avoid looking her in the eye.

Lisa is pointedly quiet. She pulls out some Band-Aids, applying them to the smaller cuts, and then finally gives me a half smile. "We're quite the pair, aren't we?"

I reach out, lift a strand of her hair, and twist it between my fingers. She turns on the tap for the bath for a minute to rinse it out, and I watch my blood swirl in lazy circles before it turns the water a cloudy pink, then drifts away down the drain.

If ever there were a moment to tell her about the pages I borrowed (or stole, depending on one's perspective) from Daniel's room, the bootprints at the base of the trees, and my ring, which somehow Rasputin used to wear, this would be it. But she doesn't seem to be exactly in the mood for more talk of the supernatural. Which gives me the oddest feeling—that we can be so far away and so close.

"Do you want to talk—"

"No," says Lisa brusquely. She roughly grabs a towel and dries my feet. "It all feels like last time. Exactly like last time." Then she throws the towel at the wall.

I reach out, firmly grab her hand in mine, and pull her toward me until our foreheads touch.

She swallows. "If I say run—"

I kiss her lightly on the lips, stopping her. "You won't have to."

"Promise?"

"Promise. But you will have to help me stand up, because I'm not all that good around blood. Particularly my own."

Lisa reaches around my waist and helps me up. The pain in my feet still throbs, but it isn't as intense.

"I don't have the energy to try to clean up that glass," she says, sounding like she's far away. I'm somewhere past exhausted, and I nod my head loosely in agreement. "Let's see if we can fit on the couch."

She helps me hobble over, and when I collapse onto the couch, its stubby legs shudder but hold.

"Scooch over," she commands. And I do. Then she curls in next to me, so lovely, so warm—I feel safe, protected. She says something else, but by then she's too far away, and I'm too far gone into sleep.

CHAPTER SEVENTEEN: AFTER I'VE GONE

I'm sitting in a Volkswagen van. In front of me is Aspinwall mansion, definitely not in its forties glory. The front lawn has almost completely been taken over by wild blackberry bushes, the front porch is rotted and sagging, and most, if not all, of the upper windows are cracked.

But there's a tall aluminum ladder perched against the peeling stucco, and a small swath of weeds has been cleared for a haphazard assortment of paint pails, two-by-fours, new windows, and gleaming copper pipes. A friendly-looking beagle pants on the front step, and it's hot—that sweltering, humid, New England kind of heat. From somewhere inside the mansion, I hear hammering and the tinny sound of a radio playing something funky.

I open the van door, it groans in protest, and I discover that the outside of the Volkswagen has been handpainted with rainbows, dolphins, ocean waves, and peace symbols. Worse still, I'm wearing faded, torn bellbottom jeans, an embroidered purple tunic, and on my wrist is some kind of hand-tooled leather bracelet with a yin/yang symbol. My chin is itchy, and when I reach up to scratch I find a scraggly beard.

Oh, the *horror*. I'm Shaggy.

"Hey, *namaste*!" calls out an airy woman's voice from the deep interior of the house. Into the sunshine steps a true flower child, with floaty blond hair, some kind of baggy paisley dress, light freckles, and a wild Susan tucked behind her ear. She beams and drifts out to where I'm standing, girlishly grabbing my hand. "You saw the sign?"

I nod.

She giggles and then hugs me lightly. She smells like freshly mown grass. "You're our first. Come in, come in."

I'm pulled up the steps, past the beagle, which only gives my feet the most cursory sniff, and then I'm in the main entry of Aspinwall. One wall is covered with the ghastly wallpaper I remember from my night there, but the others are still Italianate fresco, although mildew has spotted the figures beyond recognition.

"Wolf!" she calls out. "I'm Celia, by the way. But this month you can call me Lotus. I've been feeling very lotusy lately."

I have no doubt. But then a cold realization strikes—Celia and Wolf, the hippies from Amherst. One of them will die soon. *It's just a dream*, I tell myself.

A bright-eyed young man with long brown hair tied back by a red bandana, wearing similar bellbottoms and a leather-fringed vest (no shirt), steps out from the kitchen, a hammer in hand.

"You from San Fran?" he says, wiping his hand before reaching out and gripping mine, like we're long-lost brothers.

What the hell. "Yeah," I say.

Apparently that gives me some cachet. He's obviously impressed. "Always meant to get out there, to where the action's at. But got a little delayed with my woman here."

Celia is far from a woman—she could easily pass for a fifteen-year-old—but she giggles appreciatively and twists his hand in hers. "You can take your pick on the second floor; there are lots of rooms. But watch out, 'cause there are bad spots in the floor."

Tell me about it.

"You know anything about wiring?" Wolf asks hopefully.

"No," I reply. "I'm a writer."

This, apparently, makes me a god, because his eyes widen. Even Celia takes a step back. "For real?" she says. "I have some poems. I'm really into ants right now. You know, busy, busy ants. People are just doing, you know? Doing but not thinking. Not *dreaming*." Her eyes glaze over at the word "dreaming."

Wolf kisses her lightly on the cheek. "Busy, busy ants."

They seem like nice people. Disgustingly in love with each other and full of nauseating hope, but otherwise nice people.

"Oh," says Celia, "I found something in the kitchen!" Without further explanation, she *skips* away.

"She's a freak in bed," says Wolf confidentially.

I so did not need to know that.

A cool wind blows through the wide, spacious entry, and the beagle whimpers for no discernible reason, then Celia is back, holding an old saltine tin. The top is slightly rusted.

My heart instantly begins to beat faster. I recognize the saltine tin—it's the same one Lisa showed me.

"Oh that is *cool*, babe." Wolf's got a look in his eyes, like he'd prefer to just ditch the home repairs and explore her freaky side, which probably explains the overall lack of progress on the site.

"Not this," says Celia, pulling at the lid. "*This*."

Celia pulls out the pages wrapped in black velvet, shyly proud of her find.

"It's Greek and some other weird language," she says. "But I can read the Greek."

I must look puzzled, because Wolf says, "I rescued her from college."

"All girls," adds Celia with a visible shiver. "I was thinking we could get out the Ouija board tonight. Have some shiny time."

"You're so *witchy*," says Wolf, kissing her neck. He really can't keep his hands off her.

Just as I'm about to open my mouth and warn them, the music in the background changes to a white-noise hum and everything around me flickers, becomes staticky, like I'm watching a TV show with bad reception, and the whole world tilts, gets fuzzy. There's a piercingly bright flash of light, and then I hear a singer, a swing band; the night sky is dark with stars and my head pounds—or is that the drums?—and I get a fragmentary glimpse of the Aspinwall driveway lined with intricately carved, glowing jack-o'-lanterns. I distantly hear Amelia's bright voice calling out over the crowd, "Captain, come join the séance; you have no idea the trouble I've gone to," and then I'm spinning again, falling, falling, falling. When it stops I find myself lying on the weedy front lawn, feeling like I just stepped off a roller coaster, like I can't find my balance. Everything around me flickers but eventually clears—there, the cans of paint . . . But the ladder is gone. The beagle cowers on the front porch, whimpering—its eyes wide with terror.

I catch a wavering movement by the door, and a hazy form steps out of the shadow.

Poe.

For a moment she just looks at me with an icy stare. Water clings to her dress, drips from her fingers and onto the ground. Then she lifts her hand, beckons for me to follow, and disappears inside.

But there are sounds. Horrific sounds. Sounds that make me hesitate, wonder if I wouldn't be safer standing on the front lawn. I firmly tell myself, *This is just a dream; it's not real.* As soon as I step past the doorway I feel a deep arctic chill, and I find myself alone in the vast and nearly empty hall.

I say nearly, because Wolf's body is on the floor. Beside him, a bloody knife.

And then I see Celia. Folded over his body with grief, rough sobs—but the sound isn't right; there's something *gritty* to it—and then I realize she's not sobbing, she's snarling. A shaft of the light from the setting sun catches the glittering chandelier, refracts through the crystals, and casts a wider circle of light on the body. I can see his entrails now, covered with red slime, pulled from his stomach and lying in a heap on the floor.

Celia sits back on her heels, a look of orgiastic ecstasy on her face. Her mouth—*Christ, her mouth*—is covered with blood; her white, blousy shirt drips with it. She wipes a wrist against her face, smearing more blood across her cheek, and then licks her lips, before leaning back over the body. She starts gnawing at something in the cavity of his corpse and then uses a finger to pull out some muscle so she can get to it better.

I'm going to be sick.

The air shifts next to me, and when I turn I find Poe watching me, expressionless. A light breeze blows through the open door, lifts some papers in the air, twirls them around. One lands by my feet.

Medieval drawings. Greek and Russian typeset. The edges are burnt. They're the pages I found in Daniel's room—the pages Celia found in the saltine tin.

Poe looks at me fiercely.

You must be ready. You must see.

Not a sound, not a voice—I don't hear her speak; instead I see the words hover in the air like mist.

God, I'm sick of this ghost bullshit. "And how the fuck do I go about getting ready? Would you tell me that, Poe?"

She takes a step closer. I can see water beading her eyelashes and there's a smell, something musty and organic, like mud at the bottom of a pond.

Say my name. Say my name and I can tell you everything.

"I don't know your name."

But I do. It's there, just outside the edge of memory, like the words to a song I've long forgotten, her name. And maybe I could remember, but the sound—*oh dear God*—the sound of human teeth on human bone, the iron-rust smell of blood, Wolf's blood. It rushes out to meet me, pools darkly around my feet, and then suddenly there's the roar of the white-noise hum, and everything flickers again, crackling into shards of images.

I cover my ears with my hands, and there's a hot flash of light—
my head throbs, pulses, and when I open my eyes next I find that
I'm standing on the neatly manicured front lawn of Aspinwall. I'm
wearing a white waiter's jacket, holding a silver tray of shrimp hors
d'oeuvres. And there, underneath a shadowy bower, is Alice dressed
as Little Bo Peep, as if she just stepped out of the photograph I'd seen
her in. Her hand is lightly pressed to a vampire's chest, and he holds
her staff protectively.

"Oh, Jack, you *can't* be serious. Why on earth wouldn't I marry
you?"

The band plays.

You're gonna feel sad,
You're gonna be blue,
After I've gone,
After I've gone and left you.

"You!" An angular, slightly balding butler approaches me. "Are
you just going to *stand* there, or do you have plans to actually serve
tonight?"

"Oh, right," I mumble. I'm still dizzy, and my ears ring, but I
move through the crowd carrying my tray, wondering where Amelia
might be. But then a woman stops me, grabbing my arm. She wears
a simple white cotton dress with wide peasant sleeves, an odd choice
to go with her plain black mask and devil's horns, but then it strikes
me—this is the woman from Alice's photo. Khioniya.

She reaches out to the platter with long delicate fingers, hesitates
briefly, and then takes two of the hors d'oeuvres. She has to remove
her mask to eat, so she pulls it from her face, lets it rest on her forehead. And my body freezes.

Poe.

But not like I've seen her. Her flesh is pale but alive; it catches
the warm glow from the paper lanterns and despite the cold, a trickle

of sweat makes its way down her neck. On her feet she wears golden slippers.

"You can't run away from me that easy!" shouts a booming voice, and then Zorro appears behind her, catches her by the waist, and twirls her about roughly.

"You're a *divine* dancer," he says, trying to flatter, but she regards him with icy disdain.

"I am tired," she says coolly with a thick Russian accent, "and I must prepare for séance."

"I say, when is that? I don't want to miss the fun."

"Midnight," she replies with a catlike grin.

He leans in to kiss her, and she slaps him soundly on the cheek.

"Well, I'll see you then, you *little devil*." He laughs like he's made a great joke and then disappears back into the crowd of dancers.

Poe takes another hors d'oeuvre from the platter, places it in her mouth. "They are children playing dress-up," she says. "They want to play at being Arabs; they want to play at having séance. But it is not play what I do. It is real."

I stand still, not daring to move.

"You, you work here just tonight or all the time?" she says to me.

"Just tonight," I say quietly.

"Well," she says, wiping her hands on her dress, "if you see gardener, you give him message." She thinks for a moment, then laughs. "Tell him Khioniya says hello."

She claps me on the shoulder, not lightly, not in a feminine way, and then slips her mask back on and steps invisibly through the crowd, completely unnoticed. Delia, dressed as a fairy, runs up to greet her, and Khioniya takes her hand, kisses it lightly, and together they walk into the house.

CHAPTER EIGHTEEN: THE SECRET BOOKS

There's an owl in the room fluttering about the ceiling. It hits the window, trying to escape. It makes a gentle knocking sound in the process, but then I realize this doesn't make sense. How can there be an owl in my apartment? My tongue is dry and scratchy, like it's wearing a wool sweater, my feet ache, and I can't feel my right arm at all, because Lisa's using it as a pillow and blood probably hasn't been able to circulate for hours—not that I'm complaining. I try to open my eyes, which is hard to do; they're unwilling, heavy, and thick with sleep. But finally they open, and I find the dim morning light edging through the grimy window—God, it must be *early*—and there's no owl but the knock again, polite yet insistent, like a maid checking that the room is clear before entering.

It's a real sound.

My heart stops—Daniel?

Instantly I sit up and disentangle myself from Lisa—*Fuck, where's the gun?*—but then Daniel doesn't seem like the knocking-before-entering type. I should check the window, easy enough since I've never invested in actual curtains. The windowpane is as cold as a sheet of ice, but nobody's scrambling down the tree—a good sign—and the sidewalk is deserted.

Suddenly a man wearing a thickly hooded jacket leaves my building, briskly crossing the street. The hood covers his head, his face. Then I notice his thick boots.

Fuck.

But I need to be sure. Without thinking I grab a paperback, push up the windowpane, ignoring the blast of frigid air, and throw it at him. Not since my infamous Twinkie shot have I ever hit someone so squarely on the head. Startled, the man turns around and for a brief flash our eyes meet.

The dude from Sacred Heart Collectibles?

"What are you doing?" Lisa asks sleepily from the couch. "I'm cold."

"Lisa come here, it's that guy . . ."

But when I turn back to the window, he's gone. A Buick runs over my book, burying it in a mound of black slush.

"What guy?"

"Nothing," I say quietly, trying and failing to do the arithmetic that would make any sense of his sudden appearance at my apartment building. Of course, it is a small town, in which case I just hit an innocent man with a book projectile. Now he probably thinks I'm racist or something. But what are the odds? Slim to none. So then what did he want to tell me?

"Idiot, idiot, idiot," I mutter to myself. Columbo would never have slept in.

"Are you going to shut the window, or is this some kind of Hindu deprivation morning ritual?"

"Right," I say, pulling the window closed. Lisa's looking at me expectantly—*somebody* got some sleep.

"Breakfast?" she asks with more hope than one should in my apartment.

"Not likely."

"What about that lasagna?"

"Right . . . that lasagna." It strikes me that I never turned the oven off, but somehow the kitchen isn't on fire. A quick check reveals I never actually turned the oven on. The lasagna is still frozen rock solid.

"Looks like we'll have to pick up something," I say sheepishly, turning around empty-handed.

And then I notice something's been slipped under the door, a folded piece of newspaper.

"What's this *we*?" says Lisa, reaching down to get the remote. "I think the least you could do is cross the street to get me some donuts and coffee."

"In my condition?" Lisa hasn't noticed the paper, a good thing, because God knows what it contains. I quickly hobble over, ignoring the dull ache in my feet, and discover it's a crossword puzzle, with "Mesa" neatly written in pencil for fourteen down.

Delightful. Now someone *else* is leaving me indecipherable clues. Should only take me a few decades to work out. My head pounds, and I'm starting to give that move to Florida some serious consideration—I'm getting tired of every waking (and now sleeping) moment being spent on this crap. I'm not a puzzle freak like Ernest; why can't anyone come out and just *tell* me what they want me to know?

Ernest?

Vaguely I hear a click and then the newsy drone of the television.

Ernest, keeper of "The Stacks" at the *Eagle*, taught Greek for decades—maybe *he* could translate the books . . . or at least tell me what they are—

"Oh, Jesus. Dimitri?"

It's the tone that stops me dead. I look over and see Lisa slowly lean forward, ashen faced.

"Owner Fred Janson was shocked to find a trail of blood this morning when he arrived at the station to open it at five thirty A.M."

Double fuck. Another murder. I reach over for the remote and turn up the volume.

Ace reporter Jennifer is standing in the snowy field by Friendly Fred's, the gas station that's just barely a quarter mile from Lisa's house. The parking lot is filled with police cars, and there are a couple of blue tarp tents set up in the field.

Jennifer holds the microphone tightly, and in the background I can hear the buzz of a helicopter. "The community is shocked at this latest murder, none more so than Fred Janson, who discovered the body early this morning." Jennifer, of course, doesn't looked shocked—she looks like an actress auditioning for the role of her life, which of course she is.

They cut to Fred; he's small and wiry, with a deeply weathered face and cropped gray hair. "I thought maybe a dog got hit by a car, so I followed the blood to the back. That's when I found Maddy." He chokes on her name. "I've known her for thirty years. Never thought something like this would happen to her, could happen here."

Maddy. I'm not proud that I exhale when I hear her name—no one deserves to go that way—but it's not Elizabeth or Amelia.

Next they flash a series of photos of Maddy from when she was younger, and judging from the flashy white miniskirt and tight sweater, they were probably taken in the sixties. She stands arm in arm with her sister Myrna (God, poor Myrna), who even then showed poor taste in eyewear; she wore thick black owlish glasses that would probably have gotten her voted most likely to become a nun or librarian by her high school classmates.

"We have to go," says Lisa quietly.

"Go? Go where?"

Lisa closes her eyes, like it's causing her physical pain to speak. "I don't know. Somewhere else. Somewhere safe."

The television cuts to an overhead helicopter shot, shaky and not really adding much to the story except the thrill of seeing the ambulance pull away, lights flashing.

"Define safe."

"Dimitri Petrov," says Lisa, giving me a look as if I've lost what's left of my mind. "*Anywhere* is safer than New Goshen."

I drop Lisa off to pack (her street is jammed with enough police vehicles to ward off an army), trying to justify in my own mind the small white lie I left her with (I need to go to the bank for some cash, when in fact I'm going to run the books by Ernest), and the even larger, nowhere-near-white lie of the gun in my glove compartment (what will Elizabeth think when she discovers it's gone? That Daniel broke in and stole it?).

When I get to the office, the bored security guard actually looks at me for a moment, and there is something almost fearful in the way he appraises me. Apparently the police aren't the only ones thinking I might be the killer. The elevator dings, and I've never been so happy to step inside it.

I really don't want to push the button for the third floor, not because I don't feel bad for Myrna—I do—but because I'll be in close proximity to the energy of mourning. Definitely not my favorite thing, but after all my immature cracks, I feel like I owe her. While the elevator ascends I try to think about something else, namely white-sand beaches, fresh coconuts containing fruity alcoholic beverages, and turquoise ocean waters. Lisa and I strolling down the beach, watching the sunset. She'd be wearing a bikini of course . . . maybe white with red polka dots. Would the company credit card work in Miami? I wonder how long we could ride on it until Mac notices the charges from Florida and cuts me off.

My reverie is interrupted by the rude chime of the elevator when it hits the third floor, and the first thing I notice as the doors open is how quiet it is. Either the phones aren't ringing—hard to imagine, given the breaking story—or they're being answered on a different floor. Even the grinding of the old laser printers is gone, so that for the first time I can hear the hiss of the radiator and the ticking of the fabulous fifties clock.

Bob approaches me first, wearing a black polo shirt tucked under a belt that's cinched three notches past reason; the straining seams around the buckle look like they can't possibly hold on much longer. He holds out a sweaty hand, which I reluctantly take, although even Bob would probably think it in poor taste to palm his standard buzzer. "Glad you could make it. Such a sad day, sad day."

I see Nate in the corner staring at the wall and drinking something from a small paper cup, an appropriate expression of sadness arranged on his face. And then I see Myrna standing stiffly by the water cooler, surrounded by office staff I've never encountered, all seemingly frozen in place. Her dress is lumpy and black, adorned with that awful brooch in the shape of a turtle I last saw Maddy wear, and there are sad bits of cookie crumbs dotting her unusually red lipsticked lips. The mood is somber, and even Mac seems subdued; his normal shout is reduced to a reasonable decibel, and he clasps Myrna by the elbow, as high, apparently, as he can reach.

"Take the day," says Mac. "We'll hire a temp to cover."

Myrna sniffs loudly into a tissue, and now Mac is nervously at a loss for words, as if this is the extent of his experience with female consolation. Both he and Nate notice me at the same time. Mac looks relieved to have something else to talk about. Nate glares.

"Look who's here," says Mac, coming over to grip *my* elbow, as if I've suffered a loss, too. "Great story you dialed in the other day. Made me crazy that it was so late, but worth it, kid. You've got the knack."

Nate crushes the paper cup in his hands and throws it at a trash can. He misses.

"Tough on Myrna," says Mac in an even softer tone. "They can't have the funeral until the autopsy is done. Specialists coming in from DC. Myrna said it'd be weeks." Then, even more quietly, Mac whispers, "And you were right; we're doubling our ad rates. Maybe when Myrna has had a chance to, you know . . ."

Myrna blows her nose loudly into the tissue. It sounds like someone just strangled a goose.

"Get a little past her grief," continues Mac, "you could do an interview. Victim's side of things. Could be very touching."

I can hear him mentally subtracting his net from his gross; it's making me sick just to stand next to him. Instead of replying, I walk over to Myrna.

"I'm so sorry," I say, and she peers at me with more than just a little distrust. I'm ashamed to say I've earned it. "Your sister was"— *What's a positive word I can honestly use here?*—"*special.* One of a kind."

Apparently that works well enough, because Myrna starts to sob again, but she also holds out a hand appreciatively and grasps my arm before dabbing at her eyes with the same tissue.

Obviously this is all more than Nate can take, because, looking furious, he digs his hands into his jacket pockets and storms out to the stairway without uttering a word.

"A sensitive kid, my Nate," says Mac wistfully.

Sensitive, my ass.

After I stay on the third floor for what seems to be an appropriate amount of time, I start to quietly make my way for the elevator— God knows I don't want to take the chance of running into Nate on the stairs.

If I thought the third floor was quiet, then the basement is like a tomb. No one is sitting at the gray metal desk, and I have a brief panicky moment where I think maybe Ernest finally went and died, which would make me the winner of the office pool, but a holder of indecipherable texts. Then I hear soft shuffling footsteps in the utility closet. A waft of smoke drifts out. He's, like, ninety-five, and he's a *smoker?*

"Ernest?"

Ernest pokes his head out of the closet and sheepishly waves away at the small cloud that follows him. "Bad habit. Going to kill me one of these days."

"*You* are going to outlive us all."

"One can only hope," he says dryly. He drops the cigarette on the floor and rubs it out with his heel. "Now," he says with a raspy voice, "out with it. What do you want? You look like a student who deserves a *C* but wants me to change his grade to an *A*."

I do a cursory check behind me—looks like we're alone, so I decide to start with what should be the easiest to translate, the inscription in my father's pocket watch. I take it out and gently pull off the back to reveal the inscription. "Can you tell me what this means?"

My heart starts to pound. Is this just another pointless clue that will lead to another that will lead to another, like some kind of karmic Möbius strip? Or will it actually reveal something of consequence about my father?

Ernest gives me a hard look. "I take it you didn't study the classics?"

I shake my head.

"I swear, the state of education today," he mutters, taking the watch and examining it closely. "You need to get this fixed. You notice it's going backwards?"

"I had noticed that, thanks."

Then he doesn't say anything; he just stares quietly, not even blinking, and I start to think maybe he's one of those old people who fall asleep standing up with their eyes open.

"Umm, and the inscription says?"

"This would have taken one of *my* students about six seconds. 'Glance into the world just as though time were gone, and everything crooked will become straight to you.' Nietzsche."

 "But what does it *mean*?"

"Hell if I know," he says brusquely. "I taught languages, not philosophy."

Great—this is just *great*. I hold back with difficulty the impulse to take the watch and throw it against the wall—a measure that would at least provide me a small amount of gratification.

Ernest moves on to what must be his new crossword puzzle and pulls a chewed pencil from behind his ear. "Nine-letter word, convert to vapor," he mutters.

"Sublimate," I say. I wonder if there's any point in even showing him the books.

He looks at the word going down. "You're right," he says, as if this is a big surprise. Then he sighs. "Okay, what else do you have? There's something in the bag, right, that you want to show me?"

Feeling particularly hopeless, I pull out my book and the battered pages wrapped in dusty velvet, which maybe someone tried to burn because trying to decipher them was a *freaking waste of time.*

Ernest weighs the leather book in his hands, turns it over, and runs a finger down what's left of the spine. "Hand sewn, I can tell you that," he says. With a little more interest he carefully opens it to the first gilded page, measuring the thickness of it between his thumb and forefinger. "Nice paper. The Russian print looks like moveable type, but the Greek is much, much older . . ." Then, most surprising of all, he lifts the book and takes a deep, almost perverted whiff. I wonder if maybe Ernest has some kind of book fetish.

"You're smelling my book."

"Nothing like the smell of an antiquarian book, son. Nothing like it. With this binding, I'm going to take a stab in the dark and say that they're the same book, just different translations from different time periods. The Russian pages are early twentieth century, but the Greek, hard to say. The paper almost feels like papyrus. Of course, that would be completely blasphemous to cut and bind such a rare document with a newer text. Possible though. And the title, of course, is very interesting."

"The title, perfect. What's the title?"

Ernest puts his head on one elbow and glances at my ring. "You realize that the watermark is the same symbol on your ring?"

"Yes, I'd *noticed*."

"No need to take a sarcastic tone. Now why do you have a ring with this particular symbol?"

I swallow hard. "I don't *know*. One of the reasons I was hoping you could translate the book . . . now you said the title—"

"Is very odd," he says, pushing his glasses back with his forefinger.

I try to restrain the part of me that wants to leap over the counter and wrap my hands around his ninety-five-year-old neck, and I take a deep breath instead. "And the title is—what?"

"*The Secret Grimoire of Grigori Rasputin: The Book of Seraphs.*" Ernest carefully flips through the next few pages.

"So it's about Rasputin?"

"Mmm, no. It's attributed as being written *by* Rasputin. Very odd, because as far as I know Rasputin never published anything. But all this looks very hand done." He glances at me over his glasses. "Which would mean it's the only copy. Or one of only a few. And if *that* is true, then this is a very, *very* expensive book. Where did you say you got it?"

"I didn't," I say brusquely. "But why is it in Greek *and* Russian?"

"Well, whoever translated it from Greek obviously wanted to keep the original text. Always good to keep the source material in case there are errors in the translation. But I am very curious as to how you obtained—"

I push the velvet-wrapped pages toward him. "This might be another copy actually. But the pictures are different."

Ernest raises an eyebrow and casts a glance over his shoulder, like we're in the middle of some kind of illicit drug deal, but he can't resist and unwraps the velvet. As soon as he sees the charred first page, he sucks in his breath.

"Oh my," he whispers.

"Is it the same book?"

"No, no . . . I wish I had some tweezers to lift the pages. These are in very bad shape indeed. But so . . . compelling."

My heart starts to race. "So then what's the title of this one?"

"Fascinating" is all he says.

"Ernest?"

"Oh. Yes. The title of this one is *The Secret Grimoire of Grigori Rasputin: The Book of Fiends.*"

"What's a grimoire?"

"Well, to *really* say what *these* are"—he gently lifts a page and turns it over, completely absorbed—"I'd need some time to fully study them. Weeks maybe. There's so much here . . ."

I lean in closer. "Ernest, I really don't think I have weeks. If you can't—"

Quickly he clutches my arm. "No, I didn't say I couldn't, just . . . well . . ."

"Well, what?"

But already Ernest is feverishly talking to himself, as if I'm not there at all. "It's not like I'm exactly overwhelmed in The Stacks," he mutters.

"Ernest!"

He jumps, completely startled, and almost drops the pages.

"Ernest," I try in a quieter tone. "*What* is a grimoire?"

"A grimoire is a book of spells."

"Please tell me you're kidding."

"Why on earth would I be kidding? Wouldn't be such a far stretch to think that Rasputin was intrigued by the occult, given his reputation. It was quite the rage all through the late eighteenth to early twentieth century, back when the division between science and mysticism was not so clearly defined. Technically, the translation is 'experiment,' but not the kind of experiments you're familiar with. Science has its genesis in alchemy, you know. All those attempts to turn lead into gold or create an elixir for immortality led to modern chemistry. Even Newton dabbled in—"

"So you're saying I have a book of spells," I say, interrupting. "Perfect. Just what I always wanted." My heart sinks as my mind conjures up images of green-skinned witches with pointy hats and a peculiar hatred of girls from Kansas with small terriers. Or worse yet, the Wiccan sort who attend Renaissance festivals and wear blousy peasant shirts.

Ernest reads my tone. "They aren't those kind of spells."

"Nothing about eyes of newts or toes of frogs?"

"Macbeth," he says, obviously impressed. "Your education wasn't a complete disgrace. No, these are much more interesting than anything even Shakespeare could imagine. Basically, you have one book for conjuring and releasing seraphs, or angels as they're more familiarly called, and then another for conjuring and releasing fiends, or demons. Should make for a fun Halloween party one of these days."

"Halloween—not exactly my favorite holiday."

"Oh right, of course. Apologies. I forgot about your near-death experience," he says cheerfully. "I'd say the *real* value of these—besides the price you could probably get at auction—would be the notoriety from discovering books penned by Rasputin himself. I'm sure it would create quite a literary stir in the world of scholarship, and for the translator, well, it'd be quite the feather in the cap, so to speak . . ."

His voice drifts off, and I can see Ernest imagining a much better obituary than the one I currently have filed away in the event of his death.

"But it's also quite possible they're clever forgeries," he adds reluctantly. "I do have a friend who could authenticate the books, but he's on sabbatical right now in—"

"Let's just say they're authentic. If I leave the books with you, you'll translate them? Unless you have better things—"

But already Ernest is rewrapping the pages in an almost possessive manner. "Of course I will. Much more fun in any case than my crossword puzzles. And if they are genuine, I'll be immortal in the only realm it matters. Academia."

"I need to know what they mean—*soon*."

"You understand normally this kind of undertaking would take months, if not years—but if I scan some of the pages and let Google do the rough translation . . ."

"I don't have months, Ernest. I have hours."

"Well . . ." he says reluctantly. "I could have some partials done by tomorrow. At least give me a day."

I sigh.

"There are no shortcuts with these kinds of things, young man." He grabs my elbow with a surprising degree of strength and ushers me toward the elevator; it's clear he's eager to be rid of me so he can get back to the pages. "But I appreciate your keen enthusiasm . . . Have you ever considered going back to college and actually getting your degree? With your knack for discovering material . . ." At this he licks his dry lips. "And you will tell me where you found these books, won't you? Before we're finished?"

I nod. What's one more lie added to the others? And in that moment I realize I'm changing in some core inner space I'd never been aware of before. And that thought truly scares the shit out of me.

CHAPTER NINETEEN: REFUGE

There is a rustic, lakeside summer cabin that Elizabeth knows of, a friend of a friend's electricity-free, phone-free artistic retreat that's only a half hour away. This is where I take them, Lisa in the front seat, saying nothing and staring hard out the window, Elizabeth equally silent in the back, while Amelia happily makes her doll play air guitar for the benefit of Buddy, who's either really into it (not a single bark or growl since he laboriously climbed onto the backseat) or long past caring.

The cabin is a place they have never been. It goes unsaid, but weighs heavily, that it's a place Daniel wouldn't know about.

The road winds through small towns, smaller towns, and then it's just a few scattered farms with looming red barns. The wind pushes snow across the road, and it snakes over the recently plowed asphalt. The sun is setting behind us, glinting against the ice in the barren trees. I don't want to stop. Ever. I want to keep going, maybe drive south through the stripped mine towns of Pennsylvania, the Smoky Mountains, and down into the heart of Florida, until we reach Miami—palm trees and Cuban restaurants. I could reasonably kidnap them all, couldn't I?

Somehow I don't think Elizabeth would go for it.

But once we get into the backwoods, some of the heaviness lifts. I've always found that when life is starting to turn to crap, it's never a bad idea to change the scenery, if only for half a day or a night. There's something comforting about seeing different things, different people; it makes life seem less claustrophobic, less pressing. The first six months after my parents' death I put ten thousand miles on my Mustang. Sometimes I'd go find a park I'd never been to or a café I'd never eaten at and hang out for the day, people watching. It was good to think that I could literally pack everything I owned in a suitcase and walk away from my life, start again.

"Right here," says Elizabeth.

We turn off on a road that's barely a road. The branches are low, and twigs scrape at the sides of the Mustang. Then there's a clearing and a small two-story cabin. The sagging front porch and unpainted clapboard exterior make it a little too *Deliverance*, in my humble opinion. I half expect to see an overweight man in dirty overalls break the front glass window and aim a shotgun at us.

But Elizabeth sighs with relief. "Here we are."

I note that the snow is perfectly undisturbed, except for a few deer prints. A good sign. Behind the cabin stretches the lake, a flat expanse of snow-covered ice; wind has created drifts of snow like mini–sand dunes.

Amelia jumps out of the car and drops backward on the pristine snow, waving her arms and legs. "I'm making snow angels!" Of course she's barefoot.

"Jesus Christ, Amelia, do you not *know* how to wear boots?" says Lisa.

"They make my feet itch," replies Amelia happily.

Lisa mutters something incomprehensible, but there's a welcome color in her cheeks as she digs under the car seat for the boots.

Elizabeth notices too and catches my eye. We silently agree that this was a good idea.

"Well," says Elizabeth cheerfully, stepping out of the car. "Let's go scare off the bats and get some canned beans going."

The inside of the cabin isn't too awful. It's sparse, the twiggy wooden furniture looks like it's been feasted on by termites for decades, but there's a good stack of firewood next to a rock fireplace and no sign of mouse droppings or other critter occupation.

A few trips to the Mustang bring in our essential supplies—luggage, hot dogs, canned beans, instant coffee, oil paint, four loaves of Wonder Bread, two red Maglites, a guitar case, paintbrushes, matches, peanut butter, one ten-inch-by-eight-inch tom (Amelia solemnly corrects me when I call it a drum), marshmallows, hot pepper jelly, one half-empty bag of dog kibble, and my thousand-page doorstop of a novel, "Rasputin: Secret Tsar of Immortal Zombies." I'm planning to scan it to see if I've inadvertently incorporated information that could prove useful, while Ernest's translating the books.

By the time the sun has completely set, Elizabeth's got a good fire roaring, the hot dogs are only mildly charred, and we each have a bowl of steaming baked beans, heated up in the cans they came in.

"I don't want to share a bed with Lisa," says Amelia, picking out one bean that is too brown (she only likes the light brown ones) and tossing it into the fire. "Her feet are too cold."

One of the first things Elizabeth pointedly did after we brought the suitcases in was assign rooms. She gets the smallest upstairs bedroom, Lisa and Amelia are to share the other, and I've been given a sleeping bag and a place by the fire. I have a feeling it's quiet retribution for making off with her daughter the night before, but I don't care. Travel had always been my father's realm. My family never took vacations together, or went camping, not even a day trip. In a strange way, this is almost fun.

"*My* feet are too cold," says Lisa. "Yours are like icicles, 'cause you never wear boots."

"Are not."

Lisa reaches over and grabs one of Amelia's bare feet, tickling the bottom. "Tell the truth."

Amelia falls to her side in a peal of giggles, dropping her beans on the wooden floor. "Icy feet, icy feet!"

"Tell the truth!" says Lisa, laughing and reaching for Amelia's apparently even more ticklish waist.

Elizabeth shakes her head ruefully. "A waste of perfectly good beans."

It's astonishing how easy they are with each other, considering. Like there's a groove they naturally fall into, a congenial warmth. Long ago I convinced myself that happy families are a myth, a construction that only exists in television sitcoms and syrupy Hallmark cards. It was easier to believe no one is happy than to think that maybe I was missing something. And even though I'm still somewhat on the outside looking in, I don't mind. It's enough just being this close. I once had to read a story about a man who made a pact with the devil—he gave up his soul in exchange for a clock so he could stop time at the happiest moment in his life. Of course the man couldn't choose his happiest moment. There was always something to look forward to—falling in love, marriage, the birth of a child—so the man ended up dying before he stopped time.

I wouldn't make the same mistake. I'd stop it now, because the truth is I could stay here, like this, forever.

———

Everyone's gone to bed, the logs are comfortably smoldering, I'm in my sleeping bag, and at about page 595 of my novel when I hear a creak on the stairs.

I look up. Lisa's standing on the bottom step, holding a red Maglite. She's wearing an oversized gray sweatshirt and pair of boy shorts. Impossibly sexy as usual.

"You're still up," she says.

"So are you."

She sighs. "Amelia kicks. I'm going to have bruises on my legs in the morning."

"I don't kick."

"Yeah, well, you're in deep shit. Surprised my mom hasn't manacled you to the floor."

"Trust me, I get that."

Lisa crosses the room and settles on the floor next to me, hugging her knees. "What are you reading?"

I blearily rub my eyes with my fingers. "Nothing interesting."

"Looks like some kind of manuscript," says Lisa, peering at the type. "Your novel?"

"If you want to call it that."

"I want to read it."

Sound effect of screeching cars crashing into each other.

"Umm, really," I say as politely as possible. "You know that would actually take days. Days and days. Long, tedious, boring days. Weeks maybe."

"That's *completely* unfair," protests Lisa.

"Life's not fair."

She gives me a look then, a look that sets off more than a few alarm bells, but before I can react she's grabbed the first two hundred pages. I try to get them back, but she wiggles expertly out of my grasp. I feel like a fourth grader playing keep away.

"C'mon, give it back."

"No, wait," says Lisa. "I played my drums for you, now I get to read your writing."

"Lisa, I'm really not—"

She shushes me dismissively and settles closer to the warmth of the dying fire, holding her flashlight steady to read. I fall back on the floor, lift a cushion, and mock suffocate myself.

While I wait for death to come, I wonder why I really brought my novel along—the odds of it containing any factual information about Rasputin are slim. And scanning it again has only confirmed that it's not the Great American Novel; it's not even an averagely acceptable novel—no, it's a thousand-page albatross that I've been lugging around for years, like one of those sad patents for mobile bathtubs and gerbil shirts. Lisa reading even a bit of it is excruciating, to say the least.

"Wow," she finally says.

It's an unqualified "Wow," the kind of "Wow" you say when a friend has just gotten an irreversible bad perm, because what else can you say when it's horrible beyond fixing, and there's nothing to do but wait and let it grow out?

"I know," I mumble from beneath the cushion.

"It doesn't sound like you. It feels like it was written by someone in their late fifties. 'Rasputin gazed at the fire; oh, the weight of it, the future, here was the fate of Russia in his hands. Could he heal Alexis, and therefore the nation?'"

"I wanted it to be serious," I say defensively.

"But then later he's a zombie killing peasants."

I groan. "Okay, okay, it's a thousand-page piece of rambling shit. I admit it. But if I let go, it's like I wasted two years of my life."

"Letting go is part of the artistic process," says Lisa with the optimism of someone who actually has artistic skill.

"Well, the process sucks."

Suddenly the crackling starts to get louder, and I peek out from under my cushion. Lisa has just tossed a good chunk into the fire.

"Holy crap!" I jump up and—damn!—burn my hand while trying to rescue it. Who knew cheap paper was so flammable? *Snap, crackle, pop*; in goes another chunk. "What are you doing?!"

"I'm liberating you," says Lisa calmly.

"The way we liberated Iraq; the way China liberated Tibet? Hey, give me that!"

Holy mother of God, she's got about three hundred pages in her hand.

"Let go," says Lisa. "It's time to let go."

"*Jesus*, Lisa," I say, really irritated now, and I try but fail to wrestle the next chunk away from her. For a relatively small person she's pretty strong. Or I need to work out more. Or maybe just work out.

The flames crackle happily like they're overdosing on speed, and the pages curl before turning to a blackened lump. It's really kind of beautiful in a sick way. I can suddenly see the attraction of cremation and funeral pyres; there's no going back once something is burned. It never felt real, on a certain level, the death of my parents. I tossed my scattering of dirt after their coffins were lowered into the ground, but I never saw their faces, and maybe I should have in spite of what Lucy said. She thought I should remember them the way they were—"The accident wasn't kind" is how she put it—but a part of me never let them go. I reach my hand toward the fire and let it hover over the pages. See how close I can get before I feel the burn.

"I wanted to make him proud of me, for once," I say quietly.

Lisa gently pulls my hand back. "Who?"

"My father." Suddenly the heat from the fire seems to jump—I can feel a burning flickering up my arm, reach into my chest, land in my stomach. I grab the next hundred pages and toss them in. It's amazing how powerful it feels to pass anger and dip into pure, crystalline rage. "My father." Fuck it, I grab about five hundred pages and jam them in over the rest of the burning mess. Now the flames are wild, they lick at the top of the mantel—they want to escape, these flames, take a walk, transform everything in their path to blackened soot.

"Okay, Dimitri," says Lisa, trying to pull me away from the fire. "We've gone from catharsis to borderline insanity. Come back from the edge."

I hear her faintly but grab the last of the pages and stuff them in roughly while black smoke starts to drift from the hearth, too much for the chimney to handle. Now Lisa forcefully pulls me back.

"My father," I whisper and start laughing. I'm not sure why, but I can't stop.

Lisa grabs my face and turns it to hers. She looks so serious, and that strikes me as hysterically funny. Even the tears in my eyes are funny to me. I wipe them away with the back of my sleeve.

"You know it was the first time they were coming to see me? Almost four years in college, and they'd never visited." My chest shakes with laughter, and the room starts to tilt.

She wipes my forehead, like I'm a fevered child. "You do love me, right?" Lisa asks. "You said that last night, that you loved me."

Oh Christ, she heard that? It's like someone just dumped a bucket of cold water over my head—I'm instantly serious. "You were supposed to be asleep."

"I wasn't *that* asleep," she says.

"And?" I ask quietly. An owl hoots in the distance.

She rubs the back of my neck with her calming hand. "And I can honestly say that if your father wasn't proud of you, then fuck him."

I close my eyes. It feels good just to hear the words "fuck him" in the same sentence with the word "father." I lean in, let my forehead touch hers. "And?"

She knows what I mean. "And I guess love you too."

I lightly kiss her lips, reach my hands behind her back, and stroke the skin that's warm from the fire. "And?"

"What, are you deaf?" says Lisa breathlessly. "I just said I love you."

I pull her to me, jubilant, and explore the soft arc of her neck with my lips. "I know," I say. She tastes like a lovely addiction. "Say it again." I pull her sweater up over her head. Outside the wind rattles the panes.

"I love you," whispers Lisa, running her hands through my hair.

Together we fall to floor and let everything that needs to burn, burn.

CHAPTER TWENTY: THE CABIN

It's night. I'm in a thicket of enormous trees. There's a small log cabin in front of me, and a warm glow shines from its sole window. A large brown horse snuffles under the shadow of an eave; it's tied to a pole, and its head hangs low, somber. Beside it is a sleigh, and I see something that chills my heart—a small body covered with a red cape. A tiny bluish hand dangles from the sleigh's edge, miniature icicles hanging from its fingers.

"No," I whisper to myself. "Not here, not now."

I'm alone. Or not. By the sleigh, partially hidden in the shadow, is a familiar figure.

Poe.

I close my eyes. Christ, she's followed me. Why can't she leave me the fuck alone? I will myself to wake up—I try to find the thread that will lead me back to consciousness, to the sleeping bag on the floor, to Lisa—but when I open my eyes the cabin is still there. The wind blows a sprinkling of snow off the roof. From inside the cabin come the soft, repetitive tones of voices chanting. *Russian* voices.

Now she's got me hooked. And even though I know that on a certain dangerous level I'm being manipulated for reasons I still don't understand, I quietly approach the front door.

The chanting instantaneously stops. Suddenly the door swings open, and a boy who looks about ten stands in the doorway. His clothes—gray handwoven pants and a thick, roughly sewn white shirt—are drenched with water. He doesn't see me—instead he looks through me out into the dark wood, like he's scanning for an intruder.

"No one is there," he says to someone inside. There's something strange about his speech. The lilt is unmistakably familiar, just like my father's, but the words themselves are completely foreign, although I understood him perfectly well.

In my dream I can understand Russian?

"Good," says an old and weary voice in the same thick Russian. "Then shut the door before more trouble comes."

Guess that's my cue.

The boy reaches out to shut the door, and I nimbly step past him into the small one-room cabin. A bit of scattered snow follows.

The planks of the cabin look hand-hewn, and from the beams hang a variety of dried flowers, plants, and leaves neatly tied with coarse string. On top of a narrow, rustic table is a flickering candle, a wooden bowl and pestle, a few odd-looking roots, and glass jars filled with ground herbs.

And in the center of the room is a taller boy tied to a bed with thick straps of leather that bind his hands and feet. He appears to be unconscious. His fevered flesh is pale and sweaty, and his eyes are closed. A weary-eyed man sits next to him on a simple wooden stool. He wears the same woolen pants, a roughly woven white shirt, and his brown hair and beard are flecked with gray. The smaller boy walks over to the crackling fireplace, which snaps an occasional spark as the logs gently burn. Water from his clothes drips onto the floor, and a small pool gathers near his feet. He holds out his hands to warm them.

The man coughs, and something on his hand catches a glint of firelight. The ring. My *father's* ring. For a moment I can't breathe.

The man turns and beckons for the small boy to approach. The boy swallows but does as he's told.

"Rasputin, this isn't your fault. It is *mine*," says the man gravely.

Rasputin's eyes fill with tears.

"It was not Dmitri who drowned your sister. It was the demon inside him, a demon he called because he read the books. I should have taught him years ago. If I had, he would have known then how dangerous they can be. I will not make that mistake with you. Do you understand?"

The boy nods his head mutely.

"Bring them to me."

The boy crosses over to a wooden trunk. He lifts out two battered books, both bound in rough calfskin, and reverently hands them to the old man.

"These are old books, Rasputin, very old. So old we don't even know where they came from. But my father gave them to me to safeguard."

He gently opens one of them. "I want you to promise me something. That you too will safeguard them when it's your time. That you will never share their knowledge with anyone but your *own* children."

"I promise," whispers Rasputin.

"We use our knowledge of spirits to help people, to heal them, and I will teach you how to be a healer like me. We can do *wondrous* things, my son. But there are good *and* bad spirits that haunt this world. Remember the man who saved you?"

The boy nods solemnly.

"He looked like a man, but really he was a good spirit in the man's body. The man died of a fever. And when I couldn't save his body, I called a good spirit, Nachiel, to come help protect our family."

"He didn't protect Maria!" blurts the boy.

"He tried. But he was too far away when Dmitri said the words that conjured another spirit, a bad one. Too late for your sister, but he was able to save *you* from being drowned."

"And Dmitri," whispers the boy.

The old man drops his head then, a wave of grief obviously overcoming him. Dmitri moans softly and turns his fevered head to the other side of the pillow.

"And Dmitri," says the boy more firmly. "It wasn't him that tried to drown me. It was a bad spirit from the bad book."

"Yes," says the old man quietly. He raises his head and looks at Rasputin closely. "The bad one called Sorath. He hates our family. Do you know why?"

The boy shakes his head.

The old man raises his hand, holding out the finger with the ring. "*This* is why. I'm going to tell you something now, something that's hard to believe. When my father gave this ring to me, he told me he was *two hundred years old*."

The boy sucks in his breath.

"And I know he was telling the truth, because *I* have walked this earth now for one hundred and fifty years."

"How?" the boy whispers.

The man slowly runs a hand through his beard, as if he's looking for how to begin. "A long time ago, before my father was born, or his father's father, a healer in our family conjured a demon, Sorath, and made a trade. If Sorath stole into the Garden of Eden and brought back a bit of apple from the Tree of Knowledge and a twig from the Tree of Eternal Life, he would be given the body and soul of the healer's daughter, who was very beautiful and very good."

Rasputin edges closer, his eyes wide.

"But after Sorath returned and handed over the twig and piece of apple, he discovered that the daughter had died during the night and her soul had passed on—she'd been very ill, but the healer had hidden it from Sorath. The man had known when he'd made the pact that she wouldn't live much longer than a day. Sorath was enraged, but the man had the twig and the apple, so he couldn't be killed and he couldn't be tricked—he now possessed powers that made him the equal of any spirit, good or bad. The man forged a special ring, preserving the twig within the band, and he took an ordinary red stone, carved out its center, and placed the small piece of apple inside. So the ring has two special qualities. The twig from the Tree of Eternal

Life makes the wearer immortal as long as he wears it. The apple from the Tree of Knowledge gives the wearer the ability to communicate with the spirit world, a world where he can see the past and sometimes the future. He can even slow the effect of time for the ones he loves so that they don't age as other people do. That's why Sorath hates us."

The boy hesitantly holds his own finger over the stone.

"*But!*"

The boy instantly draws his hand back like he's been burned.

"Immortality is not always a gift. Sometimes it feels like a curse. Especially when death comes for the people you love. And the spirit world is dangerous for humans. You can't see them, but they can see *you*. And sometimes bad ones want to do you harm."

"But you can get rid of the bad spirits?" asks the boy softly. "Make them go away. Right?"

"Yes. With the books and the help of a good spirit, I can almost always get rid of the bad one. But when you have to touch the dark soul of a demon, it leaves its mark on you. And that's what Sorath really wants, in the end. For one of us to turn . . . to become *like* him."

"I'll *never* be like him."

The man smiles grimly. "That's good, Rasputin. I know you won't. But there's something else, too. Something that will be hard for you to hear. Usually, when a bad spirit possesses someone so close to our family, someone we love . . . " He takes a deep breath, and his own eyes tear up. "Usually when I make the bad spirit go away, it kills the body as it leaves."

"*No!*"

The man grips Rasputin firmly by the shoulders. "I *could* do nothing," he says, his own voice cracking, "but it wouldn't be Dmitri. It would never be your brother. It would be a monster, and it would kill and kill again to gain more strength, more power. Maria was just the first. If we don't perform the exorcism, it will say anything—*do* anything—to claim five more souls. And then I wouldn't be *able* to make it leave. A demon that murders six within the cycle of one moon is invincible."

The boy wrests himself from his father's arms and backs away, sobbing. "No! I don't want the books! I don't want the ring! They're Dmitri's; he's the oldest!"

"Son," says the old man.

"*They're Dmitri's!*" the boy screams. He bolts out of the house into the dark woods, sobbing. I watch the shadows gather behind him, until he's disappeared entirely.

Then I hear footsteps behind me. I turn and find a thin, reedy man, also wearing wet, roughly sewn clothes, solemnly standing in the doorway, a knitted cap in his hands.

"Should I find him?" he asks softly.

"Let him go, Nachiel. He needs time," says the old man with a quavering voice. "And we have a long, hard night ahead of us."

He reaches for one of the jars, slowly pinches out what looks like a bit of black ash, and bends over Dmitri, using his thumb to spread a thick line across the boy's forehead.

Suddenly Dmitri awakens with a howling scream. His eyes bulge, and his body begins to seize wildly, straining against the straps that bind him. Nachiel quietly shuts the door behind him.

The man opens one of the calfskin books. "Let us begin."

A hand reaches out for my arm, startling me, and I turn to see Poe behind me, her eyes fierce with a burning, luminous intensity. She leans in toward me and softly whispers in my ear.

"*Say my name.*"

The words hang like vapor, then burst into flakes of snow, creating a whirlwind—a blinding white arctic storm that stings my face and my eyes. Poe grips my arm so tightly that it feels like she could break the bone.

But I pull hard against her. "No," I want to say. "I need to know what happens next. If the boy survives."

But then I remember what I learned from the book *Rasputin: Mad Monk or Mystic Prophet?*

He doesn't.

———

Poe hasn't let me go, and now she's shaking my arm furiously, as if she's hoping to dislodge it from its socket. I open my eyes to the cold remains of a fire, charred logs, and curled, black pieces of paper. The room is freezing or a couple of degrees below, and a thin veil of early morning light is just starting to creep through the front window.

"*Dimitri,*" says Lisa in a hollow voice.

Oh, it's Lisa shaking me awake.

"What?" I grumble.

I look over—Lisa grips her cell tightly; her hand visibly trembles. Her lips are a straight line, pressed so tightly together they've turned white.

"What?" I ask again, more softly.

Lisa closes the phone with a snap, her face pale.

There is, of course, only one question. "Who died?"

"They found Nate," says Lisa, her eyes starting to tear. "In the alley behind the *Eagle*. At least they found most of him . . . but his head . . ."

She can't finish the sentence.

CHAPTER TWENTY-ONE: MAGIC SQUARE

First Lisa, then Elizabeth tries to talk me out of going back to New Goshen, but I know what I have to do—although *know* might be somewhat of an overstatement. But it was leaked to the press that a series of numbers were scrawled on Maddy's and Nate's backs, which means that there will probably be two more murders, bringing the death toll to six. I need to get my hands on whatever Ernest has managed to translate. I'm a believer now that Daniel or this Sorath is coming for me.

Either way he's too late. Because now I'm coming for him.

Lisa pensively leans against the hood of my Mustang. She's barely spoken three words to me since I firmly told her I was going, no room for debate. She's wearing jeans and just the sweatshirt from the night before, and she pulls the arms over her hands to keep them warm.

"You'll keep your cell on?"

The barest of nods. Lisa squints hard at the frozen lake, trying to ice me into making a different decision.

I quickly lean in and kiss a cold cheek.

Nada. I don't exist.

"You'll be safe here," I say quietly. "He has no idea where you—"

Lisa raises her hand. "We don't talk about that."

The curtain called Daniel once again falls between us. But there is one more thing I have to say, just in case. "I kinda borrowed your mom's gun. It's in the glove compartment. I'd feel better if you had it."

Now Lisa glares at me. If looks *could* kill, my heart would be flatlining.

I swallow.

Lisa reaches into her sweatshirt pocket and pulls out a small cardboard box, tossing it to me. "Probably would be more useful with an ammunition clip, don't you think?"

Ammunition. *Right.* And then the realization strikes me. "You knew."

"Stealing the gun without the bullets was a bit of a giveaway. Very amateur. You take the Glock—I've got the Taser and I'm better with a shotgun anyways."

"Shotgun?"

"You didn't really think there was a guitar in that guitar case, did you?"

God, I love this woman.

So it is a shard in my heart when she just walks away as I start the engine, not even turning back for one last wave. But then it's pretty clear, even though Lisa won't—maybe can't—admit it that she thinks Daniel is the killer. Which means she just gave me a loaded gun I might use to kill her brother.

A hard trade.

I try not to wonder how—if ever—she'll forgive me.

———

New Goshen is a ghost town. I drive past the deserted Goodwill, past empty garage structures, past Sacred Heart Collectibles, Giovanni's Liquor, and E-Z Pawn and Loan. All have CLOSED signs. Only one homeless man shuffles down the street, and he glances nervously as I pass by, grips his shopping cart tighter.

The only real signs of life are the news vans lined up in front of the *Eagle*, with white satellite dishes and national television news logos. Three reporters stand on the sidewalk being filmed as I pass, and even more crews are placing parking cones on the street, setting up lights and tripods, their equipment connected by thick cables to a large generator that rumbles from the back of a massive diesel truck. A few locals are cashing in with hastily set up folding tables and handwritten signs, like "COFFEE & DONUTS 4 SALE, TWO DOLLARS" and "NEW GOSHEN MURDER MAPS." In the back of my mind I can see the television executives in corporate offices with city views, calculating all the advertising cash this horror show will rake in, like Mac after the first murder. News is just news until it happens to you. Then it's tragedy.

Obviously Ernest's not at work today, and what with the offices at the *Eagle* being cordoned off with yellow tape, he probably won't be there tomorrow, either. More than a minor snag—Ernest has the books, but I don't have Ernest. I didn't *exactly* make friends with my coworkers—my YouTube posting of last year's disastrous office Christmas party didn't add to my popularity, which reminds me that there *is* one coworker who might know where Ernest is, plus I've been to his house.

Mac.

To save money, the *Eagle* held the Christmas party at Mac's house, and after Nate spiked the eggnog, Myrna sang Madonna's "Like a Virgin" for the karaoke portion of the festivities, writhing on the floor with the microphone trapped between her ample thighs. But one of Mac's many threats has always been that he's memorized our home addresses, so that if we give him any shit, he'll know where to throw the Molotov cocktail. If anyone knows Ernest's address, it's Mac.

I find Mac's two-story saltbox home, gray with white shutters, but there's a cop standing watch outside. New Goshen must now have the highest cop-to-citizen ratio in the country. I keep driving, trying to look inconspicuous, like that's possible in a normally quiet suburban neighborhood that's now deathly quiet—everyone's gone. I park around the corner, open the car door, and step out onto the sidewalk for a moment.

Take the gun, yes or no?

OBITUARY WRITER STRANGLED BY GRIEVING FATHER

Better safe than sorry.

I slip the gun into my jacket pocket, briskly cross the street, and scale a low brick wall into the backyard of an empty Colonial. I jog across the lawn, a light scattering of snow crunches beneath my feet, and then pry apart a boxwood hedge. The pine branches pull at my jacket and scratch my face as I step through into Mac's backyard. All the lights in the house are on even though the sun is shining.

I knock on the sliding glass door.

A figure shuffles into view. God, Mac looks old. He squints at me, wearing a thin flannel bathrobe and old leather slippers. There's a start of gray, stubbly five-o'clock shadow on his chin, and in his right hand is a shot glass filled with amber liquid that slops over the side as he slides the door open.

"Dimitri, myy boyy," he slurs. "Kind of you to drop by. Even in this ungodly hour. Come in, come in."

"I'm sorry about—"

"Have a drink," he says. "Itz a drinkin' kind of morning, if you know what I mean. But you do, dontcha, son? Two dead parents, you not even out of college." He stares at a spot in the carpet and looks lost for what to say next.

"Sure," I say. "I'll have that drink."

He claps me on my shoulder, and I follow him into the kitchen. There's a sad attempt at some scrambled eggs burnt in a pan.

"Whatz your drink, son?"

"Whatever you're having."

He raises his glass to me. "Smart boy. I've broken out the Elijah Craig for breakfast. You a bourbon man?"

"I can be."

"Right you arrrre," he says, pouring and slightly missing the plastic cup. "All out of clean glasses. Nate was supposed to do the washup yesterday." He hands the drink to me, and I take a sip. Liquid fire pours down my throat, and I start to cough.

"Takez some getting used to." He swirls the ice in his glass reflectively. "Dark days, my son, dark days."

A slight alcoholic buzz starts. I need to get what I came for before I'm forced to drink the whole thing. "I'm sorry about Nate, Mac. I really am."

Mac's eyes tear up, and his voice is thick when he says "Nice of you to say. I know you two didn't always see eye to eye." He pauses for a moment, takes a sip. "What kinda sick bastard would kill a kid like Nate? And do what he *did*. I juss can't, I can't . . ."

The words hang, then fade into silence. Mac swirls the ice in his highball glass again; it makes a light tinkling sound. "Shit. Do you think itz that psycho brother?"

I pause. "Yes."

"Shit," says Mac.

A longer pause this time. "God, I remember when that happened, when Daniel tried to kill his sister. What a sick fuck. They should have electrocuted that motherfucker. Thatz what they did in the old days with evil motherfuckers. Fried them. Now they have more rights than regular tax-paying folks." He pounds the table with his fist, and his voice breaks. "Itz not *right*. Itz not fuckin' right."

There's a clock in the kitchen, one of those fifties black-and-white Kit-Cat clocks; its wide bubble eyes move back and forth to the tick of each passing second, like it's looking for something, someone. I need to move this along—quickly.

"Mac, I know this isn't good timing. In fact, it's really bad, awful timing. But I need Ernest's address. Do you know where he lives?"

"Ernest, why you askin' about Ernest?" asks Mac suspiciously.

"It's . . . complicated."

"Just funny you ask," says Mac. "Nate was excited about somethin'. Said he was onto a big story. Said I'd be impressed."

"What kind of a story?"

"Christ," says Mac, taking a long sip from his glass. "Fuck if I know. Somethin' about these old books and Rasputin. He overheard Ernest talking about it in The Stacks."

Ernest? The Stacks? I remember that Nate had left the office the day I came to give Myrna my condolences and talk to Ernest, but I thought he'd gone outside for a smoke. Had he been hiding out in The Stacks? Did he eavesdrop on our conversation? Christ.

"Thatz all he really wanted, for me to be proud of him. And I never told him. Never." Mac covers his eyes with his hand and his shoulders shake with grief.

"He knew," I say, the only thing I can think of.

A bitter laugh. "Thatz sweet of you, kid. But no, he didn't. I may be drunk, but I'm not that drunk. Give me another bottle of bourbon and maybe I'll agree with you."

"Mac," I say quietly, "the address?"

He shrugs his shoulders. "Beats the shit out of me."

"Oh," I say, trying to hide my disappointment. "I thought, you know . . . you memorized our addresses . . ."

"The Molotov cocktails bit? I don't mean half the shit I say, kid."

"Right," I say hollowly. *Now what?*

Mac swallows, looks to the floor. "If you want to go to Nate's room, pay your respects . . . it's upstairs, first room on the right. Don't worry about waking up the wife; she's taken enough Valium to down an elephant."

"Sure, Mac, I'd love to." If Nate was working on a story about Ernest, maybe he's got an address written down. A long shot, but then I'm fresh out of other ideas. I leave Mac in the kitchen dully staring into the bottom of his plastic cup, accompanied only by the lonesome sound of the Kit-Cat clock tick-ticking away.

——

Nate's room. Barbells in the corner. A calendar on the wall with a voluptuous model in a white bikini—she reclines on the hood of a red Corvette, her blond hair cascading over the grille while she arches her back, seductively holding a finger to her red lips. A twin-sized bed, simple oak, with crumpled black sheets and a white and navy-blue plaid comforter. Crude shelves nailed to the wall hold an assortment of empty beer cans, each a different label, and the stink of old beer and unwashed gym socks makes me want to crack open a window, but I can't without attracting the attention of the police officer outside.

But there's also a desk, which must have been far too small for his muscular body, and a manual typewriter. Nearby is a mesh trash can full of crumpled paper. On the desk sits a thick dictionary—it looks well used. Also a copy of *The Elements of Style*. I gently unfold the first folded ball at the top of the pile.

It's a crossword puzzle. There are quite a few erased letters—he got most of the words wrong the first time—but it's complete. The next folded ball is also a completed crossword puzzle. Which is strange, because his biggest complaint about my writing was the long words I used. On the third crumpled ball I find notes in the margins, neat handwriting that's easily recognizable—Ernest's. Maybe he was working with Nate, because the next page appears to be a vocabulary list: "precipitous," "equivocate," "unction," "obdurate," "rubescent." Maybe that's why he'd gone down to The Stacks in the first place: not to eavesdrop but to learn.

Christ, Nate was trying. He was really trying to be a better editor.

The very idea collapses my legs from beneath me, and I drop to the floor, my back sliding against the wall. Blood rushes to my head; I can feel it pounding thickly—and a visceral heat, a burning rage, starts to roil in my stomach. I reach into my pocket for the gun. The cool, smooth handle feels heavy, and good.

Then I catch a glimpse of a slip of paper that has fallen behind his desk. I reach out, unfold it, and find a handwritten note scribbled with the blood-red Sharpie I'm so used to seeing on my copy.

Ernest. 125 East Elm Street. 4 P.M. Bring the smokes.

I jam the paper in my back pocket and race out the door.

———

The Cape Cod homes on East Elm Street are small and simply kept; a few have gables, and all of them have neat stamps of front lawn. The towering elm trees are old and big. Their thick branches create an arch and cast spotted shadows on the recently shoveled sidewalks. But the street is completely deserted; not a single car in a driveway or a barking dog—not even a cat in a windowsill.

What if Ernest's gone too?

I step on the gas, passing by 130 East Elm Street—empty; 128 East Elm Street—empty; until I see 125, the only Cape on the street with wooden shingles. I sigh with relief when I see that under a white metal carport is a light blue Prius, its trunk open. I pull over to the side of the road and watch for a moment.

Ernest comes out the green front door, trying to heft a cat carrier into the backseat. He slips, and I jump out of the car and jog over, worried he could break a hip. But as soon as he sees me, his eyes grow wide with terror and he almost drops the cat; it yowls a complaint as it slams against the wire screen. Maybe Ernest thinks I could be the killer.

"Here," I say, ignoring the fear in his eyes and grabbing the handle of the cat carrier. "Let me help you with that."

Ernest's lip trembles, and he nervously glances at his front door.

This is just plain *ridiculous*. "Ernest, do I really look like the spleen-eating type?"

"And what, pray tell, *does* the spleen-eating type look like?" asks Ernest.

"Seriously, Ernest, if half a century of smoking hasn't killed you yet, I don't think a serial killer has a chance."

He gives just a hint of a smile. "Lung cancer I could handle," he says. "Let's just say the beheading got my attention."

"Well, when I murder you I'll be sure to remember that. No beheading, I promise. But where should I stab you first? Do you have any preferences?"

Ernest sighs wearily. "Smart ass. Get the cat—I don't want Herman to freeze to death in the car. And come inside. I have something for you."

Suddenly I get a prickly feeling, like someone's watching. I quickly look up and down the street—no one's there. Maybe it's the quiet that feels wrong; it's like a neutron bomb has hit—all the people are gone but the buildings still stand.

I grab the cat carrier (Herman is a victim of too much kibble largesse—the damn thing must weigh about sixty pounds) and follow Ernest into the house. I'm immediately struck by the sheer quantity of books. Shelves line the hallway and the small living room. There are even shelves built into the wall by the stairway, all stuffed with hard and softcover books, each looking well read, with cracked and sun-faded spines.

"It's a good thing we don't get earthquakes," I say. "You'd be buried alive."

Ernest chuckles and crouches down to let Herman out from his cage. "Some people have children. I have books. Much more interesting and they never ask me for money."

We watch for a moment as Herman waddles over to a spot on the carpet and starts to lick at his long gray fur.

"No," continues Ernest, "the biggest danger here is fire, of course. This place would go up in about five, ten minutes tops." He says this with no regret, as if that were an interesting possibility he might entertain just to see if he is right or not.

"So you said you had something for me. The translations?"

"Yes . . . well," says Ernest, and instantly his smile fades. He gestures me into his living room awkwardly and says, "Here, sit." The only place I can see is an ottoman covered with books, which I gently place on the floor: *Greek–English Lexicon of the New Testament: Based on Semantic Domains*; *Dialogue Concerning the Two Chief World Systems*; *Thus Spake Zarathustra*.

"A little light reading?" I call out. I can hear him puttering about in the hallway. There's an antique rolltop desk across from the otto-man where I'm sitting, but before I can snoop, Ernest shuffles back into the room with a paper Stop & Shop bag in hand.

"There was a day when writers actually *read*," he grumbles. "They could quote Keats and Socrates. Now anyone with a keyboard and a fifth-grade education can call themselves a writer."

I feel this slight is pointed at me in particular, but I don't take the bait. Instead I politely wait as he settles in a dusty green armchair next to the desk. He gently pulls out the leather-bound book, then the velvet-wrapped pages, and hands them to me.

"You should burn these," he states matter-of-factly.

I'm shocked. Ernest, obvious bibliophile who actually sniffs books like an addict, is advocating I go *Fahrenheit 451* on them?

"Why?"

"Why indeed," says Ernest mildly, as if he's trying to remember himself. He lifts the knees of his pant legs and then leans back in his chair, crossing a leg. "I don't know how it happened, but I'm an old man, Dimitri. I was born in 1921—just after the First World War; the Great War they called it, as if any war could be great. But when I was about your age, I couldn't wait to sign up for the second one, the war that would end all wars. I'd heard the horror stories, but to be honest, that wasn't why I went. You see, I had naïve ideas about heroism, valor, and honor. And I didn't want to miss my *chance* to prove myself."

I can't help but note a tone of bitter irony at the word "chance."

"And I got it, all right. Boy, did I get it." He pushes up his left sleeve, and what I see stuns me. A straight line of numbers tattooed in faded blue ink, the exact color of the blue veins I can see through his translucent skin.

"My plane was shot down over Poland. Not many survived the camp. And what I saw . . . Well, what I saw will be the stuff of my nightmares until the day I die. You can't possibly comprehend what a place like that turns you into. What I did to survive. It took decades for me to forgive myself."

For a moment he seems to drift away, and a shadow falls across his face. A hushed quiet hangs between us until he smiles grimly. "'Beware that, when fighting monsters, you yourself do not become a monster . . . for when you gaze long into the abyss, the abyss gazes also into you.' That's Nietzsche again, by the way. Knew his stuff, that man."

"I thought you said you weren't a philosopher."

"I'm not anymore. I like to take things as they are these days. Wake up, eat my oatmeal, feed the cat. Simple things. Living under the shadow of pure and unadulterated evil has that effect. But reading these books of yours, well, I got excited again by ideas, by new possibilities . . . until I started to get the distinct impression that these books were somehow reading *me*. And it felt like I was living under that shadow again."

"I'm not sure I understand—"

"You don't need to. And you don't want to. Just leave it alone. Move on. Be a young man with a pure conscience. Have a happy life."

I mentally replay the scene from the night before, sitting by the fire eating lukewarm beans with Elizabeth, Amelia, and Lisa. How even there I felt like I was on the outside looking in. I pensively play with the ring on my finger. "Maybe happy lives are for other people. Other families."

"'Happy families are all alike; every unhappy family is unhappy in its own way.' Tolstoy."

I meet Ernest's eye. "You want to know where I got this ring? My father. Of course, he didn't bother explaining what it meant."

"Maybe your father didn't want you to know. Maybe he thought you were better off *not* knowing."

I'm momentarily stunned into silence. I can feel all my memories suddenly reshuffling themselves, trying to reshape themselves from this new perspective—his distance, his silence, the almost militant absence from my life. How delightful it would be to think that it was somehow all for my benefit, that he was trying to protect me from some great danger. A part of me would like to believe it but can't.

"Too bad he never mentioned that," I say with a bitterness that surprises even me.

Ernest sighs deeply.

"Are you saying you didn't translate them?"

"I translated what I could in the time I had. I'm a scholar," says Ernest grimly. "You give a scholar an unpublished esoteric book by a famous historical figure, and they're going to translate it. Over in the desk you'll find a journal."

I stand slowly and walk over to the desk, rolling up the top. Sitting on a leather ink blotter is a gray linen-covered journal. Ernest reaches down, and I'm amazed that he's able to lift Herman to his lap; I'd have thought the weight would dislocate a few discs in his lower back. He doesn't look at me while I flip through the pages.

I read the first line. Ernest's handwriting is neat and precise. "The man has now become like one of us, knowing good and evil. He must not be allowed to reach out his hand and take also from the Tree of Life and eat, and live forever. (Genesis 3:22)"

The room seems to shift slightly then, and for a surreal moment I wonder if I'm just dreaming, that I could be asleep but don't know it.

"This isn't possible," I mutter. I turn the page and find a neat table of contents that gives me pause:

"Apparently the death curse works best with the blood of a newborn baby burned in its placenta," says Ernest coolly, stroking Herman.

"Are you serious?"

"There's some interesting mention of spleens as well. The epicurean human organ of choice for demons. Apparently makes them more resistant to exorcism. By the way, your *Book of Fiends* is missing quite a few pages. The ones dealing with exorcism, judging from the table of contents."

For a moment I'm speechless. Possibly a first in the life of Dimitri Petrov.

"But it's not—it can't be *real.*"

"Whether it's real or someone believes it's real, what does it matter? Look at this." He holds out his tattooed arm for my inspection.

My heart clenches. The first row of a grid I've become all too familiar with.

6 32 3 34 35 1

"Interesting, wouldn't you say? Ever seen them before?"

"Yes," I whisper.

"Are you feeling all right? Your face just went a little pale there."

I swallow and try to center myself. "Define all right."

"Yes, well," continues Ernest, "according to my translation, these numbers are the first row of what the books call a magic square. Each magic square represents a demon or angelic spirit. So let's see how your math education pans out—add up these numbers and what do you get?"

Focus. I do the math quickly. "It's one hundred and eleven." A strange low humming begins to vibrate through the room, rising up from the floorboards. Although Ernest doesn't sense it, Herman apparently does. The cat leaps to the floor and frantically scoots behind a bookshelf.

"I haven't seen him move that fast in a decade," says Ernest. "One hundred and eleven is the summation for that *row.* But look at the whole table. I flagged it for you."

Quickly, with a trembling hand, I turn to the page he's marked with a Post-it.

Impossible. I add up the rows once, twice, three times to be sure. What I'm thinking could not be possible. "Six hundred and sixty-six."

"Puts the whole 'evil empire' in a new perspective, doesn't it? Not many know that Hitler was intrigued by occult notions. I had the distinct misfortune to be a part of an experimental control group. Now I wonder if they were scientific experiments, or . . . the other kind."

"But how—"

"Who knows, maybe it's all just a strange, random coincidence; life is full of those. Or maybe not. Either way, I'm taking it as a sign to leave it alone. I strongly suggest you do the same."

My heart begins to beat erratically. "So let's say, *completely* theoretically, someone used this book and conjured a demon. Why would anyone want to do that?"

"*Theoretically,* you could make it do things—your bidding, so to speak. If you had the strength and ability to control it."

"And if you didn't?"

"Then I imagine it would control you."

A dark chill shudders down my spine, and I hope to God that somehow the real Daniel is not aware of what his possessed body is doing. I can't imagine recovering from that kind of horror.

"How do you do . . . the whole exorcism part?"

"Like I said, those pages were missing. Ask a priest," says Ernest irritably while slowly getting to his feet. "I think I've done enough here. And I still have packing to do, young man, so, if you'll excuse me . . ."

"Ernest, you have to tell me—"

He waves a hand dismissively. "I should have been on the road an hour ago."

Reluctantly I stand up, slipping the journal into the paper grocery bag. "So the second book . . ."

"The second book is all about how to fight the monsters." He pats me genially on the shoulder while unmistakably also walking me to the door. "Good luck with that. Now I am going to search for my cat and try to coax him back into the carrier. It's not an easy task. He hates that thing; makes him think he's going to the veterinarian."

He opens the door pointedly. "No offense."

"None taken." I step over the threshold. Thick, darkening clouds now cover the sky, like the mother of all storms is about to hit. And before he can shut the door in my face, I add, "Thanks, Ernest. I really mean that, honestly."

Ernest slumps slightly and seems to age a decade before my eyes. He glances nervously over his shoulder, as if he too feels someone might be watching, then leans in and says quietly in a rush, "Theoretically, if all this *is* real, then you'd need to conjure a seraph, or angelic being . . ."

My mind immediately flits to the dream—Nachiel, the good spirit's name was Nachiel.

"Because if this . . . *demon* exists, it will use anything and anyone to try to control *you*. Both books make that clear." Then he grips my arm tightly. "When the abyss looks at you, it wants to draw you in. Become *like* it. Understand?"

"I'm not sure . . ."

He lets go of me. "Just don't lose sight of who *you* are. Like I did."

And with that he swiftly shuts the door.

I stand for a moment on the cement front porch, clutching the paper grocery bag in my right hand. I have stepped past surreal into something the word "supernatural" doesn't seem broad enough to cover.

Of course, if anyone probably knows how to exorcise a supernatural being, it'd be a supernatural being.

Good thing I know exactly where to find one.

———

It takes a few minutes of jiggling with the key and muttered swearing before the bolt unlocks. But when the door swings open to my crappy apartment, I'm momentarily stunned. It looks like it was hit by the proverbial tornado.

The couch is on its side, torn to pieces, piss-yellow stuffing scattered across the floor. Every drawer from the kitchen cabinet is open or tossed aside. The one lamp that still worked is broken, *more* glass on the floor, and the egg-shaped chair—*Christ*, the egg-shaped chair looks like someone has taken an ax to it: the amber plastic is shattered into spidery cracks, like a broken windshield. I drop the grocery bag on the floor and walk through it all in a daze, cataloging the damage. Who the hell could have done this?

Right. My non-rent-paying supernatural roomie.

"Goddamn it!" I roughly shove the couch over, back into place. "I told you to leave my fucking stuff alone!" Poltergeist bitch from hell.

I stride over to the fridge to see what she's got to say for herself, but the magnets are scattered wildly and randomly on the floor—no message.

Then I notice that the refrigerator door itself is open, barely.

Ketchup leaks onto the floor.

But it's not ketchup; a part of me knows that. Ketchup isn't so runny. Ketchup isn't such a dark red color. Ketchup doesn't drip in small, perfectly rounded drops.

I take a breath. Pull the handle.

Nate's head is perched on the top plastic shelf. It stares at me blindly with opaque, runny eyes. His mouth is open. On his purple swollen tongue is an antique postcard, a sepia print of a mansion I'm all too familiar with.

Greetings from Aspinwall.

A small black fly has landed on it. Suddenly the fly jumps away, buzzing up Nate's left nostril.

Daniel was here.

CHAPTER TWENTY-TWO: NIGHT VISION

Why oh why isn't Lisa answering her cell phone? My heart is racing as I peel through the streets, blowing through red lights and stop signs. And the postcard in Nate's mouth—oh, God, the postcard—with a note written on the back in a familiar script which turns my stomach.

catch me if you can

And I can't shake the feeling that the boundary between dreams, reality, and nightmares is blurring. It wasn't a dream, this race—or it *was*, but now it's real, it's crept into my waking life, and I'm obviously *losing*. I'm too slow, too stupid—*fuck*, why didn't my father tell me about all this shit? Good people are dying, and I'm like some dumb kid in the classroom; Daniel's always five steps ahead of me.

My cell phone buzzes in my pocket. I yank out my phone. I see the number, and a wave of sickening relief washes over me. *Finally* Lisa.

"For Christ's sake, Lisa, where the hell have you been?"

"Dimitri?" asks a quivering voice. "Is that you?"

Not Lisa. Elizabeth.

"Yes," I say, "yes, it's me. What's wrong?"

"Is she with you? Please tell me she's with you."

Fear stops my heart. "What do you mean? She's not there?"

"Oh God oh God oh God," says Elizabeth in a rush.

"You're sure?" I ask quickly. "You're sure she's not there? She's not upstairs—"

"I've looked. I've looked everywhere. I thought maybe she went for a walk—but there are bootprints, Dimitri. A man's."

"Okay," I say, trying to keep my voice calm for her while I almost rip my hair out with my left hand. Fuck. Fuck. *Fuck.* "Call the police, okay? Right now, and have them call me. I'll leave my cell on—"

"Dimitri, I can't lose her—"

"You won't. *We* won't. Just do what I say, okay? I'm going to look for her."

"Oh God," she says in a small voice. But she gathers herself. "I'll call them. I'll call them right now. But find her, Dimitri. *Find* her."

Click.

I slam the dashboard five times with my fist, almost break my hand, but it feels good, the pain. It feels good.

———

I miss the Aspinwall entrance the first time I drive by. I have to stop and backtrack before I find it again. Encroaching shadows obscure the front gate, like it doesn't want to be found; like the wild underbrush has finally taken over and reclaimed it. I pull over to the side of the road and open the car door. All is quiet and still. There's a thick metal padlock on the rusting gate, so I do the most convenient thing, which is to grab the gun and shoot the motherfucker. This feels good too.

I jump back into the Mustang and screech down the Aspinwall driveway, running over fallen tree limbs and bits of overgrown weeds. I swear, once I find Lisa I'm going to burn the place down myself, and whatever's left after that I'm going to knock down with a bulldozer. I want to kill this house, *murder* it if such a thing is possible. I'm driving so fast that the car slides when I hit the brakes, and I come close to hitting one of the columns at the entry.

"Lisa!" I shout as I open the car door.

Nothing. Silence. Not a bird, not a sound, not even a tree limb overhead moves. Everything is as still as death itself. Then my eyes fall on a strange spot of color by the door—a red Maglite.

Just like the one I saw Lisa with.

My heart clenches. "Lisa!"

No response. I grip the gun in my right hand and cautiously approach the door, half expecting Daniel to open it for me. But he doesn't. In fact the door seems to be locked, so I pick up the flashlight, hold it over the gun (another little trick I picked up from watching cop shows), and then kick it in. This also feels good.

"Lisa!"

Only my voice echoes in the cavernous entry. It feels much darker than the last time I was here. I flash the light through the chandelier, and something small scurries away—a mouse or a large cockroach; it's impossible to tell. I step into the hall, and the floor creaks beneath me. Dust swirls in the beam of the flashlight, and it all looks exactly the same—or almost the same, because there's a thin layer of snow dusting the floor where the roof opens up to the sky. And there are footprints. With dragged, scuffled marks.

I take another careful step forward and flash the light into the living room—there's the dark hole that opened up under Maddy, along with a couple of empty beer cans, probably Nate's. And then something else—a dark gray lump. I flash the beam across it and discover Nate's famous night-vision camera.

"Daniel! I know you're here!"

Nothing.

Slowly, like I'm walking on ice, I test the floor before each step until I'm close enough to the camera that I can reach out for the strap with my foot, pull it to me. It's dusty and the lens is scratched, but when I hit the power button, the red light comes on. Do I push PLAY? Do I want to know?

I push PLAY.

A greenish-gray image comes into view. It's out of focus, and at first all I can see is what looks like a chair in the Aspinwall basement; to the right is the skanky mattress on the floor, with the candles in the wine bottles, still unlit. But then the focus adjusts and I can see something move on the chair—someone's tied to it. I hear a muffled sobbing.

Lisa? I grip the camera tighter, hold my breath.

A shadow lights one of the candles, and then I can see that it's not Lisa in the chair, it's a man, but I still can't see his face, because his head droops over his chest. Off-camera is a scratching sound, then a hiss. The man whimpers, but he doesn't struggle against the ropes tying him to the chair, as if he's already given up, given in.

"Now," says a voice, high and reedy. "Are you ready?"

The man nods his head dully and raises his head.

Nate. His eyes bulge with wide-eyed terror, and his mouth is covered with duct tape.

"Good," says the voice. Then a tall, thin man comes into view that I immediately recognize from my dreams and from Lisa's pictures. Daniel. He wears black jeans and a thin white T-shirt. Although the temperature must be freezing, he doesn't look cold. In fact, his movements are remarkably easy, relaxed, almost clinically detached.

He briskly rips the tape from Nate's mouth. Nate reels back in pain. Daniel casually crumples the tape in a ball and tosses it to the corner.

"Please," groans Nate. "*Please . . .*"

Daniel ignores him. Instead he crouches down and peers into the camera lens, getting closer. He walks out of the frame and then adjusts the tripod. The camera angle rears up to the wooden ceiling, then back down again, centering Nate exactly. Daniel steps back into the frame again; his head cocks slightly to one side, examining, but he must not be satisfied, because he walks out of the frame again. This time the camera is lifted and moved a few steps closer; everything goes fuzzy as the autofocus readjusts. The zoom rushes in, rushes out.

"Still not right," he says.

Nate's lips tremble as Daniel steps up behind him, grabs the chair roughly by the back, and then brutally shoves the chair forward. The autofocus clicks in, and I can now see the gash on Nate's forehead; dark blood drips down his cheek.

Daniel approaches the camera, apparently checking the viewfinder.

"Better," he says quietly.

"Please . . ."

"I heard you the first time," says Daniel coolly. The camera pans slowly from the gaping wound to Nate's terrified eyes. A trickle of sweat dripping down his forehead glistens in the candlelight.

"Think we can do this in one take?"

"I don't want—"

"What you want or don't want is irrelevant. Now, like we practiced."

Nate swallows. "The sins—"

"*For* the sins, Nate. Christ, can't you get anything right?"

Nate's eyes roll back in his head like he's about to pass out. Daniel strides over to him, grabs the collar of his jacket, and slaps him across the face—hard.

"For the sins of your fathers," blurts Nate.

"For the sins of your fathers," repeats Daniel calmly.

"You, though guiltless . . ."

"Though guiltless."

"Must suffer."

The word "suffer" dissipates into silence, and then Nate starts to sob in earnest. I cover my mouth with my hand. This can't be happening. It can't.

Daniel claps Nate enthusiastically on the shoulder, like a parent rewarding a child who just hit a home run. "See, that wasn't so bad, was it?"

Nate's head hangs forward while his shoulders shake.

"I asked you a question," says Daniel with a veneer of threat.

"No!" Nate raises his head and visibly tries to quiet himself enough to say, "No, that wasn't so bad."

Daniel smiles, but his smile isn't real. It's the wicked grin he flashed me in my dream before he ran off to kill my parents. He steps out of the frame, and then there's the sound of something unzipping, like a duffle bag.

"*Nate*," I whisper, like I can somehow warn him, change what I know is coming next. But then he must know it, too, because his eyes grow wide again, and he struggles powerfully against the ropes that bind him.

"*No!*" he screams. "No, you promised, you said . . ."

I watch in horror as Daniel slowly approaches holding a long, slim knife that glints in his pale hand.

Nate uses his feet to kick the chair back, pushing it slightly across the cement floor, but Daniel doesn't seem to notice or care. Instead, he looks directly into the camera—at me, I'm sure. He smiles and cocks his head, like he can step through the lens, like he can hear my rolling, panicking heart.

"I *see* you," he says mockingly, and I pull back as if he can. "I see you. Do you see me?" He jabs the knife at the camera, at *me*, and an ice-cold shiver skitters down my spine.

Nate pants heavily, pushing himself as far away as he can in increments of inches, like there's still a way out.

"Still don't really know how this works, do you?" Daniel continues softly. "You don't know shit and you blame your father, but really, it's your *mother's* fault. Your father didn't tell you anything, because your mother wouldn't let him. All because she thought you'd be safe then, safe from *me*." He chuckles to himself. "And you know, it might have worked. But then you put on the ring, didn't you? *You* opened the door. Extended an invitation."

What is he *talking* about?

"Not that I'm complaining. It's nice to be back. Refreshing." Daniel takes a deep breath and pats the flat blade of the knife idly against his chest, like he's luxuriating in the fresh air. "They're dead now, aren't they? Your parents. Dead and gone, leaving you all alone, helpless and ignorant. So unfair. Because in spite of everything you've been through, you still don't know who your father was, let alone your mother. Poe—that's what you call her, right?—has been giving you hints, I know. She's been a very *naughty* girl. Hard to say what's she's up to though, considering she hates your tribe almost more than I do. Emphasis on *almost*."

Nate's pushed his way out of the viewfinder, and Daniel stops suddenly, looks in his direction. "Nate! You don't *really* think you can get up the stairs tied to a chair?"

"Fuck you!" blubbers Nate. "Fuck you, motherfucker!"

"See," says Daniel, pointing the knife at Nate, like a teacher using a ruler for emphasis. "That's *exactly* what I'm talking about. You people suffer from baseless optimism. You always think there's a way out, but there's not. There's *no* way out. Not for Nate, not for your father, not for me." He turns to the camera, looks at me directly. "Not for *you*." His eyes strike me then, almost make me drop the camera. In the hazy night-vision image I can see that they're deep, empty black orbs—each a complete and absolute abyss.

"We're all just playing a game. We didn't make the rules—those were written by others long gone. Pawns, all of us. If you don't believe me, check the basement. You might just stumble across someone you've come to know *well*." Daniel laughs quietly at this, but I don't get the joke.

Then a dark thought pierces my heart. *Lisa?*

"Nate!" Daniel yells. "Nate!" He watches something offscreen, and there's something feral about the way he stands coiled and ready. I can hear the desperate scraping of the chair being dragged across the floor. Daniel shakes his head. "Crazy-ass people," he mutters. "Nate! C'mon, man, don't be pathetic." With that he tosses the knife in the air with the calm expertise of a juggler; it rotates once, twice, and he catches it easily when it falls. He steps off-camera.

"*Nooo!*" screams Nate. "*Nooo!*"

I lean against the wall, holding on to the camera with trembling hands. This isn't happening, this isn't happening—but it is. Nate screams again, no words this time, just a piercing, chilling screech, which is cut off abruptly by a gurgling, choking sound. Something cracks—the chair, a bone, I don't know. After a few gruesome moments, Daniel reappears in the viewfinder, his mouth and shirt covered with dark blood.

He brings his face close to the lens. Holds up Nate's severed head. "It's nothing personal."

The screen goes black.

———

Fuck, fuck, fuck. I race through the entry, and a floorboard starts to give way beneath me, but I leap over it, launching myself into the kitchen, skidding across something wet and slippery—another dusting of snow. And then there it is—the door to the basement. I brace myself for the scalding knob, but this time it's cool in my hand, the way it should be, and I don't know if this is a good sign or bad.

My stomach reels as soon as I hit the first step—the rails are covered with blood, the stairs are sticky with it—but I charge down into the darkness.

"Lisa!" I scream.

Nothing. Silence.

My solitary flashlight darts frantically over the floor—*God*, there's so much blood. The mattress on the floor is sodden and dark; the cement walls are spattered with it, like the basement has been used for a slaughterhouse. Did they all come here willingly to meet Daniel? Did he trick them into a late-night visit to Aspinwall? Or did he force them here so he could take his time—relish their terror before killing them?

Is he here now?

I cast about in the gloom with my light, but if it's a trap, I don't care. My hand runs over the cool metal of the gun in my jacket. All I need is one good shot, just one.

And then—*there*, the chair, along with the tripod, and near the tripod a massive black duffle bag just like the one Nate brought that Halloween night, which now seems like a lifetime ago. *Fuck* Mac and his stupid-ass assignment—*God*, I wish I'd never come.

"Lisa," I whisper. Nothing but emptiness.

Then it hits me. The well. *You might just stumble across someone you've come to know well.* What if she's there, unconscious but still miraculously alive?

"Christ, Christ, Christ," I whisper as I rip into Nate's bag, hoping his apocalyptic planning includes something I can use. I find black rubber gas masks, along with some roadside flares. I light one of these and toss it on the cement floor—the orange light licks at the blood on the walls, creating an eerie effect. And then, *yes*—there's some bright yellow nylon rope, along with an assortment of climbing hooks, plus two glow sticks and a Mylar blanket, which will come in handy if one of us survives the water and doesn't die of hypothermia. Sweat trickles from my brow in spite of the cold. I take the gear and carefully make my way to the edge of the well. When I get to it, I drop the rope and tentatively flash the light down; it disappears absolutely into quiet blackness.

No one knows I'm here. If I make it down but can't get back out, then these will be my last moments alive. Unless wearing the ring really does make me immortal; not a theory I'd like to test.

"Lisa!"

Nothing but my own voice, a ghostly echo. I have to try. Daniel knew I would.

I find a ceiling beam to tie the rope to and then loop it around, fastening the end tightly with the climbing hook. I tug on the rope twice, hoping it will hold. Then I crack one of the glow sticks, dropping it into the black abyss. It seems to fall in slow motion. It illuminates the slimy bricks on its way down, then there's a faint splash when it hits the dark water below. It's too far to see anything except the green glow as it gently bobs for a moment and then sinks deeper. I take my jacket off, place the gun and Maglite on top of it, and wrap the rope tightly around my waist.

My plan is to try to rappel down, a sick joke because my only experience with climbing was an obstacle course in high school that used thick seafaring ropes with large knots the size of a cat's head. I close my eyes and ignore the panic that is seeping into my chest—every survival instinct I possess is screaming at me that this is a very, *very* bad idea. My mouth fills with the memory of the brackish water, and my lungs suck at the air as if these are my last breaths. I stand at the edge of the well, crack the last glow stick, hold it in my teeth, and give the rope three more good tugs. Then I take the first step over the edge.

My boots slide against the frozen slime on the bricks and the rope burns my hands—the first five feet are a jolting freefall, but then I find a ledge to brace myself against. I adjust my position and slowly make my descent. My warm breath hovers in front of me, a little pocket of mist.

Finally I can see the calm surface of the black water. There's no body floating facedown, but then he could have tied her to something heavy. Maybe's she's at the bottom in the thick silt, floating like a reed in the water. I could still pull myself up and call for help, let the firefighters or rescue workers search with the proper equipment and take the risk, but it would take them too much time to get here. I don't want to wait to know whether Lisa is dead—I don't think I could take it—and if she is there, I should be the one to find her. See her first.

Fuck it.

I unwind my hand from the rope and let myself freefall the next ten feet.

The shock of the cold water knocks all the air out of my lungs. I have to use the rope to pull myself to the surface, where I take a couple of deep, frantic breaths. I put the glow stick back in my mouth and then kick my way back down into the water.

The light from the glow stick is ethereal, and something in my mind switches off the cold. I don't resist it—I let the numbing pain wash over me as I plunge deeper into the darkness, until my hand finally touches the muddy bottom. I dig around in the muck with my glow stick, but nothing's there. Lisa's body isn't there. A wave of relief rushes through me—maybe she's fine, maybe Daniel was just fucking with me—but just as I'm about to pull myself back up to the surface, something small and oddly angular catches my eye. My lungs burn, but I wave my glow stick over it and then gently tug at it with my free hand, creating a cloud of fine silt.

Two horns. A headband of some kind, like a costume prop. And then I see long golden hair entangled in the mud. My hand seems to reach out of its own accord, and as my fingers grasp the hair, I register something else as well, cold and hard—a rock of some kind. Or a bone. I pull it free.

A skull with empty eye sockets. Something flutters now, loosened from the silt—a black ribbon—and when I pull it I discover that it's attached to a black mask. I've seen this before—this mask, these horns. Alice's photograph from that Halloween night at Aspinwall in 1941. And in my dream.

This isn't Lisa's body. It's Khioniya's.

It's Poe.

My glow light suddenly goes out, leaving me in complete and utter darkness. Cold fingers that I am expecting grip my leg fiercely, pulling me down. But this time I don't resist. This time I let her take me.

I am ready. It's time for me to see.

CHAPTER TWENTY-THREE: SÉANCE

There's the rumble of an engine, and then a flash of light as a shiny Packard rolls by. I'm standing in the circular driveway of Aspinwall. Carved jack-o'-lanterns glow from either side of the front entrance, and for a moment I watch as the partygoers mill about the lawn: New Goshen's rich and famous, circa 1940. Each wears an elaborate costume. It must be Halloween, the night of the murders. There goes Zorro—he's lost his mask and is chatting up a mermaid. A knight in full armor clangs about awkwardly, his sword catching the dress of a Greek goddess and causing her to spill her wine on an Elizabethan lord. A woman dressed as Little Red Riding Hood leans against the doorway, where she takes a lazy drag on a cigarette, looking straight through me.

She also doesn't seem to notice the dripping, ghostly figure standing right behind her. As soon as I do, Poe turns, disappearing inside the foyer.

After a breath I follow.

Once I'm inside I have to stop for a moment, because what I see is absolutely stunning. I've only been in the great hall of Aspinwall long after it was ruined by weather and neglect, but tonight it looks like a castle, a true home for royalty. The chandelier is sparkling, and the mahogany staircase is polished to a high shine, as are the wooden floors. The Italianate frescos, now blighted by mold and mildew, are bright and airy, something you'd see in Venice painted by a master.

Dimitri. A cold whisper.

Watery footprints appear on the floor, a trail to follow. But I know where we're going. Time seems to slow as I wind through the crowd, past a woman dressed as Marie Antoinette, past a pencil-mustached man wearing a large sombrero, past a vampire chatting up a medieval princess, past a clown. I push through swinging doors into the bustling kitchen, unnoticed by a cook in a white starched apron intensely carving a beef roast and the waiters loading up silver trays with fluted champagne glasses. The "baby criminal" sits in the corner, well hidden under a table. He furtively pulls out a cracker from a saltine tin, obviously famished, and the Roman nose is unmistakable. A. Bennet—he must be Lisa and Daniel's artistic grandfather, Archibald. I wonder how he gets a hold of the *Fiends* grimoire?

But that's not what I'm here for. I glance over at the door to the basement. The footprints disappear behind it.

I find that at least the stairs are in better shape than the last time I went down them, and they aren't covered with blood—a serious improvement. And while the Aspinwall basement is still cold and vast, there are wooden shelves filled with jars of preserves, cases of wine and champagne, chopped wood for the numerous fireplaces. It feels *inhabited*.

A round card table has been placed in the center of the cavernous room. There's a silver candelabra with thin, tapering white candles that give off a warm, flickering light. Around the table sits a bizarre cast of characters, as though extras from multiple genres of MGM films have gathered for some kind of smoke break. Not only is Khioniya here, alive and wearing her mask and demon horns, but the séance is attended by Little Bo Peep, Zorro, a Roman soldier wearing a metal breastplate and loincloth, the Tin Man, and two identical pale geisha with red, vibrant lips. Amelia holds court in a stunning Mardi Gras gown. She turns her head, and one of the feathers brushes through the flame of the candle, almost catches on fire.

"Oh no!" she cries, snatching it off quickly and throwing it on the floor.

And for the first time I see her face—shock freezes me instantly in place. Holy mother of God, this isn't possible—this can't be *possible*.

Because it's my mother's face.

She laughs then, a high, tinkling laugh I remember so well. It's a sound that pierces my heart, reverberates through my rib cage like a drum. I want to drop to the floor; I want to cover my ears; I want to disappear like a ghost.

"*You must see.*" Poe lurks in the shadow under the stairs.

"A close call," says the Tin Man cheerfully, stomping on the smoldering mask.

"Mom?" I gasp.

She can't hear me. Christ, she can't hear me.

Suddenly Khioniya moans dramatically. Her eyes roll in the back of her head, and she whispers, "These be the symbols and the names of the creator, which can bring terror and fear unto you. Obey me then, Sorath, by the power of these holy names and by these mysterious symbols of the secret of secrets."

Oh *shit*. Did she just say Sorath?

Although no one else seems to notice, I feel a vibration in the air, a quivering hum that ripples through the basement and almost knocks me off my feet.

Little Bo Peep giggles nervously.

There's a click as the door at the top of the stairs opens. Soft steps tread lightly down the wooden staircase, and the flames of the candles drift sideways. I turn to see Delia coming down the stairs, moving slowly like she's dazed or sleepwalking. She's dressed like a fairy—on her small back are delicate filmy wings, and her cheeks are dusted with something that sparkles. But in her right hand is no magic wand. Instead she clutches a large, menacing knife.

"*Who called me?*"

Was that Delia's voice? A strange combination between a whisper and a hiss.

Little Bo Peep giggles again. "This is so *scary*," she says, clutching Zorro's sleeve.

"Delia," says Amelia, "what are you doing up? You were supposed to be in bed by nine."

No response. The hand that holds the knife twitches, like it's on the receiving end of an electrical pulse.

"*Delia*," says Amelia more firmly.

"Who!" Delia shrieks. Her head jerks like a puppet on a string from one face to another. And then I see her eyes—not the eyes of a little girl or a human. No, what stares back at my mother are two pitch-black orbs, fathomless, empty pits devoid of life or expression.

"Delia?" whispers my mother.

Khioniya stands. Her face is pale, triumphant, and exalted. "I, Khioniya Kuzminichna Gueseva, have called you."

Delia's head jerks to register Khioniya. "*You* cannot command me."

"Oh great lord," says Khioniya in a proud, defiant voice. "I would never dare. I only ask to be your humble servant, your instrument. But there is one here who wears the ring, who would command you and bind you."

Amelia stands, pushing her chair back roughly; it grates against the cement floor. "*Enough.* Enough of this, Delia, I don't know what kind of game you're playing, but it's not funny and you're scaring our guests."

"*He* is here?" hisses Delia.

There's a dark rumble beneath our feet then, and this time the shelves with preserves start to tremble. Jars drop to the floor, smashing their contents, and the air smells sickly sweet, a mixture of summer strawberries, grape jelly, and honey.

"Yes, here," says Khioniya, her voice now hesitant.

Delia smiles.

Oh God, oh God, oh God. My panicked heart starts to race, but my mother just stands there with a look of utter confusion—she has no idea the danger she's in.

"So, Khioniya Kuzminichna Gueseva, *humble servant*," Delia says mockingly. "I'm not sure you've entirely thought this whole thing through. Because if *he* is here, he *can* command me. Unless . . ."

"Unless?" stutters Khioniya.

"Don't pretend." Delia glances around the room. "Very convenient, all in one room. Six plus a spare. Who will I start with? This one?" She takes a menacing step toward Little Bo Peep and snarls.

Little Bo Peep, no fool, clatters up the stairs, the door slamming shut behind her. The other guests nervously look to Amelia, as if they're unsure what the polite thing to do is. On the one hand, they're obviously uncomfortable, but on the other, they don't want to commit a social faux pas.

"A shame," says Delia with a dark grin. "I've lost a sheep. But then you're my *servant*, aren't you?"

Khioniya swallows, obviously losing her nerve. She frantically looks to Amelia, points a shaking finger. "Her," she whispers. "You can have her."

"But what about *you?*"

Delia steps toward her; there is something feline about the way she moves, soft and deadly. "Won't you offer yourself?"

Khioniya edges backward, aware that any sudden move could be her last. "You know I would," she stammers, "but you only *need* six—"

"*You* called my name," says Delia. "And I have come for *you.*" Delia pauses, tosses the knife up in the air; it turns once, twice, and when it falls she catches it easily in her small, outstretched palm. "I have come for *all* of you."

Chaos reigns as all the guests simultaneously jump up from their seats, pushing each other out of the way as they race up the stairs, all pretenses at social graces gone. Only Amelia stands still, immobilized by shock. But the door at the top won't open.

The Tin Man frantically pounds at it with his fist, screaming, "Let us out! *For God's sake, let us out!*"

"No," whispers Khioniya. She nervously glances behind her, no exit, nothing between her and the back wall except the well, which is uncovered and circled by a low brick wall two steps away.

Delia's head cocks to the side. She smiles and lunges.

But Khioniya has already made the calculation. She races to the well, her feet barely graze the ridge of it, and then she's gone. Her scream echoes against the stone walls, then a splash and silence.

"Well," says Delia calmly, "I guess I'll catch up with her later." She turns to the panicked guests. "Anyone else care to go for a swim?"

The Roman soldier pushes his way to the front of the line as the stairs groan beneath their collective weight. He throws the whole force of his body against the door and it rattles but holds.

Suddenly, faster than I can register, Delia charges at the two geisha, who cringe by the stairway wall, easy targets, since they wear awkward wooden slippers and their legs are hampered by thick silk kimonos. Delia expertly slashes their throats; their bright red blood matches their bright red lips, and they crumple to the floor almost simultaneously, like broken flowers.

With a feral growl, she pounces next on Zorro, pulling him backward down the steps, and with an unimaginable strength, slices his neck like she's cutting through butter. Blood spurts up over her face, the walls, the stairs, and he collapses to the floor. She roughly pulls up his shirt, cuts into his belly, and digs into his torso with her tiny hand almost absently while she sings in a strange lilting voice.

> *On a mountain,*
> *Stands a lady,*
> *Who she is I do not know.*

Finally Delia finds what she's looking for, the still-pulsing spleen. She rips it out, takes a large bite.

The Roman soldier at the top of the stairs shouts "It's jammed! The door's jammed!"

Still Amelia stands, frozen. She hasn't moved; she hasn't taken a breath since Khioniya dropped into the well. Delia licks the blood from her fingers, a childish gesture, like they're covered with cake batter.

"*Run!*" I scream at my mother, but she can't hear me, see me.

Desperate, the Tin Man spots Little Bo Peep's staff on the ground. He stumbles his way back down the stairs—I can hear the *clink* of the tin coverings on his knees—and eventually he reaches the bottom. He snatches the staff and holds it over his head threateningly.

Delia smiles, her teeth bloody. "Oh *please*," she says. "You can't be serious." Seconds later she's at his throat, and this time she doesn't even bother with a knife—she just tears at his jugular with her small teeth while he uselessly tries to club her with his arm.

At this the Roman soldier falls to his knees, gripping the doorknob, hopelessly trying to turn it. He starts to whimper. Delia laughs in delight and bounds up the outside rail of the stairway, like some kind of freakish gymnast. He drops into a fetal position, trying to protect his body with his costume armor, but this just leaves the back of his neck exposed. I hear a loud crack as she wraps her tiny hands around it and twists; then she throws the limp sack of his body down the stairs.

Finally, a flicker of movement from Amelia. Her right hand twitches. Slowly, almost imperceptibly, it reaches into her silver, glittering purse. Pulls out a lighter. Her eyes flick to the shelves on the wall.

"No!" I shout. I instinctively dart forward, reach out my arm, but something, someone holds me back. Poe.

"*You cannot change what is done.*"

Still, is it just my imagination or do my mother's eyes meet mine for a split second? Does she sense my presence before she pulls a bottle of rum from the shelf and smashes it against the wall? There's just the faintest click as she strikes the lighter, dropping the flame onto the broken glass, and the flame explodes into a roaring fire, licking its way down to the other cases of liquor stacked neatly by the wooden shelves.

This gets Delia's attention.

For a moment she freezes, the glowing flames reflected in the dark orbs of her eyes. She focuses on Amelia.

"Oh for Christ's sake, *run*," I whisper.

And miraculously she does. Or tries to. But as soon as she darts for the stairs, Delia leaps, grabbing her roughly by the neck, and throws her onto the burning pyre. I watch in horror as the flames catch at my mother's glittering dress, her hair. She screams in pain as she struggles to stamp out the fire, a piercing shriek that wrenches my heart from my chest. This is real, this *happened*, and there's nothing in the world I can do to change it, to save my mother.

Suddenly the door at the top of the stairs flies open and there stands—my father? But it's my father as I've never seen him before. He wears an expression of complete raging fury—he looks powerful, invincible, like an angry God. In his left hand he holds a burning candle, and on his right hand the ring glints, catching the reflection of the fire.

His voice booms, "I exorcise thee, O creature of fire, by him through whom all things have been made, so that every kind of phantasm may retire from thee, and be unable to harm or deceive in any way, through the invocation of the most high creator of all."

"How do you like your meat," Delia snarls, shoving my screaming, burning mother to the bottom of the stairs. "Medium or well done?"

"Such are the words!" shouts my father, and with that, he blows out the candle.

Instantly the basement is hit by a massive wind with the force of a tornado. It pulls the ash and debris into a swirling cloud, knocks over the shelves, and whips Delia's hair from her small, blood-smeared face. She opens her delicate mouth and releases a sound that's hard to describe. It's like the roar of a jet turbine or some kind of sonic boom; it's the sound Daniel made in my dream before the avalanche, and it shakes the earth beneath the house. I watch as the brick wall surrounding the well collapses and a large wooden beam falls from the ceiling, drawing the fire upward. Then, abruptly, Delia falls to the floor, unconscious.

My father drops the extinguished candle and races down the stairs. The fire now creeps across most of the ceiling, and above I can hear the panicked cries of servants and partygoers. Captain Aspinwall appears at the doorway dressed as a pirate. He shouts down through the haze of smoke.

"Have you seen my daughter, my wife?"

"Here!" my father shouts as he takes off his shirt to damp the flames on my mother's inert form; his body is surprisingly wiry and muscular, like a gymnast's. He gently lifts the hair from her raw, burned neck, and she whispers something unintelligible before closing her eyes.

Covering his nose with his handkerchief, the captain rushes down and spots Delia on the floor, covered with blood. "My baby, my baby girl," he cries. Her eyes flutter and then open.

"Daddy?"

My father covers my mother's now apparently lifeless face with his shirt; it's hard to tell if she's breathing. The captain clutches Delia to his chest, looks over to where my father is kneeling beside my mother's body, and catches his eye. There is a wordless exchange. My father shakes his head solemnly. Delia coughs. Fighting back tears, Captain Aspinwall lifts his daughter and carries her past the bodies, dodging the growing flames, up the stairs and out into the night air.

For a moment I think stupidly that my father is just going to sit there, let them both burn, because he doesn't move, doesn't stir. All the rage is gone; in its place is an exhausted, haunted look, like he knows too much, has seen too much. It's my mother who reaches out with a trembling hand, touches his leg. Quietly, gently, he lifts the rag from my mother's face. She nods imperceptibly, and then he takes her hand and gathers her in his arms. She looks so small as he carries her up the stairs, like a child herself.

"*Say my name.*" Through the fire, Poe walks toward me, strangely triumphant, her pale face illuminated by the flames. "*Say my name and we will have our revenge.*"

But I don't say her name. Instead another word escapes my lips: strange but familiar.

"Nachiel."

Suddenly there's a blazing pain like my ribs are being crushed, like someone has implanted a firecracker in my chest and lit it.

Poe's eyes grow wide. "*No,*" she hisses. She reaches out an arm, but there's nothing to reach for.

I'm gone again.

CHAPTER TWENTY-FOUR: NACHIEL

For someone who's not sure if they're immortal, you sure take some chances."

I'm lying on the cement floor of the basement, wet and cold—no, make that freezing; I can't feel my feet or my fingers. The road flare is still burning, providing a small modicum of heat and giving off enough flickering light for me to see the man crouched next to me.

The guy from Sacred Heart Collectibles?

I take in his ordinary dark jeans, brown T-shirt, and gray baseball jacket with an electric blue embroidered logo, "Supreme Being," but there's something else about him that's harder to place. Like his eyes. They're a deep, wintry gray, and I can actually feel them probing me, like a delicate finger is brushing through my thoughts.

"Fuck," I mutter, but even that small word causes pain to shoot through my chest. I spit out some brackish water and then vomit the content of my stomach—what little there is.

"Not easy pulling you up out of that well," says the man cheerfully. "Good thing I got to you first or you could've been on the way to the morgue again. Assuming they ever found you. Knew this spirit once, been possessing a body for years, right? Decided he wanted to do some cave exploring, live a little. But then part of the cave, it collapses on him, and he's stuck there, like, for a century. Skin was crazy white when he came out, like one of those weird albino fish that live at the bottom of the ocean."

I try to sit up—more pain.

"Might have broken a rib there. Sorry."

"Feels like you broke all of them. Who *are* you?"

"Me? Who do you think?"

When I don't immediately come up with the answer he looks offended. "*Nachiel*," he says as if I'm very, very stupid.

I start to laugh bitterly but have to stop because the pain's too intense. *This* is Nachiel, my protective spirit? A retail sales clerk? No wonder everything's so fucked up. "Great job. How many people have been murdered now?"

"I watch over *you*. Who do you think scared Daniel off when he was in Lisa's house or when he climbed the tree outside your window?"

The bootprints around the tree. It never occurred to me that there might be more than one set.

"The rest I'm not allowed to interfere with," Nachiel adds. "Rules of engagement."

"Rules of engagement. Next you'll be talking about collateral damage."

He shrugs. "Free will always results in collateral damage. Not my call."

I consider this for a moment. What if he's not really a good spirit but is working with Poe, or worse? How would I know the difference?

"So what happened on Halloween when I almost drowned? Had a night shift at Sacred Heart you couldn't get out of?"

"You were off the radar. I had no idea where you were," replies Nachiel defensively. "None of us did until you called."

Now this is *truly* unbelievable. "*I* called. When the *fuck* did I call any of you? I didn't even call Poe or Khi—"

"Stop!" shouts Nachiel with an intensity that instantly silences me.

He takes a breath. "You have to be *very* careful what you say. You have more power than you realize, wearing that ring. Never say a spirit or demon's *true* name unless you're ready to meet them. And when you give a command, watch how you phrase your sentences. Do you remember what you said at Aspinwall before all hell broke loose?"

Not exactly at the top of my mind; something about spirits . . . doing something? "I said—"

"For *fuck's* sake, don't say it again. Seriously, got enough to deal with. But you *do* remember?"

"I think I get general the drift. So *that* made all *this* . . . happen?"

He sighs, like I'm an idiot finally catching up. Which I am. "Exactly. You opened the door to *anything* supernatural that had touched that place. Poe came through, possessed Maddy—"

"Then the floor gave way, but she wasn't possessed afterward."

"Because you told her to leave Maddy alone. Nice bit of intuition there. But the whole thing rang a pretty loud bell in the spirit world. Sorath sensed your connection with Lisa. He needed to find a host, someone he could use to emotionally manipulate you, and he'd already possessed Daniel once. Makes it easier."

"Once?"

"Daniel found *The Book of Fiends*, or what there was of it, at Aspinwall. He conjured Sorath . . . thought he'd be smart enough to control him. Of course he wasn't. After he tried to kill Lisa, your father was able to perform the exorcism. But it was his last. It . . . drained him. He never fully recovered."

I lean the back of my head against the cement wall, fighting a wave of dizziness. It all fits, but then that's what bothers me. It's too perfect.

"And you didn't just *tell* me all this in Sacred Heart because . . . ?"

"You hadn't called me by name yet. Rules of engagement. If seraphs could just walk around telling people what they should know, it'd be a different world. You have to admit though I dropped you a pretty serious hint."

In a very odd way, probably because my life is very odd at the moment, it makes sense.

"And my father. Why the fuck didn't *he* bother to tell me? Didn't think I could handle it?"

Nachiel pauses for a moment.

"Honestly, your father didn't want a son."

I burst out into laughter, the bright, bitter kind. "Oh well, that makes me feel *so* much better. You're an amazing help, Nachiel. Wish I'd conjured you before. Could have used some help slitting my wrists."

Nachiel sighs, then joins me on the cold cement floor. "Look," he says quietly, "this is dark, dark stuff. Not the kind of stuff you'd ever wish on anyone, not your worst enemy, certainly not the people you love. You can exorcise demons, but once they've connected with someone, they're more accessible. Easier to find."

I think about Daniel's victims. How each of them in some way had been touched by Sorath. None fared well.

"A lifetime exorcising demons isn't much of a life," he adds grimly.

"Who wouldn't want to be a part of all this?" A bout of serious coughing starts then, making me double over again with pain. Nachiel reaches into his pocket and pulls out a flask. He hands it to me, and I choke back a swig of liquid fire. It takes out the cough but does nothing for the dull ache in my heart.

"He was *hoping* it would end with him. But then there was the fire. He rescued your mother, nursed her back to health. They both became different people. Better people. But because they grew close, and Delia had been possessed once . . . Well, Delia would have been too tempting of a target for Sorath if your mother ever returned. She was devastated of course."

"I was her consolation prize."

"One I know he never regretted."

I know then, by the sickening drop in my stomach, that it's true. All those years I was angry at him. Wasted. And while I now have one living relative, she suffers from dementia and I'll never be able to meet her for the same reason our mother could never see her.

My inheritance," I mutter. Suddenly I remember how pale my father was after his unexplained trips, how he'd be in bed for days, as though he were suffering from cancer. Even dealing with Poe gives me a splitting migraine. I've finally found out what my father's "thing" was. Exorcising demons. It's an empty victory.

Nachiel looks at me intently. "He was ready to move on, knew he wasn't much use anymore in the demon-exorcism department. They planned to come out and visit you. He was going to give you the ring, pass it on as his own father, Rasputin, did before him."

"Funny, I found it under the dresser."

"Well, your mother, *she* had other ideas. Slipped the shoebox out of the car when he wasn't looking."

Click, click, click go all the pieces of my fragmented life.

"But she didn't get old."

"Not as quickly as she would have," says Nachiel. He slips the flask back in his pocket. "Time is just another force of nature. One that with a little education you'll be able to . . . adjust is probably the best way to describe it."

"And the grimoires?"

"Your father left *The Book of Seraphs* with Lucy for safekeeping during his trip. She happens to own your favorite store. If you define favorite as bad, kitschy religious memorabilia."

"Sacred Heart Collectibles."

"You disappeared after the funeral and she didn't know how to get it to you. Funny, because she reads the *Devonshire Eagle* every day, but your byline is D. Peters. By the way she doesn't know about all this. Would be dangerous for her if she did. But *The Book of Fiends* is a little more tricky."

I give him a hard look. "Define tricky."

"Well, your father separated the *Book of Fiends*—never kept the pages for conjuring demons and exorcising them in the same place. Young Archibald Bennet, not knowing how to read at the time, stole the half for conjuring demons, and we all know how *that* went."

"So the other half for exorcising demons . . . ?"

"Unknown," Nachiel says. "Which makes me very, very uneasy. Your father always stashed those pages in the strangest places. You didn't run across them when you cleaned out the house?"

"I would have mentioned it."

"Well it doesn't mean you don't have them. Probably in something you'd take with you if something happened. Think about it for a sec. What would you never leave behind?"

"Wish I'd known when I packed my boxes, because what I took was random."

"I said think about it, not complain about it."

I groan. "Poetry magnets. High school yearbook. Bunky." Wait— Bunky *was* heavier than he should have been. But what kind of sick bastard would stuff their son's favorite stuffed animal with a grimoire?

Oh, right. Probably the same kind of sick bastard who'd steal a grimoire from his girlfriend, along with her mother's gun. Like father, like son.

Nachiel says nothing then, watching me carefully, and I'm overwhelmed with the impossible weight of it all. All I want to do is quit, find a corner somewhere to curl up and sleep, let it all fall away. *Enough.*

But then where would that leave Lisa?

Wincing with pain, I grab my jacket, slip the gun in my pocket, and shakily get to my feet, using the cement wall to hold myself steady.

"So how do we save Lisa?"

Nachiel though doesn't move, doesn't stand to join me. "That's just it, Dimitri. We don't."

———

I hobble up the Aspinwall stairs as quick as I can, ignoring the pain that's like a fire burning in my rib cage. Ignoring the useless sales clerk behind me. Protective spirit, my *ass*.

"You still don't understand . . ."

I pretend I don't hear him.

"She's just a pawn, collateral to force you into a trade. He wants *you*, Dimitri—he wants you to invite him in. Then he'll possess you and the powers of the ring *through* you. He'll be able to conjure any demon or angel, make them do whatever he wants."

I storm through the basement door and into the remains of the kitchen. Christ, it's nearly as dark upstairs as it was in the basement. How long was I in the well? "Then we need to save her so I won't be tempted." I click on the Maglite.

"Fuck, Dimitri, it's not that easy. He's killed five people—"

"Five?"

"Ernest. After you left."

I slam my fist against the wall of the foyer, cracking the plaster. "It is easy. We kill *him*."

"He only needs one more by the end of the night and then you won't be able to touch him. It's a win for him either way. You have no *idea* how evil—"

"I think I do." I stumble out the front steps.

Nachiel pulls the sleeve on my jacket. "Look, if it was your father, maybe—"

God, I'm so sick of this shit. I pull out my gun and point it at his chest. "*Try*. You can try."

Nachiel puts up his hands. "Whoa. Take it easy. Think carefully, Dimitri, and you'll see that I'm right."

"Maybe I don't care if you are."

Nachiel strangely doesn't seem fazed; he doesn't even blink as he says, "I can't let you do this. There's more than just Lisa's life at stake."

He takes a cautious step forward, coolly appraising me. Slowly he reaches out a hand, as if he's going to put it on the barrel. "You're not going to shoot me."

But it's his casual dismissal of just how serious I am that causes a wave of pure unadulterated rage to wash over and through me. My hands—seemingly of their own accord, because there's no thought behind what they do next, like they've gone rogue, like they're a separate consciousness—it's my hands that make the call to pull the trigger. I *do* shoot him.

The only thing more shocking than the loud crack that almost shatters my eardrums is that the bullet seems to have no effect whatsoever. Nachiel doesn't flinch.

The reality of what I've done sinks in. "Holy shit, holy *shit*," I say, rushing to his side. "I didn't mean . . ."

Nachiel sighs a deep, world-weary sigh and unzips his jacket. I see a small bloom of blood starting to stain his T-shirt, which he pulls up, revealing a ragged, oozing hole. Casually he digs into his chest with a finger, winces slightly, and then pulls out the slug. Blood now spurts with serious intent.

"Christ, I just *got* this body," he mutters irritably, like I only spilled coffee on his shirt. "You have no idea how hard it is to come across one legit."

I frantically look around for something to press against the wound—nothing but snow in all directions—and then I realize *I* must be delirious. Because where the bullet hole was just a few seconds ago, there's now a healed, smooth stretch of brown flesh. Only the blood on his hands and T-shirt remains. They're still wet.

"How?" I gasp.

Nachiel pulls his shirt back down, wiping his bloody hands on his jeans. "When an immortal spirit possesses a body, the body can't die until it leaves. In about three seconds that's going to lead you to a depressing realization."

A realization? Then it does hit me. Sorath has possessed Daniel's body. Which means his body is immortal. Which means my gun is just a useless toy, a prop.

"Even if I wanted to help," adds Nachiel more softly, "I wouldn't know where he's taken her. I'm sorry, Dimitri. We have to go."

I don't doubt him, not now. Which leaves me only one remaining card in my very small playbook.

"*Khioniya Gueseva!*" I scream at the top of my lungs. The words echo through the barren woods, startling an owl into flight. I let my arms drop to my side, raise my face to the clouds above like I'm calling the sky itself to fall on me. "I said it! I said your name! *Khioniya Gueseva!*"

Nachiel closes his eyes. "We are *so* fucked."

———

There's a crack like thunder, and a powerful wind blows through the trees, causing them to sway and scattering snowflakes that swirl into a cloud that hovers above us before it drops. The air before me shimmers slightly, the way hot air over asphalt shimmers in the summer, and gradually I see a shadow behind it, wavy like something caught beneath ice. Another loud crack and then a foot, delicate and deathly blue, steps through the shimmering air, followed by a leg, which reaches unsteadily for the ground, as if it's accustomed to a different gravity, the gravity of water. As soon as the foot reaches the snow, the rest of Poe—Khioniya—falls through, along with a wave of water. She collapses onto the frozen earth in a fetal position.

It's like witnessing some kind of ethereal birth.

Crouching on the ground she looks up at the sky, at the moon glowing through the clouds—her long blond hair hangs in wet clumps around her face. "I forgot," she whispers in a Russian accent. "I forgot the moon. How do you forget something like that? The moon?"

Now what do I do?

Nachiel crosses his arms over his chest. "Don't even look at me. This is your brilliant idea."

But I remember his instruction to keep the orders simple. "Stand," I say. Seems relatively safe.

As if her body has no choice but to obey, she jerks to her feet, and for a moment she wobbles, holding her arms out for balance. She puts one hand to her face and touches her own cheek. "I'm cold." A burst of dark laughter. "I did not think I would ever feel cold again. I have had so many years of heat. Burning, blistering heat. Here," she says, reaching out her fingers to me. "Touch me. Do I feel so cold to you?"

I regard her warily. "I think I'll pass."

"Of course," she says, observing me closely with glittering blue eyes that raise the hairs on the back of my neck. Her eyes flit to Nachiel, and she quickly tries to hide a look of disdain.

"You have good reason not to trust me. I am bound to the dark one. But you could change that." She takes a soft step forward. "You could bind me to *you*. Or you could give me my freedom." She looks wistfully at the snow. "Imagine that, free will. I would not be so careless with it again."

At this Nachiel snorts. "Free will? So you can try to kill him again?"

"I do not try to kill him," she says tersely. Then to me: "You ask *me* who I was. You say, *what the fuck does this all mean?* So I show you. And you see now, yes? You see."

Nachiel takes a step toward her. "What were you trying to *show* Rasputin when you stabbed him?"

"Oh, that is different," she says calmly. "I do try to kill *him*. Most definitely. I was angry person then."

"That's kind of an understatement," I say.

"You would be angry too," she replies hotly, "if you had been prostitute as girl no more than ten. I was not *born* bad person. No one is. I have regrets," she adds bitterly. "I have almost a hundred years of hell for regrets."

If that's true then she might have a point, and for a fleeting moment I almost get a sense of her, Khioniya, as a person. Maybe she's just a victim, another notch on Sorath's belt of destroyed lives.

But she mistakes my silence for a no.

"*Men.*" She spits the word, like a curse.

Then again, maybe this isn't the time to have empathy for my grandfather's would-be killer. Which means it's time to ask my question—the reason we are here after all, in this place, this moment.

"Where is Lisa?"

Poe backs away fearfully, shaking her head. "Nachiel is right. No matter what you do, he will kill her."

Nachiel appears visibly shocked.

"He wants *you*, Dimitri," she continues. "He wants your power. You do not know what he is planning—"

"*Tell* me," I say, not a question—an order. "Tell me where Lisa is."

She glances nervously overhead as if someone—or something—is listening in. Then she takes a step closer to me and whispers quickly, "The garden. Where your father grew roses. Do not step on the . . ."

But suddenly the words are choked off, her mouth tries to form them but there's no sound. And there's no mistaking the genuine panic in her eyes as she tries frantically to speak, to no avail. Suddenly she makes writing motions with her hand, looking around for something to use, and I see a lone stick. I grab it and toss it to her.

"Quick, write it down."

I step closer as she scratches furiously on the snow: "*Do not step on the numbers.*"

Suddenly she drops the stick, her face racked with pain, and she clutches her neck with her hands, as if someone or *something* is choking her.

"What's happening, Nachiel, what's happening?"

"I don't—"

The air behind her seems to rip open then, there's a slice of red flames, and behind it I see another form, a dense, looming shadow with demonic horns. An invisible force knocks Poe hard to the ground and then starts to drag her by the legs backward, into the dagger of red light.

"Stay!" I command. But still she slides toward it, clawing desperately at the frozen earth, looking for something to hold on to.

I grab her frigid hands.

"They're trying to take her back," says Nachiel quickly.

She looks me directly in the eyes, and I get a brief flash—a glimpse of a little girl in a ragged dress, barefoot; she's pushed against a brick wall by a soldier in a neatly pressed uniform, and he smiles lewdly at her before pressing a small brass coin into her dirty palm.

"Nachiel!"

"Dimitri, don't be stupid. She tried to kill you, your grandfather—"

There's a cacophony of growls, and a scaly arm reaches out of the flames, wraps a claw around Poe's left foot, dragging her harder. I'm losing ground as my boots slide in the snow.

Should I let her go? A part of me—more than I would like to admit—agrees with him.

But then the sickly sweet smell of rotting flesh wafts by, and I hear a high, inhuman clicking sound, something bestial and unnatural. Poe silently mouths one word: "*Please.*"

Well, this ring is supposed to let me command spirits, right? What did my father say when he exorcised Sorath? My mind scrambles for a few useful words—*Think, Dimitri,* think.

"Khioniya Gueseva, I release thee!"

A rumble from within the red light. Seems promising. "I *release thee*! I *release thee*!"

Instantly Poe is freed, and together we fall back into the icy snow. There's a high, keening screech, which causes the nearby trees to quiver, releasing flurries of snow. The red slice of light flashes brighter and then disappears.

"Damn," says Nachiel. "How'd you swing that?"

"I have no idea," I say, trying to catch my breath.

A gentle breeze ruffles the dead tufts of grass that push out through the snow.

Poe sits up, her lips trembling. "Can I ask favor?" she says quietly.

"I thought I just did you a big one."

"Yes," she says with a grim smile. "But I have one more. Let this be the end of Khioniya Kuzminichna Gueseva. She died in the well many years ago. She was not always a good person in life. And in death she was forced to do bad things. Evil things. Give me a new name."

"I already have," I say. "Poe."

"Like the writer?" She thinks for a moment. "Yes, I like that. Now, we must hurry. I can sense where Sorath is, but when he learns you have broken my bond with him . . ."

She doesn't have to finish her sentence. We all know what he'll do.

CHAPTER TWENTY-FIVE: THE GREENHOUSE

We don't run, we fly through the snowy wood. Nachiel ploughs through the brush, Poe's bare feet barely touch the ground—and when they do, they leave no trace—but what's surprising is how *strong* I feel. My heart pounds, but in a rhythmic, controlled way. Sweat trickles down my back, my wet clothes are plastered to my body, but it's a welcome chill, because my mind is icy, laser sharp. I *want* this fight—I'm ready.

And then we reach the fragile, overgrown stone steps leading to the abandoned garden. Thorny bushes pull at my jeans, a few pierce my skin, but I don't care; I'm beyond caring.

Poe scouts the ground; she can move faster than we can. She raises her hand and points to the far edge of the garden, where a lone and barren sycamore twists up and over the wall. She takes off for it like a shot. We race to join her. There's a small narrow path through the crumbling wall.

"I still wouldn't trust her," says Nachiel quietly, before we get too close.

"I don't know if I trust either of you."

"Why does *that* not surprise me?" he mutters.

Poe pauses in front of two pairs of footprints—the smaller prints sometimes drag, as if the maker of them had been forced to keep moving against their will.

Fear almost ruptures my heart. I start to follow, but Poe stops me.

"Listen," she whispers.

For what, I don't know—all I can hear is a babbling brook nearby, my own heaving breath, and the occasional crack as a frozen limb falls to the snowy earth with a muffled thump. The prints clearly keep going directly ahead.

"What are we listening for?" I whisper.

She raises a finger to her lips and then nimbly climbs the nearest tree, crouching on the highest branch. For a moment she sits there, frozen.

Nachiel stands still, watching her carefully

I place my palm against the bark. "What's she doing?"

"Probably signaling Sorath so he knows we're coming."

"If you're going to be such a pissant, you don't have to come."

"Is that a threat or a promise?"

Poe quickly drops down again. "A false trail," she whispers, her brows furrowed.

"Maybe you can call another murderous spirit," says Nachiel. "Ask for directions."

"Your jokes not funny." She peers closely at a bush, points to a broken twig. "This way." She plunges into the woods where there is no path.

Nachiel pointedly catches my eye. A warning. But I ignore him and follow after.

———

The element of surprise, obviously, won't be on our side—I make as much noise crashing through the woods as a drunk elephant—but the ring feels solid on my finger, like a talisman.

We run. We stop. Poe looks for signs, listens for sounds I can't hear, and then we run again, up hills and down hills, across the babbling brook. My feet slide on the icy rocks, plunge into the freezing water, numbing my feet, but I don't care. A branch scrapes my face; I don't care. Clouds pass across the shining face of the moon, cast the forest into darkness. I trip and fall, but I don't care. Just please God, let her still be alive. Please.

I am now keenly aware of last times. There was the last time I saw my parents, in the rearview mirror of my Mustang as I drove off for my final semester of college. The last time I saw Nate at the *Eagle*, crumpling a paper cup and tossing it a trash can. The last time I saw Ernest, closing his green front door, thinking he was going somewhere safe. If I don't save Lisa, then the last time I saw her was outside the cabin, and she didn't even look at me as I drove away. That's not something I'm prepared to live with, especially if I really could live forever.

Poe stops abruptly, raising her hand. My ragged breath heaves and drifts in the air like smoke.

In front of us looms the broken ruin of a huge, whimsical Victorian greenhouse that's been overtaken by blackberry bushes, small, gnarled trees, and dead ivy. From the center rises a decorative ironwork cupola, looking like some kind of lost Arabian turret. Most of the glass is broken, and large jagged slabs of it poke through the snow around the low stone wall. The exposed wooden beams are gray and weathered, listing slightly to the right like a ship being blown by a strong wind. Two moss-covered statues of cherubs stand guard either side of the open door, their noses and fingers broken.

Nachiel looks wary. Like something might come out and bite.

Daniel's voice rings out in the crystalline air. "Khioniya, my *humble servant*. How's tricks?"

He's here. The thought has the strange quality of an echo, so that I'm not sure if it's my thought or someone else's.

"And you brought Nachiel. It's a regular family reunion."

"Whatever you do, don't let him play you," Nachiel says quietly.

I nod. Together we walk into the ruin.

There, standing just under the turret, is Daniel. He's even thinner in person, if such a thing is possible, his cheekbones sharp and pointed like a starving man's. His eyes are two black orbs, a vacuum where humanity should be. Standing next to him, unbearably close, is Lisa, her beautiful hair twisted in his tight, bony fist. He holds a sharp knife to her throat, pressing it just enough to make an impression but not enough to cut. Yet.

And then I notice something else, a dark pattern on the snow that covers the remains of the greenhouse floor. It's a grid of numbers laid out with some kind of dirt. Daniel is standing in its center. A magic square.

"Nicely done, Khioniya. Everything in place exactly as planned."

Nachiel is obviously scanning the numbers. He turns to me, alarmed.

"You lie," Poe hisses. "And you no longer control me. I am bound to him now."

"At least that's what we want him to think, right? He really bought it, didn't he?"

Poe turns to me, a frantic look in her eye.

"I *release thee*," says Daniel. "You really thought that would be enough? Christ, did you even bother to read what little Ernest translated?"

"I was cramped for time."

"Too bad for you. *Kneel!*" shouts Daniel.

Poe instantly drops to her knees.

A shudder runs through me. Was Nachiel right not to trust her? Or is Daniel too strong for her to resist? Suddenly I'm one card down in a game I don't really know the rules of.

"You might be your father's son, but you're not your father's equal, not by a long shot," Daniel says coolly.

"Never said I was," I reply carefully.

Lisa's warm brown eyes plead with me. "Dimitri," she gasps, "he's going to kill me anyways, no matter what you do."

"Now that's not true," says Daniel. "I'm a reasonable person. There's always room to negotiate. You have something *I* want. And I have something *you* want."

Nachiel takes a step forward. "Sorath, I'm not going to let you—"

Daniel mutters something softly under his breath, and instantly Nachiel's blown back through the air like he just stepped on a land mine. There's a crack as he lands on a pile of metal rods.

I hold my breath.

But after a moment Nachiel sits up, cradling his arm, which is bent at an unnatural angle, obviously broken. Now I'm two cards down.

"I'd just sit this one out if I were you," says Daniel with a leering smile.

"You said something about a trade," I say quickly.

"Yes, a *hard* trade."

"So what do you want?" I let my arms relax just a bit. If I can push the gun out of my pocket without him seeing . . . I might not be able to kill the motherfucker, but a shot to the head would certainly be distracting.

"No cheating!" shouts Sorath. The tip of his knife pricks Lisa's pale skin, and a bead of bright red blood trickles down her throat.

Instantly I freeze.

"You're family is *always fucking cheating*! Do you have any idea how *irritating* that is?"

Anger churns in my stomach, and it takes every ounce of my resolve to keep my hands relaxed, to not give in. "Why don't you just tell me what the *fuck* you want?"

"I think you know. For the sins of the fathers—"

"Yeah, yeah, yeah, I *got* the message. Beheading Nate was a little unnecessary, don't you think?"

Daniel cocks his head, thinks a moment, and then smiles as if I've just paid him a compliment. "It was, wasn't it?"

"You *promised* me," gasps Lisa, a few tears beading her eyes. "If I said run, you'd run. Dimitri, I swear to God if you don't keep your promise, you're *so* dead."

"If only it were that easy," says Daniel mildly. "Poe, why don't you tell our friend Dimitri here what I used to make this magic square."

Poe's mouth is forced open, like a puppet's. "Ashes," she whispers.

Daniel cocks his head, smiles. "Not just any ashes. Why don't you be more specific?"

Poe gives me a frantic look as she says, "Human ashes."

Nachiel tries to stumble to his feet. "Dimitri, remember—"

"You know," Daniel interrupts genially. "They really didn't smell so good, your parents. All those months underground weren't kind to their bodies. I had beetles in my car for *days*. So I think this is an improvement, actually. I mixed them in a very nice organic peat mulch to make them stretch. The even numbers," he says, pointing to the ground, "are your mother. And your father, well, he was always a little odd anyways. Taking the ring off, bad idea. Sent a nice ping out into the spirit world, and then it wasn't too hard to possess your mother long enough to grab the steering wheel of the car. So sorry for your loss."

I start to jolt forward with a surge of rage—I could tear his throat out with my *teeth*—and a look of maniacal triumph crosses Daniel's face.

Which is why we all miss the exact moment when Lisa stealthily reaches into her jacket pocket for the Taser. All I see is a small arc of blue light followed by a crackling zap, and suddenly Daniel's dropped the knife, his back arching while his eyes grow wide with shock. And for a split second something flickers across Daniel's expression, something human. His hand shudders, like there's a fight for who controls it, and the trembling fingers relax just enough for Lisa to pull her hair out from his fist. Gasping, she falls to the ground and starts to crawl away.

I look to Poe and, hot damn, she *is* on my side, because before Daniel can reach with a trembling hand for the knife, there's a white flash, and she's pinned his arm to the ground.

Lisa is still crawling away—one hand reaches out beyond the boundary of the numbers—and now I'm past rage, past reason, and I pull the gun from my pocket, aiming for Daniel. The gun feels good in my hands, slick and cool, and all my fury rushes from my heart—this is for Lisa, this is for my mother, my father. Rage flows down the length of my arms to my hands like a white-hot electric current. My finger catches the trigger.

And I forget. I forget what Nachiel said. What Poe said.

I take a step.

My foot touches the numbers.

And everything—instantly—stops.

————

Time doesn't exist. Sound doesn't exist. Everything is frozen, motionless. Even the minuscule flakes of snow, disturbed by the falling glass, hang midair like they're suspended in some kind of viscous liquid.

Everything except Daniel. Except Sorath.

I want to scream at Lisa to run, but I can't move or speak—I'm frozen in place too. And all I can do is watch as Daniel slowly frees himself from Poe's grip, blood rushing down his arm from a gash, falling onto the snow and creating dark shadows. And all I can do is watch while he stands up and runs a bloody hand through his hair.

He grins at me. A demented, heart-piercing, maniacal grin.

Slowly he bends over, picks up the knife. Takes his time wiping the snow from its edge on his pants. Stares at me.

No. Oh God, *no.*

It's just like the video, only this time I'm a captive audience and I can't turn it off. I can't even close my eyes as he nonchalantly walks toward Lisa, his feet sinking into the snow with each step. She too is frozen. I have no idea whether she's aware, as I am, that Daniel is coming up behind her. I hope to God not. Slowly Daniel kneels by her side, almost lovingly brushing the hair from her forehead while my whole being is ablaze with fear—this can't be happening; this is *fucked up*; this is so fucked up. The rage is gone; in its place a cold, chill abyss, which brings on the dull realization that he tricked me.

This is what he wanted. If he can't possess me, he'll make sure I suffer. Lisa will be his sixth and final victim. *For the sins of the fathers . . .*

Daniel tosses the knife in the air. It rotates once, twice, before he expertly catches it. He looks me in the eye—he *marks* me—as he pulls back her head.

As he slits her throat.

As he places a finger to her bleeding neck.

As he lifts his finger to his mouth and licks it.

He murmurs something, a word I can't hear, and suddenly the ashes of my parents rise and mix with the floating snow to create a whirlwind. It's blinding, like being in the middle of a sandstorm. I would fall to my knees, but I still can't move.

And then he's gone.

I know this because the ash falls, the snow falls, and I can hear the wind again blowing softly through the trees. Poe jumps to her feet, Nachiel cries out, and now my legs finally move, and I stumble toward Lisa, her blood darkening the white snow. But when I reach her, cradle her lolling head in my arms—oh God.

There are no words.

There are no words.

No words.

CHAPTER TWENTY-SIX: LIFE SUPPORT

Frantically I try to staunch the flow of blood from the gaping wound on Lisa's neck, but there's too much, too much—it seeps through my fingers, hot and sticky, drips down my wrist onto the snow, turning it a deep, profane red.

"*Please,*" I whisper. "Oh please don't. Don't go, Lisa. *Don't go.*"

I press my trembling hands against her neck while her skin turns pale—*This is all my fault; oh God, this is all my fault.* Her eyes are half-closed and glassy; they are beyond me, beyond this world, this moment. She warned me, oh God she *told* me not to go messing around with Daniel's numbers, but did I listen? She said she knew how it would end, and now it's too late.

"Nachiel, *do* something."

Nachiel places a weighty hand on my shoulder, his broken arm miraculously healed.

"You can save her," I protest, sweat beading my forehead. "I've seen you—"

"It doesn't work that way. A spirit can only heal the body it possesses."

A shudder runs through me. "Christ, I don't know what to do," I say, my voice breaking. "It's all my fault. I've killed her, the one good thing—"

"*Dimitri,*" says Poe with a fierce intensity. "Her life force is still there. Faint, but there. It will not be for long."

I glance up and see that Poe's eyes have changed; they're lighter now, a pale wintry blue. And I notice the morning is coming. Warm slices of sunlight reach through the trees, glint against the broken glass, and a small flicker of hope lights in my chest. "Cell phone," I say quickly. "There's a cell phone in my jacket. We can call an ambulance."

Nachiel looks down. "It won't get here in time."

Lisa's warm blood flows through my fingers, and she's lost so much already. *Why* didn't my father tell me more about this goddamn inheritance? But then he did. The inscription in the watch: "Glance into the world just as though time were gone: and everything crooked will become straight to you."

Which gives me an idea. How can I make time disappear? Maybe it's not the most brilliant idea, but it will have to do.

"She's going," whispers Poe.

No, she's not. The rest I'll have to work out later.

———

To say Nachiel's pissed is an understatement. For the first time I'm actually glad to be immortal, because if I wasn't, I think he might actually go over to the dark side and kill me. Cradling Lisa in his arms with a strength I envy, he charges through the woods—I have to jog to keep up. Not easy, since my feet are frozen and my teeth are chattering. I really need to get a decent winter jacket one of these days.

"Uh, where are we going?" I venture to ask.

"Nate had medical supplies in his pack," hisses Nachiel through his teeth.

But I really don't care if he's pissed, because Lisa, while still pale and unconscious, is now *breathing*, and with each soft breath I'm pushed a few more steps past punch-drunk into the giddy arms of hope. It only took a few seconds for the gash in her neck to heal, and although her shirt is covered with blood, her face is peaceful, almost like she's sleeping.

I trip over a rock, nearly slamming hard into a tree face first, but Nachiel doesn't miss a step. He takes the next hill with long steps and momentarily disappears from view.

"Hey, Nachiel, wait up!"

I've got a migraine so fierce that I might need to stop sometime soon to vomit, but I'm so euphoric I don't care about that either. Lisa is alive. Lisa is breathing. Lisa is—

"Do you have any idea what you've done?" mutters Nachiel as I catch up to him.

"I've saved Lisa's life?"

Nachiel glares at me.

"Okay, yes, I understand that we have a small technical difficulty with Poe, but Lisa's breathing, okay? Her heart's beating. You told me yourself a body possessed by an immortal spirit can't die. So this is like life support. Only—creepier."

Nachiel stomps down through a small gulch. "That's a pretty big technical difficulty. Think Poe's going to give up a nice human body after all those years in hell so you and your girlfriend can go live happily ever after? Sound like something she'd do? But I guess you know her *so* well, after what? Talking to her for five minutes? Or was it ten?"

"I am an *excellent* judge of character," I reply hotly.

"You shot me in the chest."

"I'm *almost* an excellent judge of character. But I apologized. Plus we can exorcise her if we have to."

"We don't have the missing *Fiend* pages," says Nachiel tersely. "And even if we did, you remember what happened to the first Dmitri?"

Oh right, those minor details.

"If I remember correctly," I reply, "my great-grandfather or whoever said *usually* the body dies when a bad spirit vacates someone we love. Usually. Usually isn't always."

"Usually is usually. As in almost all the time."

"Okay, give me the percentage," I say, panting as I try to keep up.

"Ninety percent. Ninety percent of the time people die."

My heart does skip a beat at that news. "But that's still a ten percent chance of surviving. Ten percent is better than zero percent. What was I supposed to do, just let her bleed to death? No way. Not gonna happen. Besides, I've got a good feeling about this, and—"

"For all you know, as soon as she regains consciousness Poe will stab herself in the neck and save Sorath the trip."

"She's not *like* that anymore."

Nachiel snorts derisively. "Changed her colors that fast after nearly a hundred years on the dark side? I don't think so."

"Plus she has to do what I tell her to. Right?"

"What you have is the spirit of a psychotic murdering fool who despises every fiber of your being in complete control of your girl-friend's body."

"Well when you put it that way . . . So how *do* we get her out of Lisa's body?"

"By any means necessary." Nachiel plunges ahead of me into the thick brush, disappearing again.

"Well everything happened so fast," I say, pushing my way past a low-hanging branch, "I didn't exactly have time to think things all the way through. Easy enough for you to criticize *now*—"

But I'm stopped short at the sight of a hunter who is standing four feet in front of me, completely frozen, his mouth hanging open in shock. He wears one of those stupid L.L. Bean plaid flannel caps that cover your ears, a puffy bright orange coat that any deer with a lick of sense would steer clear of, and a large, well-oiled rifle is slung over his shoulder. I look down and realize the degree to which I'm covered with Lisa's blood.

And great, there's no sign of Nachiel—he's vanished entirely, leaving Lisa curled up neatly on the snow. And to someone who didn't just see her turning blue a few moments ago, she probably looks like a fresh corpse.

The man nervously reaches for the tip of his rifle.

"Hey," I say, holding up my hands and taking a step forward, which makes him take two back. "We—I mean *I*—just found her. She's alive but badly hurt. But we need to get an ambulance. Fast."

The man twitches his finger toward his gun, keeping both eyes firmly on me. "Were you talking to someone?"

"No, just a bad habit. I talk to myself when I'm freaked out."

He stares at me closely, assessing.

"*Please*," I say with the ache of truth in my voice. "She's the love of my life. I just want to get her to the hospital. I just want to get her help."

Slowly the man's hand drifts down from the gun to his right front pocket. He pulls out a cell phone, but he keeps me dead center in his sight. He presses a few buttons, slowly raises it to his ear.

"There's a girl here, seriously injured. We need an ambulance . . ."

But I don't hear the rest of what he says, because I've dropped to my knees, utterly spent. I press my forehead to the cold ground, and when I sit up on my heels I reach out for Lisa's hand, the faint pulse in her wrist an echo of my own beating heart.

———

After I've given my statement to the police, a strange amalgam of truth and lies needed to cover what they'd never believe—"Yes, I went to Aspinwall to see if Lisa was there"; "No, I didn't see anything suspicious, I just found her lying in the snow"; "Yes, she was unconscious, and it looked like she'd been bleeding from her nose"—I'm finally allowed to visit, or at least look through the glass of (with police supervision), the hospital room where Lisa is hooked up to a series of machines I'm familiar with. After a blood transfusion, her lips have gone from deathly white back to their normal rosy pink, and there's even a faint glow in her cheeks. The doctors have given her a serious dose of sedative drugs—something I'm grateful for, because who knows what Poe would say or do if she was conscious.

But my 10 percent chance of getting Lisa back feels smaller with every passing minute. I press my finger to the glass and wish I could go sit beside her, but they're not letting anyone but family in.

The police pointedly asked me for my bloody clothes, which I was more than happy to get rid of anyway, and I was finally given a blue set of surgical scrubs after I flat out refused the offer of another ducky hospital gown. I'm sure they're wondering how on earth anyone could lose that much blood from just a nosebleed, but given the lack of any visible injury, there is no other explanation yet. They've got a series of MRIs and brain scans planned, and there's serious talk among the doctors about a tumor or possible hemorrhage, which is good because it will give them something to do instead of look at me oddly, like I'm surrounded by an invisible haze of bad juju.

Suddenly I'm almost knocked over by what feels like a small bear gripping my legs. I look down into the beaming face of Amelia and see she's actually wearing loosely tied sneakers. One red, one blue.

"Are you a doctor now too?"

"Yes," I say seriously. "My specialty is shoe removal. It's a very complex operation. Many people suffer greatly when their feet are confined by shoes."

Amelia holds up one foot hopefully.

"Oh no you don't," says a warm voice behind me. I turn to see Elizabeth, looking relieved but also haggard. "It took me two hours getting her into them." She leans forward and gives me a dry kiss on the cheek. "You look like shit, by the way. You should get some sleep."

"Nana, you said the S-word. Do *you* have a record deal?" asks Amelia slyly, obviously happy to have caught an authority figure breaking a rule.

"Not today, love," replies Elizabeth in a distracted tone. She gazes into the hospital room, a few years of sleepless nights recorded in her distant stare. Along with Lisa, there are two others hooked up to machines: an elderly woman who was just wheeled in from Crosslands making her next stop in the Quadrant of Death; and a blond teenage girl who, I understand from overheard snippets of conversation between nurses, is a runaway in a vegetative coma after a drug overdose.

"You can go in," I say. "I'm just stuck in the nonfamily zone. Give her hand a squeeze for me."

Elizabeth swallows hard and looks at me closely. "You didn't see him? Daniel?"

There's no passing a lie by this woman—she should have been a detective. I try for a moderated truth. "I thought I did. For a second." And I do think I got a glimpse of the real Daniel in that brief moment before Lisa was able to break free.

Elizabeth nods weakly. And I realize that while one child is safe now, the empty loss of the other still aches fiercely. The manhunt for Daniel is on now. Rumors of the video were leaked to the press, so it's headline news across the nation.

"Go on," I say softly.

"Can you watch Amelia?"

"I want to go in too!"

Elizabeth quickly hugs Amelia's tiny body tightly; tears bead her eyes, as if she can somehow hug Daniel through her.

"C'mon, Amelia," I say, grasping Amelia's small hand in mine. "This floor's no fun, and it smells like pee. Let's grab a gurney and find an empty hall to race it in."

"You said *pee*," says Amelia, covering a giggle with her hand.

Elizabeth quietly mouths *thank you*, and then gently opens the door to go sit next to her daughter. Or at least her daughter's body possessed by the spirit of a dead Russian woman with a penchant for knives and conjuring demons.

Something I plan on rectifying as soon as the night shift starts.

———

A couple of hours after I call Nachiel, he shows up. Somehow he's managed to snag some surgical scrubs himself, along with a white lab coat and a fake ID with his picture clipped to his front pocket. Of course he didn't bother to knock before entering the closet-sized break room, which somehow accommodates a twin-sized bed that the real doctors use to sleep between shifts. I finally managed to get a couple hours myself—deep, beautifully unconscious sleep.

"Did you find Bunky?"

"Just so we're clear," he says, unzipping a duffel bag and tossing a Coke and a Snickers in my general direction, "I'm only here to make sure you don't make things worse. But I take no responsibility for what happens to Lisa tonight."

That means he did.

"Nice to see you, too," I say, cracking open the Coke and taking a deep sip. "Thanks for bringing dinner. Very thoughtful."

Nachiel glares at me, locks the door, and props a folding chair under the knob—I guess he *really* doesn't want someone walking in inadvertently. He sits down sullenly while I peel off the wrapper of the candy bar and take a bite. It's the first thing I've eaten in I don't know how many days, and for a moment I just bask in my caffeinated sugar high.

"So what's next?" I mumble through the caramel.

"I don't know. You're the man with the plan. Why don't *you* tell *me*?"

"Oh come on. Don't pretend you haven't done this whole exorcism thing before."

"You're right. *I* have done this before."

Oh dear Lord, I feel a lecture coming on.

"To start with, I can't remember *anyone* in the *entire* history of your family who has ever done anything as idiotic as *invite* an evil spirit to possess the body of someone they love . . ."

I was so right about the lecture. I wonder if the ring has given me some psychic mind-reading side benefits.

". . . with the *asinine* idea that they would then be able to success-fully exorcise that spirit—"

"Okay!" I interrupt. "Okay, I *get* it. My bad. So given this terrible situation I've created, what would you recommend we do next? *Tell* me."

Nachiel fumes, but unfortunately for him I'm the one who can command spirits. He pulls an assortment of items from the duffel bag, some of which I recognize and others I don't. There's a vial with leaves, a small stone mortar and pestle, Bunky, *The Book of Seraphs*, a long white candle, a cigarette lighter, and a large container of salt. Finally he slowly pulls out a very ominous-looking needle containing clear liquid of some sort.

"Is all this really necessary?" I ask.

"Make yourself useful and grind the leaves," he says in a tone that doesn't leave much room for discussion. I reach out for the mortar and uncork the vial, then make the mistake of taking a whiff—the leaves are beyond rancid; they smell like a skunk that just crawled out of a sewage tank.

"Are you serious?"

"Do I *look* like I'm serious?" He pulls off poor Bunky's head with-out even a hint of remorse and removes the rolled pages.

"Yes," I say, reluctantly pulling out a leaf with the tips of my fingertips, "you look like you're serious." So whether this is really nec-essary, or I'm just being punished, I crush the leaves with the pestle, creating a fine granular ash and a pungent vapor that would probably stop the heart of a fully grown elephant.

"The fact is we don't know what we're dealing with here—which side Poe's operating from. The exorcism to release a good spirit is *com-pletely* different from the one used to exorcise a negative one."

"Well, she seemed—"

"Seemed isn't good enough. *Seemed* will take your ten percent chance of getting Lisa back alive down to zero. You think someone who spent the last hundred years in hell is going to tell you the truth?"

"Well when you put it that way—"

"We have to *know*," says Nachiel. He picks up the lethal-looking needle and points it at me. "Which means *you* can't get squeamish at the last minute."

"You're not sticking me with that."

"You're right. *You're* sticking *Lisa* with it."

I smile until I realize he isn't kidding. "What is that? Some kind of truth serum? I thought those were bunk."

"Nope. Epinephrine. You need to inject it right into her heart."

A thought that makes mine skip a beat. "Wouldn't that be . . . dangerous?" What if I miss and hit her kidney? I'm starting to think that maybe it wouldn't be *too* awful letting Poe stay. Maybe she and Lisa could work out some kind equitable body time-share.

"Define dangerous," says Nachiel, leaning back in the chair. "Dangerous to *me* is inviting an evil spirit to possess someone I *care* about—"

"I *know*," I say, holding up my hand. "Okay? I heard you the first time. I'm just wondering why."

"Her body is heavily sedated, and we need to jolt it suddenly into consciousness without giving Poe time to think. Once she's awake I'll be able to tell whether she's for real, or if she's still reporting to Sorath."

"All I'm saying is that this seems a little extreme."

"*Extreme*," says Nachiel, leaning forward and taking the mortar and pestle from me. He taps the crushed leaves into one of the vials. "You haven't even *seen* extreme yet. But you will. You will."

CHAPTER TWENTY-SEVEN: A HARD TRADE

It's late. the hospital is deathly quiet, and we pass unnoticed through the hallways with relative ease until we get to the sixth floor, Lisa's floor. As we step out of the elevator, a thin and very intimidating nurse sitting behind a desk watches us closely. Her gray hair is pulled back so tight it actually stretches the skin on her cheeks, and I can feel her scanning Nachiel's fake ID. Her eyebrows furrow slightly at the surgical mask I swiped from the break room. But just as she's about to push a button on the phone, something starts beeping down the hall in the opposite direction, and she has to jump up to investigate.

"Did you do that?" I whisper from behind my mask.

Nachiel pointedly ignores me. We are apparently past the lecture phase and have moved on to the passive-aggressive silent-treatment phase.

I sneeze, causing another nurse to glance up as we pass her in the hallway. The mask makes my nose itch, but without it I'm way too easy to recognize—morgue guy with the mysteriously anemic girl-friend. I give her what I hope passes for a professional surgeon's nod.

"You know, I was thinking," I say quietly to Nachiel's impenetrable wall of silence. "I'd feel a whole lot better about stabbing Lisa in the heart with a needle if we got a second opinion. Are there any other spirits I can call? Maybe a recently deceased pulmonary surgeon?"

Nachiel glares at me.

"Just to make sure we're, you know, headed in the right direction with this. Not that I'm questioning your obvious exorcism experience."

"You don't just call spirits whenever you want."

"I think—"

"And you'd *know* that if you'd been *paying attention. You* see more, but more sees *you,* too. But if you want to shoot a flare gun into the spirit world announcing your location at the present moment, be my guest."

Oh yeah, I'd forgotten that part.

"I know what I'm doing," says Nachiel tersely. "So just *shut up* and do exactly what I tell you."

I'm wondering what Nachiel's definition of "good spirit" is; he's starting to get a little totalitarian. But as we slip into Lisa's hospital room, I don't care, because there she is—or there she is *almost.* In body if not soul. Her heart's hooked up to a monitor, and there's an IV with clear fluid connected to her right arm, but otherwise she looks remarkably healthy, like she might wake up at any moment and start deriding my taste in music.

Nachiel quickly starts to pull out his exorcism gear, dropping it onto a beige metal rolling table. "Pull the curtain."

I do, cutting us off from view of any nurse who might pop open the door. Probably a good precaution, since the candle Nachiel lights is definitely against hospital rules; he places it right in front of a sign that says OXYGEN IN USE. NO SMOKING. NO MATCHES. NO OPEN FLAME WITHIN 50 FEET.

"Is that a good idea?"

Nachiel pointedly ignores me and briskly takes out the container of salt and pours it in a circular line around Lisa's gurney, until he's encircled it completely.

"Do I want to know why?"

Finally he glances in my direction. "Prevents any interference. If we have to perform the exorcism, then we don't want some other demon jumping in."

I neatly step on the inside of the line myself. No sense taking chances.

Next Nachiel pulls out the ground ash. He takes a pinch and then smudges a line across Lisa's forehead with his thumb. Her nose twitches, but otherwise there's no sign of consciousness. He flips through *The Book of Seraphs*, chooses a page, and leaves the book open to it. Then, somewhat more gingerly, he picks up the *Fiend* pages and places them neatly on the table next to the flickering candle.

"God, I hate even touching these," he says quietly.

Carefully he turns the delicate pages over until he finds the one he's looking for. He gently places it on the table as well, moving a small electric clock over it to act as a paperweight.

"Okay," says Nachiel, wiping a hand across his forehead, which is lightly beaded with sweat. "You're going to have to pull the electrodes off carefully and put them on your chest; otherwise, we'll have a bunch of nurses running in with a crash cart. Her heart rate is going to spike when you inject her."

"Right," I say.

Nachiel looks at me expectantly.

"*Right,*" I say with a sigh. I glance over my shoulder; the old woman is mumbling something unintelligible in her sleep, and the teenage girl is safely in her vegetative coma. I suddenly recognize her—I saw her at the crosswalk on Ocean and Main, looking cold and alone. But that has to be random. A coincidence.

"Dimitri?"

"Right," I say again. More pressing business to take care of.

I pull off the top of my scrub and take a deep breath. I slip my hand down the front of Lisa's hospital gown—*God*, her skin is soft (*Don't think about it; not the time or place to get distracted*)—and just as her heart pauses between beats, I quickly rip an electrode off her chest and place it on mine without setting off a single alarm. One down, three more to go.

I take another deep breath and quickly remove the rest of the electrodes from Lisa's chest. There's one small blip on the last one, but not enough to create an alarm. For a moment I watch the electric signature of my own even heartbeat.

"Not bad," says Nachiel. He reaches into his duffel bag and pulls out the needle. It's gotten longer since the last time I saw it. I swallow hard.

"Just jab hard with one hand, like this," he says, making a stabbing motion, "and then press the epinephrine in."

I ridiculously practice a few times, like I'm a baseball player out on the field swinging the bat at warm-up. Although maybe that's not the best analogy, because I never was good at baseball. Whenever I actually hit the damn thing, it would shoot straight up over my head and then land somewhere behind me with a sad plop.

"There is no way in *hell* this can possibly work," I say desperately.

"Keep your hand firm; don't use the wrist. You just want to jab, but if you twist, you'll rip—"

"No talking about ripping, please." A droplet of sweat trickles down my back. "I'm nervous enough as it is. Okay?"

"Okay."

"*Okay*," I whisper. Feeling as prepared as someone without any medical training, not even a basic CPR course, can, I gently tug at the top of Lisa's hospital gown, lowering it enough to get a direct hit into her upper chest without revealing anything rated *R*. I try to recall my basic anatomy course, looking for which side the heart is on. Little to the right? Left?

"Here," says Nachiel, gently touching Lisa's skin just to the left of her breastbone where a mole I'm fond of marks her.

"Hey! Hands off my girl."

"I'm just trying to show you—"

"Well consider me shown," I say irritably.

"*Okay*. Now you want one smooth motion."

"One smooth motion."

"Whenever you're ready."

I inhale deeply. There's a silence then, like the moment right before a symphony starts to play, an ethereal hush. I put one hand down on the rails of the gurney to brace myself and lean over. I exhale deeply. Inhale deeply. Raise my hand . . .

"And is there a *reason* I'm doing this and you're not?"

"*Dimitri*, I swear to God, if you say one more word I'm going to jam that thing in your head. Now *do* it."

Fuck it. My arm swings wildly, and I plunge the needle into Lisa's chest—there's not as much resistance as I would have imagined—and I press the epinephrine in, hoping I'm not injecting into a lung. As soon as it's empty I slowly pull the needle back out. There's a small bead of blood where the needle entered.

Nothing happens.

But just as I'm about to turn to Nachiel, ask him what's wrong, Lisa bolts upright in the bed, nearly knocking me backward. It sounds like she's choking—her chest heaves with gasping breaths, her eyes bulge, and one hand frantically pulls at the bed sheet, like it's operating with a will of its own. Oh *fuck*, I did hit her lung.

Nachiel stares at her with a fierce intensity.

"Is she okay? Nachiel, is she okay?"

My heart starts to race, skipping the occasional beat, and Lisa's fair skin starts to turn pale. But *still* Nachiel says nothing, as if none of this is happening; as if he's somewhere else entirely, another planet perhaps. Lisa's hand jerks uncontrollably—it reaches out to me and almost pulls off an electrode.

"Lisa?" I ask faintly.

"Where," Lisa says in a hoarse voice, "am I?" The throaty accent is unmistakably, freakishly Russian, and my heart sinks like a stone—*Christ*, what I've done to Lisa is far, far worse than any demon could dream up.

Now, though, Nachiel springs into action—he pulls the rolling table toward him so fast that the candle's flame shears sideways. He gives me a hard look, shakes his head somberly, and my heart starts to throb when I see him pulling the paperweight off the page from *The Book of Fiends.*

Meanwhile Poe seems to have finally mastered Lisa's renegade hand. She holds it directly in front of her face with an expression of pure delight, like a child with a new toy.

"A body," she says in wonder. "I have a body again."

"Poe," I say firmly, "that wasn't the deal. You have to let go. You can't stay in Lisa's body."

"I have flesh," says Poe in a hushed voice. She raises the hand to her cheek, closes her eye like she's savoring the feel of it. "It's beautiful. So beautiful."

"*Poe.* I really appreciate you stepping in and keeping Lisa's body alive, but it's time—"

Poe's eyes suddenly grow wide, and they dart from my face to Nachiel's. I can see her registering the candle and the pages. "What is that *smell?*" she says, wrinkling her nose. A finger hesitantly reaches up to her forehead, touches the smeared ash.

Nachiel catches my eye in a meaningful way and says, "Just repeat after me." He begins to intone. "I exorcise thee, O creature of hell."

Reluctantly, I say the words too. "I exorcise thee, O creature of hell." Instantly a migraine starts, pressing in and making me feel slightly nauseous.

Nachiel continues: "O tormented and lost soul who has turned to the side of the Dark Night."

"O tormented and lost soul who has turned to the side of the Dark Night."

"*No,*" whispers Poe. She clutches my arm, the same icy, viselike grip I'm familiar with. Her eyes plead with mine for mercy. "He is *wrong.* I am *not* evil."

"I dispel thee. I send thee back into the hellfires."

"I'm sorry," I whisper. "I dispel thee, I send thee back into the hellfires."

Poe's bottom lip trembles, and I can't help but think of what we're sending her back *to*; I can almost hear the growls that erupted from behind the red curtain of light, almost feel the razor-sharp claw that reached out for her.

"The *same*," she breathes miserably. "You're all the *same*. You *use* me."

"I dispel thee, I invoke the power of the light."

"I dispel thee, I invoke the power of the light."

Lisa's body suddenly starts to seize—her back arcs wildly, and I try to hold her down without losing my connection to the heart monitor, which is now spiking from my own racing pulse. White foam beads the edge of her mouth; my 10 percent chance of getting Lisa back is dropping down to zero with each passing second.

"*No*," she moans.

Nachiel, though, is untouched, unmoved. "By the power of the light . . ."

The light gets so bright it hurts my eyes, and the floor seems to tilt. This feels wrong. It all feels so wrong.

Lisa's eyes roll in the back of her head, and her mouth hangs slack as Nachiel picks up the candle.

"*Wait!*" I shout.

"There is no waiting," says Nachiel. "Either we do this or—"

"We don't," I finish for him. "I get that. But Poe *helped* me."

"She helped *herself*. She hasn't changed—she has no intention of voluntarily leaving Lisa's body."

"If she has free will, then she can make her own decisions. Right?"

Nachiel inhales deeply. "There isn't *time*."

Poe's eyes flutter and then open, darting fearfully from me to Nachiel, then back to me.

"I propose a trade."

"What kind of *trade*?" spits Poe. "I have traded everything there is for a woman to trade, and it has never done me any good."

"I'm not talking about that kind of trade. I can offer you a *life*—if you swear to use that life to undo some of the harm you've done."

Poe regards me suspiciously. "You are trying to trick me again."

I shrug. "No, it's not a trick. But you can't have Lisa's body. That's taken."

Poe slants her eyes at me. "Then whose?"

"I'm wondering that myself," says Nachiel.

I nod behind me at the teenage girl in the coma who's hooked up to a ventilator and heart monitor. I'm officially retiring the word "random" from my personal lexicon. "The nurses say she's a Jane Doe. Runaway, no ID. She's brain-dead, and they're going to remove her from the ventilator tomorrow morning. One of the doctors asked me if I'd write up a small obituary with just her physical description for the newspaper. See if anyone would claim the body."

Nachiel glances over at the girl, scanning her. "Her spirit *has* been gone for some time, but that doesn't mean this is a good idea."

Poe cranes her head to take a look, considering. "I would find her acceptable," she finally says.

"But Poe," I say, reaching for her hand. Tentatively, she lets me hold it. "If you *ever* give me a reason to regret this . . ."

"I will not. You are the first man I have ever known to give me so much for so little." She seems to choke slightly at the last word, "little," but then recovers quickly and glares at Nachiel. "Plus I will enjoy proving *this* one wrong. He seems a little—how you say?—up stuck."

"Stuck up," I correct, "although somehow the way you put it seems just as appropriate."

"Kid's got jokes," grumbles Nachiel. "For the record, I'm completely against this."

"Noted," I say.

He sighs and blows out the candle. Gently he puts the page back from *The Book of Fiends* and picks up *The Book of Seraphs* instead. "Let's see what page transferring bodies is on."

I notice, although I pretend not to, that Poe keeps hold of my hand, like a tether.

————

Much to my great disappointment, Lisa doesn't regain consciousness immediately once Poe's spirit has left her body, although much to my great relief, she doesn't die either. Just after Nachiel finished his chant, Lisa's eyes briefly fluttered, then gently closed, and there was only the slightest exhalation of breath, a soft *ah*, as a haze of blue mist rose from her body. It passed right through me, like a shivery wave of cool water, and then floated over to the girl in the coma, gently drifting down until it settled on her skin like morning dew, then disappeared.

But that was five eternally long minutes ago, and neither has moved since. Did it work?

"Lisa," I say, smoothing her forehead. No response. Her skin feels colder, and I notice that she's lost some of the color from her cheeks. I turn to Nachiel, worried.

"Give her some time. Her body's been through a lot," says Nachiel.

"How much time?"

"As much as she needs. You'd better get those electrodes back, though, in case a nurse comes."

I sigh but do as he says, making sure that not a single beat is missed. Then I gently lift her hospital gown back into place, which I notice features gamboling teddy bears. Something I plan to tease her mercilessly about as soon as she comes to.

"You might want to put your shirt back on too," says Nachiel.

"Good point," I say, grabbing the top of my scrubs from the floor. I brush off some of the salt and pull it over my head while Nachiel packs away the books and the candle. The needle he tosses into a red bin marked BIOHAZARD, and I briefly wonder how the hell can *anyone* get well in a hospital when all the signs read like they're equally applicable to a nuclear facility.

Nachiel slides the bag over his shoulder.

"You're not going, are you?"

"Someone's got to start thinking about what comes next," he says, looking pointedly at Poe's new body, still safely hooked up to the ventilator and heart monitor.

My chest seizes. "I can't leave before Lisa wakes up."

Nachiel grins and pointedly ignores me. "I'll be back later. Try not to do anything *too* stupid while I'm gone, okay?"

"Poe's right. You *are* up stuck."

"Don't even *start*," says Nachiel. He pauses for moment, gives me a serious look, and then reaches into his bag. "There's something else you should have."

I back up a few steps. "No more books. I need a little vacay from the whole conjuring/exorcism thing."

He gives me a half smile. "Nothing like that." He pulls out a large, fairly crumpled photograph, its edges yellowed with age, and holds it out to me.

Quietly I take it from him.

It's a familiar arrangement, the same photo of Aspinwall I found in the *Eagle* archives. I see the neat rows of servants lined up in their starched aprons and severe expressions. But this is obviously the original, because my mother's face isn't rubbed out. I can see her delicate features clearly. She's smiling and her eyes are warm, friendly.

"And there," Nachiel says softly.

I almost can't take my eyes off my mother's face, but I do and look to where his finger is pointing. It's the figure that was cut off in the newspaper image; I can now follow the arm holding the trowel to the tall, thin man holding it. His dark wool pants are stained with dirt, and I discover the gaunt, ragged face of the Russian gardener. The gaunt, ragged face of my father.

I swallow.

"It took me years to track down all the photos they appeared in and destroy them. There couldn't be any trace, you understand. But I kept this one for you."

I nod, temporarily unable to speak. "Thanks," I finally manage.

Nachiel puts an arm on my shoulder and then starts for the door.

But before he opens it, I casually ask, "Hey, Nachiel. Where did my father go during the day all those years?"

He smiles at me. "You mean when he wasn't traveling the world to exorcise some demon, save the world, that kind of thing?"

"Yeah," I say, trying to sound like it's just an offhand question, no big deal.

"Your father was the gardener for the Wharton Nursery. In the next town over, ten minutes from your house."

Not the response I was expecting. "Well, why didn't he tell me *that*?"

Nachiel shakes his head. "He wasn't proud of it. He worked with his hands, in the dirt. In a way he was like any other immigrant; all he wanted was for his son to have a better life than he did."

I swallow hard and fidget with the edge of Lisa's sheet. And I quietly pocket that idea to think about later.

"See you soon," says Nachiel, giving me a wave before slipping out the door.

I pull up a chair and settle myself in, keeping hold of Lisa's hand. There's the soft hiss of the ventilator, the *blip, blip, blip* of the heart monitor, and the gentle hum of the air conditioning. Warm sunlight streams through the window, not a cloud in the sky.

And just as my own eyes droop, just as I start to feel the deep pull of sleep, Lisa's hand moves ever so slightly in mine. Instantly I'm alert, and I watch breathlessly as her eyes quietly open.

"Lisa?"

She pulls her hand from mine, turns her head, and smiles beatifically at me, reaching out as if to gently stroke my cheek—before swiftly balling her hand into a fist and punching me in the arm, *hard*.

"Ow! For Christ's sake, Lisa, what the hell was that for?"

She can barely speak but somehow mutters in a raspy voice. "You *lied* to me."

Holy shit, who's possessing her now? "When did I lie?"

"You *promised* me. You said if I told you to run, you'd *run*. And you didn't."

"I thought we were speaking figuratively, not literally," I say, rubbing my arm, which will soon sport a bruise—for someone who just had a blood transfusion, she's got an amazing right hook. "Besides, I think I should get a little cred for saving your life."

She glares at me and punches me again.

"Okay, I lied! I'm sorry I lied. I'm an evil, lying man unworthy of you. Just stop hitting me, please. You wouldn't be so abusive if you knew what you just put me through."

"I'm the one who's plugged into a heart monitor."

"Hey, that's *my* line, you can't—I distinctly remember saying that when I came to in the hospital. Plagiarism is not attractive."

"Neither is lying."

I groan and lean my forehead against one of the railings of the gurney. "I *said* I was sorry," I mutter in the general direction of the floor.

"Well, *that* sounds a little more sincere." I feel her fingers brush through my hair. "Just next time . . ."

"There can't be a next time," I say, lifting my head. "I couldn't take going through something like this again."

"Me neither," she says quietly. One of her hands tentatively reaches for her throat, and I can sense her surprise when she doesn't find a bandage.

"See? I did save your life," I gloat. "Maybe someone deserves an apology."

She looks uncertain. "How?"

"Because I'm the *man*, that's how."

"Well I'm not going to apologize to someone who refers to themselves as 'the man.' By the way, you look like shit."

"Yeah, well you almost went and *died* on me."

"Now you know how I felt."

"Just enjoy the fact you're not being fitted for a coffin and scooch over. You can thank me later."

"Hmmph," grumbles Lisa, but she does make room on her hospital bed, and I climb in, wrapping my arm around her. It feels warm and good. Just as I start to drift off again, she says in a small voice, "Dimitri?"

"Yes," I mumble, halfway between being awake and asleep.

"You might think I'm crazy . . ."

"I'd never think you're crazy."

"Well . . . I think I saw him. Not in the greenhouse, I mean. After I passed out."

I know who she means, but still I ask "Who?"

"Daniel. *My* Daniel."

My eyes open, and I look into hers.

"It was like I was walking in a gray mist. And I could see someone far off watching me. Not in a creepy way; a good way, like he was waiting for me. And he waved, just like Daniel used to when he was onstage, and he saw me in the crowd."

I stroke her hair gently.

"He's still in there, you know."

"I know," I say quietly. "I know."

"Did they find . . . him?"

"No," I say. "Not yet."

"It's not random, is it? It *is* all connected . . . Do you think . . . ?" She can't finish the sentence, but I know what she wants to ask. There is, after all, only one question.

"I don't know," I say, gently kissing her on the lips. "Maybe we can get him back. We can try at least."

She nestles into the crook of my arm then, and as daylight comes, and the morning light spreads across the polished linoleum floor, we fall asleep together, into whatever dreams will come.

EPILOGUE

The nurses are shocked when they discover that not only is Lisa conscious, but so is the girl they were about to humanely remove from life support. The confusion is so great that no one even bothers to kick me out of the room. After a cursory check of Lisa's vitals, a steady stream of doctors and nurses flow through the room periodically all day to check on the Jane Doe, who not only is sitting calmly upright with clear light blue eyes, but can answer their questions intelligently, albeit with a funny accent.

When she tells a doctor her name is Poe, like the writer, I have to turn my head away so that I don't give away a smile.

"And your first name?" asks the doctor.

"Poe," she says firmly.

"So your last name is . . . ?"

"No two names; just one. Poe."

"*Okay*," says the doctor, scribbling something down anyways—a note for a psychiatric appointment perhaps. "And how old are you?"

"Eighteen," says Poe firmly. At this the doctor looks confused, because physically Poe looks about fifteen, with a childishly thin body and soft chin, but the clarity and maturity with which she meets the doctor's gaze is clearly unnerving him.

"Would you like me to schedule an appointment with a social worker?"

"That will not be necessary," says Poe in a polite yet unmistakably dismissive tone. "Thank you."

Lisa, though, is not amused in the slightest. As soon as I fill her in about the true identity of her new hospital roommate, she keeps glancing at her with obvious suspicion.

"And you trust her?" she whispers during one of Poe's interviews.

I shrug. "We'll see. All I know is that I had to get you back."

"Yeah, well, I hope you've disinvited her from your apartment."

I smile. "What, you jealous?"

Lisa narrows her eyes at me. "I'm just saying."

"You don't have to worry. Nachiel's on it."

"Nachiel? Who's Nachiel?"

I lean over and kiss her lightly on the forehead. There's so much to explain, and I'm incredibly thankful that I'll now have the time to do so. "You're beautiful."

"Ahh," says Lisa, "that's the drugs talking."

"I'm not taking any drugs."

"Well, then why are you looking at me like that?"

"Maybe because I love you."

"Yeah, well after the hell you just put me through, you should."

"The hell *I* put *you* through . . ."

But even as we mildly argue, my heart is floating peacefully in my chest, lofty as a child's balloon.

———

After the FBI has combed through Aspinwall for any shred of possible evidence, a committee is formed by the local council, and it's determined that the mansion poses a hazard to the community. Finally the funds are allocated to demolish it. I'm given the story to cover, one of my last before Lisa and I start packing for Hawaii. Nachiel said we should disappear for the next few months, and Hawaii is the farthest away from New Goshen we can get without leaving the United States. I'm looking forward to finally seeing Lisa in that polka dot bikini I've been dreaming of.

There are no news vans now, no trailer trucks with generators and reporters from across the country videotaping the bulldozers and wrecking ball, which smashes the remains of the hulking building into a pile of debris. I snap a few pictures but wish someone would give me a chance to try my hand in the cab of one of the bulldozers— I'd like nothing better than to knock over a few walls myself. My brief story is picked up by the AP though, and the *Devonshire Eagle* gets its highest spike in web traffic since the murders, something that immensely displeases the new corporate owners. They bought out Mac and are slowly trying to shut the paper down, because it's worth more to their balance sheet as a loss. Go figure.

But while the mansion is razed to the ground, no one dares to step into the crumbling greenhouse, not even the thickest-built, testosterone-jawed demolition expert. For some strange reason, even though it's the dead of winter and a good foot of snow still covers the floor, the long-dead rosebushes in their rusted steel containers have started to bloom—fresh, vibrantly red blossoms that drop the occasional petal, like a droplet of blood on the snow. I picked a bouquet of them for Lisa, and after a month they're still fresh and soft to the touch.

Daniel—or Sorath—has vanished, and not a single murder has been reported in the past month in New Goshen, nor has there been a similar murder anywhere else. A truck driver did report a hitchhiker matching Daniel's description on the side of the I-95, trying to get a lift south. But Nachiel is on the trail, and he says Poe has actually been useful helping to map out various places Sorath might want to hide. Still, he keeps her close—he finagled his way into a small motor home with two bunk beds, and he sleeps in the bottom bunk with a gun under the pillow *just in case she gets any ideas.*

What will happen if and when they find him is something I try not to think about. But the ring stays firmly on my finger. I'm learning to read Russian, and I find myself paging through *The Book of Fiends* late at night while Lisa's asleep, trying to understand as much as I can. Just in case.

ACKNOWLEDGMENTS

Many thanks to my family, who tolerated hours of me staring into the screen when I could have been doing something more obviously productive. I especially thank my husband, the earliest champion of my work, who has also been my refuge during the hard times. My son is the light that has kept me moving forward when it would have been easy to fall backward.

Influential and encouraging writing teachers include John Yount, Charles Simic, Carolyn See, and Diane di Prima. Life teachers include Khenpo Gyurmed Trinley Rinpoche, who kept our family in his heart, and the ever-humble Lopsang Sakya.

The journey to publication was a long one for *Poe*. Thanks to Jennifer Escott for reading an earlier version and asking the important questions. Eternal gratitude to all those who had kind words to say about *Poe* as it made its way through the 2013 Amazon Breakthrough Novel Award Contest, and the editors who chose it as the winner in the Science Fiction/Fantasy/Horror category.

Landing in the expert editorial hands of Kristin Mehus-Roe was an amazing piece of luck. Thanks also to Terry Goodman for giving me my heart's desire on the cover, and Marcus Trower for his copy-editing wizadry.

Finally I thank my parents, who adopted and raised me with love. They left this world too soon.

ABOUT THE AUTHOR

 J. Lincoln Fenn grew up in New England and graduated summa cum laude with a degree in English from the University of New Hampshire. She lives in Hawaii with her family and is at work on her next novel.